A HANDFUL OF HAPPINESS

A HANDFUL OF HAPPINESS

Evelyn Hood

LONDON NEW YORK SYDNEY TORONTO

This edition published 1993
by BCA
by arrangement with
HEADLINE BOOK PUBLISHING PLC

CN 6351

First published in 1993
by HEADLINE BOOK PUBLISHING PLC

10 9 8 7 6 5 4 3 2 1

Typeset by Keyboard Services, Luton

Printed and bound in Great Britain by
Mackays of Chatham PLC, Chatham. Kent

Although Ellerslie is a fictitious Clydeside town, and none of the characters in this book bear any resemblance to people past or present, the Dalkieth Experimental Tank section is based on the Denny Experimental Tank, a section of the former Dumbarton shipyard owned and operated by generations of the Denny family. The Tank is now part of the Scottish Maritime Museum, and open to the public.

I would like to thank the following people for the assistance they generously gave me during the research for this book; the Scottish Maritime Museum staff in Irvine and Dumbarton, particularly Niall McNeil and Anne Hobin of Dumbarton; the staff of Dumbarton Library; Mrs Margaret (Peggy) Wallace, a former Tracer and Analyst in Hydro-dynamics in the Denny Experimental Tank, and Reg Wishart, a former Clydeside shipyard worker.

Evelyn Hood

To my sons, Alastair and Simon, with
thanks for the many years of pleasure
they have given me.

E.H.

1

'It's here! The letter from my Aunt Margaret's here!' Lizzie Caldwell, who was waiting impatiently outside the Experimental Tank department, squealed as soon as Jenny emerged. 'She says we can both start on the first day of December, me in drapery and you in hosiery. We're going tae Glasgow!'

Jenny's heart stopped as though an unseen hand had gripped it, then started to pump twice as fast. 'Let me see!'

'She says one of us is in drapery and the other in hosiery,' Lizzie said as she handed the letter over, 'but since it's my aunt that got us the places I should have first choice.'

Jenny pulled off the gloves she had just smoothed over her fingers so that she could relish the feel of the letter she drew from the envelope. In the four years since the beginning of the war, letters from men serving in the forces had become commonplace among the people who lived in the crowded shipyard tenements. Jenny's brother Maurice, stationed in France, sent letters to his mother, and once Jenny herself had received letters with her name on the envelope – but not now. Robert Archer was as dead to her now as though he had been killed in the fighting.

Maureen Malloy, who had come out of the office with Jenny, was squinting so closely at the letter that her chin dug into Jenny's shoulder. 'Stop starin' at it as if you're expectin' it tae speak tae ye, and open the thing!' she ordered.

Like the envelope, the single sheet of paper was of fine quality, and bold black writing flowed imperiously across the page in neat lines. Although she wrote a good hand herself – fine handwriting was high on the list of qualifications demanded of the women employed in the tracing office – Jenny was impressed. This letter had been written by none other than Lizzie's Aunt Margaret, the stylish supervisor of the ladies' wear department of a large and important emporium situated in Buchanan Street, in the heart of the city of Glasgow. Aunt Margaret had, as Lizzie was fond of saying, 'pulled herself up by her own bootstraps.'

She repeated the phrase proudly, for the umpteenth time, when

1

the letter was returned to her and the three girls began to walk home. By now most of the other Tank workers had gone and the street was empty. The double doors that led directly from the wax-model room on to the street had been closed and locked by Mr Duncan, the Tank superintendent.

'I don't see how anyone could pull themselves up by their bootstraps without draggin' the feet from under themselves and fallin' on their arses!' red-headed Maureen said, with a snigger. Maureen's parents had come over from Ireland as newlyweds; their many children, though born and raised in Scotland, had inherited their parents' easy-going Irish natures.

'That's all you know about it!' Lizzie shot back at her, her round, pale face flushing with anger. 'And that's why you'll always live in Ellerslie and probably stay in the tracing office until you get married and raise more brats than you can afford just because your priest says you should!'

'I can think of worse things tae dae,' said Maureen unrepentant. 'All I want's for my Jacko tae come home from the war an' get back intae his old job in the shipyard. An' we like weans, both of us. I hope we have lots!'

'Please yourself.' Lizzie put her snub nose in the air. 'Me and Jenny'll be in Glasgow, learning to live like ladies.'

Maureen slipped a hand through Jenny's arm. 'You'll write tae me, won't you, Jen? When you can find the time tae let go of your bootstraps, that is,' she added, with a sidelong glance at Lizzie, who pretended not to hear her.

'Of course I'll write. And I'll send a fine christening present every time you have another brat,' Jenny promised, making Maureen giggle and Lizzie flounce by stressing the final word. She knew that it was wrong of her to tease Lizzie, but at that moment she was so excited that she wanted to pull off her hat and throw it into the air, to run and jump and swing round the gas-lamp posts and sing for joy. She was going to Glasgow, to a huge city where nobody knew her, and there she could be whatever and whoever she chose.

She was getting away from Ellerslie and the overcrowded tenement flat where she had lived all her life, away from her father and his drinking and constant criticism, away from her faded, exhausted mother, who had never known anything but worry and who broke Jenny's heart with her continual fear of poverty and the workhouse. Away from Gran's twisted face with the spittle running down her chin.

As the girls turned on to the bridge that spanned the river running through Ellerslie they passed a small knot of people studying the

2

billboards outside a newsagent's shop. 'Tide Turns For Allies!' said one of the boards, while the other proclaimed, 'Kaiser's Army Crumbling!'

'I wonder what'll come first – us going to Glasgow, or the war ending?' Jenny linked her free arm through Lizzie's so that the three girls were swinging along the footpath in line.

'It'll be a great way to end the year,' Lizzie's anger at the teasing had gone. 'Peace for the world, and a new life for you and me. For the three of us, with Molly and Jacko getting married,' she added magnanimously.

Jenny felt a twinge of guilt at the ease with which she would leave her family behind, but compensated by reminding herself that she would send money home to help them. The truth of it was that she would miss her job at the shipyard more than she would miss her family. She was proud to have been considered fit for a position in the Experimental Tank section – small though Dalkieth's shipyard was, it had been the first Clyde yard to install a tank where models of their designs could be tested before the actual ships were built. Only the mighty John Brown's Yard at Clydebank had followed suit so far.

A short distance along the riverside from the bridge the three girls reached their destination, four rows of tenement buildings in the form of a square. A hundred years earlier the son of the Dalkieth who had set up the shipyard had bought this land on the opposite bank of the river from the original town and built houses for his workers on it. He had built them in the form of a square surrounding a large back court, and had named the four streets James, George, William and Anne, after himself and his wife and two sons. Since then other tenements had sprung up around them, but the original buildings, now old and shabby, were still occupied by Dalkieth employees and their families.

Maureen said goodbye at the corner of Anne Street and went off to the tenement building where she lived with her parents and countless brothers and sisters. Jenny and Lizzie, arm in arm, continued on along George Street, planning their dazzling futures.

'Just think—' Lizzie squeezed Jenny's arm, 'we'll be in Glasgow in time for Christmas. We'll need tae give in our notices at the end of the month. Are you sure your da'll let you go?

'He'll have to for my mind's made up. And my mam'll be pleased for me. Alice has turned thirteen now – she can help with my gran as well as I can.' Though Jenny spoke lightly, guilt sparked in her again.

Alice, the clever member of the family, was still at school, and had a lot of studying to do. But she would manage. She would just have to manage, once Jenny was no longer there.

3

'Maurice'll mebbe be back home by the time I leave. Once he's back working in the shipyard again they'll not need my wages so badly.'

'D'ye think he'll marry that Lottie when he comes home?'

'He'll have to, now. He'd not leave wee Helen fatherless and he knows fine that she's his bairn.'

Lizzie's voice was suddenly self-righteous. 'My mother says Lottie's nothing but a slut.'

Jenny bit back a sharp retort. Lizzie was her best friend and she had just got her a new job in Glasgow. Anyway, Jenny herself had little time for her brother's sweetheart. Secretly she thought that Maurice could have done better for himself than Lottie, who was lazy and selfish. But that was Maurice's problem, not hers. She would soon be out of it all, living her own life in Glasgow.

She parted with Lizzie at the closemouth and ran up the dark, narrow stairs to the second-floor flat she had been born and raised in, suddenly longing to share her good news. She would ignore any sarcastic remarks her father might make about it – she would soon be away from him and his ill-tempered tongue.

She lifted the door latch and burst into the tiny dim hall, calling as she went, 'Mam – the letter's come for Lizzie. There's places for both of us where her aunt works. We're starting in Dec—'

She stopped, suddenly aware that the place was silent apart from her own voice. At this hour of the day there was usually the sound of the hacking cough that was the legacy of her father's bad bout of pneumonia eighteen months earlier, and Helen's high, clear, little voice and a babble of talk from her mother and Lottie and Alice.

'Mam?'

There were only two people in the kitchen instead of the expected crowd; no smell of cooking, no bustle by the range where, for once, the pots were missing. Only the big kettle emitted its usual faint plume of steam. Marion Gillespie, Jenny's grandmother, was huddled as usual in one of the two fireside chairs, a shapeless mass of wool with an untidy white head at one end and scrawny ankles at the other. Faith Gillespie was in the other fireside chair, the one normally reserved for her husband, who was still the master of the house, though since his illness he had been demoted in the yard and now worked as a storeman instead of at his own trade as a fitter.

In her faded skirt and blouse, her hair well streaked with grey, Faith was almost unnoticeable, a shadow of a woman with little substance to her. 'Mam—'

Faith lifted her head and looked at her daughter with pale blue eyes.

4

'What's wrong? It's not Helen, is it?' Jenny, who adored her little niece, felt fear catch at her throat.

'It's no' the bairn.' Faith's mouth trembled. 'The poor wee bairn, that's never even seen her fath—'

Her voice broke. She held out a hand and with a twist of sudden fear Jenny saw that it held a crumpled buff form. She knew well enough what that meant. Many a home up and down the street had received one. Jenny's sister Bella had had one six months earlier, though in her case it had not been notification that her man was dead, but that he was being returned to her a cripple.

For the second time within half an hour she scanned a sheet of paper. This time she had to read it three times before the words sank in. 'Oh, Mam!'

Faith's head came up, her fingers reaching out to snatch the form back. 'He's not dead, only missin', it says that here,' she said fiercely. 'Not dead. He's comin' back tae us. It was just – a wee bit of a shock, that's all, comin' just when everyone's sayin' that the war's over and our men'll be home soon.'

Jenny wanted to put her arms about her mother, but the Gillespies weren't a touching family, so she could only stand over her mother helplessly, saying again, 'Oh, Mam!' while the pleasure of her own news leached out of her. 'Where's Alice and wee Helen – and Dad?'

'Alice took the bairn round tae Mrs Malloy's. I needed time tae think. I don't know where Lottie is, but yer da went out tae the pub.'

'He would. That's where he aye goes when he doesn't know what else to do.'

'That's enough,' Faith said, with only an echo of her usual sharpness. She allowed nobody to criticise her husband.

'I'll make a cup of tea.' Jenny fetched the old caddy, so well handled that its original picture had faded away, and measured tea-leaves into the pot, trying, as she worked, to come to terms with the news. Maurice, a young and self-conscious stranger in his uniform, watched her from the carved wooden frame on the sideboard. Behind his likeness she could see her own face in the small standing mirror and realised that she was still wearing her hat and coat. She took them off and put them over the back of an upright chair, automatically smoothing her already neat dark hair, which was drawn into a bun at the nape of her neck, straightening the collar of her ivory working blouse, finally meeting her own blue eyes in the glass and turning away quickly from the truth that she read in them, but didn't want to acknowledge.

'Someone should tell Bella.' Faith's voice fretted at her as she put

5

cups out on the table. 'I didnae like tae ask Alice tae dae it, she's only a bairn herself.'

'I'll go to Bella's in a wee while.'

'What was it you were saying when you came in?'

'Nothing, Mam.'

'What was it?' Faith insisted. Jenny put the pot on to the brass stand that Maurice had made when he was an apprentice in the machine shop at the shipyard and turned to face her.

'I said that Lizzie had heard from her aunt. She's got places for us both in that big shop where she works in Glasgow.'

Faith stared for a moment, as though trying to make sense of the words, then a sudden flash of fear passed over her face. 'You'll no' leave us?' she said at once. 'You'll wait till Maurice comes home?'

Jenny swallowed hard. For as long as she could remember her mother had been afraid – of poverty, of illness, of the shadow of the workhouse. She had never known the luxury of security, even after marriage rescued her from the home where she had been abused and half-starved. As a shipyard worker's daughter, then a shipyard worker's wife, Faith Gillespie had never known what it was to be free of insecurity and nagging financial worry. She had buried two sons in infancy, had almost lost her husband to pneumonia, had had to see her only surviving son go off to war, and had then had to take in his pregnant sweetheart when the girl's own parents threw her out.

She had spent most of her marriage being bullied by her strong-willed mother-in-law and, when the woman had succumbed to a stroke, it was Faith who had had no choice but to find room for her in her own over-crowded home.

'You'll no' go?' she said again, insistently, reaching a hand out to Jenny.

'Mam, the job's waiting for me. I'll send money home every week, mebbe more money than I'm getting just now—'

'Ye'll have tae wait – just till our Maurice comes back!' The words were wrung out of Faith's throat.

'Faith?' The latch lifted on the outside door and Mrs Malloy, a solid dumpling of a woman, came through the hall and into the room with a rush, filling it almost before she had cleared the door, her face heavy with the news she had just heard. 'Oh – Faith,' she said, and the old woman sleeping uneasily in the other chair stirred and woke with a whimper of fright as Mrs Malloy's passing rocked her like a small boat in the wake of a steamship.

'It's all right, Gran.' Jenny's arms went out automatically to support Marion as she slipped sideways and almost fell from the chair. Carefully, she eased her grandmother upright then fetched a cloth and wiped spittle from her chin. Marion's eyes, which until short months before had had the ability to terrorise with one look, wandered for a moment then focused on Jenny. She gave a garbled grunt.

'She'll likely want tae use the commode, poor old soul,' Mrs Malloy whispered, then, raising her voice, she boomed, 'All right, hen, we'll see tae ye in a wee minute. I'll just make some tea first.' Although she still retained her Irish accent, Mrs Malloy's speech was peppered with Scottish words and phrases.

'It's already made.' Jenny heaved the large, battered teapot from the range with a skill acquired over the years. As she poured tea she heard her mother say behind her, 'He's not dead, Molly, only missing. He'll be home, just like he promised. He'll come home tae look after us all. He's not dead.'

Bella Kerr, Jenny's elder sister, lived a few closes further along George Street in a 'single-end', a one-roomed flat on the upper floor. As Jenny climbed the stairs she could hear her brother-in-law's raised voice and her hands closed into fists in her pockets.

Patrick had been a riveter in the shipyard before the war, a cheerful young man who had swept quiet, timid Bella off her feet. While the early radiance of marriage still glowed in their faces, Patrick had been called up; then sent home a cripple with one foot badly damaged and all his zest in life replaced by a bitter resentment against the entire world. He could only get about with the aid of crutches now, and steadfastly refused to go outside where people could see him and pity him. Bella had to work hard, cleaning shops and offices, to support them both.

Silence fell behind the scarred wooden door as soon as Jenny knocked on it. After a moment Bella peered out, then stepped back as her sister pushed the door wide.

'What's amiss?'

'It's me that should be asking you that,' Jenny said bluntly, noting Bella's reddened eyes and the way she was rubbing at one wrist. 'I could hear you all the way up the stairs, Patrick.'

He glowered at her from the chair where he spent almost all his time. 'Mebbe they should've shot me in the throat, then. I wish tae Christ they had.'

'Pat, don't!'

Patrick Kerr turned away from his wife's anguished face, one hand plucking restlessly at the shabby rug over his knees, then looked back quickly at Jenny when she told them why she had come.

'God – poor old Maurice,' he said, his voice dull with shock.

Bella took her shawl down from its hook on the door. 'I'd best go round,' she began, then hesitated. 'Will you be all right, Pat?'

'I'm no' likely tae run away, am I?' The bitterness was back, in his brown eyes as well as in his voice, and the hand that had been fidgeting with the rug dug into the thin material, gripping at the crippled leg below.

'I'll stay if you—'

'For God's sake, woman, will ye stop moitherin' me an' go if ye're goin!' he shouted, so suddenly that Jenny jumped.

'But—'

Jenny's hand closed over her sister's wrist and then, as Bella winced, she relaxed her grip. 'Come on, Bella. Pat'll be fine on his own for a wee while.'

As they began to go down the hollowed stone stairs there was a noisy rush of water as someone flushed the cistern of the privy on the landing. The door opened and Daniel Young, a widower who lived with his son on the ground floor, began to emerge then stopped abruptly at sight of the two young women, his jacket dangling from one hand. His pale thin face went beet red with embarrassment at being caught leaving a privy.

He ducked his head in acknowledgement then cleared his throat nervously, and began to descend towards his own flat, scrambling into his jacket as he went. Then he hesitated and looked back at Bella.

'Is something wrong?'

'It's our Maurice – there's been a telegram.' Her voice shook.

'He's missing, just,' Jenny put in swiftly.

'He'll probably be all right,' said Daniel, but his voice lacked conviction. They all knew that few missing men reached home. 'D'ye want me tae sit with Patrick while ye're out?'

'I'd be grateful. He's in a low mood.'

'I'll just tell the laddie, then I'll go up,' he said, and hurried on down before them.

'He's a good man, Daniel,' Bella murmured gratefully as the sisters passed his door. The brasswork on it was gleaming. 'Not many of the men Pat used tae work with bother now.' Tears brimmed up in her eyes and she wiped them away with a corner of the shawl as she stepped into the street. 'And now there's Maurice. This damned war, Jenny – will it never leave us be?'

'It's nearly over, they say.'

'Aye, but—' Bella's voice broke. 'Nothing'll ever be the same again!'

'Lizzie got the letter from her aunt in Glasgow today.'

8

'What letter?' Bella asked blankly, then recollection flooded back into her small, pinched face. 'The place in Glasgow?'

'It's all arranged. I'm supposed to be handing in my notice at the end of the month.'

The same fear that she had seen in her mother's eyes came into Bella's. 'But things've changed now, Jen! We were counting on Maurice coming home. If he's—' She stopped, then said, in a rush, 'Ye cannae leave us just now, Jenny. Not the way things are!'

'I'll mebbe not get the chance again.'

'But how'll Mam manage without your wage comin' in?'

'I can send money,' Jenny said desperately. Already the words were beginning to sound hollow to her own ears.

'Ye'd need tae be paid a lot tae afford tae keep yourself and send enough home.' Bella put a hand on Jenny's arm, her chilled fingers pressing into the flesh. 'Now that Dad's makin' less money workin' in the stores instead of on the ships there's not enough comin' in as it is.'

'He'll have to stop spending most of his money at the pub, then,' Jenny said bitterly.

'You know he'll not do that. An' with Patrick not earning I can't spare anything. It's hard enough tae pay the rent as it is.'

'I need to get away, Bella!'

'Later, when things are better,' Bella's voice was pleading. 'You like your work in the tracing office, don't you?'

'Yes, but—'

'When things are better,' Bella said again, her hand tightening on Jenny's arm.

Looking down at the work-reddened fingers clutching at her sleeve, the broken nails and bony knuckles, Jenny knew that her sister was right. Despair washed over her; she felt like a prisoner about to start a long sentence for a crime that she hadn't committed . . .

2

It was a long, wearying evening. Neighbour after neighbour called to offer condolences as the news spread round the streets, each bringing something – a plate of home-made scones, a packet of biscuits, half a loaf, a 'scrapin'' of margarine. Jenny and her two sisters were kept busy making tea, for it was the custom on such occasions to offer hospitality to every visitor.

Faith, still frighteningly calm and dry-eyed, assured each sympathiser, with growing determination, that her son would be found safe and well and sent home.

Alice had come back from the Malloys without little Helen, who had already been tucked into the wall bed that the three Malloy girls shared, and was to stay there for the night. Lottie returned home halfway through the evening, her red-gold curls and vivid tawny eyes lighting up the room as soon as she walked into it.

When the news was broken to her she looked blankly from one face to the other. 'Missing?' she asked at last. 'Missing in action? Maurice?'

'It means that they don't know where he is, Lottie,' Mrs Malloy said, and the girl glared at her.

'I know fine what it means!'

'It's all right, hen. He'll come back tae us,' Faith said for what seemed to Jenny to be the hundredth time. The neighbours exchanged furtive glances then nodded their heads vigorously. One of them put a gentle hand on Lottie's arm, but it was shaken off.

'And what if he doesnae?' Lottie demanded, dry-eyed. 'What's tae happen tae me then?'

There was a general hiss of indrawn breath from the group of women.

'Stop thinking about yourself for once,' Jenny said sharply, and Bella chimed in, 'What about Mam – how d'ye think she feels?'

'She's all right, she's got her man – and she's got you and Alice,' Lottie said sulkily. 'It's me that'll have no place tae go tae if Maurice doesnae come home the way he promised. He'd no right tae go off tae fight an' leave me with a wean!'

11

Jenny took a step forward, her hands fisting by her sides. Lottie had always been selfish, but until then none of them had realised just how deep her selfishness went. Jenny started to speak, then stopped, swallowing the bitter, angry words back, unwilling for her mother's sake to cause a scene at such a time.

'We'll see ye all right,' Faith was saying, 'You and the wee one. We'll look after ye till Maurice comes home.'

'Aye, no need for you tae fret, Lottie,' Mrs Malloy chimed in, a steely edge to her voice. 'I'm sure *you'll* land on yer feet, whatever happens.'

Lottie gave her a venomous look, appropriated a scone and a cup of tea that Alice had just poured for Faith, and announced that she was going to bed.

'An' don't you worry yersel' about yer wean – she's stayin' wi' me the night,' Mrs Malloy tossed the words after her but they were ignored as Lottie slammed the kitchen door behind her, leaving a shocked silence in her wake.

'I knew she was a hard bitch, but I didnae realise she was as hard as that!' someone finally muttered, and Faith half-reared from her chair, roused out of her apathy by the need to defend her beloved son's sweetheart.

'It's the suddenness of it!' she snapped back, 'It's just the way it took her!'

'Ye're right, Faith, ye're right,' Mrs Malloy soothed, the edge gone from her voice as she stooped over her friend. 'Don't get yourself all upset, now.'

Behind Faith's back the other women exchanged looks that spoke volumes.

Long after Bella went home to Patrick, Teeze Gillespie lurched up the stairs and into the kitchen, drunk as a lord, loud-mouthed, aggressive, scattering the last of the well-meaning visitors and sending them off to their own homes.

'Make yersel' useful,' he commanded his wife thickly as the final caller fled, 'Get me somethin' tae eat!'

'I'll do it, Mam. You stay where you are,' Jenny said, but her mother had already scrambled out of the chair so that Teeze could sit down. Frying potatoes and onions on the range while Alice set the table and Faith fussed nervously around the sink, Jenny thought longingly about Glasgow, and the new life she had planned.

When the meal was ready and Teeze eating it the two girls helped their mother to pull the truckle bed out from under the bed in the alcove, then to undress and wash their grandmother. With the bed in the middle of the floor the kitchen seemed to shrink to the size of a cupboard. The corners of the low bed hacked unwary ankles as the three women manoeuvred the invalid out of her chair and worked over her.

It was a relief when Jenny was free to go to bed in the small, narrow room that she had all to herself. It had been Maurice's room before he went off to the war and there was only space in it for the bed and a large orange box that Jenny used as both a table and a storage area for blouses and underwear. Her skirts and the one dress she owned were hung on nails hammered into the wall.

Most of the shipyard workers' houses boasted two or three handsome pieces of furniture, for the Dalkieths were, on the whole, good to their employees, and when a ship came in for refurbishment it had always been their policy to sell off the discarded furniture, made of the finest timber by skilled craftsmen, to their workers at nominal prices. Most of the other yards either sold the furniture to second-hand dealers or scrapped it.

Before the war, when Teeze and Maurice were both bringing in wages, the Gillespies had owned several pieces of furniture from the yard, including the handsome sideboard that still stood in the kitchen. But the fitting bay, open to the bitter winds that swept down the river had been well named 'Pneumonia Bay' by the men who worked there. Teeze Gillespie had succumbed to pneumonia about a year earlier, and the determined fight he had put up, insisting on going off to work day after day when he wasn't fit for it, had almost killed him and resulted in permanent damage to his lungs. Now he worked in the stores, sweeping floors and running errands and dedicating most of his reduced wage to the local pubs.

With Maurice fighting in the war and Alice still at school, money had become scarce; one by one the pieces Faith had delighted in and polished every day had been sold and replaced by orange boxes begged from local shopkeepers. Only the sideboard remained as a symbol of those better days.

Jenny blew out the candle – there was gas-light only in the kitchen – and lay in bed, thinking of her handsome, outgoing brother. It was hard to believe that he was dead but, unlike her mother, Jenny knew that they would never see Maurice again. Wee Helen would grow up without knowing her father.

The tears came unexpectedly and she wept for fatherless Helen, then for Maurice, and finally for herself and the way her hopes and plans had been dashed. There would be no going off to Glasgow for her, no new life. She knew that now.

One day, mebbe. But not yet. Not for a long time . . .

'Ye don't mean it!' Lizzie's voice was incredulous. 'Ye're surely not going tae turn down the chance tae get out of here and start a new life!'

'How can I, now that Maurice is – Maurice won't be coming home?'

Jenny, Lizzie and Maureen were crossing the bridge on their way to work. The sky overhead was threatening and, glancing over the stone parapet, Jenny saw that the water hurrying below on its way to the Clyde was yellowish grey and sullen. The weather suited her mood.

'She cannae leave her mam just now, Lizzie,' Maureen agreed. 'Mebbe in a month or two—'

'It'll be too late, then,' Lizzie snapped, walking faster, so that the other two had to run a few steps to catch up.

'I just need to get things settled here.'

'And you expect my auntie tae keep the position open for you, do you?'

'No, of course not. But mebbe there'll be another place later.'

'I don't suppose there will be. And you neednae think I'll stay here just because you're staying, Jenny Gillespie,' Lizzie said, sticking her chin out and increasing her pace until she was almost running. Jenny trailed miserably along behind her, swallowing back the tears. Life was so unfair. All she asked for was just a handful of happiness, but each time she grasped it, it ran through her fingers like sand.

'Ach, don't be so childish, Lizzie!' Maureen panted in exasperation when Lizzie finally slowed down and allowed the other two to catch up with her. 'Jenny's not doing it on purpose – she wants tae go tae Glasgow, but how can she, the way things are at home?'

They had reached the huge, wrought-iron main gates to the yard. The men started work half an hour before the office staff, so the steady flood of people crowding in at the gates had ceased. Now there was only the office workers and the inevitable knot of men waiting patiently outside the gate, anxious-eyed and shivering in the wind, in the hope of getting a day's work.

'Me childish? I like that! Who is it that's been fair desperate tae get out of Ellerslie ever since Robert Archer jilted her? Not me,' said Lizzie, and marched into the yard, leaving Jenny shocked and winded with the sudden pain of betrayal. She and Lizzie had been friends since their first week at school; they had grown up together and it was Lizzie who had helped Jenny through her grief when Robert had gone off to work in the English shipyards then chosen to marry an Englishwoman.

'I didn't – I don't care about Ro – about him,' she said feebly, but

Lizzie had gone beyond hearing, stamping across the cobbled yard, her solid, broad behind swinging and swaggering beneath her blue serge skirt.

'She walks like one of they cows they drive through the streets tae the market,' Maureen said, but Jenny, stricken, couldn't even manage a twitch of the lips as she moved on round the corner and along the street to where the yard's Experimental Tank section was situated.

'Ach, pay no heed tae her, hen.' Maureen caught up with her and slipped a hand into the crook of her elbow. 'She's just jealous because no man's ever looked at her. Why else d'ye think she's so set on goin' tae Glasgow? It's because she's heard that the men there arenae all that choosy!'

It was hard to stay downhearted for long in Maureen's company, and this time a faint, shaky grin tugged at one corner of Jenny's mouth as the two girls stepped over the wooden threshold into the wax room, which opened directly to the street. 'Maureen Malloy, you're terrible!' Jenny protested, her gloom lifting a little despite herself.

'I know that, but it's folk like me that keep the confessional frae gettin' dusty!' said Maureen.

The furnaces had been lit early to start the slabs of wax melting and the room was already cosy. Baldy Devine, one of the moulders, was working at the clay bed, the long trough where clay was shaped by wooden templates into a mould, then covered with canvas sheeting before liquid wax was poured in to make the finished model. He glanced up as the girls came in. Baldy was famed for having more hair on his wizened little face than his head; even his enormous grey walrus moustache exuded sympathy.

'We're all awful sorry tae hear about your Maurice, lass,' he said, and Jenny nodded.

'Thanks, Baldy.'

'Bearin' up, are ye?'

'I'm fine, Baldy.'

His brown eyes warmed in a smile. 'That's the ticket, hen.'

The model room was small, and there was only a narrow space between the clay bed and the large cutting machine where the exact measurements were cut into the models to guide the men who then shaved the surplus wax away, flake by flake. Neil Baker, one of the naval architects, was perched beside it on a small revolving stool, one plump hand resting on the lever that operated the sharp instruments within the machine. Although he was only in his early twenties Neil was already running to fat and his buttocks overhung the stool.

He glanced round, then leaned back as Jenny approached, ostensibly to study the plan pinned on the machine for his guidance. All the tracing office girls knew Neil of old. Normally Jenny would have squeezed past his broad back, ignoring his leer as their bodies were forced together by the narrowness of the passage, but this morning she hesitated.

'Sorry,' he drawled, and wiggled slightly on the stool, swinging it round so that her thigh would have to press against his knee as she tried to ease by him. 'There – you can surely manage past now.' His pale blue eyes ran deliberately over her and, despite her coat, buttoned to the throat, Jenny felt as though she had nothing on but her underclothes. 'You're not that fat.'

'No, but you are.' Maureen edged her way round Jenny then pushed past Neil, managing as she went to jab him in the ribs with an elbow, shoving him against the cutting machine. He opened his mouth to object, but instead let out an almost womanly squeak of outrage and leapt off the stool as Maureen unexpectedly reached down and grabbed a handful of his rump.

'You'd be worth a shillin' of anyone's money in the pork butcher's, Neil,' she said loudly then caught at Jenny's arm as Baldy and the other men in the room howled with laughter, pulling her past the naval architect, who was too busy coping with his own embarrassment to savour the brief contact between them.

'Bitch!' he snapped, crimson-faced.

'Bugger,' Maureen retorted calmly. Amused faces peered over the railings of the gallery above, where the joiners and cutters worked.

'Can I go next, Maureen!' someone shouted down.

'The first yin's free, the rest o' youse'll have tae pay for the pleasure,' she yelled back, laughing. 'Come on, Jenny. He's like a dirty old man, that one,' she went on loudly as they climbed the short flight of wooden stairs to the next level. 'Just because he's a naval architect and his dad's one o' the gaffers he thinks he's somethin' special.'

Before crossing to the stairs that led up to her own office Jenny paused and glanced down into the model room. The melted wax was beginning to pour in a pale gold river into the clay bed through the pipes leading from the two small heating tanks on one wall. Jenny had been working as a tracer for four years now, but she still found the process of model-making fascinating, and the work she did, analysing the results of the tests run on the wax models in the tank, made her long to know more about the whole complex business of designing and building ships.

She turned to glance at the tank itself, stretching three hundred

16

feet away from her. The truck that spanned the water's breadth was on the move, backing up the length of the tank, with Mr Duncan, the tank superintendent and a naval architect by trade, standing on the small platform. Jenny lingered, waiting until it reached the far end. There it paused, then came clanking and rumbling towards her, driven by the steam engine at the far end of the tank, the model under trial clamped firmly on to the underside of the truck. As always, there was a breathless moment when it seemed that this time the truck would burst through the buffers at the end of the tank, then it came to a stop with a final bone-shaking clang as Maureen called her name from the second flight of stairs. Reluctantly, Jenny went to join her.

Senga, the third tracer, was already in the office and Miss McQueen, the supervisor, was hanging her jacket up carefully.

'Are you sure you should be at work this morning, Jenny?' she asked with unexpected sympathy. 'I heard about your brother. Could your poor mother not be doing with you at home?'

'She'd as soon everything was just as usual, Miss McQueen.' Jenny took her own coat off and hung it up, then reached for the smock that each girl wore to protect her clothes from the coloured inks they used.

The supervisor nodded. 'In that case, so would I – and that means, Maureen Malloy, getting on with the work instead of fidgeting with your hair,' she added with a sudden switch back to her usual tone. Maureen jumped, then scrambled up on to her high chair at the sloping desk running the length of the office wall as Miss McQueen doled out the morning's work.

Senga and Maureen were set to analysing the results of a series of trials carried out the previous day in the tank, which meant that they had to work their way through a great bundle of paper, collating the detailed results from each experiment on to four or five sheets which would then go back downstairs to the small drawing office where the naval architects worked. Jenny was given the more precise task of finishing off a pencilled line-drawing, going over each line in coloured ink and tidying up the architect's scribbled notes.

It was the sort of elaborate task she normally revelled in, requiring precision and care. The details before her had to be meticulously recorded, as the completed line-drawing would be used by the designers, then the engineers, platers, boilermakers and everyone else involved in the building of the ship. Ever since Lizzie's final malicious comment about Robert her heart had felt as though it had been scrubbed with a hard-bristled brush dipped in strong disinfectant, a raw ache that slowly began to fade as she worked. It thrilled her to know that in the noisy, busy yard outside great sheets of metal would

17

be bent to the correct shapes then riveted together on the massive stocks. Plate by plate, pipe by pipe, the ship would rise towards the sky until eventually it was completed. And she, Jenny Gillespie, would have played her part in its birth. Time flew past as she worked, then as she laid down a pen for a moment and stretched stiffened muscles Lizzie's voice intruded unexpectedly, 'Ever since Robert Archer jilted her—' and Jenny knew that the pain that she thought had finally gone was still with her.

It was Robert Archer, Maurice's friend, who had first aroused her interest in the craft of boat-building, firing her with his own enthusiasm. Robert, himself a naval architect, had helped her to study for the examination that had won her a place in the tracing office. Their shared love of ships had turned to love for each other; or so Jenny had believed. But she had been wrong, she thought now, flexing her stiff fingers, trying to push the thoughts out of her mind, and failing.

An orphan who lived with an elderly relative, Robert had been made welcome in the Gillespie household, for Faith's sympathies were stirred by the way his knobbly wrists and large, strong hands stuck out of sleeves that were far too short for him, and by his cracked and battered boots, with string for laces.

'He's neglected, poor wee laddie,' she said, although Robert, who had grown up rather than out in his early teens, was already a good half-head taller than she herself. His burning ambition was to know everything there was to know about shipbuilding, and to be master of his own yard one day.

'I'll do it, you just wait and see,' he insisted firmly when Maurice and Teeze, both content to work for others, laughed at him. Jenny, looking at his determined young face, the glow in his grey eyes, had believed him.

At first he was almost unaware of her existence, for she was only Maurice's young sister and he himself, older than Maurice, was some seven years her senior. But as time passed and he completed his apprenticeship he became aware of her interest in anything he had to say about his work.

By that time, Jenny's talent and liking for arithmetic and drawing had begun to baffle her mother and annoy her father. 'What's the sense in a lassie knowin' how tae dae her sums an' paint pretty pictures?' her father taunted time and time again. Her attempts to justify herself usually ended in a boxed and ringing ear and, 'Ye want tae learn tae keep a civil tongue in yer head instead, girl! What man's goin' tae want tae marry a shrew?'

Only Robert understood. He began to encourage her and help her

18

with her homework, sometimes even sitting at the kitchen table with her, patiently unravelling some mathematical problem while Maurice, who like his father had little time for book learning, was out with this girl or that, enjoying himself. When she was about to leave school it was Robert who had suggested that she should sit the Dalkieth examination.

'They're good people tae work for. Willing tae encourage folk that work hard. You've got a sharp brain, Jenny – you should at least try the examination.'

The pattern of lines on the stiff paper before Jenny merged and faded as she thought of the day she heard that she had come top in the examination and been rewarded with a place in the Experimental Tank's tracing office. The day Robert had first kissed her. Dazed with success and excitement she had run to tell him and had found him coming down the stairs of the building where he lived. As he stepped from the final stair Jenny, scampering through the close, ran full tilt into him and he had to brace himself and catch her in order to prevent a collision.

'I did it!' she crowed into his chest, broader now that he had started earning a wage and justified better feeding. 'I came first! I'm to report to the tracing office on Monday!'

She looked up to see her own triumph mirrored in his normally serious face. 'Jenny, I'm proud of you!' He enfolded her in an unselfconscious bear hug, then held her back a little. 'What did your father have to say?'

Some of the pleasure left her. 'He just grunted.'

Robert, his hands still on her shoulders, shook her gently. 'He's just jealous – you know how the men in the yard are about the Tank. They all think the folk that work there are toffee-nosed.'

'I wish he could have been pleased with me, just this once.'

'Pay no heed. I'm pleased for you, Jenny. I'm proud of you,' said Robert, and then he kissed her, a light kiss that took them both by surprise. For a moment Jenny experienced sheer astonishment, then a great wave of happiness swept over her. Her arms tightened about him and he kissed her again, taking more time about it.

'That's never happened to me before,' she said shakily when he finally released her.

'Was it – did you not like it?'

'Of course I liked it, you daft lummock!' said Jenny, and he gave a yell of laughter that started a child wailing behind a nearby door, and a woman snapped her irritation. 'Come on—' He took her hand and pulled her out of the close and along the street, not stopping until they reached the bridge—

19

'Are you not finished yet, Jenny?' Miss McQueen asked, irritated, her voice shattering the memory of the bridge, and Robert's arm about her shoulders. 'I promised Mr Duncan that drawing by noon. You're not usually so slow.'

'I'm sorry, Miss McQueen.' Jenny picked up a pen. It was a piece of malice on Lizzie's part, she thought as she worked; she had managed to forget Robert altogether, and now everything had come back to her, as vividly as though it had happened only yesterday instead of four years earlier . . .

Just before the threat of the coming war hardened into reality William Dalkieth, the owner of the shipyard and a man of great intelligence and ambition, had decided to send three carefully selected young employees to one of the yards in the North-East of England to learn more about shipbuilding for the eventual benefit of the Dalkieth yard.

Robert, one of the chosen three, had eagerly accepted the offer. Sitting at the long, sloping desk, watching as one ink-stained hand held a ruler firmly in place and the other drew a blue line over the thick graph paper, she could hear his voice as clearly as though he, and not Maureen, was sitting on the neighbouring stool.

'If I stay here I'll be no more than an ordinary worker for the rest of my days. If I take this chance, who knows what could happen? We'll write to each other, Jen. It'll work out well for both of us, you'll see!'

There was one consolation – because of the work he was doing he was of value to the English yard and wasn't, to Jenny's relief, taken into the armed forces. But after six months his letters began to taper off. Then came the terrible day when he wrote to tell her that he wanted to marry an English girl he had met.

She had torn up all his letters then, put him out of her life and gone through the misery of knowing that everyone in the tenements and the Experimental Tank section knew that Jenny Gillespie had been jilted.

Eventually, the gossip had ended and somehow, she had survived.

3

In November a party was held in the big back court to celebrate the end of the war. Teeze got very drunk and tried to fight Mr Malloy then collapsed, and was carried upstairs by half a dozen men and slung into the alcove bed.

Before she went to her own bed Jenny stood at the narrow window in her room, brushing her long curly hair and looking out at the uneven pattern of lamplit windows on the other side of the court. Figures crossed and recrossed most of the windows, and she could hear the faint skirl of music, for the party had moved indoors, scattered through most of the tenement flats. With Maurice still missing, the Gillespies had little to celebrate, though Lottie had gone off with a group of revellers, leaving Jenny and Alice to put wee Helen to bed.

'Are you asleep?' Alice whispered through the bedroom door.

'No. Come on in.'

As Alice, barefooted and in her nightgown, a shawl wrapped around her shoulders, closed the door behind her the flame of the single candle in the room dipped and swayed. The moving light reflected brilliant colour from the mass of red and pink roses decorating a fat teapot on the orange box, the flowers seeming to move as though brushed by a summer breeze.

Alice perched on the edge of the bed. 'I couldn't sleep for Dad's snoring. That teapot's bonny, Jen.'

'It's for Miss McQueen. It's the first time she's ever asked me to decorate anything, so I wanted it to be specially good.' As a schoolgirl Jenny had learned the art of china painting from an elderly neighbour. She enjoyed the detailed work, which needed the same attention and precision as her job in the tracing office, and neighbours who couldn't afford to buy pretty china often bought pieces of plain white delft for her to decorate. She charged a nominal fee for her work, just enough to pay for the paints and brushes that she used.

'I wish I could paint like that,' Alice said wistfully. She knew better than to touch the teapot; it had to be left to dry, and then Jenny would

21

bake it in the kitchen oven until the colours had set. 'Lizzie was fairly queening it at the party, wasn't she?' she added tartly. 'You'd have thought the whole thing was to celebrate her going off to Glasgow instead of the end of the war. Give me the brush.' She took charge of it and began to brush her sister's hair. 'You should've been able to go to Glasgow too, Jen, instead of being stuck here because of us. It's not fair – why did the war have to do this to us?'

'It's happened to thousands of folk. Even the Dalkieths lost Mr Edward in the fighting. Their money didnae protect him. When it came down to it, he was just the same as our Maurice.'

Her head bounced on the stem of her neck as Alice drew the brush again and again through her crackling hair. 'But Edward Dalkieth didnae leave responsibilities the way Maurice left us with Lottie and wee Helen. I'd not blame you,' said Alice fiercely, 'if you hated the lot of us for being so dependent on you. Lottie does nothing to help.' Her mouth, usually smiling, took on a downward droop. 'And it'll be almost a year yet before I'm old enough to leave school and get a job.'

Jenny took the brush back. 'You're going to stay on at school as long as you can. Maurice and me already decided that.'

'But that was before he—'

'Alice, you should still try for the scholarship to the Academy, the way Maurice wanted.'

'But the scholarship only covers the fees, not the uniform I'd have to wear, and mebbe the books as well.'

'We'll worry about that when the time comes. The first thing is to try for it. One day you're going to do better than any of us. You're going to get out of Ellerslie—'

'I don't want to, Jenny. I like Ellerslie.'

'At least you'll get out of this poky wee place and live in one of the grand houses—'

'With a garden and a drawing room and a maidservant?'

Jenny picked up a piece of wool and began to tie her hair back. '*Two* maidservants. And a carriage.' They slipped easily into the game they had played together for years and never tired of.

'No, a car,' Alice insisted. 'A big car, all gleaming and sleek. With a driver.'

'A handsome driver with black leather gloves—'

'I'll send him to fetch you for afternoon tea twice a week,' Alice offered grandly.

'I'll wear my furs and diamonds. But until I get them, lend me a bit of your shawl – I'm freezing.'

Alice giggled, and re-arranged the shawl so that they were both wrapped in it.

22

'That's better.' Jenny blew out the candle and they sat in silence for a moment, looking out at the windows across the court.

'Jen,' Alice whispered at last, 'Shouldn't someone tell Mam that our Maurice's probably dead? Is it right to let her go on hoping?'

'Hoping's all she's got, pet. Let her hold on to it. She'll let go in her own good time.'

'But—' Alice was stopped by a mighty yawn. Jenny began to unwrap herself from the shawl.

'Go to bed – and don't you fret about anything but yourself and your schoolwork.'

'Och, I can manage the work fine.' Alice stood up, adding wryly, 'Brains are all I've got.'

'Alice!'

'It's true – and I should know it because I'm the one with the brains. You're the pretty one of this family, and Bella's pretty too – or she was before Patrick got hurt. But me—' Her hands gleamed in the light from the other windows as she indicated her sturdy body, her straight brown hair, her broad, freckled face. 'I'm brainy.'

When she was alone, Jenny got into bed. One by one the parties still going on in the crowded tenement flats came to an end, the revellers calling to each other as they crossed the dark courtyard on their way home, some laughing and some cursing as they stumbled over broken flagstones or walked into clothes-poles. The outer door opened and closed, marking Lottie's return.

Jenny fell asleep before the last of the lights in the windows opposite finally winked out.

The old year, the last year of the war that had brought heartbreak to almost every family in Ellerslie, died, and nobody mourned it. The womenfolk scoured and white-washed their homes as usual, to make sure they were clean for the start of the new year, and dumplings and rich, dark, fruity black buns were made for the New Year celebrations. There were fewer parties than usual, though, because so many of the tenement families were still in mourning for sons and brothers and husbands lost in the war.

1919 brough bitter winds that numbed the hands of the men working on the first peacetime ship in Dalkieth's yard. Teeze, searching for some way of gaining the stature he had lost when he had had to give up his trade, developed an interest in the problems faced by shipyard workers in general. Although trades unions were now commonplace on Clydeside none of the men who worked in the Dalkieth yard belonged to a union because it had always been the Dalkieth family's way to keep their employees informed of matters that concerned them, and to listen to grievances and deal with them at once.

But the war had changed many things. Men who had faced death defending their country were more determined than before to have their say. George Dalkieth, who now ran the yard, was a man who had never had the workers' respect, a man who was known for his lack of interest in anyone's opinions but his own. He was also a man who had stayed at home in safety while his brother and many of their employees fought in the front lines.

Since the war ended many of the Dalkieth workers had begun to feel that the time had come for the trades unions to represent their interests. A small group of men from the various sections in the yard fell, during that winter, into the habit of gathering in the Gillespie kitchen when the public houses closed, to talk about the business of the yard and argue over the changes that they felt were needed.

In the narrow streets by the river there was the usual outbreak of chest complaints, but at least they were spared the Spanish influenza that was still ravaging the country in the wake of the war.

'It's wary o' comin' here in case it catches somethin' worse than itsel',' someone said with a flash of irony one night in the Gillespie's flat.

A gust of laughter followed Jenny out into the hall when she went to answer yet another knock at the door. Daniel Young stepped into the hallway, muttering a greeting and dragging off his peaked cap. She stood back against the wall to let him pass; as she followed him into the kitchen she saw that the thin coat he wore was darkened over the shoulders with rain.

'Give me your coat, Daniel.' She took it from him and hung it up in the hall as Faith poured out a mug of strong black tea for him.

'Ye should have brought the laddie with ye, Daniel,' she said, lifting the condensed milk tin. Daniel stopped her with a raised hand.

'I'll have it as it is, Mrs Gillespie. The boy's got his schoolwork tae dae. He's fine on his lone.' The men gathered about the range eyed each other. Everyone knew of Daniel's burning ambition for his son, a clever boy who had never been allowed out to play with the other children. He took the tea with a nod of thanks and leaned against the high mantelshelf, as there were no more seats vacant. In contrast to the other men in the room, he was formally dressed in a neat shirt and a suit that looked as though it had been well brushed just before he came out. His straight dark brown hair was smooth against his skull and he wore a tie which was faded from many washings, but spotlessly clean. Even before he went off to join the Navy Daniel Young had been particular about his appearance. He went off to work each morning looking as though he was going to an office instead of a shipyard and he came back in the same neat condition at the end of the day. It was said that he visited the local public baths each afternoon before going home, to bathe himself and change out of his working clothes.

Jenny, who was working on a sugar bowl and milk jug to match the teapot she had painted for Miss McQueen, sat down at the table and picked up her paint-brush. Her gaze was drawn back to Daniel as she mixed more paint. He was talking with animation, using an index finger to underline the points he was making. His eyes glowed with enthusiasm and for once there was some colour in his thin face.

He glanced up suddenly and met Jenny's eyes. His voice faltered for a moment, then picked up as both of them looked hastily away as though caught committing some crime.

A discarded newspaper swept towards Jenny's ankles as she hurried down the street. It was a Saturday, and the week's work had just ended. She side-stepped out of the paper's reach then ducked in at the close, glad to be out of the cutting January wind that had scoured the street clear of the usual knots of men, women and children.

Coming up the stairs, she could smell the herring that they always had on Saturdays, dipped in oatmeal and fried with onions, then served with boiled potatoes.

In the warm kitchen Alice was setting the table for the midday meal while her mother attended to the pots on the range. Marion slept uneasily in one fireside chair and Teeze, home before Jenny, read his newspaper in the other, with Helen playing placidly between their feet.

'Jen!' Helen carolled the name joyfully as her aunt came into the kitchen. She scrambled up from the rag rug before the range, tipping herself on to her hands and knees, her round bottom sticking into the air, her face tense with concentration. She was fifteen months old now, and just learning to walk without holding on. Pushing down hard on her hands, she managed to rock skilfully on to her heels then, upright at last, she swayed for a moment before steadying herself and toddling across the floor.

'There's my clever girl!' Jenny lifted her, holding her close, burying her face in the silky-soft russet hair, then released her when Helen, who could rarely be still for a moment, squirmed to be set down again. The little girl toddled back to her rag doll, losing her balance at the last minute and collapsing on to the rug with a thump, tumbling first one way, against Teeze's ankles, then the other, brushing against Marion's stick-like legs.

25

'For Christ's sake, can a man no' get a bit of peace in his own house?' Teeze rustled the newspaper and scratched at one armpit. 'I'm surrounded by damned females!'

'Mind yer gran!' Faith Gillespie squalled at the same moment, rushing to move Helen six inches to the left, away from the old woman. Marion's body twitched as she woke suddenly, disturbed by the angry voices more than the bump she had received from Helen. She whimpered and struggled, and would have slid sideways if Jenny hadn't caught her shoulders.

'Come on, Gran, heave up a bit. That's better.'

Faith immediately brushed her daughter aside and bent over the old woman. 'It's all right, Mam, I'm here. Ye're all right. We'll get ye washed, will we, and then ye can have some broth. Alice, damp that cloth and hand it over here. Jenny, ladle some broth out for yer gran and yer dad.'

Marion Gillespie's bones had felt as brittle and delicate as a bird's; Jenny, watching her mother fussing round the old woman, recalled the way the colour had drained from Faith's face each time this same woman had marched into the house in the old days, her dark eyes cold, her back straight, her head, with its coronet of white hair beneath a black hat, held erect.

Marion had raised her son single-handed after her husband died young – possibly, quick-witted Alice claimed, his only way of escaping his wife – and from the day of Teeze's marriage she had done her best to make his wife's life miserable, visiting at least once a week, carping and fault-finding. Her domination had ended one day six months previously. While attending to a customer in the butcher's shop where she had worked since her husband's desertion she had paused, looked about her uncertainly, then dropped to the floor like a stone. She hadn't uttered an intelligible word since, or been able to do anything for herself. Faced with the shame of letting his mother go into the workhouse asylum, Teeze had had no option but to find a place for her in his own home. Having done his duty he ignored her, leaving her entirely to his wife.

Carefully, tenderly, Faith spooned broth into Marion, mopping at her chin between every mouthful. Alice fed Helen and Jenny saw to her father's needs, for Teeze never sat at the table for a meal, but stayed in his chair while his womenfolk danced attendance on him.

It wasn't until the rest of the family had been fed and Helen and Marion washed and settled, the baby in her crib and Marion in her chair, that Faith and Alice and Jenny were able to sit down at the table for their own meal.

'Where's Lottie today?' Jenny wanted to know. When Faith

shrugged she persisted, 'Is it not time she was staying in more, seeing to her own bairn?'

'For all the good she is, she's as well out of the way,' Faith said indifferently.

'But it's not right that she should be out enjoying herself instead of help—'

'Hold yer tongue or it's you that'll be out of here!' Teeze snapped.

'Aye, leave it, Jenny,' his wife said quietly. 'It's easier tae just see tae things myself than tae try tae make her dae them.'

Jenny, aware of the exhaustion on her mother's grey face and the way Faith pushed her food around the plate, too tired to eat it, subsided. But Lottie's laziness was beginning to rankle and, when the meal was over and the dishes washed and she had sketched some possible patterns for future china painting, she found that her annoyance over Lottie's selfishness made her too restless to concentrate on anything.

When Helen woke from her nap Jenny fetched the little girl's coat, noting as she pulled the buttons across Helen's tummy to meet the buttonholes that she would soon need a new one, then the two of them set out on a visit to Bella. It took some time to get as far as the close because Helen, proud of her new ability, insisted on going down the stairs on her own, one step at a time, clutching at the iron railings and breathing heavily in concentration.

Patrick was in bed and Bella washing clothes in the small, stained sink. She wiped her hands on her sacking apron and drew the curtains that shut the alcove bed off from the rest of the room. 'He's had a bad day, poor soul.' She returned to her work, knuckling her hands round the collar of one of Patrick's shirts and rubbing hard.

'He's not the only one, by the look of you.' Jenny, peeling Helen out of her coat, eyed her sister with concern. 'Where did you get that bruise on your cheek?'

Bella bent her head quickly over the basin. It's only coal dust. I've just made up the fire.'

'Bella—' Jenny began, then glanced at the curtained alcove. 'Come on out for a wee while. I've some things to get from the corner shop and you look as if you could do with a breath of air.'

Her sister finished scrubbing at the shirt and started to wring the water out of the heavy material. 'I'd best stay here. Pat might need me.' She shook the shirt out and hung it over the clothes-horse by the range.

'At least sit down and let me finish the washing for you. You look exhausted.'

'It's all right, I've only got my working skirt to do. You could mebbe unravel that for me.' Bella pointed, then paused to draw an arm across her face before returning to her work.

'That' was a man's jersey, shrunk and already coming apart at cuffs and waist. But the wool was good enough; all it needed was careful washing and drying and it could be used again.

'Mrs McColl gave it to me,' Bella explained as her sister picked up the jersey. 'She's awfy good tae me. She puts the word round her friends, and they pass their unwanted stuff tae her for me.'

'So she should be good tae you, you work hard enough for her.' Bella spent one full day a week at Mrs McColl's big house, doing the heavy work. She also cleaned out Mr McColl's offices every Friday evening. Once, when the sisters were in the town together, Bella had pointed out Mrs McColl, a large well-dressed woman who looked far more able to do her own heavy work than thin little Bella.

'She pays me for what I do.'

'Not much.'

'It all helps. Don't you go criticisin' your elders and betters, Jenny Gillespie,' Bella said with a flash of spirit. She looked at Jenny. 'Ye're bein' awful nebby today.'

'I am not!'

'You're gettin' as bad as Miss Galbraith,' Bella teased, and they looked at each other and laughed. Miss Galbraith had been the terror of the local school when Bella and Jenny were pupils, an elderly woman with a permanent scowl and a voice that grated like a file on metal. Whenever one of the sisters tried to bully the other she was accused of becoming like Miss Galbraith.

'I wonder what happened to her?' Helen had settled down on the rug with a box of buttons. Jenny managed to locate an end of corrugated gray wool, and started ripping at the jersey, winding the growing strand round her knuckles. 'You never think of what happens to your teachers outside of school, do you? She's mebbe dead by now.'

Bella finished wringing out the skirt and spread it over the clothes-horse alongside Patrick's shirt, which had begun to steam gently in the heat from the range. The room smelled of wet clothes. 'If she is, she'll be giving them a hard time, wherever she ended up.'

As the dirty water gurgled noisily down the drain she dried her hands and arms and came to sit by the range, lowering herself into the chair carefully, as though she was an old woman with creaking bones. Helen immediately fisted her small hands over the legs of the chair and hauled herself upright, arms outstretched. Bella lifted her up and cuddled her, burying her face in the baby's rich red hair.

Lottie came into Jenny's mind, young and strong, drifting through

28

life with never a thought for anyone else, even her own daughter or her missing lover, while Bella uncomplainingly worked herself into exhaustion for the sake of a man who had been damaged and embittered by the war.

'Her hair might be like Lottie's, but her face is that like our Maurice's,' Bella said over Helen's shoulder, her blue-grey eyes wistful. 'Lottie's lucky, having such a bonny bairn.'

'You're young yet, Bella, you'll have bairns of your own.'

'It takes love tae make bairns – an' money tae raise them,' Bella said almost inaudibly. The light from the window made the bruise on her cheek more noticeable, and Jenny felt a stab of helpless anger. Bella was a gentle soul who wouldn't harm a fly. It was wrong of Patrick to take his frustration out on his wife, she thought, but she had the sense to hold her tongue. Her interference would only upset Bella further. 'I got a letter yesterday from Lizzie,' she said instead.

'How is she?'

'If she's to be believed, Neilson's Emporium's as near as anyone'll get to heaven on earth.'

Her sister's small rough hand, still damp from the washing, reached over and touched her own.

'I'm vexed for you, Jenny. You should be in Glasgow too, away from all this worry.'

'Och, life was never meant to be a bed of roses for the likes of us. We're used tae disappointments.'

'You've had more than your share. First Robert, then—'

'Robert was a long time ago,' Jenny said sharply.

Bella stared at her sister over Helen's head. 'You sound different.' She leaned forward a little, then said, 'You look different. I've noticed it ever since we heard about Maurice. Harder, somehow.'

Jenny hauled viciously at the wool in her lap. 'Is it any wonder? Bella, if you hear of any other cleaners needed, let me know.'

'Ye're surely not thinking of givin' up workin' in the Tank, are ye?'

'It's not for me, it's for Lottie.'

Bella gave a yelp of laughter, a rare sound these days. '*Lottie?* I can just see her down on her knees scrubbin' floors!'

'It's time she earned her keep, and the bairn's. She can't expect tae sit around the house eating food bought with someone else's wages. I've tried hinting that she should think of finding work, but it does no good. She just ignores me and goes her own way. But now things'll have tae change whether she likes it or not,' said Jenny with determination.

'Is that what Dad says?'

'Him? He doesnae fret himself about how we're all tae live. He

29

leaves that tae poor Mam – and she's too worn out tae take Lottie on. Bella – with Dad not earning so much now it's my wages that's making the difference at home. I don't mind supporting Helen and Gran, for they're helpless. But Lottie's well able to work. It's time she was doing her share.'

'Once Alice is old enough to leave school it'll be a help.'

'Alice should try for a scholarship in the spring . She could go on to the Academy – be a teacher, mebbe. She needs to get her chance – she's the clever one of the family.'

'So was Maurice.'

'Not clever enough tae keep himself frae gettin' killed.' Jenny picked carefully at a snarl in the wool. 'You'll let me know if you hear of any job that Lottie could do?'

'Aye.' Bella reluctantly began to loosen her arms from about Helen's warm little body. 'I'll make a wee cup of tea.'

Jenny put the shrunken jersey aside and stood up. 'No, I'll do it. I sit on my backside for most of the day.' She carefully measured a small amount of tea-leaves from the caddy then hoisted the kettle from the range and poured boiling water over them. 'You do more than you're fit for.'

They had kept their voices low, but even so Patrick Kerr, wide awake behind the thin curtain that hid him from their gaze, heard everything. He squeezed his eyes tight shut against the memory of the terror in Bella's eyes earlier, just before his fist had connected with her cheekbone, and against the frightening rage that had mauled him mercilessly over the past months.

But the anger still managed to force itself to the fore, filling his head, flooding the darkness behind his eyelids with a crimson glare.

4

Isobel Dalkieth stood in the big bay window of her drawing room. Although it was night outside and the room behind her was brightly lit by electricity the heavy blue velvet curtains were open and the dark window acted like a mirror, reflecting Isobel herself, straight-backed and handsome in unrelieved mourning black that would have overwhelmed most women but only served to complement her white hair, fine skin and clear green eyes. She looked past herself into the night, picturing in her mind's eye the terrace, the sloping lawn and the river beyond.

Like some of their own employees, the Dalkieths lived on the opposite side of the river from the main town, though in their case the surroundings were much more affluent. Isobel could see lights twinkling on the other side of the river and reflecting on the water; electric lights on the upper slopes where the wealthier townspeople lived, gas lamps nearest the shore where the tenements crowded together. She turned her head towards one of the side windows from where, by day, the bend of the river and a glimpse of the cranes and stocks of the Dalkieth yard could be seen.

'Here's to the first peacetime vessel in the yard, and a new beginning.' Fergus Craig, a quarry-owner, a member of the Dalkieth Board of Directors, and Isobel's brother, came to stand by her side. The window reflected him as an imposing man, also silver-headed, and tall enough to hold the extra weight brought upon him by increasing age and comfortable living.

Isobel accepted the glass he offered and sipped at her malt whisky appreciatively. She had never been one for wines. 'A poor beginning, Fergus.'

'Surely not. The order book's filled and the future looks secure. With the war behind us at last there's a new prosperity ahead.'

'With wages higher than they've ever been, and the spirit of anarchy in the country? Nothing'll ever be the same, or as good as before, you mark my words.'

There was a sudden pattering against the window as a shower of

February rain slashed across the glass, distorting the lights opposite. Isobel shivered and turned back into the comfortable room as Fergus put his own glass down and drew the curtains together. 'It's natural for you to be in low spirits after what you've been through those past few years, my dear. But things'll change – and for the better.'

'Not for me. I've lost the best of them, Fergus. First my husband, then my son. George should have been the one to go to war.' Isobel's voice was harsh. 'But no, he insisted on staying behind to look after the yard when his father became too ill to oversee things himself.' She sank on to one of the two velvet-covered sofas flanking the fireplace. 'No matter that Edward was the better master. George was set on saving his own skin – and now he's all I've got left, God help me.'

'You're too hard on the boy. I remember a time when George was your favourite.'

Isobel shrugged impatiently. 'Edward was born to follow his father into the business, but George was mine, my little one. He wasn't raised for responsibility. That's the trouble, now that he's the only one left.'

'It may be the making of him.'

'Or the ruination of the yard. If I'd only known what was going to happen, Fergus.' Isobel stared into the flames. Her father, a quarry-owner, had himself been a director of Dalkieth's shipyard, and it had delighted him and the Dalkieths when Isobel and William Dalkieth married. Her ambition had matched her husband's and it had been a good marriage, a true partnership, until William's death from heart trouble only months before his elder son Edward was killed in France. Now, Isobel looked ahead and saw a bleak future for the shipyard that had meant so much to her husband.

'I will *not* let George destroy the yard, Fergus. Not after all that William and Edward did for it!'

'Then do as I suggest – as William himself would suggest. Bring young Archer back from Tyneside. Make him the office manager so that he and George will have to work in tandem and George won't get everything his own way.'

'But he's the youngest of the men William sent south; too young, surely, to take on such responsibility,' she protested.

'He's the only one available,' her brother pointed out. 'Grey died in an accident and McGarrity has no wish now to come back to Scotland, but Archer's willing. Sometimes age has little to do with it. William kept a close eye on the lad when he sent him to England, and I've continued to do so. He's learned a lot and given a good account of himself – and he's hungry for success.'

A frown tucked Isobel's finely shaped brows together. 'He's the same age as George.'

'But more – mature. Archer's had to make his own way in life, and he's done it with confidence.'

'I'll grant you that it would be good to have a man we could trust in the place. A man who'd look after our interests until such time as George matures – if he ever does.' Isobel took another swallow of whisky, then said, 'My real hope, I suppose, is that this new wife of his'll give him an heir, a boy I can train to take his grandfather's place. In the meantime, I must make sure that there's still a yard for such a boy to inherit.'

Fergus Craig eyed his sister warily. He had always been a little afraid of Isobel's iron-clad determination, which verged at times on ruthlessness. Though he himself had little time for his nephew George he was sorry for both the young man and his wife. Isobel set standards that few people could live up to. 'I'm sure that George will provide you with many heirs.'

'I sincerely hope so,' she retorted tartly. 'After going through the embarrassment of his divorce I deserve some compensation! Thank God his father wasn't alive to suffer the shame of it. But then, if William had still been alive, George and Catherine would never have been allowed to contemplate divorce.' She swirled the remains of her drink round in the glass, then asked, 'What d'you make of my new daughter-in-law, Fergus?'

'She seems suitable. I hope that George finds happiness this time.'

'Catherine was never the right woman for him. Her people had a lot of money, and that mattered to George far more than it should have. Fiona comes from more ordinary stock and she has a lot to learn, but at least she's got ambition, far more of it than George has. Harnessed properly, it could be put to good use. She may become an asset – if,' Isobel Dalkieth added slowly, 'she plays her cards well.'

The rain-shower returned to throw itself against the windows again. Craig, eyeing his sister, judged that it was time to guide her thoughts back to the matter at the forefront of his own mind. He seated himself opposite her and leaned forward, elbows on thighs.

'About young Archer—' he began.

'Me? Go out scrubbin' other folks' floors?' Lottie's voice was outraged. 'I'll do no such thing!'

'Then you'll have to find yourself something more suited,' Jenny told her. 'I'm not going to go on working to support the likes of you when you're well able to bring in a wage.'

'Hoity toity – just listen tae her!' the other girl mocked, throwing a glance at Faith, who clattered dishes in the sink, carefully keeping out of the confrontation.

'I'm tired of the way you just do as you please in this house without putting a penny into it, Lottie.'

'It's not my fault Maurice was killed,' Lottie said sullenly, 'If he'd come home—'

'Our Maurice hasnae been killed!' Faith spun round from the sink, eyes blazing. 'He's missing, that's all. He'll be on his way home now that the war's over – he'll be here soon.'

'We know that, Mam,' Jenny told her levelly. 'But until he does come home we need more money now that Dad's not earning what he used to. I'm making almost as much as he is now.'

And all my wage goes into the house, while he drinks most of what he does earn, she thought, but such things couldn't be spoken aloud in her mother's presence. Only Faith had the right to criticise her man's drinking, nobody else.

Alice came through from the bedroom where she had been studying. 'What's going on?'

'Nothing. We're just sorting a few things out, aren't we, Lottie?'

'Aye, well, if I must work it'll not be scrubbin' the floors under other folks' feet,' Lottie sulked. 'I'll find somethin' better.'

'You do that. If you don't, I'll go ahead and find something for you. And there's another thing,' Jenny went on relentlessly, 'I'm going to move into the big bedroom with you and Helen. Alice'll have the wee room, so that she can get on with her homework in peace.'

'I'm not sharin' a room wi' you!'

'Then you can find somewhere else to sleep.'

'But it's not fair on you, Jenny,' Alice protested 'I can manage fine.'

'You need peace to get on with your work. You need that wee room more than I do. And don't forget,' Jenny turned back to Lottie, 'if you haven't found work by the end of the week I'll find it for you.'

'Are you goin' tae allow her tae order us all about like that?' Lottie appealed to Faith. 'Next thing you know she'll be puttin' her old grandmother out in the street because she cannae earn her own keep.'

Faith picked up a shabby piece of towelling and began to dry her hands. 'Jenny's right. It's her wage that's keepin' us alive.'

Avoiding Jenny's eye, she shuffled in her down-at-heel slippers to tuck the blanket more securely round her mother-in-law's knees. 'Things have changed,' she said quietly. 'They've changed for all of us.'

Lottie flounced out in a rage and Jenny, inwardly shaking, went to the tiny room she had just given over to Alice. She sat down on the bed and began to pull the pins out of her hair, looking around at the claustrophobic, damp-stained walls as she worked, close to tears at the thought of having to give up her privacy and share a bed with Lottie.

Alice tapped at the door and came in, subdued. 'Jen, I can't take your room away from you.'

'Of course you can, it's all decided. We'll change over tomorrow – and not another word.' She began to comb her hair, then tutted with annoyance as the comb tangled in it.

'It's because it's curly,' Alice took the comb and began to ease it through her sister's tumbled dark-brown curls.

'Why can't it be straight, like yours?'

'Curls are better.'

'They're not.' Jenny took a handful of hair and tugged at it. Then, struck by a sudden thought, she bounced to her feet. The comb, pulled from Alice's hand and still caught in her hair, hit off her cheek as she knelt down to rummage beneath the bed, bringing out a tin box. She opened it, and produced the scissors she used for dressmaking.

'Alice, I want you to cut my hair.'

'What? I can't do that!'

'Then I'll do it myself.' Jenny pushed her sister aside so that she could see herself in the room's small mirror.

'Jenny – what'll Mam say?'

'I doubt if Mam'll even have the time to notice. Anyway, it's my hair, not hers, and I can't be bothered pinning it up any more. It'd be easier to look after if there was less of it.'

Alice had one last try. 'You've got such bonny hair – it's a crime to cut it.'

Jenny pulled the comb free and tossed it on to the orange box, remembering, with a stab of pain, a night years before, just before Robert Archer left for England. She remembered the wind rustling the leaves overhead, the lumpiness of the ground beneath her shoulders, Robert's hand loosening her hair, drawing it over her shoulders. She remembered the touch of his knuckles against her neck, the husky note in his voice. 'You've got such bonny hair, Jenny. Promise me that you'll never ever let anyone cut it off.'

'It's a crime to waste the time I have to waste on it every day, when there are other things to do,' she said now to Alice, and took a firm grip on a clump of hair, discovering how difficult it was to tell by her own reflection where she should position the scissors.

35

'Wait – I'll do it, if you insist,' Alice took the scissors from her. 'You'll only chop it and make yourself look ugly. Now—'

She turned Jenny's head to one side, selected a lock of hair, and began to cut. 'I just hope you won't regret it when it's too late.'

The noise of the scissors biting their way through her hair crunched in Jenny's ear. A dark curl fell to her hand and from there to the floor.

'I'll not regret it,' she said steadily. 'Times change, folk change. I'm different now, Alice, and it's time I looked different.'

Lottie sulked and pouted until the last moment, then found a job as a barmaid in a public house two streets away.

'It means I'll no' be here tae see tae the bairn at nights,' she pointed out triumphantly.

'I'll see tae her,' Jenny said, and added, catching and holding Lottie's gaze with her own, 'I usually do in any case.'

True to her word, she had changed rooms with Alice, and now slept in the larger room, which reeked of damp and stale sweat and Lottie's cheap perfume. Alice, thrilled at having a place of her own to study in, had squeezed another orange box into her new room to use as a desk.

Jenny now had to keep all her possessions under the bed in boxes and bags, because Lottie's things were strewn about the small room; there were long red hairs each morning on both pillows of the bed they shared, and in little tangled clumps on the floor where they had been carelessly dropped after being pulled from the other girl's unwashed brush and comb. Gathering them up each day and carrying them into the kitchen to throw them on the range Jenny was glad that at least her own hair was now short and easy to keep clean and neat.

At the end of Lottie's first week at work there was another confrontation when she came in after everyone else had gone to sleep to find Jenny still awake in the bedroom.

'I'm waiting for your wages.'

Lottie glared, then said truculently, 'I'm no' givin' my money tae you.'

Jenny held her hand out. 'If you give it to Dad he'll only drink it instead of using it to pay the rent and buy food.'

'I'll give it tae yer Mam mysel', then.'

'No, I'll give it to her, since it was me that saw to it that you started earning your own keep,' Jenny said, and waited, her hand out, until Lottie sullenly handed over the money. Jenny pushed it around her palm with a forefinger. 'There's a shilling short here.'

'Four shillin's, that's all I get paid.'

'I went into the public house yesterday and asked the landlord. He

36

says it's five. It's not Mam you're dealing with now, it's me,' Jenny went on as Lottie's mouth dragged itself into an ugly square.

'Ye're a right bitch, Jenny Gillespie!'

'Mebbe so, but I'll still have that other shillin' out of you.'

'How am I tae manage if I give ye all my wages?' Lottie whined, and Helen stirred in her shabby cot then settled again, thumb in mouth.

'You get tips from some of the customers. Think yourself lucky I don't take them, too,' Jenny retorted heartlessly. When Lottie had handed over the missing shilling she tucked the coins into a small purse, which she put beneath her pillow.

She gave the money to her mother the next morning and Faith took it without a word. Subtly, the balance of power had shifted in the crowded house. It was a small victory that gave Jenny little pleasure but, nevertheless, it was a victory.

The real battle came the following week, when Lottie deliberately handed her second week's wages to Jenny in front of Teeze, who was slouched in his usual chair. Soon he would take himself off to the pub and his wife and daughters would start on the ritual of the Friday night cleaning.

'The money's all there, just as you wanted,' Lottie said loudly, with a sly, sidelong glance at Teeze. His head came up with a jerk and Faith, spooning some left-over custard into Marion's slack mouth, mopping the resulting trickles with a well-stained cloth, let the spoon clatter back into the bowl, her eyes anxiously darting from her daughter to her husband.

'What's she givin' her wage tae you for?'

Jenny looked her father in the eye. 'Because I told her to.'

'Here, give it tae me.' He held out a large hand, scarred from a lifetime of working on the ships.

Jenny shook her head. 'The rent man'll be coming tonight and I want to make sure he gets what's due to him. Then the rest'll go to Mam. You'd not want to see us all thrown out on the street, would you?'

'That's my business, no' yours!'

'Jenny says it's hers,' Lottie put in, swaying over to the sideboard to study herself in the mirror.

'Hers? Since when did you run this family, madam?'

'With you not earning so much and Maurice not here I'm bringing in a fair amount of the money,' Jenny told him levelly. 'I'm going to make sure it goes where it's needed.'

The newspaper Teeze had been reading was thrown to the floor. 'I said give it tae me!'

'So's you can spend it in the pub?'

His eyes took on a familiar red glow and he lurched out of the chair, one hand beginning to swing up. 'Ye cheeky wee—'

Helen began to whimper and Alice snatched her up and held her close, her own eyes round with apprehension.

'Teeze, don't!' Faith put the bowl down and jumped up, catching at her husband's sleeve. With a growl, he pushed her away.

'Stop it, Dad!' Jenny's knees were weak with fear and the anticipation of the heavy blow, but she knew that the only way to save herself was to stand up to him. She forced back the memory of past beatings and took a step towards him although her instincts clamoured for retreat. 'We're both too old for that now. Hit me, and I'll hit you back.'

'By God an' ye'll no'!'

'I will. I mean it!'

His arm began to lower in sheer surprise. 'Lift a hand tae yer faither, milady, an' ye're oot o' this hoose,' he blustered.

'If you want me out I'll go, with pleasure. But I'll take all of my wages with me. How are you going to keep yourself and the rest of them out of the workhouse on what you're earning now – let alone keep the pub going?'

'Jenny!' Faith moved to stand in front of her husband, her tired face twisted with anger. 'Don't you dare talk tae your father like that in his own house! It's not his fault he had tae give up working in the fitting bay.'

'I know it's not – but it's happened, and now it's my wage that's mostly keeping us,' Jenny said mercilessly. 'So it's up tae me tae make sure there's money for the rent and the food from now on.'

Teeze's face, already red with anger, seemed to swell and throb as though it was going to burst. For a moment Jenny thought that she had gone too far and that her father was going to take a seizure, then, with a snarl he pushed his wife away from him so hard that she stumbled against Jenny, who had to catch her. He snatched up his shabby jacket and slammed out of the house, leaving a shocked silence behind him.

'Are ye satisfied now?' Faith asked her elder daughter at last. 'Did ye enjoy humblin' the man in front of everyone?'

'Mam, if he got hold of Lottie's wages you know he'd only drink the money away.'

'One day you'll be old an' past bein' able tae work as hard as ye once did. See how ye feel about it then!' There were tears in Faith's eyes.

Jenny picked up the bowl as her grandmother whimpered and pawed fretfully at the air. She dipped the spoon into the custard then Faith's hands wrenched bowl and spoon away from her, spattering the two of them.

'I'll see tae yer gran,' she said with quiet dignity. 'Ye'll not take everythin' intae your own hands – not yet. Ye can get on with yer work. And so can you two,' she added to Lottie and Alice.

'I've got my own work tae go tae,' Lottie said, and flounced out. Jenny fetched the tin of black-lead and the brush from the bottom of the cupboard and began to work on the range while Alice poured the last dregs from the teapot into the special enamel mug Jenny had decorated with bright flowers and fat, cheerful elves when Helen was born. She diluted the tea with warm water from the kettle, stirred in a spoonful of sugar and a spoonful of condensed milk, and handed it to the little girl, who received it in eager hands. Then Alice tipped hot water from the big kettle into the basin and started washing the good plates, those that were kept on show on the range of shelves on the dresser and only used for special occasions. Helen, well used to the Friday night ritual, retired out of harm's way underneath the table with her dolly and her mug.

When she had finished attending to Marion, Faith turned her attention to cleaning the sideboard. Nobody else was allowed to touch Maurice's photograph; each day she dusted it, and on Fridays it was thoroughly polished. A jug that Jenny had once decorated sat by the side of the photograph at all times, filled with bright paper flowers. The sideboard now had the look of a shrine.

'Why don't you sit down, Mam, and have a rest for once?' Jenny suggested, but the proferred olive branch was spurned.

'The day I'm no' able tae see tae my own house is the day you can turn me out,' Faith snapped, and got on with her work. Marion, her fingers picking continually at a hole in the rug across her wasted legs, watched the activity going on about her with vacant eyes.

Throughout the warren of tenements the same routine of cleaning and scrubbing was going on. Although it was early March and dark outside, the sound of voices floated up from the courtyard, where women and children, working in the lights from the surrounding windows, were hanging up rugs and carpets so that the week's dust could be beaten out of them. Anyone who neglected her Friday cleaning was considered by her neighbours to be a dirty slut. Even the children had their own tasks, depending on their age and ability. Only the men were exempt from the Friday night cleaning as it was considered that they worked hard enough all week to support their

39

families and were entitled to do as they wished during their time away from the shipyard. The fact that the womenfolk worked just as hard, some with outside jobs as well as families and homes to see to, was ignored.

When Jenny had finished with the range she was glad to escape with Alice to the back yard where they hung up the rugs on their washing line and took turns thumping the dust out of them.

'She did it on purpose – Lottie,' Alice said breathlessly as she wielded the carpet beater. 'She gave you the money in front of Dad just tae start a row.'

'She didnae win, though.'

'Not for the want of trying,' Alice said, but Jenny's attention had been caught by a lone figure struggling to hang a carpet over a rope at the other side of the court.

'Is that not Walter Young? He'll never be able tae handle that carpet on his own. I wonder where his father is?'

Since his wife's death Daniel Young had taken over all her housekeeping duties, even the Friday night work. Every week he and Walter were to be seen polishing windows and beating carpets, and Bella had told Jenny that Daniel even took his turn of cleaning the stairs and the communal privy.

'It doesnae seem right for a man tae have tae take on all that extra work after puttin' in a day in the yard,' Bella had said, her small face screwed up with concern. 'I've offered tae dae it, but he'll no' let anyone else help him.'

Walter's carpet, Jenny noticed, was getting the better of the struggle; with a brief word to Alice she hurried across the courtyard to help the boy. Between them they subdued the carpet and got it on to the line.

'Have you got more to bring out?' Jenny asked.

'Just the one from my room, and a wee rug.' The boy's face was flushed from embarrassment as much as from the struggle.

Jenny picked up the carpet beater. 'I'll start on this one and you can bring the others. Go on,' she said briskly when the boy hesitated, and he ducked his head and did as he was told.

'Is your father not here to help you tonight?' she asked when the other carpet and a smaller rug had been hung over the rope and she had relinquished the beater to Walter. At her urging he had rolled his shirt-sleeves up, revealing pale and stick-like arms. Daniel and his son were always immaculately dressed, and never usually had their shirt-sleeves unfastened, no matter how hot the weather may be.

'His head's awful bad. It happens sometimes, he'll be all right in the morning.'

'I'll help you to carry your carpets in,' she said when they had finished, adding, as Walter started to protest, 'I'll tell you what – you help me and Alice upstairs with our rugs first, then we'll help you with yours in return. That's fair, isn't it?' She took his arm and led him across the yard, weaving around groups of women taking a moment to gossip and rest before getting on with their work.

Faith had swept the floors and was washing the cracked and faded linoleum when Jenny and Alice and Walter arrived. They stacked the rolled rugs on the landing, ready to be laid once the floors had dried, then went back downstairs to attend to the Youngs' carpets.

The two girls carried the large carpet between them while Walter hurried ahead with a rug under each arm. He erupted back out of the flat as they reached the door. 'I can manage fine now,' he started to say, but Jenny marched past him. 'We'll help you to lay the carpet.'

Daniel Young, his face ashen, his eyes dark shadows, sat on the edge of the wall bed. As Jenny and Alice edged into the room, the rolled carpet between them, he leapt to his feet, a duster falling from one hand, a brass candlestick clanging from the other. He made an involuntary move to pick them up then stopped short, clutching at his head.

'Lie down, man! You look like death warmed up.' Jenny dropped her end of the carpet and pushed him back on to the bed then gathered up the cloth and candlestick. 'Just sit still for a minute while we get this carpet down. Alice, you and Walter take that end and I'll unroll it—'

The room smelled of polish and black-lead and disinfectant. The few pieces of furniture had been pushed back against the walls in order to remove the carpet and wash the floor; all were glossy with care. Daniel Young's house didn't suffer from neglect even though there was no woman in it.

When the carpet and furniture were back in place Jenny plumped up the cushion on one of the two fireside chairs and went over to the bed. 'Come and sit down here, Daniel, and Walter can make you a cup of tea.' She looped her arm about him with an ease born of caring for her grandmother and helped him to his feet. His body was wiry beneath her touch, the muscles tense. 'Alice, you'd best go back and tell Mam I'll not be long. D'you get headaches often, Daniel?'

As Alice left, Daniel started to shake his head then thought better of it. 'Never like this. It's as though every bone in my face was aching like a rotten tooth.' His voice was muffled and he held his head in his hands as though frightened that it was going to fall off.

Walter was already pouring water into the teapot from the kettle that all the tenement dwellers kept simmering on the range. Jenny

41

stopped him as he went to the sink to refill the kettle. 'Put some hot water into a basin first – this one'll do. Have you got a clean bit of cloth?'

She added a little cold water from the tap then tested the temperature with the tip of a finger. It was stingingly hot, but her hands could take it. She dipped the cloth into the bowl as Walter poured cups of strong tea then wringing it out she formed it into a pad. 'This is hot, but it'll help you.' She pressed the wadded cloth over Daniel's forehead and heard him draw in his breath with a faint hiss as the heat touched his skin.

'Hold that in place for a while, and don't talk,' she instructed, then blew on her tingling fingers before taking the cup Walter was holding out to her. She seated herself on the other fireside chair with a reassuring smile for the boy, who perched on the edge of one of the four upright chairs set round the table. He managed a nervous grimace in return.

Sipping at her tea, Jenny listened to the measured ticking of the clock and the sound of voices from outside, taking in the room in a series of casual glances. A landscape hung on one wall, and there were some ornaments around, including a china figurine and the pair of candlesticks Daniel had been polishing. On the dresser stood a photograph of Daniel in uniform, and another of him and his wife, their young faces solemn, Mrs Young seated, Daniel standing with one hand resting possessively, yet formally, on her shoulder.

Jenny remembered Molly Young only vaguely, for the woman hadn't mixed with her neighbours. The Youngs had always kept themselves to themselves, so much so that Bella was convinced that Molly might have been saved if only she had been able to bring herself to ask for help before it was too late. She had died of pneumonia about fifteen months earlier; Daniel, at sea at the time, had arrived home far too late for her funeral. The neighbours had scraped together what money they could spare to give the woman a decent funeral, for the tenement people believed in looking after their own, even those who hadn't mixed with them, and Bella had taken Walter in and cared for him until his father took over.

Daniel's breath hissed out in a tiny sigh of relief, and Jenny saw that he was sitting back more comfortably in his chair, his body relaxed.

'How do you feel now?' She took the mug from his hand and refilled it.

'It's getting better,' he said through lips that had begun to regain some of their colour. His eyes were still closed; when she took his hand in hers and clasped his fingers round the mug the lids flew open and he stared up at her. She had never realised that Daniel's eyes

42

were so dark, or, she thought when he swiftly glanced down at the mug, away from her, that his lashes were so long.

'Walter, away through and finish off your own room,' Daniel ordered, adding in embarrassment as his son went out, 'I wasnae able tae manage it. And now I'm taking up too much of your time.'

Jenny took her empty cup, and Walter's, to the sink. 'To tell the truth, it's nice to be away from the rest of them for a few minutes. There's times when they feel like an awful responsibility.'

'It's a shame that Teeze had tae take the pneumonia so bad. He was a good worker.' His words did more than anything else to make her feel ashamed of the way she had spoken to her father earlier. 'Leave the cups be, I'll see tae them.'

'I might as well rinse them through,' Jenny began, then stopped as his hand landed on her arm and she was firmly but gently drawn back from the sink.

'Ye've enough to do,' said Daniel evenly, one hand still clasping the cloth pad to his face, 'I'll not have ye runnin' after me an' Walter as well.'

She was glad to see that he looked and sounded stronger. 'I'll get back home, then. I don't want to leave Mam and Alice with all the work.'

'Aye,' said Daniel, adding awkwardly, 'Thank you for your kindness.'

As she went through the close and back into the courtyard she knew, without looking back, that he was standing in the doorway. She could feel the intensity of his gaze between her shoulder blades.

5

On the stocks the first peacetime ship to be built in the Dalkieth yard for four years, a passenger steamer for a Far East company, was taking shape. Other vessels filled the slips, and the Experimental Tank was kept busy, as shipowners who had had to wait for pre-war orders to be filled or were anxious to replace tonnage either grown old during the war or sunk in battle clamoured for new stock.

Though there was still no word of Maurice, Faith Gillespie refused to give up hope. She devoted more and more time to her mother-in-law, and Jenny began to hurry home during her dinner hour in order to help with Helen and Marion. Lizzie still wrote now and again, telling of the wonderful new life she was leading in Glasgow, each letter finishing with words of sympathy for Jenny, stuck in Ellerslie.

Patrick became more and more withdrawn, reminding Jenny of a coiled spring that might, if it was triggered, lash out in all directions. Bella continued to maintain that the bruises she bore now and then were caused by her own carelessness, walking into a door, or tripping on the dimly lit stairs.

Sometimes Daniel Young was in the Kerr's single room when Jenny called, talking to Patrick about this and that, touching on each subject without digging too deeply, chatting easily without waiting for a reply. On these occasions Patrick seemed a little easier, even contributing some conversation himself, but as soon as the other man left he retired into his shell.

'He used to be so full of fun,' Alice said one evening when the sisters were walking home after a visit to Bella. 'I was jealous of Bella, being loved by someone like him, but now – it breaks my heart to see his unhappiness.' Her hand, through Jenny's arm, tightened. 'What if he's like that for the rest of his life? How'll Bella stand it?'

'Don't think about it, pet. We'll just have to take one day at a time and hope for the best.'

'Hoping's like wishing on stars – it's not going to change things,' Alice's voice trembled. 'Pat and Bella need more than hope.'

A gas-light at the other end of the street flickered on, spreading a warm gold pool over the uneven and cracked paving stones below.

45

The lamplighter with his long pole was a shadow in the gathering darkness, leaving the lamp and moving across the street. As another lamp burst into light Jenny threaded an arm round her sister's solid waist.

'Let's have a three-legged race,' she said on a sudden impulse, then, without waiting for Alice's reaction, 'One, two, three – go!'

Passers-by stared and some clucked their tongues at the rowdiness of youth as the sisters barged along the street, tightly linked, lurching on the cobbles, giggling breathlessly, their inner ankles fastened together by an invisible thong.

'That's the way, lassies!' the lamplighter called cheerily as they swung past him. They could hear his rusty laughter fading behind them as they swung round the corner, jostling in and out of the puddles of light, managing to keep the pace going until they reached their own close. There, they fell away from each other, laughing, leaning against the stone walls, dragging in deep breaths of night air before, at a more sedate pace, they went upstairs, Alice in the lead.

Someone else entered the close below and began to climb, taking the stairs two at a time. As they reached their own door and Alice put her hand on the latch a voice from the half-landing spoke Jenny's name.

Alice turned sharply at the sound but Jenny froze, staring at the scratched door panels without seeing them. She didn't need to look round; she knew that voice, would always have known it, anywhere.

'Jenny?' the man on the stairs said again, beginning to climb the final flight. Looking at her sister, seeing the shock on Alice's face, Jenny knew that it wasn't a dream. He was really there.

'I'll – I'll tell Mam we've got a visitor,' Alice said on a rush of words and slid into the house as Jenny finally turned, her body feeling strangely stiff so that she had to pivot round on her feet, shifting from heel to toe, heel to toe, until she was finally facing him.

He had reached the top step and was close to her by that time, older, better dressed, more assured, yet still the same.

'Hello, Jenny.' Robert Archer held a hand out to her, taking off his curly-brimmed bowler hat with the other hand. 'You're looking bonny.'

His grip was firm, dispelling her final doubt that he was really there, instead of down in Tyneside where he now belonged.

'You're staring at me as if I was a ghost,' he said, his square face breaking into a grin that showed the chipped front tooth which had always seemed endearing to her.

'I – I didnae expect to see you back here.' She had feared that her voice was going to fail her, but it didn't, though it shook a little.

46

'Bad pennies aye come back, did you not know that?' His eyes flickered beyond her to the open door. 'Are you not going to invite me in, then?'

The kitchen was a flurry of activity, with Faith and Alice darting about, scooping up toys and clothing. They stopped short when the door opened, their arms filled, their faces as guilty as if they had been caught robbing the place. Robert walked in as though he had been there only the day before.

'Mrs Gillespie, it's good to see you again.'

At the sound of his voice Faith's face wavered. For a moment Jenny thought that her mother was going to burst into tears, then a tremulous smile broke through and, thrusting a rag doll and a tattered basket of mending at Alice, who already had her arms filled, Faith took both Robert's hands in hers.

'My, ye're a sight for sore eyes, laddie! What are ye doin' back in Ellerslie? Ye'll have a cup of tea – Jenny, put the cups out. Take off yer coat, man, and sit yersel' down—' In a flurry of words she led him to Teeze's chair and waited while he took off his thick topcoat. Taking it from him, folding it in her arms, she asked, 'Ye'll have heard about our Maurice?'

It was then that Jenny, taking off her own jacket and fetching the cups, realised why her mother was so pleased to see Robert in spite of the way he had jilted her daughter. He had been Maurice's best friend, and seeing him again was reassuring. If Robert could return to Ellerslie, so could Maurice.

'Aye, I heard.' His face was suddenly sombre. 'I'd have written, but I didnae know what to say.'

'He's only missing, not dead,' Faith told him hurriedly, putting his coat over the back of a chair and fetching the picture from the sideboard. 'He'll be back home before we know it.' According him a rare honour, she handed the photograph to Robert, who shot a swift glance at Jenny before taking the frame into his capable hands.

'Aye, I'm sure he will, Mrs Gillespie. Maurice was always one for waiting till the last minute. I mind when he was a first year 'prentice in the engine shop he was last in the gate so often in the mornings that come New Year's Eve everyone knew Maurice was bound to be the Skittery Winter – the last man in on the last day of the year.' His mouth softened into a smile at the memory and Faith leaned forward, hanging on his every word like a starving bird eyeing a crumb. 'I made some excuse tae be in the engine shop that mornin',' said Robert, his voice relaxing into the Clydeside accent, 'an' we were all waitin' for him – all set tae bang on metal sheets an' yell an' give him a red face.

47

So the bold Maurice comes slidin' in quiet-like an' goes up along the side of the wall so's not tae be seen.'

Faith's face split into a beaming smile that took years off her. 'Aye, I mind that day as if it was yesterday – the mess he was in when he came home.'

'That's because he was just passing under the stairs leadin' tae the upper gallery when the rest of the 'prentices leaned over and emptied a pail of oily water over him.' Robert roared with laughter and Faith joined in, her laugh squeaky and stifled from lack of use. 'He'd never thought tae look up – but then, mebbe it was as well he didnae or he'd have got it in his face.'

Faith mopped at the tears that had come easily to her eyes then took the photograph back and set it carefully on the sideboard. 'Och Robert, son, it's that good tae see ye! Are ye here for long? Where are ye stayin' now that yer auntie's gone?'

Robert took a cup of tea from Jenny, his grey eyes studying her face. She turned away, flustered, then to her horror she heard him say, 'I'm back home for good, Mrs Gillespie. The Dalkieth directors sent for me.'

'You're going to work in the yard again?' Jenny said in dismay.

'Aye. I see Mrs Dalkieth tomorrow. I'm staying in a lodging house until I know just what's to happen.'

'A lodging house? My, but that'll cost you a fair bit. You could—' Faith started to say impulsively, then hesitated. 'We've no' got much room, son, but—'

'I'm fine where I am, Mrs Gillespie, don't you fret yourself about me.'

Marion woke with a sudden start, mumbling something. Faith was by her side in an instant.

'It's all right, Mam, it's just a friend of our Maurice's come tae see us. Alice, give me a hand here, we'll take yer gran through tae the other room,' she added hurriedly as Marion's mumbles grew louder and more urgent. Jenny would have helped, but her mother waved her aside. 'We'll manage. You stay with Robert.'

As she and Alice escorted the old woman out, Faith's free hand deftly scooped up the bucket Marion used as a commode. Then Jenny and Robert were alone.

'Who's that?'

'My gran.'

'The old bat that used to worry the life out of you all?'

'She'd a seizure nearly a year ago.'

'God,' said Robert. 'The poor woman.'

Jenny fussed with the teapot, pouring herself a cup of tea, but at last she had to turn round, to look at him sitting at ease in her father's chair, his long legs stretched out over the rag rug, his eyes on her.

'You've cut your hair.'

She began to reach a hand towards her head then realised what she was doing and pulled it back. 'I didn't like it the way it was.'

'I did,' he said, his gaze intense. She wanted to look away, but instead she made herself meet his look boldly, returning it, studying him as he was studying her.

'It makes you look more – more grown up. You look well, Jenny.'

'So do you. Tyneside's treated you well.'

'They've got some fine big yards there. I learned more than I would have here.'

'Including all about marriage.' The words were out before she could stop them.

There was a pause, then, 'I was talking about shipbuilding,' he said gently. But now that the first shock of seeing him was over the thought of Robert living in Ellerslie again, where she might see him every day and be reminded of what might have been was beginning to hurt. She needed to gather all the pain up at once, like grasping a nettle, and get it over with once and for all.

'You should have brought your wife to meet us.'

'She's still in England.' Robert let the silence grow for a moment or two, then added, 'I'm ashamed, Jenny, of the way I behaved towards you.'

She was sitting on one of the upright chairs. Now she put her cup down abruptly and got to her feet. 'No need to be. You said yourself in your last letter that we were both too young to know our own minds.' She lifted the teapot, pouring out more tea for herself when he shook his head. 'You were right.'

'I was a fool!'

'Did you like the English shipyards?' she asked, abruptly changing the subject.

'Well enough, though the work was hard. They sent me from one department to another and filled my head with so much knowledge that I was fair dizzy at times. But I'm grateful to Mr Dalkieth for giving me the chance to better myself. I was sorry to hear of his death, and Mr Edward's.' He paused, shooting a glance at the closed door. 'And Maurice's,' he added quietly. 'You know he'll not come back, don't you?'

'I'm not daft.'

'And neither's your mother. She'll come round to the truth in her own time, poor soul. Mebbe it's easier on her this way.'

Another silence fell between them. Jenny risked a quick glance at

Robert's brown herringbone suit, the striped shirt and neat blue tie, the watch-chain suspended across the front of his waistcoat. His clothes were smart and looked expensive, his hair well groomed and his face clean-shaven apart from a neat, dark moustache that made him look mature, and far more prosperous than he had before he left Ellerslie.

Through the wall they could hear Marion's squawking and Faith's soothing answers. Then to Jenny's horror there came the unmistakable sound of a full bladder being emptied into a metal bucket.

Robert cleared his throat then said, 'Are you still working at the Experimental Tank?'

'Yes.' Jenny spoke loudly to drown out the noise, which seemed to be going on and on. 'The Tank's very busy just now, we've got more work than we know what to do with. Miss McQueen's still the supervisor – and Mr Duncan's still in charge.' Dear God, Jenny couldn't ever recall Gran taking so long over the bucket before.

'I might as well tell you now, Jen – there's talk of me becoming the office manager.'

'What?' She had been fidgeting with her sleeve, unbuttoning and buttoning the cuff in order to keep her eyes from him, but now she looked up, full into his face. 'But you're a naval architect!'

'I told you, I've been a lot of things in the past four years.'

'Why you?'

The question was blunt to the point of rudeness, but it didn't seem to bother him. 'With Edward Dalkieth gone, they need someone who knows the shipbuilding business well, and knows Dalkieth's into the bargain. Apparently the old man had me in mind for works manager eventually, with Edward in charge of the office. But I understand that George Dalkieth holds that position.'

The embarrassing noises through the wall had stopped, but now the wail of a small child startled from sleep could be heard. Robert, who had borne Marion's ablutions calmly, tensed in his chair and stared at Jenny, colour surging into his face. 'That's – you've never—'

'It's Maurice's wee girl.'

'Maurice had a bairn? I didn't know that. For a minute there I thought it was yours.'

'How could she be mine?'

'It was possible – as I mind,' Robert said quietly, and Jenny felt her own colour deepen, this time with anger. She jumped to her feet.

'You've got a right nerve, Robert Archer!'

He cringed back into the chair in mock fear, putting up his arms to protect himself. 'And you've still got a temper, Jenny Gillespie,' he said. And, for a moment, a dangerous moment, time dissolved and it

50

was as though they had never been apart. Then Jenny gained control over herself and stepped back, moving away from him as far as possible, until she felt the edge of the table pressing into her backside.

'Lottie and wee Helen live here,' she explained stiffly. 'When Lottie's parents discovered that she was expecting they put her out. Maurice was going to marry her as soon as he came home, but—'

'How on earth d'you manage with them as well as your grandmother to look after? I heard that your father had had to move out of Pneumonia Bay and into the stores.'

'We manage fine,' she told him sharply just as Alice and Faith brought Marion back in. Robert got to his feet at once and hovered round the three of them until the old woman was settled.

'There, Mam,' Faith said. 'Jenny, away and see if you can get the wee yin tae sleep again.'

Alice had gone back into the hall. As Jenny, glad to be away from Robert's gaze, left the kitchen her sister paused at the front door on her way to the communal privy on the landing, bucket in hand.

'What's he doing here?' she whispered.

'Just visiting.'

'He'll be here tae see you.'

'Don't be daft, Alice, he's married!' Jenny snapped, and went into the bedroom, where Helen was struggling to climb out of her cot, her face flushed and wet with tears. As Jenny went in the baby managed to tread on the hem of her threadbare gown. There was a rending sound and a great rip opened down the front.

'Come on, lovey, you're all right.' Jenny swept the little girl into her arms and Helen pushed her warm, tear-wet little face against the hollow of her neck, clinging to her, stiffening when Jenny tried to put her back into the cot. Finally Jenny gave in, picking up the blanket and wrapping it round her to hide the tear in her gown before carrying her into the kitchen, where Helen took one peek round the room, saw that there was a stranger there, and buried her head in her aunt's neck again. Jenny sat down by the table and left her mother to deal with Robert.

Faith was telling him about Patrick and Bella when the outer door opened and shut then Teeze came into the kitchen on a familiar flurry of wheezy coughing.

'Teeze, will ye look who's here?'

'Eh?' He peered across the room, his drink-reddened eyes screwed up in an attempt to focus as Robert rose.

'It's Robert – you mind Maurice's friend Robert?'

'How are you, Mr Gillespie?' Robert held out his hand.

Teeze stared at it, then at the visitor's face. 'Get out of my house.'

51

'Teeze!'

'Hold yer tongue, you,' Teeze told his wife, taking a lurching step across the room, his gaze fixed on Robert. 'So ye're back, are ye – an' all dressed up like a gentleman intae the bargain.' The words were slurred but their delivery carried all the bitterness that had been eating into Teeze Gillespie ever since the pneumonia had taken away his strength and his self-respect. 'Ye jilt my daughter for some Englishwoman an' go through the war safe an' sound in the shipyards while better men than you die in the mud – then ye come walkin' in here an' expect me tae shake ye by the hand?'

Robert's face had gone white to the lips and his hand had fallen back to his side.

'Teeze Gillespie, you hold your tongue,' Faith screeched, trying to drag her husband back by the sleeve. He shook her off with a bull-like roar.

'Don't you tell me what tae dae in my ain hoose!'

'Dad,' Jenny said warningly, 'Robert's going to be the new office manager at the yard.'

'I don't care if he's goin' tae be Christ on a golden throne,' Teeze said thickly, 'I'll decide who's welcome in my own house – an' he's no' welcome! Get out afore I throw ye out!'

He drew his right arm back, his hand fisting, then swung at the man standing before him. Faith screamed, her own knotted fists flying to her mouth, and Helen let out a fresh wail, while Marion added a terrified keening to the noise. Robert fended off the wavering blow with ease and, at the same time, gripped his assailant's shoulder with his free hand, swinging round so that Teeze, caught off balance, suddenly found himself sitting in the chair that Robert had just vacated.

'I think he needs to get to his bed,' Robert said. 'I'm sorry about this, Mrs Gillespie, I shouldn't have come here. I'll not trouble you again.' And with a nod at Jenny and Alice he gathered up his hat and coat and gloves and walked out of the room.

As the outer door closed Faith snatched a dish-cloth from beside the sink and swiped at her husband with it. 'He's Maurice's friend! I wanted him here!' she screeched, then her thin body jerked as her husband reached up and caught at her wrist, digging his fingers in.

'I'm no' done for yet! I'm still the master o' this house, an' I'll say who comes intae it!'

'D'ye understand nothin', ye drunken fool? He's tae be one o' the bosses – he could lose ye yer job if he wanted tae.'

'I'll go down on my belly for no man!' Teeze roared back at her, then the coughing began and he let her go and doubled over, fists held to his face as the harsh barks of sound tore relentlessly from his damaged lungs.

'Alice, don't stand there like a sack of potatoes, fetch me a cup of water!' Gently, Faith dabbed at her husband's forehead with the towel. Her mother-in-law, startled by all the noise, began to flail the air with her good arm.

'It's all right, Gran, there's nothing wrong.' Alice crouched by the old woman's side, crooning soothingly.

When Teeze's coughing fit had subsided he pushed his wife to one side and got back on to his feet, his head swinging low on his shoulders as though his neck had collapsed, his eyes moving from one of his womenfolk to the other. Jenny was reminded of a bull she and Robert had seen once in a farmyard, glowering over a half-door.

'Christ almighty, will ye get tae yer beds, all of ye!' he ordered, and pushed past them to stump out of the flat and downstairs to the privy.

The glow generated by Robert's arrival had gone out of Faith. 'Jenny, put the bairn back in her cot,' she said in a flat voice, 'an' help tae get yer gran tae her bed.'

They could dimly hear a fist crashing against wooden panels and a familiar voice yelling. Some poor soul must be using the privy, and Teeze had never been patient when it came to waiting his turn.

In bed later, listening to Helen's soft, regular breathing, Jenny recalled the look on Robert's face when he'd heard Helen crying. She remembered the warmth of his hand clasping hers the Sunday before he left for England, and the way Ellerslie Water had looked, transformed by the setting sun into a ribbon of glittering gold as it hurried on its way from Loch Lomond to the Clyde. Leaving the town behind, the two of them had turned aside from the path to where a thicket of rhododendron bushes stood, their great crimson blossoms brilliant against shiny dark leaves. They circled the clump of bushes until they reached a certain spot where Robert held a branch aside to let Jenny duck beneath it into a short leafy tunnel. At the end of it lay the special place they had discovered a few months earlier, a hollow in the middle of the apparently solid group of bushes.

He spread his jacket on the ground for her to sit on, then stretched on his back beside her. Sunlight shining through leaves tossed by a slight breeze cast moving shadows over his face and throat. 'I like this place,' he said. 'There's nobody fighting in the street outside or spewing into the gutter on the way home from the pub.' His hand sought and found hers, their fingers lacing together. 'One day, Jenny Gillespie, I'll build you a house in a quiet place like this.'

'How can you, when you're going away, and I'll never see you again?' Her throat was choked with unshed tears.

His free hand touched her hair and she felt him loosening the ribbon that held it.

'Don't be daft, of course I'll be back. Jen, I'm not going tae end up like most of the men here, watchin' the ships growing on the stocks and wondering if I'm going tae be laid off once they're finished, or waiting at the yard gates every morning in the hope of getting work. Worrying in case a gaffer takes a dislike tae my face, being dependent on someone else for the very bread I eat.'

'You'll forget me!' She began to get up and he pulled her down again, holding her as she struggled against him, his face firm and warm against hers.

'I could never forget you.' He kissed her, and her tears were wet on her face and on his as she stopped fighting him and instead tightened her arms about him, hungry for more kisses to remember when he was far from her.

When the kisses came she opened her mouth beneath his and felt a shock run through her as their tongues met and entwined. They rolled together on the ground, clinging, kissing. Her blouse came free of her skirt, then Robert's fingers were on her bare skin and she was moving against him, wanting to feel his touch all over her body, moaning when his hands finally covered her breasts.

They made love to each other clumsily, but with a shared sense that they belonged together and that there could be nothing wrong in their coupling. Later, as they wandered back along the riverbank, dazed with the wonder of what had happened to them, Robert said huskily, 'If I sent for ye, Jenny lass, would ye come to me?'

'I've got my own apprenticeship to go through,' she said reluctantly. Drunk with love as she was, dazed with the joy of what had just happened between them, she was still a shipyard worker, keenly aware of the value of an apprenticeship and the need to see it through.

'Aye, you're right. We'll have to wait a wee while yet.' Then, turning her into his arms, kissing her again, he added, 'But it'll seem a long wait.'

Lottie came home, blundering into the bedhead, cursing beneath her breath.

Jenny blinked as the other girl lit the stub of candle and began to undress, dropping her clothes carelessly on the floor. 'You're late.'

'Neil Baker was in the pub tonight. He walked me home.' Lottie stretched her arms above her head and the candlelight outlined the curves of her semi-nude body and picked out the rich, red tints of her tumbled hair. 'There was someone else in the pub tonight, too, late

54

on,' she said, a sly note in her voice. 'Robert Archer that used to live round the corner.'

'I know. He was here.'

'Oh aye? I heard that you used tae be sweet on him.'

'He was a friend of Maurice's,' Jenny said curtly. 'I left some water in the basin for you.'

'Ach, I'm too tired tae be bothered washing.' Lottie blew out the candle and flopped into bed. Her skin smelled of drink and tobacco smoke. She yawned loudly and tossed herself into a comfortable position before settling down. Within minutes she was asleep while Jenny, now wide awake, relived the fear she had gone through after Robert went away to Tyneside, the realisation of what might result from their loving, the tearful relief when her monthly bleeding came as usual.

Recalling again the shock in his face when he first heard Helen wailing she smiled wryly into the dark. Poor Robert, thinking that his past had suddenly jumped up at him like a jack-in-the-box. For a moment she wished that she had had the wit to frighten him, to make him think, even for a moment, that Helen was his child. Then another thought came to wipe the smile from her lips. If what he expected came true, Robert was going to be the new office manager. He would visit the Tank section often.

If only she had been free to go off to Glasgow with Lizzie, Jenny thought, turning over restlessly in bed. Then she would have been well out of the way by the time Robert came back to Ellerslie. But now it was too late. She was trapped like a mouse in a cage, with nowhere to hide, nowhere to go.

6

The door of the tracing office opened and one of the draughtsmen looked in. 'The ghost's walking,' he hissed, then withdrew.

Kerry Malloy, still in her first week, gave a shrill scream of 'Mammy!' and tumbled from her high chair, bringing a sheaf of papers down from the sloping desk with her. Senga only just managed to stop an inkwell from toppling over and spilling while Jenny scrambled from her own chair to scoop up the flurry of papers and Maureen hauled her sister up from the floor.

'God save us, ye eejit, what d'ye think ye're doin'?' she wanted to know, setting the girl on her feet and spinning her round to examine her overall for stains. Kerry's hair had come adrift from the black ribbon that was supposed to control it and her blue eyes were wide with fright. 'He said there's a ghost—'

'It's only something they say here in the Tank, Kerry,' Jenny explained, trying not to smile too broadly. 'It means that one of the bosses is in the building.'

'How was I to know th – ow!' Kerry squeaked as her sister brushed her down with a firm hand, pushing her about as though she was a sack of potatoes, then started to retie the ribbon round a handful of her red hair. 'I can do that myself – I'm not a wean!'

'Get on with it, then – and tidy that desk before Miss McQueen comes back and finds the place looking like a bear garden,' Maureen fretted.

'The poor lassie's only been in the office for a matter of days, Maureen.' Jenny felt heart-sorry for Kerry, who was crimson with mortification as she struggled back on to her high stool.

'Who was it that begged Mr Duncan and Miss McQueen to take her on in my place now that Jacko's home and we're to be wed? It's me that'll be blamed if she's not suitable.'

'Of course she'll be suitable. Come on,' Jenny began to untie her smock as she crossed to the coat-rack in one corner of the small office. 'The launch party'll be downstairs any minute now and we want to get ready before Miss McQueen comes back. Down you get, Kerry – carefully, mind.'

Maureen gave her sister a final glare as Senga helped the younger girl to scramble from the chair she had only just settled into. Then, deciding that Kerry had been sufficiently humiliated, she smoothed her own fiery hair and reached for her jacket.

Although it was a working day there was a festive air about the yard. In honour of the first peacetime launch in almost five years the employees were to have a half-day holiday; already Jenny was picturing herself at the party to be held in the back court of the tenements, in the new yellow dress she had made for the occasion.

'Wait a minute – Kerry, have a peek outside and make sure old McQueen's not comin' yet,' Senga ordered. 'Maureen, mind what you said you'd do on the day of the launch?'

'Sure I mind – an' I'm not afraid to do it, so there!' Giving a final tug at her jacket Maureen hopped on to a tall chair that stood alone by the coat-rack, well back from the high angled desk where the tracers worked.

Kerry gaped from the doorway. 'What're you doin'?'

'Gettin' meself pregnant.' Maureen, beaming from her perch, swung her feet.

'That's surely not how you go about it?' asked fifteen-year-old Kerry, wide-eyed, and the three older girls collapsed in gales of laughter.

'Did you not tell her about the chair either?' Jenny asked when she could speak, wiping the tears from her eyes. 'They say that everyone who sits on that chair has a bairn within the next nine months, Kerry. That's why it's never used.'

'Aye – even Miss McQueen's terrified of sittin' on it by accident, an' she's fifty if she's a day, an' never as much as said yes tae a man in her life,' said Maureen, setting Senga and Jenny off again.

Kerry gazed from face to face with mounting suspicion. 'You're all having me on. It takes more than an old chair tae make bairns.'

'You mean you don't believe what they say?' Senga asked with mock horror, while Maureen jumped down and invited. 'Sit on it, then.'

As Kerry backed off, shaking her head, she turned to Jenny. 'You try it.'

'I will not. We've got enough in our house without another mouth to feed.'

'It doesn't really make you pregnant, does it?' Kerry left her post to reach out a cautious finger and stroke the broken shiny leather of the chair seat.

'You wait and see – I'll be bouncing a babby on my knee by Christmas.'

'I already know that, Maureen Malloy,' Kerry retorted. 'But that's Jacko's fault, nothing tae do with you putting your backside on a harmless old chair!'

Maureen's face went scarlet. 'Ye wee midden, ye promised not to say anyth—'

She stopped abruptly as the door opened and Miss McQueen burst into the room like a ship in full sail, her plump face brilliant with two red spots over her cheekbones.

'The launch party have arrived. Quickly now, girls, line up and let me have a look at you.'

She fussed over her staff, tugging at a skirt fold here, settling the collar of a blouse there, until she was satisfied that they all looked presentable, then said briskly, 'Remember that this is a very important day for Dalkieth's shipyard. Are you ready? Follow me – and no noise!'

The clank and hiss of the steam engine on the floor below grew louder as they stepped out of the tracing office then filed in procession along the narrow corridor, forming, Jenny suddenly thought, a wake to Miss McQueen's sailing ship. A giggle bubbled its way up to her lips and was swallowed back.

'Wait!' A few steps down from the top of the wooden staircase the supervisor dramatically threw out an arm to stop them. The line broke up as the girls crowded forward, peering inquisitively over her meaty shoulders to the timber-floored area below. Jenny could only see a row of trousered legs and well-polished shoes, indicating that the drawing-office staff were already lined up to meet the launch party, and two men working self-consciously on an upturned twenty-foot model on the gallery just above the wax room, paring away the unwanted wax, curl by honey-coloured curl, to bring the hull down to the lines already cut into the model by the cutting machine. The floor round their feet was thick with shavings which would be swept up and returned to the melting tank to be used again.

From somewhere out of sight she could hear Mr Duncan, the Tank Superintendent, explaining to the guests in his slow monotone how the Tank itself worked. Then came the rapid swish of the truck racing up the length of the tank, followed by a clang as it came to a standstill and a subdued murmur of interest from the onlookers. Some of the excitement of the moment ebbed away from Jenny as another voice began to speak. She had forgotten for the moment that Robert, recently appointed office manager, would be with the visitors.

Mr Duncan's face, red with the stress of the occasion, peered up from the bottom of the stairs as he beckoned to Miss McQueen and her staff. The five of them flowed down the wooden staircase to the lower floor where they formed a line between the launch party and the stairs leading down to the wax-model room.

'In order to produce the best design possible the designer must study the environment in which the vessel will operate.' Robert's voice was clear and assured, and as Scottish as ever, though his pronunciation had improved. As she took her place in the line at the stairs Jenny risked a glance at him. He was elegant in a dark grey suit, seemingly not in the least overawed by the presence of the guests, who included Isobel Dalkieth, widow of the former owner, and her son.

'By testing a scaled-down design model several times under controlled conditions in the Tank we measure anticipated wave resistance, speed, and a number of other factors,' he was saying. 'This means that we can discover the flaws and strengths of each design before time and money goes into building the ship itself. As Mr Duncan has told you, we can simulate any size or strength of wave in this Tank.'

Robert hadn't come back to the Gillespie house since Teeze had ordered him out and, although he visited the Tank section frequently, to Jenny's relief he had made no effort to single her out. He was apparently doing well in his new job, though she had heard that he had had to battle against an initial and understandable resentment from many of the men he had worked beside in the old days.

'It's not right for a man tae move out of his own class.' Daniel Young had voiced the opinion of many of the shipyard workers only the night before, when a group of them gathered in the Gillespie flat. 'George Dalkieth's a fool, I'll grant ye that, but he's got his mother tae keep him right – and he's a Dalkieth. It's not easy for men that mind Archer when he was no better than anyone else tae take orders from him now.'

Jenny had held her tongue for as long as she could, but finally her patience had snapped and she had rounded on Daniel and the others. 'What's wrong with a man working hard to better himself? Surely it's better to take orders from someone who's worked his way up and knows what he's talking about than from a man who's a boss just because he was born into the right family.'

They had all turned and gaped at her. Daniel opened his mouth to speak, then closed it again when Teeze growled from his chair, 'Ach, pay no attention tae her – she's altogether too big for her boots these days. An' I'd've thought,' he had added vindictively to his daughter, 'that ye'd be the last one tae speak up for Robert Archer, after the way he walked out on ye.'

Jenny's face burned as she remembered how first one man, then another, had sniggered at her father's words, then they had returned to their discussion, shutting her out with their broad backs and hunched shoulders. Daniel had hesitated, eyeing her narrowly, then he too had turned away.

'These young ladies are our tracers and analysts, specialising in hydro-dynamics,' she heard Robert say now as he advanced towards the bottom of the staircase, the launch party following, the ladies in bright colours, the men sombre in grey and brown suits. 'Dalkieth's is the only firm in the country to train females for this work. They analyse the figures from the Tank experiments and draw up graphs of the results for the naval architect. They also see to the final line drawings – a highly-specialised skill. Miss McQueen—'

The supervisor bobbed forward in a flurry of excitement to meet the dignitaries and introduce her staff. Jenny was too interested in their clothes to feel nervous. Mrs Armstrong, wife of the manager of the company whose ship was being launched, wore a bright blue coat and skirt that did nothing for her sallow complexion, and a flower-pot hat in darker blue.

Old Mrs Dalkieth, straight as a ramrod and still strikingly attractive despite her silver hair, was immaculate in stylish black mourning. Mrs George, the second wife of the only Dalkieth left in the shipyard, also wore mourning, a smart two-piece black silk costume edged with rich ebony fur. She had added a dash of colour – a lilac blouse trimmed with pale grey beneath the jacket, and a pale grey drift of feathers about the broad brim of her hat.

Her blue eyes looked at and through the women lined up before her and, as she turned away, the presentation over, the delicate scent she wore lingered behind her and the feathers on her hat danced slightly.

'The wax model is made in a mould; you will see this process downstairs,' Robert took up his narrative skilfully as he led the party towards the joiners' section. 'It's then put into the cutting machine, where lines indicating the exact measurements are cut into the hull. These men—' he had come to a halt before the workers on the gallery, 'then pare the model down carefully until they reach the depths indicated by the cutting machine. The model is then ready to be fastened beneath the Tank truck and tested.'

'She's beautiful, Mrs George,' Kerry said enviously a few minutes later as the four girls left the Tank building by a side door and set off in the direction of the launch area, leaving the guests to descend the wooden staircase to the wax room. 'And not a freckle in sight, lucky thing. My mam says Mr George divorced his first wife because she couldnae have any bairns to follow him into the business. I wonder if this one can?'

61

'You shouldn't gossip about your betters, Kerry,' Senga said crushingly.

'She's got a lovely slim figure, hasn't she?' Kerry rattled on.

'But a cold face,' Maureen put in. 'Come on, our Kerry, or we'll not get a good view of the launch.'

'You're not bothered about the launch, Maureen Malloy,' Kerry retorted. 'You're just wanting to make sure that you can stand beside Jacko!' As the other two girls forged ahead she hung back. 'Jenny, me and the rest of them at home have saved up and brought two cups and two saucers for our Maureen and Jacko's wedding gift. Could you paint them for us? I can bring them to your mam's tonight, after the party.'

'What d'you want on them?'

Kerry thought for a moment, then said, 'Bluebells. She loves bluebells. With green leaves.'

'And mebbe a butterfly, to add some more colour?'

'It sounds lovely. Could you do them in the time? I'd have got them sooner but it took a while tae make up the money.'

'I'll manage.'

'Thanks, Jenny.' Kerry squeezed her arm as they swerved to avoid one of the many puddles left by the night's rain. 'Look, she's found Jacko right enough. Come on—' and she dragged Jenny over to where a group of men from the joiner's shop stood. Jacko, who had been one of the first to return to Ellerslie after the war and take up his old trade as a joiner in the shipyard, good-naturedly made room for them, one arm about Maureen. It was good, Jenny thought, to see her friend so flushed with happiness.

The town of Ellerslie had been built on both banks of the Ellerslie Water, a river spanning the half dozen miles or so from Loch Lomond, its birthplace, to the River Clyde. Dalkieth's shipyard lay on the east bank, close to the mouth of the river, at a point where it broadened just before meeting the Clyde. The stretch of water wasn't large enough for the yard to compete with the giants of the Clyde shipyards, such as Fairfield's and John Brown's, but three generations of Dalkieths had gradually built up a reputable yard specialising in cross-Channel steamers as well as passenger and cargo boats, all of a size that enabled them to be launched safely from the yard.

Ship number 1462, the twelve-thousand-ton *Tanamura*, waited on the slipway, her great bulk supported by props, the Dalkieth house-flag, with its blazing gold 'D' against a crimson background, fluttering and snapping at the mainmast. After launching she would be towed round to Pneumonia Bay to be fitted out. Only when she was ready to leave the yard would she officially become the property of the company that had commissioned her and fly their flag.

The open ground beneath the vessel seethed with employees who had come to watch the launch; men black as night from the forge, their teeth and eyes gleaming white, dungaree-clad platers and riveters and caulkers and joiners, men from the engine and boiler shops, designers and draughtsmen and timekeepers as well as women from the offices and the upholstery and glass departments. In contrast to the dull colours of the crowd, all in their usual working clothes, the bunting and flags on the launch platform were all the colours of the rainbow under the May sun.

The buzz of excitement grew louder as the launch party finally emerged from the Tank section and made their way to the decorated platform, the ladies cautiously negotiating the wooden stairs. Mrs Armstrong named the ship in a voice that didn't reach Jenny's ears, then the bottle swept forward on the end of its lanyard and there was a cheer as it burst against the ship's stern with a sudden flowering of foam. There was a moment of breathless anticipation, then another, louder cheer ripped into the air as the vessel began to move, slowly at first, then faster as it neared the river.

The sky went black with caps tossed high as the *Tanamura* finally met with the water, her natural element, her bows lifting, then dipping, then levelling as the huge drag chains tightened to take the strain and slow the headlong momentum that would, if left unfettered, have allowed her to plough across the river and bury her bows in the opposite bank.

Jenny, cheering as lustily as the rest, felt tears pricking at the backs of her eyes as she watched the ship take to the water. In that moment the war that had killed and maimed millions and turned life inside out for millions more was truly over. Dalkieth's had returned, once and for all, to peacetime shipping.

When Jenny got home the kitchen was fragrant with the smell of baking and plates of sandwiches and scones covered the table. Helen, a tattered piece of towelling tied under her chin to protect her clean clothes, was noisily drinking from her decorated mug and Faith was scurrying between the range and the table, her hair wisping over her flushed face.

'Thank goodness you're back,' she said as soon as her daughter walked in. 'I'm fair distracted, tryin' tae get ready for the party an' tend tae yer gran wi' the wean under my feet. I tell you, our Maurice's goin' tae have his hands full dealin' with that yin when he gets back.'

Jenny lifted the lid on a huge cast-iron pot bubbling on the range;

through a cloud of steam she made out the knotted corners of a cloth.
'A clootie dumpling!'

'I've tae dae my share,' Faith said shortly. Once she had been the
best baker in the street, but all that had stopped when the telegram
came about Maurice. Jenny hoped that Faith's return to her old skills
was a good omen for the future.

Helen, who had become more difficult to look after since she found
her feet, toddled over to the table and stretched inquisitive fingers up,
groping for the edge of a plate. Jenny scooped her back just in time
and found something for her to play with, then she made tea and
persuaded her mother to sit down for a minute. 'Is Lottie not here to
look after her?' she asked as she poured the tea.

'She was here – I didnae hear her go out. She must be somewhere
about,' said Faith vaguely, her irritation eased slightly by the hot
sweet drink. Jenny at once put down her own cup and hurried to the
room she shared with Lottie and Helen. She had learned, since
sharing a room, that it didn't do to leave Lottie too long on her own
among other people's possessions.

Lottie, dressed only in a pair of cotton cami-knickers edged with
dingy lace, jumped guiltily when the door opened and Jenny's new
yellow dress fell from her hands to the floor. She stooped to pick it up
but Jenny got there first, snatching the dress away from the other
girl's avaricious fingers, clutching it protectively.

'What d'you think you're doing?'

'I was just lookin'.'

'I made this dress specially for the party and nobody else is going to
have it.' Jenny's voice was hard. What Lottie saw, she wanted, and
what she wanted she usually took.

Lottie's lip curled in a sly grin as she looked Jenny up and down.
'Who d'ye want tae look nice for? I doubt if Robert Archer'll be there
– not now that he's such an important man.'

'Mind your own business!' Jenny examined the dress carefully and
was relieved to see that it was unharmed.

Lottie picked up a lit cigarette from a saucer on the orange box and
drew on it. 'Though I've heard that that wife of his still hasn't come to
Ellerslie.' Smoke dribbled from between her lips and her tawny eyes
danced with malice. 'Mebbe there never was a wife – mebbe he just
made it up tae stop you from pesterin' him.'

Jenny snatched up the saucer, one that she had painted herself, and
held it out. 'Take that through to the kitchen and wash the ash off it.
I've told you before not to use my belongings.'

Lottie shrugged, and put a hand out for the saucer. As Jenny
released it, it seemed to slip through Lottie's fingers and fell to the

floor, breaking into two pieces a few inches away from one of Lottie's bare feet.

'You—!' Goaded beyond endurance, Jenny dropped the dress on to the bed and snatched at the other girl's shoulders, shaking her. Lottie gave a screech and dropped the cigarette, reaching for Jenny's hair. Jenny jerked her head back, out of harm's way, and the clawed fingers caught at her blouse instead, jerking it half-off Jenny's shoulder. A button rattled to the floor as the two of them teetered on the brink of falling over on to the bed.

The door flew open and Faith came storming in, squeezing herself between the girls, wrenching them apart and glaring from one to the other. 'What d'ye think ye're doin', the pair of ye – brawling like a couple of drunken sluts in the gutter!'

'She started it,' Lottie said sullenly, rubbing at her smooth shoulders, twisting her head to examine the red marks left by Jenny's fingers.

'She was going to take my dress – and she broke my saucer!' Jenny said at the same time. Faith, glancing down at the broken crockery, suddenly noticed the cigarette and swooped on it with an anguished wail.

'Look at my linoleum! For any favour, d'ye want tae burn the house down, and us all in it?' She licked a finger and rubbed at the burn left by the cigarette.

'Who's going tae see one more mark on that old linoleum?' Lottie demanded to know. 'It's me you should be worryin' about. She could've burned my foot, makin' me drop my cigarette. And now I'll have tae wear somethin' wi' sleeves tae cover the bruises she's put on me.' She snatched the cigarette from Faith and flounced out, jostling Jenny as she passed.

'I'm sorry, Mam.' Jenny pulled the blouse back over her shoulder, angry with herself for having let Lottie provoke her.

'So ye should be. There's folk gatherin' in the back court for a party, an' you turnin' the house intae a bear garden – all over a wee saucer. One o' these days,' said Faith, getting to her feet, the pieces of china in her hand, 'ye'll mebbe know what it's like tae have real worries. Hurry up and get yerself ready then come and help me with yer gran.'

In the kitchen Lottie was washing herself at the sink, dabbing with excessive care at the fading finger-marks on her plump shoulders. She didn't look round as Jenny poured water from the kettle into a basin then carried it back to the bedroom, where she dragged the orange box against the door to keep it closed against unwelcome visitors before stripping and washing. Taking off her blouse she saw that it was torn where the button had been wrenched off. It would have to be mended before Monday.

She didn't know what had possessed Maurice to take up with the likes of Lottie Forsyth, she told herself furiously as she went down on her hands and knees to search for the missing button, which had skittered away under the bed.

Scrambling to her feet, the button clutched in her fist, she admitted to herself that she did know what had possessed Maurice. Lottie, full-breasted and slim-waisted, with her red-gold curls and her tawny eyes tilted up at the corners, was enough to tempt any man, and Maurice had always been easily tempted. Jenny, lathering hard yellow soap as best she could in the tepid water, scrubbing at her arms with the flannel, wished that he had been more selective in his choice of a sweetheart. But then Helen wouldn't have come into their lives, with her mother's lovely hair and her father's soft brown eyes and heart-stopping broad grin.

Alice tapped on the door just as she finished dressing. 'Can I come in and show you my outfit?'

Jenny pulled the orange box out of the way, and her sister came in, with Helen clutching her hand and guzzling happily at a crust dipped in tea and sugar. 'You stand by the window, Helen, and keep well clear of my skirt,' Alice warned, then pirouetted. She was wearing a pale blue muslin dress that Jenny had made over for her from a gown that Mrs McColl had given to Bella. Jenny had bought some cream-coloured lace and used it to trim the bodice and cuffs, with enough over to provide a mock fichu to fill in the low square neck.

'What d'you think?'

'It's lovely, though I say so myself.' The muslin softened the outlines of her sister's sturdy figure, and the colour of the dress complemented Alice's fresh colouring.

'Now let me see yours. Oh, Jenny, it's bonny!'

'D'you think so?' Jenny smoothed the skirt over her slim hips, comforted by her sister's admiration. The dress consisted of a strip of pale yellow crepe de chine that she had folded in two, cutting a round neck out of it and taking two strips from the side so that the dress formed a T-shape. Then, borrowing Mrs Malloy's old but reliable sewing machine, she had sewed along the sides and turned up a hem. Some dark blue braid on the neck and sleeves and a belt made from the surplus material edged with the braid completed the dress – her first new outfit since the beginning of the war.

'P'etty,' Helen said placidly. Lifting the edge of the smock she wore and looking down at her own little muslin dress, bought by Jenny, she said again, 'P'etty,' then returned to her crust.

66

'You don't think it's too short?' Jenny flattened the skirt against the front of her thighs and bent forward to examine the hemline. 'I feel as if my legs go on and on beneath it.'

Alice shook her head firmly. 'The new short skirt length suits folk like you, with pretty ankles.' Then she asked inquisitively, 'What's been going on? Lottie's moaning about being covered with bruises, though I couldn't see any. And Mam's in my room, getting ready for the party and looking more as if she's going to a funeral.'

'It was nothing.' Jenny was too ashamed of her burst of temper to admit to it. 'Just a wee argument between me and Lottie.' She ran a brush over her dark hair then fluffed it up so that it fell into soft curls round her face.

'Jen—' Alice swallowed audibly then said, in a rush of words, 'I heard today that I got that scholarship.'

'What? Oh, Alice!' Jenny dropped the brush and hugged her sister, heedless now of the need to keep their good dresses free of creases. 'I'm proud of you!'

'Me too, me too,' Helen clamoured, suddenly jealous, and had to be gathered up into a three-way embrace.

'That means you'll be going to the Academy in September!'

'It means I'll have to find a uniform, too.'

'We'll manage.' Jenny, tears in her eyes, gave her sister another hug and Helen, caught between them, gave a muffled squeak of protest. 'Now we've got more than just a launch to celebrate!'

Alice wrinkled her forehead. 'I don't know if I'm doing the right thing, Jenny. Mebbe I should just leave school when I turn fourteen in August and get some sort of work.'

'You'll do nothing of the kind. You'll get another scholarship next year then when you're sixteen you'll be able to go to college and learn to be a teacher. We'll manage fine, you wait and see,' Jenny promised.

Alice nodded, then remembered, 'Mam wants us to help her to get Gran to the window so that she can watch what's going on down in the back court.'

'She'll not be interested.'

'I know, but it makes Mam happier to think she is,' said Alice with a wisdom beyond her thirteen years. The door opened and Lottie flounced in.

'If you don't mind, I'd like tae get dressed now. In private,' she said sullenly, ignoring their finery, even ignoring Helen when she proudly caught at the hem of her smock and hauled it up over her face to display her new dress.

'Look. P'etty,' her voice said, muffled by the smock, and Alice picked her up and carried her out at arms' length to avoid getting sticky from the remains of the sugared crust, still liberally plastered to Helen's mouth and fingers.

'You're the bonniest wee girl in the street,' she said, turning in the passageway as Lottie banged the door shut behind them to add under her breath, 'You'd think she'd at least say something nice tae the bairn.'

'Not Lottie – she never sees anyone but herself.'

Faith was back in the kitchen when they went through, dressed in the same 'best clothes' she had had for many years – a dark green serge skirt and a high-necked blue blouse with carefully ironed frills at the neck and edging the three-quarter-length sleeves, a cameo brooch which had belonged to her mother pinned at her throat. She was carefully washing and drying her mother-in-law's face and hands. When Marion's hair had been brushed the three of them heaved and tugged until they managed to get her, chair and all, up to the window overlooking the courtyard.

'There, Mother, ye'll be able tae see everythin' now, won't ye?' Faith said cheerfully, ignoring the fact that in order to see out Marion would have had to get out of her chair and lean over the sink. The old woman's head lolled and a ribbon of saliva drooled from her slack mouth. Faith wiped it away.

'Mam, did Alice tell you her news? She's got the scholarship!'

'Aye, she said,' Faith said vaguely, then nodded to the table where the large round dumpling, rich with spices and raisins, released from its confining cloth and in pride of place, gently steamed. 'We'll have tae get this lot down tae the court. No sense in waitin' for yer father – he'll have stopped in at the pub.'

'But Mam, Alice—' Jenny began, then as her sister frowned and shook her head at her she gave up. A thin thread of music rose from the back court outside and Alice dashed to the window, leaning precariously over her grandmother's shoulder. 'It's old Peter wi' his fiddle. Would ye look at the weans followin' him – he looks like the fattest Pied Piper anyone's ever seen!'

Jenny joined her, balancing herself with a hand on Alice's arm. For once, the open cobbled back court that served four rows of tenement buildings was free of a forest of lines of washing. The ropes and clothes-poles had been stowed away in the four wash-houses, one built against each of the buildings that made up the court, and the space they had left blossomed with trestle tables covered with a collection of multi-coloured tablecloths and bed sheets, each table decorated with jam-jars stuffed with wild spring flowers gathered from the fields outside the town.

Peter McLellan, a boilermaker in the shipyard, had come through one of the closes from the street and was marching between the tables, his face and his bald head shining from a recent thorough application of soap and water, his Sunday suit straining over his paunch, a battered old fiddle almost lost in the multiple folds of his chins. Behind him, hopping and skipping haphazardly as they came, was a ribbon of children, their faces split by grins of excitement.

Peter's music had called to more than the children. The court was suddenly busy with women bearing teapots, trays of mugs, covered dishes and bowls and jugs. The men followed, scrubbed and dressed in their best clothes, strutting a little as they walked. After all, hadn't they built the ship that was being honoured today? Didn't they have more right to celebrate than the Dalkieths and their fine guests who would at that moment be sitting down to lunch in the shipyard offices?

'Come on—' Jenny turned back into the room to remove Helen's bib. 'Let's get you washed, milady. It's time to celebrate!'

7

The model gallery on the floor above the Dalkieth offices housed an impressive display of some of the vessels launched from the yard since its earliest years. On the *Tanamura*'s launch day most of the models had been cleared from the gallery to make way for four trestle tables, three running down the length of the gallery and the fourth placed across the room as a top table. Only a few of the larger models were left against the walls, handsome in their glass cases, for the interest of the male members of the launch party.

This was the first launch Fiona Dalkieth had attended, and so far she had found the whole business intensely boring. She saw no sense in having to climb a rickety ladder to stand on a crowded, breezy platform, one hand clutching at her wide-brimmed hat to keep it from being whisked off her head, while some simpering woman she didn't know or remotely wish to know tossed a bottle of good champagne at a ship. What was wrong with just letting the dratted thing slide quietly into the water by itself? And now she was forced to sit on an uncomfortable chair and listen to speeches before she could enjoy her lunch.

Even the pleasure of choosing new clothes for the occasion had been spoiled by Mama Dalkieth's insistence that they were still in mourning for George's brother and father. She stroked a hand down the skirt of her black silk costume. At least it was well made, and black suited her fair hair and pearly skin. And she had managed to add a dash of colour – her lilac and pale grey blouse and the cluster of grey feathers about the crown of her hat. George, who knew nothing of fashion and etiquette, had merely told her that she looked becoming, but Mama Dalkieth had looked at her very sharply when she walked into the drawing room of Dalkieth House on George's arm that morning.

Fortunately, their late arrival, carefully arranged by Fiona, had given the older woman no time to order her back to the modest house she and George shared on the outskirts of the town to find a more suitable blouse and remove the feathers.

A patter of applause signified, to her relief, that the speeches were over. The waitresses moved forward with plates of soup but even then there was a further delay while the Reverend John Stirling, no doubt as eager for nourishment as everyone else, delivered a mercifully brief Grace. But at last the company were finally able to relax with a clash of spoons against plates and the discreet hum of voices.

Fiona shifted slightly in her chair and noticed that her husband, several places along the table, was leaning forward and glaring at her. She glared back, and he made some strange circling movements around his forehead with one finger, repeating them as she stared at him, completely bemused.

'What?' Her lips shaped the word, but George's signals only became more agitated, his finger stabbing at the air above his own sleek brown hair.

'I think, Mrs Dalkieth, that your husband may be trying to draw your attention to your hat,' said a quiet voice beside Fiona.

She turned to the man on her left. 'What's wrong with my hat?'

'Nothing at all. It's most attractive, but I think your husband may have noticed that every time you move your head one of the feathers connects with my eye.'

Before she could stop herself Fiona giggled, and was answered by a grin from her companion. 'The number of guests and the size of the room means that we're all rather close to our neighbours,' he explained.

I'm sorry, Mr—' She looked at his place card. 'Mr Archer. Now I know why my mother-in-law chose to wear a small hat. I shall take mine off.'

'Not on my account,' he started to protest, but her hands were already busy with the hatpins, one elbow putting the man on her other side into imminent danger.

'Allow me,' said Robert Archer, deftly removing the second hatpin then the hat itself. Fiona took it from him and handed it to one of the waitresses after stabbing the pins through the material.

'Now some of the ladies look shocked,' said her companion.

'It's of no consequence. I don't see why women should wear hats at the table, it can be quite inconvenient – as you've just found to your cost. Also,' added Fiona as their soup plates were gathered in, 'it feels more comfortable, and I've just saved your eyesight. I think I may start a new fashion.'

The main course arrived and a waiter brought wine. The woman on Robert Archer's other side engaged him in conversation and Fiona turned to the man on her right. He answered her comments as briefly

72

as possible, being far more interested in the food and drink before him, and she soon left him to his own devices, claiming Archer's attention again as soon as she could. He was vaguely familiar and, after a moment's thought, she recalled that he had been involved in the boring tour of the Tank section before the launch.

'Have you been with Dalkieth's for long, Mr Archer?'

He shook his head. There was silver over his temples and strands of silver glittering here and there in his thick dark hair, giving him a distinguished look, but his lean, strong face was still youthful. George's hair was an uninteresting mid-brown with no silver in it as yet, although his face was already beginning to fill out and take on a florid tinge.

'I've recently come from Tyneside to take up my duties here as office manager.'

'Indeed? You don't sound like a Tyneside man.'

He had just cut a piece of meat and put it into his mouth. Fiona had to wait while he chewed and swallowed without haste before he answered. 'I was born here in Ellerslie. I followed my father into the shipyard and was apprenticed as a naval architect in the Tank section. After I'd served my time Mr George's father sent me to a yard on Tyneside to learn more about shipbuilding. I came back only a few weeks ago.'

'Why should a naval architect be brought back as an office manager?'

He didn't seem the least offended by her bluntness. 'In the past few years I've come to know quite a lot about administration among other things, and the Board felt that it made sense to have an office manager with a good knowledge of the work carried out in the yard itself.'

There was a pause, during which he attended to the food on his plate and Fiona scrutinised him in a series of sideways glances. He was quite an attractive man, she decided, and not in the least afraid of women, so he was almost certainly married. 'Is your wife happy to come back to Scotland?' she probed.

'My wife is English, and she prefers to remain in her own country among her own people.' His voice was calm and unhurried.

'So she'll be hoping that you'll change your mind about settling here?' Fiona asked with increasing interest. 'And will you? Are you willing to risk your marriage for the sake of Dalkieth's?'

'If I am, I think my wife should be the first to know of it, Mrs Dalkieth,' he said in the same bland voice, and she gasped at his impertinence, then began to laugh.

73

'You're quite right, Mr Archer, it is none of my business. I am altogether too inquisitive.'

'Not at all. You're entitled to ask whatever you wish – just as I'm entitled to keep my own counsel.' Robert Archer cut another piece of meat with deliberate precision and Fiona, suddenly realising that everyone else had almost emptied their plates, turned her attention to her own meal, wondering why George had never spoken of his new colleague. She must see to it that Mr Archer was invited to dine with them soon. With his wife still in Tyneside the poor man was on his own and it was only right that she and George should make him welcome in Ellerslie.

By mid-afternoon the large back court was filled with men, women and children, many of them dancing on the cobbles to the music of old Peter McLellan's fiddle. The thin notes straggled into the summer air, as many wrong as right, but today nobody cared. Music was music.

Daniel Young and another man had helped Patrick Kerr downstairs and into the court, his arms round their necks, his twisted foot dangling helplessly. Now he was seated on an ordinary kitchen chair near his own close, with Bella hovering round him, the anxiety on her small face emphasising her resemblance to her mother. When Jenny went over to speak to him he looked at her sourly.

'God, Peter's playing gets worse by the day.'

'What we need is your mouth-organ, Pat,' Jenny said.

'I've got it here,' Bella dipped into her pocket and produced the mouth-organ that had once been Patrick's pride and joy.

'I've already told you – I don't want it!'

'Please,' Bella said softly. 'Please play something, Pat. Just for me.'

He looked at her in silence for a long moment, then as she said again, 'Please?' his mouth took on a wry, bitter twist and he held out a hand that was almost his trademark, the skin blue and permanently scarred, knotted in places by burns received from working with rivets still hot from the braziers. Before the war as a riveter in the shipyard, Patrick had scrambled sure-footed over scaffolding, high above the ground.

'All right, then, I'll play something just for you,' he said, and Bella's eyes lit up as he put the instrument to his lips. For a moment she looked almost radiant; then all the light died from her face as her husband pursed his lips about the mouth-organ and began to play the Last Post, the sad lament played over the graves of countless dead servicemen.

74

Heads turned and faces gaped as the heartbreaking refrain rose into the air, vying with the thin pipe of the old fiddle.

'No—!' Bella said on a sob, putting a hand out towards him. He ended the lament on a harsh discordant note, and stared defiantly up into her stricken face.

'What's the matter, Bella?' he asked roughly. 'Why did ye no' dance tae my music? I'm sure ye could find plenty of new partners, men able tae whirl ye round and lift ye off ye're feet. Here, you,' he added, beckoning to a lad who had pushed his way through the staring crowd. 'Catch.'

The mouth-organ flashed silver as it sailed through the air, to be caught deftly in the boy's grimy hands.

'Patrick—' Bella spun like a distracted top, torn between staying with her husband and retrieving the mouth-organ.

'I don't want it – I've told ye that, time and time again! Now mebbe ye'll believe me! Take it, son,' Patrick ordered, and with a yelp of 'Thanks, mister!' the lad disappeared into the crowd, the mouth-organ held high in triumph.

Patrick's face twisted into a scowl as he looked at the people who were still staring and whispering. 'What else d'ye want from me,' he asked roughly. 'A hornpipe?' His finger stabbed at his twisted lower leg and foot. 'Ye've had all the entertainment ye're goin' tae get from me – now clear off!'

They muttered their embarrassment, slowly turning away as Daniel Young pushed his way through, carrying two mugs of beer. His dark eyes took in the scene and he marched up to Patrick, holding out one of the mugs. 'Here ye are, man, drink it down. Bella, you go off and enjoy yourself,' he added. 'Patrick and me'll have a wee chat together.'

'Come on, Bella, come and get a slice of Mam's dumpling.' Jenny caught at her sister's hand and drew her away. 'Leave him to Daniel for a wee while,' she advised as they went.

'Ye'd think it was his head that had been hurt, not his leg,' Bella choked out, the tears spilling freely down her pale face now. 'Jen, what am I goin' tae dae if he doesnae get any b-better?'

Jenny put an arm about her and gave her a quick hug, remembering her sister's wedding less than two years before, and Patrick, home on leave and handsome in his naval uniform, dancing with Bella to the scrape of old Peter's fiddle. She recalled the tenderness in his eyes as he looked down at his slim young bride.

'Go and help Mam,' she said, giving Bella a gentle push towards one of the tables, where their mother was in the midst of a knot of neighbours. Some of the younger married woman were there, laughing and chattering. Perhaps they could help Bella to forget her worries for a few minutes.

A storm of harsh, familiar coughing came to her ears. Her father was with a crowd of men in a corner of the court beside two beer barrels, a donation from the Dalkieths. Too much talking and laughing had set him coughing, fighting for breath, almost bent double, the beer in the tin mug he held slopping over and splashing the cobbles. Jenny walked on, and came on Walter Young, Daniel's son, standing alone against one of the buildings, watching the proceedings. Although most of the youngsters in the courtyard were dressed in casual, comfortable clothes, Walter wore his usual heavy suit, complete with shirt and tie and polished boots. Hearing the violin music swing into a familiar tune Jenny impulsively held out her hand to him.

'Walter, you're the very lad! I've been looking for someone to partner me in a dance.'

He flushed scarlet and shrank back against the wall as though trying to push his way through the stones. 'I cannae dance!'

'I can – well enough for the two of us. It's easy, come and try it.'

He swallowed hard and looked about as though for assistance. When none came he gave a stiff, wretched little nod and put his hand into hers, allowing her to lead him to the edge of the area where Alice, her face red with exertion and enjoyment, reached out to him.

'Good for you, Walter – now we've got ourselves a set,' she shouted. Walter's hand twitched in Jenny's grasp, and for a moment she thought that he was going to wrench himself free and run, then the music started and the circle they were in began swinging round and it was too late for flight.

At first Walter's movements were nervous and jerky, but he soon picked up the rhythm of the simple dance and Jenny felt him relax. At twelve years of age, growing up instead of growing out, he was as tall as she was.

'You're doin' grand, Walter,' Alice shouted as they whirled together. Jenny laughed, her yellow skirt spinning around her legs like the petals of a flower, and awakened an answering smile on his perspiring face.

When the dance ended Alice tried to coax Walter towards a corner of the court where a group of lads were trying their prowess at walking a plank of wood set up between two barrels. The wood had been well rubbed with fat and the audience was squealing with helpless laughter at the walkers' attempts to reach the far end.

'You'd be good at it, Walter,' Alice said. 'I'd bet on you being able to run across that old plank like a mouse up a drainpipe.'

But Walter, blushing once more, shook his head and escaped back to his watching place beside the wall.

'It's a shame, so it is.' Kerry joined the two sisters as they watched him go. 'He should be havin' fun with the rest of the lads.'

'His father doesnae give him much time for playin', Alice said. 'He's his heart set on Walter doing well at the school.'

'It's just his way.' Jenny felt she had to defend Daniel. 'He's a good man and he keeps that house of his like a new pin.'

'Aye, well, that doesnae seem tae me tae be man's work.' Kerry's voice was doubtful. 'My ma says it's time he was gettin' himself a new wife.' Then, after a quick glance over her shoulder to make sure that Maureen wasn't within earshot, 'I'll drop those cups and saucers in later on, will I?'

'Fine. I'd better go and see to Helen. It's not fair to leave her to Mam all afternoon.'

'Lottie's the one that should be looking out for her own bairn.' Then Alice's glance moved to a spot beyond Jenny and she added with a change of tone, 'Never you mind about Helen, we'll see to her. Come on, Kerry.' She grabbed at the other girl and pulled her away, into the crowd. Jenny, puzzled, began to turn just as a hand closed over her arm.

'Dance with me, Jenny,' Robert Archer said and, before she could protest, she had been swung into the midst of the dancers.

'You look bonny,' he said as he guided her over the cobbles, one arm about her waist. 'Is that a new dress?'

'What are you doing here?' She was aware of people staring as they danced by, nudging each other and pointing.

'I heard there was to be a street party to celebrate the launch, and I minded the fine parties we used to have.'

'That was in the days when you lived round here.'

Robert's arm tightened about her as he deftly swung her out of the way of an energetic couple who were in no mood to make room for anyone. 'I'm neither fish, flesh nor fowl, is that what you mean? Not one of the posh folk, for all that I'm working among them, and not one of the tenement folk any more. A traitor to my own kind.' His voice hardened. 'Your father made that clear the night I came to see you.'

'He shouldn't have spoken to you the way he did,' Jenny said into his shoulder. He smelled of tobacco and good soap.

'I suppose a man's got a right to speak his mind in his own house. I shouldn't have just walked in without finding out how he felt first.' Then Robert said, low-voiced, 'Not that his feelings concern me. It's yours I'm more interested in.'

77

'I have no feelings one way or the other, Mr Archer.'

'I wronged you, Jenny, I know that. But I was younger then, and my head was easy turned by everything that was happening to me.'

'I hear you've bought yourself a comfortable house.'

They were too close for her to see his face, but close enough for her to feel the laughter in his chest. 'At least you're interested enough to want to know what I'm doing. That's a good sign.'

She tried to step free of him, but he held her firmly and she had no option but to dance on. 'I'm not a bit interested, but I can't help hearing gossip now and again. And you've given the gossips plenty to talk about, coming back to Ellerslie.'

'In case you're wondering, I bought the house for my own convenience, not my wife's. She's decided that she's going to stay in England.' The laughter had gone, and when she glanced up she saw the knot of hard muscle along the edge of his jaw. 'It was a mistake, Jenny, marrying her. When the word came for me to come back here to the shipyard I could have refused and stayed where I was. I wanted to be back with my own folk, back where I belong.'

She said nothing, staring at the lapels of his smart jacket. She had learned to live without him, had almost learned to forget him. It was wrong of him to come back now of all times, just when her own life had unexpectedly reached a dead end.

'I never thought to find you still here, still unwed,' he said just then, his hand tightening on hers.

'I should have been in Glasgow, but with Maurice gone I'm needed at home.'

'Mebbe it was meant for me to come back just when I did.'

Until then she had been confused and in turmoil at finding herself in his arms so unexpectedly. But now anger seasoned her emotions. 'Home to find me waiting for you, d'you mean? You're wrong!'

'Jenny—'

'There's nothing here for you, Robert Archer – not as far as I'm concerned.'

The music ended and she tried to pull away, but again his arm tightened about her waist. 'Let me be!'

'We've got things to talk about, Jenny. You owe me that, at least.'

'We owe each other nothing.' Turning her head away from him as the music started up again and she was drawn back into the dance she found herself looking at Daniel Young, skirting the group of dancers. His head turned at that moment, as if someone had called to him, and his eyes met hers. He began to shoulder his way towards her.

'Jenny, at least listen to—'

'Sorry I'm late, Jenny,' Daniel said, arriving by her side, ignoring

Robert. 'I was talking to Patrick. You promised this dance tae me, did you not?'

'Yes – yes I did.' She stopped, and Robert was forced to stop as well, his arms falling away from her. 'Thank you, Mr Archer,' she said, and went into Daniel's arms.

'What's he doing here, pestering you?' he wanted to know as they moved away from Robert.

'He wasn't pestering me, but I'm glad you came along, Daniel.'

'He doesnae belong here anymore. Not now that he's one of the bosses. He'd have been better keeping away.'

Jenny said nothing. The last thing she wanted to do was talk about Robert. To her relief he didn't approach her again. She saw him talking to her mother, then dancing with Kerry Malloy; later he danced with Lottie, her red hair spilling over his jacket, her laughter ringing out above the noise.

She caught another glimpse of him over by the beer barrels, talking comfortably with the men, mug in hand, while Teeze stood nearby with another group, his back turned to the office manager. Then, to her relief, he left the party, shaking hands with former neighbours and school friends on his way out.

'He's not a bad fella at all,' she heard Mr Malloy say as she walked past the men later, Helen toddling along by her side. 'Not a snob, like some I could mention. If ye ask me, it's good tae see one of our own kind gettin' on in the world.'

8

Kerry, as promised, delivered two plain white cups and saucers after the street party, carefully wrapped in newspaper. When the evening chores were done on the following day Jenny put her precious box of paints and brushes on the kitchen table and started work.

Alice was doing schoolwork at the other side of the table, Lottie was at work, and Helen slept soundly in the cot in the larger bedroom. Teeze, home for once, was sprawled out in his chair by the stove, his stockinged feet on the home-made hearth-rug, his head tipped back, mouth open, snoring. Marion puffed and grunted and bubbled in the truckle-bed, which took up most of the kitchen floor.

Faith sat opposite her husband with a pile of darning on her lap, her chair turned to catch the best light from the gas mantel above her head. Her needle flashed in and out of the material in her hands, getting dangerously close to her face as time wore on and her tired eyes became less able to focus on what she was doing. She badly needed spectacles, but couldn't afford them. Instead, she wore her mother-in-law's when the old lady was asleep, and refused to believe her daughters when they tried to tell her that someone else's spectacles might not be suitable for her eyes.

The gas mantel on that wall wasn't strong enough for the delicate work Jenny was doing, so she fetched one of the two paraffin lamps that usually sat on the big dresser flanking Maurice's photograph. As the extra light flooded the table Alice lifted her head and gave a vague smile of gratitude before returning to her work.

Alice would make a good teacher, Jenny thought as she got on with her own work. She was conscientious, and she got on well with children. It was right that she should get the opportunity that she deserved. They would manage, somehow, to get the uniform and find the extra money she would need.

Kerry had stipulated bluebells for her sister's wedding gift. Jenny dabbed deep blue paint on to the old saucer she used as a palette, dipped a fine brush into it, and started work, then her hand stilled for a moment as she realised that Alice would eventually have to go to Glasgow to attend college. She would be the one to make the journey

81

that Jenny had so dearly wanted to make. A sudden stab of envy and resentment shot through her, startling her with its intensity. She drew in her breath sharply, and Alice looked up.

'What's wrong?'

'Just indigestion,' Jenny said mildly, and with a determined effort she concentrated all her attention on her work.

An hour ticked by, then another. Faith's hand slowed and stilled, and she began to nod over her darning. Jenny put down her brush and clenched then straightened her stiff fingers just as her father's snores stopped dead. Across the table, the sisters' eyes met.

'One – two – three—' Alice mouthed, and had reached fifteen before Teeze gave a great shudder then sucked in his breath again with a choking snore that brought Faith's head up with a start and almost, but not quite, wakened Teeze himself. He shifted in his chair, then relaxed again.

'Lucky you weren't painting then,' Alice murmured. 'You'd have run that butterfly straight into one of the bluebells. He'll forget to breathe in again one of those nights.'

They grinned at each other like conspirators, then Jenny picked up the cup she was working on, blessing her sister's impish sense of humour. Life would be intolerable without Alice.

When the first cup was completed she edged round the truckle bed and put it on to the mantelshelf where it could dry safely before being fired in the oven. The gaslight emphasised the delicate blue of the flowers, the twining fragile green stems and leaves, the sudden rainbow burst of the butterfly, hovering above one of the blossoms.

Jenny was cleaning her brushes when Lottie came in, blinking in the light. Her hair was tousled, her eyes sleepy and cat-like, and her mouth had the full, almost bruised look that spoke of a man's kisses.

'I'm parched. Is there any tea?'

Teeze choked into silence in mid-snore and woke up, yawning and stretching and scratching himself. The old woman in the truckle-bed stirred and Faith, brushing her darning into the old basket that had held her sewing and knitting for all the years that Jenny could remember, shushed Lottie, rising stiffly from her chair and tiptoeing to lean over the bed, her body shading the old woman's face from the light. When she was satisfied that her mother-in-law wasn't going to waken she straightened up, easing her back carefully as though it hurt her.

'Clear the table, you two, and we'll have a cup of tea before we get to our beds.'

Alice, knowing that a protest would only bring a thump on the ear from her father, began to gather up her books and Jenny carried the lamp back to the dresser. As she set it down its light washed across Maurice's elaborately framed photograph. The telegram that had come from the War Office, already yellowing, was tucked into the frame of the mirror behind the picture.

Looking into the mirror, seeing Faith's tired, worried face reflected in the glass, the lines and hollows deepened instead of softened by the shadows from the gas mantels, she wished that her mother had had the comfort of a strong religion. But the Gillespies didn't believe in religion, only in the here and now and in folks' ability to stand on their own feet, and so Faith had to settle for a handful of flowers beside the likeness of the only one of her three sons to achieve adulthood.

On the afternoon of Maureen's last day at work Miss McQueen, unable to bring herself to join in any unseemly rowdiness but equally unable to put a stop to tradition, discreetly left half an hour early, pleading toothache. As soon as the door had closed behind her the other girls pounced.

Maureen, squealing with excitement, tried to take shelter in a corner but Kerry and Senga dragged her back and held her while Jenny pinned streamers of coloured paper to her blouse and skirt and sleeves, finishing off with a large red paper heart over Maureen's left breast and a paper baby-bonnet, all carefully made at home by Senga and herself and brought in that morning.

'There!' With a flourish she completed the dressing-up by hanging a baby's bottle round Maureen's neck on a string, then stepped back and eyed the result with satisfaction.

'I'm like a dog's dinner, so I am!' the bride-to-be lamented, beaming.

'You're lovely,' Jenny told her, pushing a battered old top hat into her hand. 'Come on, then.'

Giggling they dragged her down the narrow stairs to where the men were already waiting. On the floor by the joiners' area stood a large chamber pot filled with salt. Even Mr Duncan shared in the fun, beaming broadly as he stood by his office door and watched the age-old traditional 'bottling' of the bride-to-be.

'Jump ower the chanty, hen,' Baldy shouted. 'Jump high, for yer man's sake!'

There was a roar of appreciation as Maureen, a rustling rainbow now that her plain white blouse and black skirt were festooned with paper ribbons, lifted her skirt higher than necessary to show plump calves and dimpled knees before skipping over the chamber pot to a cheer of approval from the men.

'Ye'll hae a hooseful o' bonny babies noo,' someone shouted and Maureen yelled back, 'God, I hope no'!' before the men advanced to claim their bridal kiss, each one dropping a coin into the top hat as his contribution to the wedding. Then they lifted the bride-to-be by the arms and legs and carried her, shrieking and displaying more black stocking than was seemly in a young lady, down the stairs and through the wax room and out to the street where a kitchen chair waited, tied to a trolley and decorated with scraps of coloured material.

Passers-by stopped to watch and laugh as Maureen, her bonnet askew on the side of her head, was pulled through the streets to her home in style, waving grandly to either side and having the time of her life. Most of them waved back and shouted out their good wishes, some even tossing a coin into the top hat on Maureen's lap. Children with nothing better to do trailed along after the procession, fighting over the occasional penny that missed the hat and chinked on to the pavement close to their bare toes.

'It'll be your turn next, Jenny,' Maureen called down from the trolley and Jenny, running alongside, shouted back sarcastically. 'Aye, that'll be right! Who'd want me when they'd have to take on my whole family?'

As was usual with weddings in their neighbourhood, the happy couple had a private religious ceremony with only their bridesmaid and best man present before returning to Maureen's home for a meal attended by the immediate family. Friends and neighbours, some of whom had donated tea or sugar or milk or baking for the wedding breakfast, came in afterwards to pay their respects.

Old Peter McLellan had arrived by the time Jenny and Alice reached the flat, and was already busy scraping at his fiddle. The furniture had been pushed against the walls and the centre of the small kitchen was crammed with dancers, so tightly packed together that they could only jump up and down on the spot.

On the sideboard, a handsome piece of furniture from the Dalkieth yard, the presents the couple had received were laid out for all the guests to admire. There was a condiment set from a well-to-do aunt of Maureen's, a pair of dish-towels, a pretty caddy full of tea, a home-made tea-cosy, hand-embroidered pillowcases. And, in pride of place, the decorated cups and saucers, only just completed in time and delivered first thing that morning.

'Jenny!' Maureen, in her best blue dress, fought her way through the crush and hugged her friend when Jenny and Alice squeezed themselves into the crowded room. Her face was crimson with excitement and heat; although the window had been wedged open

84

with an up-ended brick from the yard below the room was stifling. 'Thanks for painting my cups and saucers, they're that bonny! Jacko's sister's fair purple with jealousy. I'm goin' tae put them in my china press – when I get one.'

'Mam baked some scones for you. I'll give them to your mother.' Alice pushed her way further into the crowded kitchen as Maureen towed Jenny to the table by the window. 'Have a drink,' she invited proudly.

Two rows of thick, plain tumblers stood on the table, the larger holding lemonade or beer, the smaller with amber whisky in them. Jenny selected a glass of lemonade and backed into a corner as Maureen was claimed by her new husband for a dance. He, too, was red-faced and perspiring, and more than a little drunk, but even so there was something touching about the protective way he smiled down at his bride as they bumped and pushed their way round the crowded floor, colliding with other would-be dancers.

'Here's a seat for you.' Jenny turned to see Daniel Young indicating the chair he had just left.

'Thanks, Daniel.' She seated herself and he loomed over her so that she had to tip her head back to look up at him. 'Is Walter not here?'

'He's got homework tae do. This isnae a good time tae let his studies fall by the wayside.'

'But the school's closed for the summer holiday, surely?'

'I always arrange for his teachers tae give him work tae dae over the holidays,' said Daniel. 'He cannae afford tae fall behind. He's got himself work at the dairy in Denny Street for the holidays, and he studies in the evenings.'

'There's surely no danger of him falling behind. From what I hear, he's a clever lad.'

Daniel's long serious face lit up. 'He is that. His teachers are fair pleased with him. The headmaster wants him tae go tae the Academy. He'll sit the examinations next April. I hear that your sister's goin' there?'

'Yes, she is. We hope she's going to be a teacher.'

Daniel nodded his approval. 'Folk with brains should be encouraged to better themselves – even lassies,' he added.

If anyone else had spoken so disparagingly about women, Jenny would have challenged them indignantly. But somehow Daniel was different. He would defend his beliefs hotly, and a wedding party was no place to start an argument. So she merely said, 'So Walter's not going into the shipyard, then?'

He had leaned one shoulder against the wall so that his body cut her off from the rest of the room. Now his mouth tightened. 'He is not. That's no life for a lad with brains. He's not going to have oil and filth beneath his fingernails.' His own nails, she noticed, glancing away from his face to ease the ache that had begun to nag at the back of her neck, were very short, square cut and spotlessly clean.

A shrill scream came from Maureen as Jacko swung her up into his arms, scattering dancers to right and left. Startled, Daniel turned and as his body eased away Jenny saw her friend held close to the low ceiling, almost above her new husband's head, her skirt ballooning out to reveal rounded thighs. Daniel looked away hurriedly, his face reddening.

More and more people were crowding into the already packed room, for the Malloys were a popular family in the tenements. When Alice reappeared a few minutes later Jenny drained her glass and stood up, anxious to get into the fresh air. Daniel immediately emptied his own glass and accompanied the two of them. As they went downstairs, Alice dawdling behind them, he began to ask Jenny about her work in the Tank section. By the time they reached the street, meeting people on their way up to the Malloy house as they descended, she found herself talking easily. Daniel was a good listener, though a stilted conversationalist.

'It's amazing to think that a young lassie like you can tell just what speed a ship'll make, and how it'll ride the water,' he marvelled. 'It's a rare talent ye've got.'

'We just work it out from the information sent to us from the Tank. I liked drawing at the school, and mathematics, and I find the work easy enough. I wish women could go into the drawing office at Dalkieth's, though, I'd like to have done work like that,' Jenny told him as they stepped out of the close. It was late afternoon; the slice of sky above the roofs and chimneys was a clear blue and a group of chairs was clustered about every closemouth so that men and women could sit out in the sunlight for a while, the men smoking, the women with basins and bowls on their laps so that they could peel potatoes or scrape carrots for the evening meal. Without realising it, Jenny and Daniel's feet slowed on the cobbles and, by the time they reached the Gillespies' close, Alice was ahead of them. Daniel touched his cap and began to turn away then hesitated and looked back.

'I wondered—' he began, low-voiced, and hesitated, giving a sidelong glance at the people sitting nearby. Then in a sudden rush of words he said, 'I thought I'd take a walk out to the edge of the town later this evening, to get away from all this for a wee while.' One hand indicated the grey walls crowding in on them, the cobblestones underfoot, the people. 'Mebbe ye'd be free tae come with me?'

Sheer surprise confused her. 'I'm – I'm not sure if I'll find the time,' she stammered. 'There's my gran to see to, and—'

'I'll be at the corner there at about eight o'clock. If you don't come by the time the church clock strikes the quarter I'll know you've got too much to do,' said Daniel hurriedly, and strode off before she could say another word.

Alice had been loitering in the close, listening open-mouthed to every word. 'You're not going to meet him, are you?' she asked, popping out of the close at Jenny as soon as he walked off.

'Why not?'

Alice's snub nose wrinkled. 'He's awful dull.'

'He's a nice kind man and don't you forget it,' Jenny told her sister with enough of an edge to her voice to make the girl's eyes widen. She had had no intention of meeting Daniel that evening, but all at once she decided that maybe she would. It wouldn't do any harm and, after all, there was no sense in hurting the man's feelings.

His disparaging remark about Alice's intelligence came back to her mind, and was dismissed. It would be unfair of her to refuse to go for a walk with him because of a chance remark made without thought.

After all, they were only going for a walk, not courting each other.

9

After their wedding George Dalkieth had brought his new bride to the house he had bought for his first wife. It was modest in comparison with the large residence he had been raised in by the river, but it was in a select neighbourhood, and a staff of two maids, a cook and a gardener looked after the young couple very well.

Isobel Dalkieth had suggested that George should sell the place, with its memories of a failed marriage, and bring Fiona to Dalkieth House, where they could have their own suite of rooms, but they had declined; George because he had no wish to live under his mother's watchful eye, Fiona because she had made up her mind that when she moved into the big house it would be as the sole mistress, not a companion dependent on Isobel's bounty. Besides, she could control George much better while they lived on their own.

A few weeks after the launch George burst into their bedroom, waving a crumpled newspaper at his wife, who was still in bed.

'Look at that, dammit!'

'What, dear?' Fiona, who had been enjoying a leisurely breakfast, accepted the paper and studied it vaguely. He snatched it from her and folded it again and again, then thrust it back at her, his handsome face purpling, one finger stabbing at a small announcement. He had thrown himself on to the bed beside her, so close that every time he gave an angry huff she was acutely aware that he had had kippers for breakfast again. George liked to start the day with a hearty meal, which was one of the reasons why he and his wife breakfasted apart.

Fiona peered at the item that kept disappearing beneath his accusing finger and, despite the fire that she insisted be lit in the grate every morning, even in the summer, the blood chilled in her veins. Captain Harold Beasley and Mrs Catherine Beasley of Ashford House, Dunfermline, were happy to announce the birth of their first child, a daughter, to be named Alexandra Catherine. Mother and child were both well.

As she struggled to find the right words the newspaper was snatched from her hands and thrown across the room. 'The bitch!'

stormed George, getting up from the bed and pacing the room. 'The bitch! Refusing to give me an heir, then she's not married to that bounder for five minutes before she's shedding brats!'

'Perhaps—' Fiona began, then stopped short, hit by the enormity of what she had almost said.

'Perhaps what?'

'Nothing. I just – nothing.'

'Fiona,' said George through his teeth. 'I give you notice here and now – I mean to have a son, and I mean to have him soon!'

'Have I ever denied you your rights?'

'No, but we've been married for long enough.'

Now that the first moment of panic was over Fiona's mind had begun to function. 'We've not been married for a year yet. In my opinion it shows vulgar haste to have a family within the first two years of marriage.'

'I,' said George tightly, 'do not agree. You hear me, Fiona? I want an heir!'

'You shall have one, but first I would like to finish my breakfast.'

'Be damned to your breakfast!' snarled George. For a moment he stood in the middle of the pretty bedroom, which Fiona had had redecorated entirely when she moved in, his feet apart, hands fisted on his hips, then, to his wife's horror and outrage he advanced and snatched up the tray containing her lightly boiled egg and pot of weak China tea, setting it on a nearby table with a jingle of agitated china. Stripping off his jacket and unfastening his waistcoat then his trousers he moved back to the bed.

'George! What do you think you're – the maid might come in!'

'She knows better than to walk into a room without permission,' said George Dalkieth, hauling the bedclothes aside and climbing into bed. Once again Fiona was surrounded by the aroma of kippers. With a rending sound the fine lace on the bodice of her nightgown gave in to his clutching fingers.

'At least give me time to—'

'Dammit I've not got time, I'm due at the yard!' snapped George, pushing her down against the pillows that had been carefully piled up to support her back. She slid down the heap until she was lying flat on the mattress and George impatiently batted toppling pillows out of the way as he followed her, dragging what was left of her gown up around her hips. Without further ado he rolled on top of her, ignoring her breathless objections, crushing her with his weight. The strong smell of kippers filled her nostrils, and her lungs when she opened her mouth to protest further. She shut it again. Not that there was much

90

sense in protesting, for he was already rocking and plunging on top of her like a demented bull.

A few minutes later he was out of bed and getting dressed while Fiona, clutching the sheet to her chin in a belated attempt at modesty, was still considering whether anger or hurt would have the most effect on him. Since anger hadn't done much previously, she opted for hurt, catching her breath and squeezing a tear into her eyes.

It had no effect. Without glancing at her, without apparently hearing her sniffles, her husband completed his toilet, anxiously consulted the handsome watch on his watch-chain, and muttered, 'I'm going to be late.'

'George—'

Impervious to the tear that she had now managed to trickle on to her cheek, he picked up the discarded tray and put it back on the bed. 'I mean it, Fiona – I want an heir. Catherine refused to give me one, but you won't, if you're wise.' Then he left the room, and she was alone – sore, humiliated and furious.

She well knew that word of his ex-wife's child would quickly spread round the town. Everyone would know that the woman George Dalkieth had divorced because she was apparently unable to give him children had borne a daughter to her second husband with quite indecent haste. People would snigger, and no doubt wonder if George would be prepared to divorce a second wife if she, too, remained childless.

Fiona had no intention of allowing that to happen. Her father owned a large and successful emporium in Glasgow and his family had enjoyed a comfortable life, but, when all was said and done, her father was only a tradesman compared to the Dalkieths, and Fiona's marriage to George had been quite a triumph. She wasn't prepared to be sent back home in disgrace.

Despite her protests about the vulgarity of having children too soon, there was no reason why she shouldn't have been pregnant before this. There might well be a sinister warning in the fact that George's first wife hadn't had his child, but had conceived easily with her second husband.

Fiona lay among the rumpled mess of her formerly comfortable bed and thought hard. She knew that George wouldn't consider even the most carefully worded suggestion that he himself should have a talk with the family physician. To men like George the ability to father children was a God-given right, a fact. Without that ability they couldn't consider themselves to be men.

Fiona wasn't particularly interested in children herself, but the Dalkieth money meant that they could afford a good nursery staff and she had a vague idea that children brought their own blessing and that she and George would, when the occasion arose, make devoted parents.

There was still plenty of time, she'd thought, after all, he was only twenty-seven years of age and she was five years younger. But now, with the birth of a daughter to his first wife, the situation had become serious. Time was running out. If she didn't become pregnant soon she might find herself with problems.

She began to sit up then realised that George had dumped her breakfast tray back on the bed in such a way that she was almost lying underneath it. Because the sheet was over her shoulders and arms she couldn't free her hands to lift the tray away. She squirmed this way and that, but there was no way of freeing herself, other than heaving her body over and sending the entire tray, with its cold toast and egg and tepid tea crashing to the floor and ruining the expensive carpeting she had chosen personally.

She had no option but to lie still, a prisoner, until the maid tapped on the door and entered, in answer to a terse command, to find her dishevelled mistress lying flat on her bed, pinned beneath her breakfast tray, with pillows strewn over the floor and the bed looking like a battle-ground.

The widespread admiration that Maureen's painted cups and saucers had caused on her wedding day brought more work for Jenny, and filled up what little spare time there was left after she had put Helen to bed and helped her mother.

Whenever possible, she went out in the evenings for a breath of fresh air when the old woman and the baby were settled, walking down by the river most of the time, following the path that led away from the shipyard and out into the country around the town. Sometimes Daniel Young walked with her; he said very little about his own work, but was always interested in Jenny's. Despite herself, she was flattered and soothed by his admiration.

Often they walked in silence; at first Jenny, used to people talking all the time, found this uncomfortable, but soon she realised that with Daniel there was no need to talk all the time. She came to appreciate the freedom his silence gave her to concentrate on her own thoughts.

She was taken aback when Maureen, meeting her in the street one day, referred to Daniel as her sweetheart.

'He's nothing of the sort!'

'You walk out together.'

'That doesn't make us sweethearts,' Jenny protested, and her friend winked.

'It's the way me and Jacko started out – it's the way every couple starts out.'

We just happen to meet sometimes, and if we're walking in the same direction we might as well walk together.' Jenny retorted, and was exasperated when Maureen smirked.

Daniel, she soon noticed, only mentioned the shipyard when they visited Bella and Patrick, and then he talked generally, apparently unaware of the tension that always seemed to crackle through the small room, never saying anything that would remind Patrick too strongly of the work he had had to give up because of his war wounds. Patrick became more animated whenever Daniel was in the room.

'You're good with him,' Jenny said as they stepped out into the street after one of their visits. Patrick had been unusually relaxed and animated that night, and Bella's face glowed with happiness as she watched him. 'I never know what to say to him. He's so – locked in. Patrick was never like that before.'

'He's had a rough time of it. You'd need tae have been there tae know how bad it was. I tell you one thing, if it ever comes tae another war I'll not let my son go,' Daniel said with iron in his voice.

'It'll never come to that again.'

'I hope not. They asked enough of us the last time, and took more than most of us could afford tae give – and little thanks we've had for it.' The iron was still there, bitter in his throat. Looking sideways at him, she saw the sinews standing out on his neck. 'Look at young Pat back there – what sort of gratitude have they shown him? Robbed him of the right to work and given him nothin' but a pitiful pension in exchange. They'll not ever do that tae my boy – he's goin' tae be one o' the bosses, not one o' the slaves!'

In September Alice donned the grey skirt and blazer, the blue blouse and grey-and-blue striped tie worn by the Academy pupils. She had managed to buy the uniform from a second-hand shop, with money earned by working during the summer holidays at a local bakery.

Her father stared the first morning she walked into the kitchen, self-conscious in her uniform. 'What the hell's she dressed like that for?'

'It's her clothes for the Academy,' Faith was explaining nervously when Jenny came into the room.

'Academy?' Teeze said the word as though it was dirty, and Alice flinched.

'You know fine that I won a scholarship, Dad.'

'I know nothin' of the sort!'

93

'I told you myself,' Jenny cut in. 'You grunted and went on reading your paper.'

He stabbed a thick finger in Alice's direction. 'She should be out workin' for her keep, like the rest of us!'

'You're right there,' Lottie remarked from the table, where she was drinking a cup of tea, her eyes still puffy with sleep and her uncombed hair in a tangle.

Alice flushed and opened her mouth to speak, but Jenny, putting a reassuring hand on the girl's arm, said, 'She'll do better for herself getting an education.'

'And who's tae support her while she's gettin' it?'

'I will,' Jenny told him. 'It's my wages that do most of the supporting round here anyway.'

She heard her mother gasp at her impudence, but Jenny held her father's gaze, refusing to be the first to look away.

He crumpled the newspaper he was reading and threw it on to the floor, then stamped out of the room, leaving Jenny more determined than ever that, no matter how hard it was, she would see that Alice got the opportunity for advancement she had had to deny herself.

Jenny's struggle to find the money to keep her sister at the Academy received unexpected assistance a month later. She was called to Robert Archer's small but comfortable office in the shipyard's main office block and offered the job of supervisor in the tracing office.

'But – but Senga's surely the one who should take over from Miss McQueen!' she protested, after a stunned silence.

The pen in Robert's hand tapped at the blotting paper before him, flipped over, tapped again. 'You both started on the same day. There's no question of seniority.'

'She's two months older than I am.'

'But you're the one that Miss McQueen recommended,' he reminded her, adding with a lift of an eyebrow, 'Unless you think you're not capable of taking on the responsibility?'

'Oh, I am!' She had no doubt of that. And suddenly she realised that promotion meant more money and a slight easing of the family's financial situation.

'That's settled, then. Mr Duncan agrees with me that when Miss McQueen retires next month you'll become tracing office supervisor – with an increase in wages, of course.'

'You're not—' she began to say, then hesitated, reddening.

'Not what?'

'You know fine what I mean. You're not giving me the job just because of—'

94

His mouth tightened and the pen dropped to the desk. 'You think I'd have favourites? I told you – Miss McQueen recommended you and Mr Duncan supported her. There's no favouritism about it, although I have to say that I think they've come to the right decision. You're good at your work, Jenny. You deserve this chance.'

She got to her feet. 'Thank you, Mr Archer.'

'You can surely use my given name when there's nobody else about.'

'Best not,' she said, and left the room. Scowling, he picked up his pen, dipped it into the inkwell and started to write, then laid it down again and got up, crossing restlessly to the window. Below him, as he stood on the upper floor of the office block, was the woodyard with its huge piles of timber. The angle-iron smithy lay beyond them with the joiner's shop to the left and the tidal basin to the right. The river itself was hidden from his view by an intricate mass of scaffolding and half-completed ships. Dalkieth's yard had eight building berths, and now, in September 1919, seven of them were occupied. George Dalkieth and his mother had every right to be satisfied with the way things were going, yet uneasiness gnawed at Robert's gut.

He glimpsed movement below him as Jenny, neat in her white blouse and dark skirt, came out of the shelter of the office block and began to flank the woodyard on her way back to the tracing office. Watching the set of her shoulders and the tilt of her head with its short, dark hair Robert felt a sudden sense of loss. For all her quiet demeanour, Jenny Gillespie had her pride. He had no way of knowing whether it was only pride that had made her keep him at arms' length since his return to Ellerslie, or genuine indifference. He remembered the feel of her in his arms as they danced together at the back-court party on the day of the first peacetime launch, close and yet remote, willing to turn away from him and step into another man's embrace without a backward glance. It was possible that she would never forgive him for having betrayed her after his move to England. He had heard that she was walking out with someone else now; perhaps, Robert thought, the time had come to accept that he had lost her for good.

His lips tightened as he watched her move out of sight, then he turned back to his desk, telling himself that Jenny wasn't the only woman in the world. There were others, including one as erect and slender as Jenny, but with hair like silky corn framing a blue-eyed face that could slip from haughtiness to a beguiling smile in an instant.

Tonight he was due to dine at Fergus Craig's house, and no doubt Fiona Dalkieth would be there. Since his return to Ellerslie he had received a number of invitations to soirees and supper parties. His first inclination had been to refuse, for he had little interest in such goings-on, but Isobel Dalkieth had reminded him gently but firmly that he represented the shipyard now and was no longer free to please himself.

So he had attended this event and that, and each time Isobel's daughter-in-law was there, growing increasingly friendly towards the new office manager as her husband grew increasingly sullen. Fiona Dalkieth, Robert soon realised, was something of a flirt. Now that he had settled back into life in Ellerslie and had got the measure of his new appointment he was beginning to hunger for feminine company. He had enjoyed and appreciated the physical side of marriage and the warmth of a woman in his bed. He wanted that woman to be Jenny – but if she had indeed lost interest in him, then he would have to look elsewhere. Time was passing; he was in the prime of life – and his hunger was growing.

At Elspeth Craig's dinner table that evening the conversation, dominated by the men, mainly concerned shipbuilding. One of the guests, Malcolm McWalter, was an ageing man who owned a small shipyard adjacent to the Dalkieth yard. On occasion the two yards had helped each other out, but now McWalter felt that it was time for him to retire and he was anxious to find a buyer for his business. It was clear from the way he introduced the subject – and from the reaction he got from George Dalkieth – that the man had already approached George unofficially, and George was in favour of taking over the smaller yard.

'Are you sure that this is the right time to think of expanding?' Robert Archer enquired, and George gave him a withering look across the table.

'When could we find a better time? Our order books have never been so full and our profits are up. This is when we should invest and expand. Clyde shipbuilding is respected all over the world.' George thumped a fist on the table for emphasis.

'And how do we pay for this expansion? Robert asked mildly. Isobel Dalkieth took her eyes from her son and looked at him. 'During the war years the Government subsidised shipbuilding because we're an island nation and our warships were vital. They're not going to continue to subsidise us now that peace has been restored.'

There was a murmur of agreement around the table but George shrugged it off as though it was a speck of dust on his lapel. 'We borrow from the banks. Our name's good.'

'Only while business continues to be brisk.'

McWalter, seeing his chances of selling out to the Dalkieth yard under threat, cut in sharply. 'Why should it not continue?'

'At the moment importers and exporters all about the globe are rushing to replace ships either sunk in action or too old to be of use for much longer,' Robert explained. 'Commercial shipbuilding has stagnated during the past five years and there's a great need for it at the moment—'

'My point exactly,' George interrupted, his voice triumphant. Archer didn't even bother to give him a look, concentrating instead on Isobel Dalkieth and Fergus Craig, seated near each other.

'And what happens when that need has been met? That won't take long because shipyards all round the world, not just here in Britain, are working flat out to satisfy it. We must also take into consideration the captured enemy tonnage that's being handed over to commercial traders to take the place of ships commandeered for the war effort then lost.'

'That's only a stop-gap business,' George told him impatiently. 'The enemy ships are old and battle-weary; they'll all have to be replaced by new stock.'

'And once they are, there must be a lull, a recession. Mark my words,' said Archer insistently, 'Shipping companies aren't bottomless wells. Once they meet their targets the orders will slow down and the result for us may well be empty berths, men being laid off – and profits dropping.'

'Only for those yards that have refused to move with the times,' George trumpeted, his face reddening with anger. 'You're talking like a cautious old woman, Archer!'

A flash of anger brightened Robert Archer's eyes. His fingers, absently caressing the stem of a glass, tightened on its fragility. 'I was brought back to the Dalkieth yard because of the knowledge I gathered on Tyneside. There's little sense in me holding my tongue when I hear wild talk about expansion and spending money at a time when we should be consolidating what we have and planning for the future.'

'You were brought back because of your experience as a shipbuilder,' George snapped at him. 'You've little enough knowledge of the financial side of things, for all that you've been pushed into the post of office manager.'

Archer's face reddened at the deliberate slight. 'No man who's had to live on what he earns, and do without when there's no money coming in, can be accused of knowing nothing about finance,' he said, looking his tormentor full in the face. 'It's those who only know how to live on wealth earned for them by others who have little knowledge of its value.'

He knew as soon as he had said it, as soon as a rustle of movement and the sound of indrawn breath eddied around the table, that he had gone too far. George Dalkieth was by no means the only person present who had been born into money, or made his comfortable living through the efforts of other men on comparatively low wages.

'Ladies—' Elspeth Craig rose from her seat abruptly in response to a glance from her husband. 'Shall we withdraw and leave the men to their port?'

'I agree. We've been sitting here overlong.' Isobel got to her feet and swept from the room, her head high. Fiona's eyes met Robert's as she rose from her seat, and he saw sympathy in them.

'I'm afraid you spoke out of turn, Mr Archer,' she murmured later when the men had come into the drawing room. Robert was standing on his own near the windows and slowly, moving from one person to the next, she had contrived finally to reach him.

'I only spoke my mind, Mrs Dalkieth.'

'How very refreshing – and how dangerous.' Her blue eyes held his for a long moment and the corners of her full mouth flickered into a conspiratorial smile. 'I find that my husband prefers people to speak *his* mind, not their own.'

'Indeed? Are you speaking his mind now, Mrs Dalkieth?'

'George's opinions are boring. I prefer to make up my own mind about things. And,' she added, 'about people.'

'Indeed?' said Robert. Then, in a faintly mocking echo of her own words, 'How very refreshing.'

10

'You didn't have much to say for yourself this evening,' George Dalkieth complained when he and his wife were on their way back to their own house in their chauffeur-driven car.

Fiona cast him a sidelong look. 'I'm not interested in chatter about clothes and the problems of finding and keeping good servants. And I'm even less interested in shipbuilding.'

He grunted and said nothing more until they reached home. In the hall Fiona reached up to kiss her husband's cheek. 'Goodnight, dear.'

'I'll be up in a moment,'

She sighed as she began to mount the stairs. She had no doubt that he would be up in a moment. She was still not pregnant, and George was still hell-bent on proving to himself and his former wife that he was a virile man, capable of fathering a brood of children on the right partner.

A bedside lamp had been left on and Fiona's nightgown and George's pyjamas had been laid out on the satin quilt. Fiona prepared for bed swiftly and climbed in, switching out the lamp and hoping against hope that George would settle down in the library with his newspaper and a glass of whisky and delay coming upstairs until he was too tired to make love to her.

Her heart sank when she heard his heavy tread less than five minutes later. By the time he switched on the overhead light she had buried her head beneath the quilt and was giving every sign of being in a deep and peaceful slumber. The floor creaked and he grunted once or twice as he stripped his clothes off, leaving them where they lay. He had been raised by nursemaids and had never had to learn how to fold his clothes or put them away.

The light clicked off and he muttered a subdued curse as he fumbled his way towards the bed. A draft of cold air assailed her back as he thumped into it, then his hands reached out for her, tugging at her shoulder, wrenching her round to face him.

'George—' she protested, but his fingers were busy with the bows of her gown. Her own hands came into contact with cold, naked skin

99

and she jerked back in disgust. 'George, I do wish you'd put your pyjamas on! It's vulgar to come to bed naked. Only working-class men do such a thing!'

'How do you know about working-class men?' he mumbled, his fingers busy.

'George!'

'Anyway, pyjamas get in the way.' He found the hem of her gown and started to haul on it. She pressed her hip against the mattress but he levered her up and continued to peel her as though she was a grape.

'I'm tired!'

'I'll not take long.'

She knew that only too well. The bed squeaked in protest as the nightdress was hauled as far as her armpits and George Dalkieth triumphantly claimed his reward.

'All you have to do is become pregnant,' he panted as he rolled her over on to her back and covered her with his own body. 'Then you can sleep till the brat's born if that's what you wish!'

'Women can't just become pregnant by wanting to!' The words came out in a series of jerks as Fiona's ribcage was crushed and released like an accordian.

'Yes they can – Catherine proved that, the secretive bitch that she is. Anyway—' George gave a wheezy, coarse chuckle, 'I'm doing my bit.'

While he did his bit, Fiona lay stiffly beneath him, her teeth sunk into her lower lip, praying that this time she would conceive and get the whole messy business over with.

Robert Archer suddenly came to mind, with his lean body, his narrow face, handsome in its own way, those grey eyes that seemed to hold a promise of – something that Fiona would like to find out more about. Deliberately, she conjured up an image of him lying alone in his bachelor bed, perhaps staring into the darkness, thinking of her. As George pumped and puffed the picture in her mind changed until she could imagine her own fair head on the pillow beside Archer's dark one, see his eyes gazing into hers, feel his arms about her, his hands—

She whimpered and gave an involuntary shudder just as George, with a final muted roar, collapsed on top of her, almost squashing her.

'You see?' he murmured smugly into her ear, tickling it with his whisky-laden breath, 'You enjoyed it, too. That means you'll probably fall pregnant.'

It was all she could do not to heave herself round bodily and toss him out on to the carpet.

* * *

At the Board meeting a week later Robert Archer was not surprised to find himself out-voted on the decision to buy over the neighbouring yard and expand Dalkieth's with the assistance of a bank loan.

When he made one last attempt to argue against the motion put forward by George Dalkieth, Isobel said clearly and coldly. 'I feel, Mr Archer, that you're erring on the cautious side. A commendable quality, but one that has to be tempered by a degree of adventure now and again. I agree with my son that we should make an offer for the McWalter ground.'

During the four weeks Miss McQueen was training her into her new post there were times when Jenny almost gave in to the temptation to go to Robert's office and ask him to change his mind and give the position of supervisor to Senga. The thought of being in charge of the tracing office, being responsible for the quality of the work done there, terrified her. If she hadn't had so many problems at home she would have relished the thought of promotion. But sometimes she felt as though being the new supervisor was just one more weight on her shoulders, and more than she could cope with.

But once October came and Miss McQueen departed for Paisley, where she was going to take over as housekeeper to her brother, a widower and church minister, Jenny discovered that she loved her new position. With the shipbuilding industry flourishing, Dalkieth's Experimental Tank was in great demand from shipbuilders up and down the reaches of the Clyde as well as from its own yard and the tracers and analysts were kept busy from morning till night.

It took fifteen minutes for the water in the Tank to settle after each experiment, but as soon as it did, off the truck went again, backing up to the end of the Tank then surging forward with a clatter and rattle of machinery to clang to a sudden halt that almost sent the naval architect balancing on the small platform reeling. After each set of experiments another fat roll of paper was carried up to the tracing office, bearing another series of figures to be worked out and analysed by the girls.

As well as dealings with the model trials the tracers worked out the likely results before each Dalkieth ship left the slips to run the measured mile over the stretch of water off Skelmorlie, and analysed the actual results once the trials were over. Often they were working on a ship's performance while it was still running the mile, for a 'doo-loft', complete with pigeons and caretaker, was part of the shipyard equipment. An apprentice was sent aboard each ship due to run the

101

measured mile with a basket of fluttering cooing birds that were released at intervals to fly back to the loft with information fastened to their legs. As each bird returned to the loft the message it carried was brought at once to the tracing office.

Jinnet Harper, a woman in her thirties who had left the tracing office to get married during Jenny's first year there, was brought back to make up the team of analysts and tracers. The war had treated Jinnet badly; her husband had been killed in action and her only child had later died of Spanish 'flu. She was pathetically grateful to Robert Archer, who had remembered her from his own days in the Tank section as a naval architect, for seeking her out and offering her her old job back.

Thanks to Jenny's promotion and increased salary the Gillespie family's financial worries had eased a little. Alice was settling in well at the Academy, while Lottie, for all her sulking and complaining, seemed to be enjoying her work at the public house, and Teeze had said no more about her paying her wages over to Jenny.

Faith fretted just as much as before and fussed over her mother-in-law as she waited, with heart-rending patience, for Maurice to come home.

'You'd think the truth would have dawned on her by now,' Alice said as she and Jenny and Bella worked together in the brick wash-house early one Monday morning, a good hour before the shipyard siren was due to sound. The sisters had taken to combining their washing and dealing with it before they had to go about their day's duties, and while Patrick was still asleep.

Alice was turning the big mangle while Bella and Jenny fed the sheets through it one by one. Grey scummy water cascaded from the tangle of wet linen into the tub on the floor as the two of them tried to keep the folds of the material smooth so that it wouldn't bunch up and jam the rollers.

'Mebbe someone should say something. It's not right that she's still waiting. It might be better for her to face the truth,' Bella was volunteering when the door opened, letting in a waft of fresh air and Mrs Malloy, a cigarette dangling from the corner of her mouth and her arms filled with laundry.

'God, but ye're early birds, so yez are! I'll just use that water when ye've done if ye've no objections. No point in throwin' out good hot water.'

'It's very dirty, Mrs Malloy.'

'Ach, that'll no' bother me, Alice hen. Sure, my old man's dungarees are that filthy they could stand on their own. I could send them tae wash themselves if they werenae as thick as he is when it

102

comes tae followin' directions.' Kerry's mother laughed wheezily. 'Any water'll be clean enough for them.'

The sisters exchanged looks. Mrs Malloy was notorious for 'borrowing' other people's water to save herself the trouble of cleaning and refilling the big copper.

'If that's what you want, Mrs Malloy,' Jenny said, and the woman dropped her load on the floor and began to sort through it, her huge, rolling behind straining against the confines of an old tweed skirt. They could see the stitching in the seams being pulled apart.

'Who did yez say would be the better of knowin' the truth?' the woman demanded as she worked. Nothing was a secret as far as Mrs Malloy was concerned, but there wasn't a malicious bone in her entire body and many a neighbour in need had benefited from her casual generosity in the past.

'Our mam,' Alice's round face was screwed up with concern. 'We're thinking it's bad for her to go on waiting for Maurice when we all know he's not coming home.'

'Who says he's no'? Did he send ye a telegram, then?'

'After all this time—'

Mrs Malloy fisted her shiny red hands, already showing signs of winter hacks, on to her hips, the washing forgotten. 'Listen tae me, lassies – for all yez know yer poor ma might be right. He might be safe an' well.'

'But—'

The woman stopped Jenny with one look. 'God has his own ways, hen, an' don't ye forget that. Mebbe this is his way of helpin' yer poor ma tae get used tae the idea of losin' her only son. Leave her be, that's what I say. Leave her with her hopes. Ye've no way of knowin' what harm ye might do if yez try tae make her see things different.'

'D'you think our Maurice is going to walk through the door one of these days?' Bella challenged, and Mrs Malloy swung her turbanned head with its fringe of escaping greying hair in her direction.

'No – but that's my opinion, no' Faith's. She's no' daft – she'll make up her own mind in her own time. She'd not thank ye for tryin' tae interfere – an' neither would I,' she added. 'So think on. Yer ma's been a good neighbour tae me an' I'll no' see her heart broken by a thoughtless word. Here—' she advanced on the boiler and reached into the hot water without flinching to haul a fistful of sheet out. 'Get that through the mangle or yez'll all be late an' my water'll be stone cold.'

'How's Maureen?' Jenny remembered to ask as they worked together.

'Like a house-side, an' wishin' she'd never let Jacko cuddle her so

103

hard in the spring.' Maureen's mother cackled. 'But that's what we all think when we get tae her stage. Next thing the bairn's squawlin' in a cot an' there we are, daft as ever, lookin' for another cuddle.'

'Tell her I'll visit her soon.'

'She'd like that, hen. Ye've got a lot o' sheets, surely?'

'Mrs McColl that I work for gave me some old ones,' Bella said breathlessly as they all struggled to get the final sheet, a renegade, out of the water and through the mangle. 'What with Gran not bein' able tae hold herself in any more, Mam needs extra sheets.'

The Irishwoman shook her head. 'I mind the way yer gran used tae lift her feet high when she came walkin' down the street tae visit yer ma, for all the world as though there was some infection hidin' in the gutters, an' the look on her face when she had tae pick her way through the bare-arsed weans playin' in the street. Her ladyship, we used tae cry her.'

'My Mam hated her then,' Bella remembered.

'Ach daughters-in-law an' mothers-in-law never get on well thegither. Look at me an' our Tom's Rosie, stuck-up wee bitch that she is,' said Mrs Malloy without rancour. 'But for all that ye cannae fault the way Faith looks after the old woman now that she's in need.'

'I don't know why Mam's so good to her now, after the way Gran used to talk to her.' Jenny retrieved the old wooden and metal clothes tongs from the floor by the boiler and started to fish in the water for any smaller clothing that might be hidden in the steamy yellowish depths.

'One day when ye've done a bit o' livin' yersel', hen, ye'll understand,' said Mrs Malloy. 'Now – will ye let me at that water while there's still a wee drop of heat in it?'

At the end of October, just after Helen's second birthday, trouble flared at the shipyard when a section of the workforce threatened to down tools over the sacking of a lad who had been caught making tea for his 'gang'.

Daniel, who had been involved in the row, spoke at length about it at an unofficial meeting in the Gillespies' house that night, his thin face tight with anger. As well as the usual six or seven men who had got into the habit of calling in at Teeze Gillespie's home every week there were a half-dozen more, some sitting on the floor, some leaning against the walls. Tonight there was tension in the small crowded room, and an air of purpose that had never been present before.

Jenny, sitting in a corner, doing some darning for her mother, let the work drop to her lap as she watched Daniel and listened to the words that poured from his lips.

'The gaffer came by an' took a kick at the brazier. It was that swine

Baker, the one that has a son workin' in the Tank section. Sent the whole thing over, he did, an' if the poor lad makin' the tea hadnae jumped back he could've been burned, or scalded by boilin' water. Red-hot coals all over the place – an' the tea-leaves lost. It cost money tae buy that tea.'

There was a growl of anger from his listeners and one of them said, 'Any decent man, even a gaffer, would've given the lad a warnin' an' let the men have their hot drink. From what I heard, it was so cold that the fire had been lit tae melt the oil in the machines.'

'You're right,' Daniel told him. 'I went there mysel' afterwards, tae talk tae them. The wind was blowin' up from the river sharp as a knife, an' they were all shakin' wi' the cold. Poor Jamie that got intae trouble had only a thin jacket on over his shirt.' He looked round the circle of faces. 'We all know Jamie – he's only a simple-minded laddie that earns what he can by doin' whatever he's told tae dae. He was in such a state o' fear in case he lost his job that they had tae stop him from putting the hot coals back intae the brazier with his bare hands. Then Dalkieth himsel' sent word that the lad was tae be turned away, an' him wi' no chance o' gettin' work anywhere else. The men that know Jamie best went tae his office tae ask him tae give the lad another chance, but it was no use.'

'It was George Dalkieth's father that gave Jamie the job in the first place,' Teeze said, ''cause the laddie's own father had been a good worker in his time. I mind the day he died in an accident in that very yard.'

Daniel nodded. 'When we heard word o' what was goin' on we put our heads together then sent word tae the office that we was goin' tae down tools if Jamie was turned off.' His mouth was grim. 'It's no' right that a man like Dalkieth should have the power tae take another man's livin' from him without a word of protest spoken. The men that first saw Mr George were level-headed creatures with the right words in their mouths, yet they couldnae get him tae see reason – him that never missed a meal in his life or was ever threatened wi' bein' put out o' his fine house because he couldnae find the rent.'

'If it had been left tae him we'd all've walked out and be damned tae the consequences, an' mebbe more would've followed us,' the other man said. 'But Robert Archer stepped in just then, an' he up an' took Jamie's side.'

Jenny saw her father's mouth tighten at the words of praise for Robert. Daniel nodded, and gave a bark of laughter. 'I don't know who was the most surprised, Mr George or ourselves. Archer said it wasnae worth losin' time ower a can o' tea. I hear he gave that bastard Baker a right tongue lashin'.'

He looked round the circle of faces. 'If you ask me, it's high time the unions were in that yard. George Dalkieth's no' the only yin that's entitled tae his rights.'

Around the range, heads wagged in vigorous agreement.

11

At that moment Robert Archer, sober and neat in a brown suit under a warm topcoat, skirted George Dalkieth's gleaming new motor car, which stood at the foot of the broad sweep of steps leading to the front door of Dalkieth House.

An elderly butler admitted him into a large square hall dominated by a massive painting of the wife and children of George Dalkieth, the founder of the shipyard. Archer laid his hat and gloves on a gleaming table and was ushered into the library where Isobel Dalkieth waited for him behind a huge desk, her hands clasped on the spotless blotter before her. Her face was expressionless but George, who occupied a chair opposite his mother, looked sullen.

'Well, Mr Archer, you know why you're here?'

'I'm here because you asked me to call, Mrs Dalkieth.' Archer put an extra feather of weight on the word 'asked' and knew by the way her eyebrows tightened slightly that she had noticed it.

'I – asked you to call because I want to get to the bottom of an incident that occurred in the yard this morning.'

'It was an internal matter and it has been dealt with, Mrs Dalkieth.'

Isobel stopped him with a raised hand. 'I understand that there's talk of the unions being involved with our yard because of it. This makes it more important than an internal matter. I would like to hear your side of the story, if you please.'

Archer's eyes flickered towards George Dalkieth, who was scowling at the carpet and pulling at his lower lip. So the fool had gone whining to his mother for support, had he? He glanced at the empty chair near George, then back at Mrs Dalkieth. He was damned if he was going to stay on his feet like a schoolboy in the wrong.

'Sit down, Mr Archer.'

'Thank you.' He took time to settle himself before telling her calmly about the foreman who had come across a man making tea and had kicked the brazier over, tea-can and all.

'I understand that the man in question was only doing as he was asked by others. The fire was already there, and it was bitterly cold in that part of the yard. There was no harm—'

'The men know the rules about making tea in the company's time,' George snapped.

'Even so, they still make tea. I did it myself when I was working in the yards.'

'Then you should have been dismissed for it.'

'I made certain that I was never caught, Mrs Dalkieth. But the lad concerned in today's trouble didn't have the wit to avoid being caught. He was only doing as his workmates asked.'

'If he's bright enough to earn money, he's bright enough to know the difference between right and wrong,' growled George, while his mother said crisply. 'I trust you're not adopting too lenient an attitude towards the men, Mr Archer.'

'I can assure you that there's no danger of that.'

'You soon knuckled under when a group of them threatened to walk out,' George cut in.

'I saw no sense in making an issue of something as unimportant as an illicit can of tea.' Archer heard a thin note of anger come into his voice and swallowed it back. 'If the men had walked out it would have held up production. Others might well have joined them. The nature of the situation didn't call for that.'

'The working man is becoming altogether too aggressive these days,' Mrs Dalkieth said coldly. 'If we're not vigilant we'll be done for.'

'The working man has just won a war, Mrs Dalkieth. He's not in the mood to see things return to the way they were before he was wrenched from his home and his family and sent away to risk life and limb for his fellow countrymen.'

'That's a dangerous attitude for a manager to take!'

'On the contrary, I think it's a practical attitude. Men give better service to a company that recognises their self-respect.' Robert Archer stood up. 'I can assure you that I'll not allow anything to bring Dalkieth's yard into disrepute, or to interfere with the work. If you intend to bring this matter before the Board of Directors I shall be happy to justify my actions to them.'

A trace of colour stained the woman's cheeks. 'In other words, you're wondering why I chose to deal with the matter myself instead of bringing the other directors into it. I happen to agree, Mr Archer, that today's disturbance was trivial and can now be laid to rest. I merely wanted to hear your—' She stopped short, but she and Archer both knew that she had been about to say, 'your side of the story.'

'If you have no more need of me,' he began as the door opened and Fiona Dalkieth swept in.

108

'George, I can't wait any longer. I promised Mrs Tennant that I would call and it's getting late. I can send the car back for you.'

'Thank you, Mr Archer,' Mrs Dalkieth said evenly, as much in reproof to her daughter-in-law as to the office manager, who inclined his head and left the room, catching the scent of lily-of-the-valley as he walked past the newcomer.

He collected his hat and gloves and stepped out into the chilly, windy evening with a sense of relief. The house behind him was altogether too oppressive and luxurious for his liking. So George had gone running to his mama to complain that the new office manager had overstepped himself, he thought, striding down the drive. From the very first, Archer had had no doubts of the other man's antagonism. He even understood it – George had worked with his father and his brother, and now they were both gone and an outsider, a man from the tenements and a former apprentice in the yard, had appeared in their place. It was natural for George to feel that his nose had been put out of joint.

But Robert Archer also knew why he had been appointed. George was the weak link of the shipping family and Robert had been brought in as a counter-balance, someone who knew more about shipyards than George ever would. Someone who would keep the yard going while George reigned as crown prince.

From the moment Archer had met Isobel Dalkieth he had recognised her ruthlessness and ambition, her burning love of the company and her desire to keep it solvent. She had all the strength that her surviving son lacked, but it wasn't a woman's place to run a shipyard. She needed Robert Archer's knowledge and experience to keep the yard from going under when the slump came, as come it must.

And he needed the yard just as much as she did. He had worked hard for such a position, had dragged himself up the ladder inch by inch, working by day and studying by night, living hand to mouth to pay for books and tuition. He had toiled in atrocious conditions and had had to learn how to use his fists as well as his tongue and his brain. He had worked on his accent, his appearance, his bearing, and now his efforts had paid off.

And, by God, he swore to himself as he walked, he wouldn't let a wealthy, arrogant know-nothing like George Dalkieth take any of it away from him.

A thin, icy drizzle had began to fall, and he turned his coat collar up as he swung through the Dalkieth gate and on to the pavement. He had only gone some ten yards when he heard a car turning out of the driveway behind him, then a voice called his name. He turned to see that George's handsome car was keeping pace with him, the uniformed chauffeur staring straight ahead as though disassociating himself from his young mistress, who was waving from the rear window.

'Mr Archer, can I offer you a lift?'

'I'm only going to Park Street.'

'I'm driving in that direction. Stop, McFee,' she ordered, and opened the door as the car halted.

'Thank you.' Archer ducked his head and climbed in as she moved across the seat to the other side. The interior smelled of leather and lily-of-the-valley.

'You don't have a car yourself?' she asked as he seated himself beside her. This time her hat had a narrow oval-shaped brim, and she wore a coat of silky black fur. Her small face glowed like a pearl against her large fur collar.

'I've never felt the need for one.'

'Park Street, McFee.' She gave Archer a sidelong glance as the car moved forward. 'Do you rent rooms there?'

'I have a small house.'

'For your wife, when she comes North.'

'My wife has decided that the Scots are too fierce for her. She will not be joining me.'

'Oh? I'm sorry.'

'No need to be, Mrs Dalkieth.'

She let the silence grow between them, and Robert did the same, until finally she probed, 'So you live on your own?'

'A housekeeper comes in every day.'

'It must be lonely in the evenings and at the weekends.'

'I've not found it so.'

'I shall tell George to invite you for dinner one evening.'

'If you'll forgive me for saying so, Mrs Dalkieth, that wouldn't be a good idea. Men who have to work together see quite enough of each other without being expected to socialise as well.'

She pouted. 'So I must do without your company just because you and George are tired of the sight of each other?'

He smiled. She was pretty and flirtatious, and he was enjoying this little interlude, locked into the small leather-smelling space with her, behind the chauffeur's rigid back. 'I doubt if my company would be of any great interest to you,' he said, wondering what on earth such a pretty young woman could have seen in a lumbering ox like George Dalkieth – other than his money and his family's prestige.

'I don't agree.' Fiona leaned forward as the car came to a standstill, rubbing at the window with a gloved hand. 'Which is your house?'

Archer found and operated the door handle while the chauffeur was still reaching for his own handle. 'The third on the left.' He got out, then turned and said into the car's interior, 'Thank you for the lift.'

'We'll surely meet again, Mr Archer.'

'I look forward to it.' He shut the door and stepped back, watching as the car moved away. He had heard the town gossip about George's disastrous first marriage, and wondered if the people who forecast the same ending to his second marriage were right.

As he opened his front door and stepped into the narrow hall he seemed to catch the scent of her perfume again . . .

Fiona smiled to herself as she trailed her gloved fingers over the leather seat where Robert Archer had been sitting. He was the sort of man who grew more interesting with each meeting, she thought. It was a pity that George had taken a dislike to him, not that Robert – in her mind, she was already calling him by his first name – would let that bother him. He wasn't like George, who fussed and worried over every imagined insult and slight.

Fiona had already heard all about the silly business in the yard that day, over and over again. There had been no arrangement to visit Mrs Tennant, but having been left alone for far too long in her mother-in-law's drawing room she had suddenly decided that she had had enough. It seemed, from the glimpse she had seen of George's face when she walked into the room, that his mother hadn't, after all, given him the support he had looked for. Which meant that he would probably start complaining again when he came home. Then – the worst thing of all – they would have to go to bed.

Fiona shifted uneasily on the car seat at the thought. She was beginning to feel like a mare that had been put to stud. Night after night she went to sleep feeling sore and stiff and woke up feeling sore and stiff, with only her monthly bleedings affording her any peace. Not that she was allowed to enjoy her few brief nights of freedom, for George spent the time railing on at her about her inability to conceive.

Fiona was becoming increasingly aware of the fact that she was not going to fall pregnant. And, as the weeks and months passed, she grew more and more certain that the fault didn't lie with her, but with her husband.

The hands of the clock over the tracing office door stood at six o'clock. The truck on the floor below was still working, the whine and rattle of its engines only dimly heard by Jenny, who was alone in the tracing office, bent over a library book on shipbuilding, referring now and again to a line-drawing on the desk beside her.

In her anxiety to give a good account of herself she often put in extra hours at the tracing office, sometimes arriving earlier than the others, sometimes staying behind to finish a piece of work. She would happily have worked during her midday break, when the truck was finally stilled for an hour and the place was quiet, but she had to go home then to help her mother, snatching a quick meal as best she could.

By chance she had found the books on shipbuilding in the local public library and had started taking them out, trying to marry ship design as she knew it with the facts and figures in the textbooks.

After her father found one of the books and sneered at her for sticking her nose into men's affairs 'just because ye've been made up tae gaffer over a parcel o'lassies in thon place where they play wi' toy boats', she began to hide the books from his sight, and take them into the office with her. On evenings when the naval architects were working late and the other girls had gone home she could read the books without fear of interruption.

The drawing she was puzzling over reminded her of one she had seen earlier that day, pinned to the cutting machine on the ground floor. Clutching the open book Jenny made her way quietly out of the office and down the darkened stairs, meaning to slip downstairs without being seen by the men working at the Tank. But as she stepped off the final stair Neil Baker called her name, sauntering towards her. 'Are you looking for me, Jenny?'

'I was just going down to the wax room. I didn't mean to disturb you.'

'I was coming over for a drink anyway. My throat's dry.' He picked up a bottle from a nearby bench and held it out to her, saying when she shook her head, 'It's only ginger – I'd not be fool enough tae bring strong drink in here.'

'I'm not thirsty.'

He shrugged then drank from the bottle, his throat muscles moving as the liquid went down.

'What are you doing here?' he asked, capping the bottle. 'I thought everyone else had gone home. What's that you've got?'

The book was plucked from her hands and he flipped it over and studied the gilt lettering on the front. His eyebrows rose.

'Ship-design?' She had expected him to laugh, but to her surprise he asked mildly, 'Interested in design, are you?'

Jenny swallowed. 'I'd like to know more about what happens outside my department.'

'Mebbe I can help you.'

She stared at him. 'D'you mean it?'

'Why not? You only needed to ask. Here—' Neil jerked his head towards the Tank. 'D'ye fancy a shot on the truck? Nobody would know but me and the engineer, and he'll say nothing. Come on and I'll show you how it works.'

It had been a dark, brooding day, and now a wind was rising. Jenny could hear it gusting against the solid stone walls of the model room.

'I should be getting home,' she protested, but half-heartedly, her gaze moving past him to where the truck waited, a wax model slung beneath it. She had always wanted to ride on the truck.

'It'll not take long. We were just going to do a run. Watch how you go, you don't want to fall into the water.' Neil took the book from her and put it down on the bench beside the bottle then drew her towards the waiting truck. She edged after him along the narrow walkway then he jumped up on to the truck platform and reached a hand down to help her up.

'You'll have to hold on tight, there's not much space.' Neil swung himself up beside her and signalled to the engineer at the far end of the Tank. The area where the models were shaved to size retreated as the truck started its glide along the Tank, the dark water below ruffling in their wake like deep grey satin. As they went Neil briefly explained about the system of weights and counter-weights, indicating the roll of paper and the four coloured pens attached to it, waiting to record the results of the test run.

'Watch them when we're making the run. The one on the left's for control, it maintains the margin. The others show the true speed, the resistance, and the calculated speed. Take it carefully, Frank, we've got a passenger tonight,' he said to the grinning engineer as they reached the far end of the narrow Tank. Then, reaching round Jenny and taking hold of the rail so that she was tucked securely within the protective loop of his arm he grinned down at her. 'Hang on, Jenny, here we go.'

The truck accelerated fast, swaying from side to side like a tramcar; the pens connected to the mechanism holding the model fast scrawled rapid coloured lines over the revolving roll of paper and, looking down, Jenny could see the water being thrown to either side as the model knifed through it. She clung tightly to the railing, the wind generated by their speed ruffling her hair, grateful for the support of Neil's arm about her as they rocketed along. It was the most exhilarating experience she had ever known.

'Hold on,' he shouted, his mouth close to her ear, then released the

113

rail and pulled her tightly against his body as the truck reached the end of the Tank and stopped with a jerk that seemed to rattle every tooth in her head and might have toppled her from her perch if he hadn't been holding her.

Despite herself, she shrieked at the sudden stop, then turned to laugh up at him, half in embarrassment at her own foolishness. 'That was wonderful!'

'I thought you'd enjoy it.'

'You're lucky, doing that every day.'

'Ach, it gets to be monotonous. And if ye're not feelin' too well, it can be downright unpleasant.'

'I can imagine that. Thanks, Neil.' As she began to turn towards the walkway his arm tightened, holding her back.

'Stay an' have another run,' he said into her hair.

'It's time I was going home.' She tried again to move away from him and realised that his body was pinning her against the rail and one of her arms was trapped in his embrace.

'Neil, let me go.'

'You can surely spare a minute or two.' His free hand landed on her shoulder, the thumb travelling down towards her breast.

'Frank'll be wondering what's going on,' she said, and Neil laughed.

'Don't bother your head about him. It's dark down here, he can't see us.'

She tried to pull away and realised that the rail was biting into her back. 'Mebbe not, but he'd hear me well enough if I shouted.'

'You'd not be so daft—' said Neil, then ducked his head suddenly, his mouth searching for hers. Furious with herself for having been so naive, Jenny jerked her own head away then swung it back, hard, aware of pain shooting through the back of her neck as her forehead collided with his mouth. He gave a muffled exclamation and released her so suddenly that she stumbled and almost fell from the platform. One of his hands flew to his lips and came away smeared with blood.

'You bitch!' He lunged after her as she scrambled from the truck. Fingers clamped round her wrist and she was spun round to face him. She tried to pull away, the planks that formed the walkway bouncing beneath her feet. Beneath them the water, still disturbed by the passage of the truck, lapped noisily.

'Let me go!'

'Not till you've made up for hurting me,' Neil panted.

She was bending her head in desperation to bite at the hand holding her prisoner when the side door leading out to the shipyard squeaked open. Neil's fingers fell away from Jenny's wrist and she stumbled, off balance and convinced that she was going to topple into the dark water below. Her outflung hand caught at the truck as Robert Archer walked out of the shadows.

'What's going on here?' he asked, then as he came forward and got a clearer view of the two people by the truck he added in a sharper voice, 'What's happened to your mouth, Baker?'

There was a brief silence, then Jenny said swiftly, 'I – it was my fault. I didn't realise the truck stopped so suddenly. My head bumped against Neil's mouth.'

'You both know that only the naval architect is allowed to ride the truck.'

It was enough that she had let herself fall for Neil's lies, without causing further trouble by telling Robert the truth. If Neil was to lose his job, Jenny realised, he would make a bad enemy. His father, being a gaffer, had power in the area. Her life was difficult enough without adding to her problems.

'I asked Neil to let me try it,' she told Robert. 'I thought that since there was nobody else here to know it would be all right. Isn't that so, Neil?'

The naval architect muttered something, his voice muffled by the handkerchief he had pulled from his pocket to staunch the blood. Jenny put a hand to her dishevelled hair. 'I'd best be getting home. I'll just get my coat.'

Silently, his eyes on Neil now, Robert stepped aside to let her pass. Furious with herself for having been caught in such an absurd situation, she hurried upstairs and collected her hat and coat, jumping when Robert spoke coldly from the doorway behind her.

'I thought you'd have had more sense than to ask a man like that for favours.'

'I didn't—' she began, then stopped abruptly, realising that she was in danger of contradicting her earlier story. His eyes narrowed.

'You'd not lie to me, Jenny – would you? If Baker's been pestering you—'

She made herself meet his eyes. 'He hasn't.'

He studied her in silence for a moment, then said, 'From what I saw when I arrived you were fortunate I happened to come through from the yard when I did. What are you doing here at this time of night anyway?'

'I was finishing off some work.'

'You're not paid to work late,' he said curtly. 'I'm paid to work all the hours that God and the Dalkieths send, but you're not.'

'I don't mind staying on if something has to be finished.'

He put the book she had left behind down on the desk. 'Baker tells

115

me this is yours.' One finger traced the lettering on the front. 'You're wanting to learn how to be a naval architect now?'

Jenny snatched the book up from beneath his hand and held it close. 'Are you laughing at me, Mr Archer?'

'I'd not dare do that, Miss Gillespie,' said Robert, straight-faced.

'If you must know, I only wanted to find out more about how ships are designed. I was going down to compare one of the drawings with the sketch on the cutting machine—'

'—and you fell foul of Baker instead. You should have asked me. I'd have explained it to you.'

'You're the office manager.'

'Does that make me an ogre? Show me the drawing you're talking about.'

She would have liked to refuse, but instead, reluctantly, she opened the book and found the page. Robert took the book from her and studied it, then reached for a pad of paper and a pencil, drawing them towards him as he settled himself on one of the high stools and motioned her to sit beside him.

'The first thing you have to know in ship design is how the water deals with any object that's put into it—' began Robert. Below, the truck clanged into action again.

The Tank area was dark and silent when they finally went downstairs, the library book beneath Jenny's arm, her head spinning with facts and figures. In the model room, still warm from the furnaces that had been switched off when the men went home, tools were laid out neatly in readiness for the next day and the clay bed was empty, waiting for a new model to be started in the morning. A wax hull lay snugly in the cutting machine.

'I like this room when everybody's gone home for the night.' Robert paused and put one hand on the rim of the clay bed. Looking at that square, capable hand, she suddenly recalled the days before the war, and the warmth of his palm against her cheek, and glanced away from him in a flurry of confused emotions.

Outside, he locked the door and put the key in his pocket. 'I'll walk you home.'

'I can manage fine.'

'For God's sake, Jenny, d'you have to be so distant? We used to be friends.'

'I can manage,' she said again, still bothered by the sudden memory of times long past. 'Thank you for your help.'

She walked quickly away, pulling her coat closely about her against the wind. If things had been different – if old Mr Dalkieth hadn't sent

116

Robert away, if he hadn't met someone else on Tyneside – they might well have been walking home together. But not now. The past was ·past, and it couldn't ever be brought back.

A figure leaning against the wall a few yards further on, cap pulled low over his forehead, hands thrust into his coat pockets, straightened up then moved towards her. As he stepped beneath a lamp-post she saw that it was Daniel Young.

'I called in at the house and your mother said you were workin' late.' He fell into step with her. 'I thought I'd wait for you and walk you home.'

'There was no need,' she protested.

'I wanted to,' said Daniel.

12

The spring of 1920 seemed to be sulkily reluctant to take over from winter. In April wintry winds swept through the tenement buildings, which were old and unfitted to keeping out the cold. It became commonplace to hear children, day and night, choking and wheezing with the croup that had always been prevalent in the damp, low-lying west of Scotland. The elderly grew silent and bitter-mouthed, plagued by the constant ache of rheumaticky joints.

Teeze Gillespie took a bad bout of bronchitis but struggled out to his work every day, insisting that it was only a wee cold.

'That's what you said before, and it turned out to be the pneumonia,' Faith reminded him, her face drawn with worry, and he rounded on her fiercely.

'It's my body – I know what ails it, woman! Will ye stop worritin' at me an' gie me peace?' he bellowed, setting off another fit of coughing. Faith, gnawing at her bottom lip, said no more, even when Teeze had to give in and take to his bed. There was no point in recriminations once the harm was done. Instead she set herself to nursing him, boiling kettles in the hope that the steam would help to improve his breathing until the kitchen became permanently foggy and the other members of the family felt as though they were suffocating in the damp, humid air.

Jenny, taking her turn of rubbing her father's chest with turpentine liniment to try to ease his discomfort, feeling the rumbling and wheezing of tortured lungs vibrating through her fingers, saw the weary acceptance in his eyes and remembered with sudden pain the pride he had had in his strength when he worked in Pneumonia Bay. True, he hadn't hesitated to use that strength to subdue his children and his wife with unnecessary harshness at times, but Jenny took no pleasure at all in seeing him weakened and humbled. Energy and good health were the most valuable possessions a tenement dweller could have and, when they ebbed away, as they must in time, there was nothing left – no dignity, no self respect, no hope.

'Here ye are, Teeze—' Faith pushed past her, a steaming linseed poultice in her hands. Jenny, her palms stinging and burning from her ministrations, stepped aside and watched as Faith laid the poultice in place over her husband's hairy chest. Teeze sucked in his breath sharply.

'Is it too hot?'

'No.' He ground the word out. 'It's fine.'

Faith drew the edges of his clean but tattered pyjama jacket together. 'Try tae get some sleep now,' she urged, drawing the blankets up to his neck, her hands as gentle as her voice. He grunted and closed his eyes, turning his head away from the two women.

'Should we mebbe get the doctor in?' Jenny ventured as they moved away from the bed. Her mother gave her a withering look.

'An' what dae we pay him with? It's hard enough tryin' tae feed us all an' pay the rent an' keep the place warm for him an' her—' she nodded at Marion, dozing by the range, '—without throwin' money intae the doctor's pocket an' a'.'

It was true. With Teeze ill and not earning, every penny was needed. Thanks to Faith's expertise they managed to get by on vegetable broth and bread and stove potatoes, a nourishing dish cooked with margarine and oatmeal. The big fear shared by people who lived from hand to mouth was being unable to pay the rent, for a roof over the family's head had to take precedence over everything else. The money that Jenny and Lottie brought in between them managed to do that, but not to stretch to medicines or the sort of luxuries Teeze needed to tempt his appetite.

Once or twice, lying awake in the night, worrying, listening to Lottie's snoring and the occasional huff of indrawn breath from Helen and her father's continual coughing on the other side of the wall Jenny made up her mind to approach Robert Archer and ask for help, perhaps an advance on her wages, to tide them over. But in the cold light of day the pride that had kept her going after he had jilted her, and again when he came back and she had to face the sly murmur of the gossips once more, kept her silent. Anyway, an advance would have to be paid back and that would cause further hardship. They must just manage as best they could.

Alice wanted to leave school and get a job, but Jenny held out against the idea. 'If you give the Academy up now you'll be sorry for the rest of your life.'

'But I feel so useless,' the younger girl protested. 'At my age I should be bringing money into the house.'

'Think of what you'll earn when you're a teacher.'

'And think of how long it'll be before I'm earning it,' Alice said gloomily.

'It'll be worth waiting for.' Jenny knew now why Daniel was so insistent that his son should stay on at school. Her own determination that Alice should do well was becoming more important, perhaps because it seemed to justify the sacrifices that Jenny herself had had to make. 'Promise me that you'll stay on,' she coaxed, and Alice bit her lip, then nodded.

'All right, if it'll make you happy. But in return you'll have to promise that if you can't manage any longer you'll tell me so and let me look for work.'

The day came when Teeze was so bad that Faith *had* to call the doctor in. He sounded his patient's chest and asked a few brief questions, then left a prescription and instructions on the sort of diet Teeze should have.

'Send for me if the coughing persists,' he said as he was leaving, and gave a shrug of the shoulders when Teeze said huskily, 'There was no need tae call ye this time. Women are aye over fussy. I'll be back at work by next week.'

To Teeze's annoyance, his illness put a stop to his cronies' weekly meetings in his house, though a few of them continued to visit him, bringing news of the shipyard. Daniel Young was one of the most regular visitors, often bringing a bottle of beer for the invalid and making time for Teeze despite his own growing commitments as a shop steward.

Since the business when young Jamie had almost lost his job after being caught brewing tea, the demand in Dalkieth's yard for proper representation to ensure the workers' rights had accelerated. The purchase of the adjoining yard and the setting up of more machinery there added fuel to the fire. If George Dalkieth was set on the yard's growth, he must be reminded that the men who toiled to bring in his profits deserved consideration.

The unofficial gatherings that had begun in the Gillespie kitchen and in other kitchens around the town swelled during the first months of 1920 into meetings large enough to be held on open ground in the town, or in local halls run by committees sympathetic to working men. Union representatives travelled to Ellerslie to talk to the men and many of them, Daniel in the forefront, became trades union members. The pressure on George Dalkieth and the Dalkieth Board grew until by April, to George's fury, the unions were established in the yard. Daniel was one of the first to be voted in as a shop steward.

He bore his new appointment with quiet pride, and flattered Teeze by asking his advice and listening solemnly to what the older man had to say.

'Sure and there were some that were against the man because he's never mixed in with the rest,' Mr Malloy told Teeze when Daniel's appointment was confirmed. 'But he risked his job by joining the union, and he's got a good head on his shoulders.' He tamped tobacco down into his pipe and added thoughtfully, 'Mebbe it's not a bad thing that your man's a loner – there'll be no favouritism from Daniel Young, not for any of the workers or any of the bosses. We'll all know where we stand with him.'

Jenny silently agreed with what he said. Daniel's kindness to Patrick and her father and his fierce determination to gain justice for his fellow-workers had earned her respect.

'You know that your father'll mebbe never be able tae work again?' Daniel asked her quietly one Sunday afternoon when he had persuaded her to go out for a walk along by the railway line. The banking, bright with wild flowers in the summer, was dank and drab, but at least the air was breathable after the stuffy little kitchen with its smell of linseed oil and turpentine.

'I know.'

'He might manage in the summer,' Daniel went on, 'but come the bad weather he'll fall sick again. His lungs are in a bad way. It's sad tae see a good worker like Teeze turned intae an invalid before his time.'

His sombre voice, saying things that Jenny had known for weeks but refused to allow herself to brood over, suddenly filled her with despair. Life had been hard since Maurice's death, but now they were in danger of experiencing the bite of real poverty, the continual grinding struggle just to put enough food on the table, the worry of dependents like her grandmother and Helen, and now her father, the terror of hearing the rent man's steps coming through the close below and mounting the stairs, step by step.

Far away a train whistle shrilled, mocking her with the memory of the life she might have been living in Glasgow at that very moment if things hadn't gone sour. She fisted her hands deep into the pockets of her jacket and veered away from Daniel, struggling up the railway embankment, digging the toes of her best shoes into the sour-smelling winter vegetation to prevent herself from slipping back.

She heard Daniel calling her name, heard the pounding of his feet below her as she reached the top and stopped, inches from the shining rails, gulping in air, staring across the railway line to the fields and trees beyond. The train whistle shrilled again, nearer this time, and she felt the ground trembling beneath her feet in warning of its approach.

'Jenny, for God's sake!' Daniel's hand clutched at her, and she felt herself being pulled back down the slope, stumbling on the rough ground, dragged back into Ellerslie and all her problems. Above, the train whipped past them, screaming, throwing its shadow over them, going far too fast for Jenny to make out the faces behind the windows. The wind of its passing dragged strands of hair across her face and pressed her skirt tight against her legs; then it was gone, dashing along the tracks to the outside world, a free spirit, leaving her and Daniel behind.

'What d'ye think ye're doin'?' he demanded to know, his voice rough with fright. His hand on her arm was shaking, she could feel the tremors through the sleeve of her jacket. 'I thought for a minute ye were goin' tae fall under the wheels!'

'I was all right,' she started to say, then one eye began to sting, and she was blinded by sudden tears. 'My eye—'

Daniel whipped off his cap and tilted her chin up, peering into her face, pushing her hands away when she tried to cover her burning eye in an effort to ease the pain. 'Look at me,' he ordered brusquely.

She obeyed, squinting at him with one eye because the other was a blur of burning moisture. His breath was warm on her cheek. She had always thought of his eyes as deep brown or black, but in fact they were blue, though so dark that they were almost navy blue.

'It's a cinder, I can see it. Hold still, now, and I'll lick it out.'

'What?' She tried to draw back but his hands tightened on her shoulders, holding her still.

'Don't fret, I do it often in the yard. Men are always gettin' things in their eyes there. Just open yer eyes as wide as ye can and trust me.'

His face came very close, so close that it blotted everything else out. She felt the tip of his tongue probing at her eyeball, gentle as a night-moth's wing, then it flicked swiftly across the surface and away as he drew his head back. He glanced to one side, spat into the grasses by the side of the path, then peered into her eyes again. 'That's it.'

Released, she blinked cautiously once, then again. The burning pain had gone. 'You've done it! I've heard of some men in the shipyard being able to do that, but I've never met one till now.'

'It's not everyone can do it the right way,' he said with casual pride, bringing a spotlessly clean handkerchief from his pocket and mopping gently at her wet face. 'D'ye feel better now?'

'I'm fine.' She smiled up at him.

'Marry me, Jenny.'

'What did you say?' She was stunned.

'I said, will ye marry me? I admire you, Jenny, more than any women I know. It's been hard for ye since Maurice was lost, and with Teeze ill now it'll only get worse.' Daniel spoke hurriedly, the words pouring out as though once he had begun he couldn't stop. 'It's too much for ye tae manage on yer own. If ye kept on with yer work at the experimental tank we could support your family between us. And they'd have more room if ye moved in with me and the boy.'

Taken completely by surprise, she sought for the right words. 'It's too much, Daniel. I couldn't ask anyone to take on my whole family.'

He shook his head. 'I'm not makin' the offer lightly. It's something I've had in my mind for a while now, and it'd not be all the one way, Jenny. There's Walter, needin' a mother. And – there's me,' said Daniel, his voice suddenly low and unsure. 'I've been long enough without a wife, a woman about the house. I'd be honoured if ye'd take me for your husband.'

Dazed, she turned and began to walk swiftly back to the town. He fell into step with her and she was grateful that he made no move to touch her. 'I'd not expect an answer right away, it wouldnae be fair on you.'

'I don't know, Daniel—'

'Just say ye'll think about it an' give me yer answer in a day or two. If it's no,' said Daniel steadily, 'I'll accept it and not bother ye again. Ye've got my word on that.'

'Aye,' said Jenny, still so confused by the sudden turn events had taken that she didn't know what she was saying. 'In a day or two.'

When they parted at her closemouth he took her hand in his and shook it formally then turned and walked away without looking back, his shoulders square. He hadn't put his cap on again and his dark head, still bare, was held high.

She didn't love Daniel, Jenny thought as she tossed in her bed that night. She had known love with Robert; fleetingly, it was true, but she could still remember the sweetness and the joy of it. But, on the other hand, Robert had also taught her the bitterness and emptiness of rejection.

It was well past time for the public houses to close, but Lottie hadn't arrived home, so she wasn't there to grumble at her bedcompanion's restlessness. Jenny moved her pillow to a more comfortable position and knew that she couldn't marry Daniel. It wouldn't be fair on him – there were other women who would make better wives, women who wouldn't burden him with their own responsibilities.

Through the wall her father began another series of deep lungtearing coughs. She heard her mother's voice, then a faint whimper from Marion. Jenny eased herself from the bed, the linoleum icy beneath her naked feet, and reached for the old coat that hung from the nail on the door.

In the kitchen the light from the single candle on the table gave the shadowy, crowded room a bleak appearance. Faith was kneeling on the bed, spooning some of the soothing syrup Jenny had bought for Teeze into his mouth and Marion was flailing about in the truckle-bed, grunting and trying to get up.

'All right, Gran – I'll help you.' Jenny stooped over the bed and drew the blanket back, relieved to find that for a mercy Marion hadn't wet the bed. The old woman floundered like a fish in a net, her nightdress caught up. Jenny's hand brushed against naked, skinny thighs, then she got Marion in the firm but gentle grip that she and her mother had learned by a hit and miss method and levered her into a sitting position. Faith joined her and together they managed to get Marion on to the shabby commode that someone had loaned them.

'Thanks lass,' Faith whispered across her mother-in-law's tangled head. Her own hair was lank about her face, her eyes sunken shadows in the candlelight. 'Och, leave it be till the morning,' she said when they had got Marion back into bed and Jenny was lifting the bucket from the commode. 'We don't want tae waken the neighbours at this time o' night.'

Teeze had turned to face the wall and was asleep, breathing noisily. Jenny picked up the bottle of syrup and held it to the light before putting the stopper back in. It was almost finished. If she bought more, would their supply of oatmeal and potatoes last out until the end of the week, when she and Lottie got their wages? Was there enough milk left to do Helen and Gran tomorrow?

Faith took the bottle from her. 'Go back tae bed, hen. You've got your work tae go tae in the mornin'.'

'Mam, Daniel Young's asked me to marry him.'

Fear poured into Faith's eyes. Her mouth trembled, then she asked huskily, 'What did ye say tae him?'

'Nothing, yet.'

'Jenny, lass—' Faith put a hand on her daughter's arm. 'D'ye want tae marry a shipyard worker an' stay in the tenements for the rest o' yer days, aye worryin' about lay-offs an' the rent an' feedin' the weans?' Her fingers tightened. 'It'll no' be long till Maurice comes back an' then ye can go off tae Glasgow the way ye wanted tae. Once Maurice comes back—'

'Mam—' Jenny put her own hand over her mother's icy fingers, suddenly realising what Faith was thinking. 'Daniel's thinking about all of us, not just himself. He says that if I could keep on my place in the tracing office, between us we'd be able to look after all of you, and Walter.'

'He said that?' Jenny could see the tension draining from her

125

mother's stooped body. 'He's a good man, Daniel. Ye could dae a lot worse than accept him.' There was little doubt about the reply she wanted Jenny to give Daniel now that she knew of his offer to help to support her family.

'Mam—'

Teeze snuffled like a bull and heaved himself over in the bed, 'For Christ's sake, it's like a madhouse in here. Get tae yer beds, the pair o' ye!'

Tired as she was, Jenny's thoughts started racing again as soon as she returned to her own room and she realised that she was as far from sleep as ever. Daniel's face seemed to hover against the grey square of the window, his eyes boring into hers. She recalled his casual comment at Maureen's wedding party about Alice's intelligence, and how angered she had been at the time. Then she thought of his offer to help to support her family as well as his own if they married, and the sudden hope on her own mother's face when she heard about it. Not many men could bring themselves to be so generous.

She blinked, and Daniel's image fragmented and was reshaped into Walter's anxious young features.

'There's Walter needin' a mother,' Daniel had said. It was true. The lad did need a woman in his life, softening the edges of his father's ambitions, making a proper home for him. If she married Daniel, Walter would be her stepson. And there might be other children eventually, when they could afford them. She wanted children, had always assumed that one day she would have babies of her own.

Lottie came in, stripping off her dress and clambering into bed, bringing with her the usual stink of alcohol and tobacco smoke and another aroma that often hung about her body when she returned very late – a musky, vaguely unpleasant smell. She dragged at the blankets, settling herself into the lumpy mattress with all the grace of a pig in a mudhole. In the morning, Jenny knew, her face would be clown-like with the smudged make-up that she rarely washed off before going to bed.

Jenny moved as far to her own side of the bed as she could, and remembered that marriage to Daniel would mean an end to having to share a bed with Lottie.

It was still dark when she stepped out of the back close early the next morning on to cobbles damp with the night's rain. Figures crossed and recrossed the lit windows of the surrounding tenements as the people inside prepared for another day's work. Daniel, his face puffy with sleep, his shirt open at the throat, his braces dangling, opened the door in answer to her soft knock. At sight of her he reddened and began to haul his braces up over his shoulders.

'Jenny? Is there anythin' wrong?'

'I came to give you my answer.'

'At this time in the morning? It could have waited till – come in.' He stood aside then said as she hesitated, 'The boy's out on his milk round. I'm just gettin' his breakfast ready.'

'I'll not keep you.' She stepped past him, along the hall and into the kitchen. The table was set for two and a pot of porridge bubbled on the range; even at that early hour the kitchen was neat and spacious compared to the Gillespie kitchen, where the truckle-bed would still be in the middle of the floor. Textbooks and exercise books were stacked carefully on the sideboard beside the photograph of Daniel and his wife. She turned to face Daniel and saw the apprehension in his eyes.

'D'ye want a cup of tea?'

'No. I just came to say that I'd be honoured to be your wife, Daniel.'

The colour ebbed from his face, then flowed back. His eyes widened and he swallowed hard, his Adam's apple bobbing beneath the skin of his throat. She had never seen Daniel without a collar and tie before; his open shirt and loosened cuffs gave their meeting an air of intimacy that suddenly embarrassed her. She glanced away from him, at the school-books, the photograph of Daniel and the solemn, dead girl whom she was to replace and, finally, at her own fingers, twisting nervously together.

His own hand came into her line of sight and took one of hers. She thought for a moment that he was going to embrace her and turned to him, relieved that he had taken the initiative, to discover that just as he had done the day before, he proposed only a formal handshake.

'I'm – pleased,' said Daniel gruffly. 'Will I make the arrangements, then?'

'Mebbe you should.'

'I'll call on Teeze after work an' ask his permission. I like tae dae things properly,' said Daniel, releasing her hand.

They stood for a moment, as awkward with each other as strangers, then Jenny said, 'I'd best get back, then.'

'Aye.' He opened the door and waited for her to pass him. On an impulse she rose on tiptoe and kissed him, feeling him flinch back slightly in surprise as she put her hands on his upper arms. His face was smooth and clean-shaven, his lips cool and firm.

'I'll do my best to be a good wife, Daniel.'

'Aye,' he said, then she was out in the close again, making her way back to the home that she would soon leave as a bride. Suddenly, in the space of a few hours, she was a woman on the threshold of marriage.

13

Teeze Gillespie was highly pleased by the news, for Daniel was one
of the few men he respected and he considered that his daughter had
done well for herself.

'Ye're more fortunate than most,' he told Jenny when Daniel
visited him that evening to ask formally for his approval of the
marriage. 'Ye've got a fine man here – see an' be a good wife tae
him. Alice, away out tae the pub an' get a few bottles o' beer.
Here—' He reached into his pocket then hesitated, his face
tightening.

Jenny, watching the shame beginning to touch his eyes, opened
her mouth to offer to pay for the beer and was forestalled by
Daniel's easy, 'Man, it's my place tae provide the drink tonight, no'
yours. I'll give the lassie the money – an' this is a special wee gift for
yourself.'

Teeze's face, sagging with relief, brightened as he accepted the
small bottle of whisky. Faith even managed a slight smile as she
hurried to fetch glasses and speed Alice on her way to the public
house. The word went round the tenements almost immediately and
when the public house closed men began to congregate to drink the
health of the engaged couple. Wives arrived, led by Mrs Malloy and
Maureen, who had put on weight since the birth of her son and
looked more like her mother than ever.

'I never thought you'd end up with Daniel Young,' she
whispered, drawing Jenny into a corner, her eyes bright with
curiosity. 'Are ye sure ye're doin' the right thing? He's such a quiet
man.'

'There's nothing wrong with being quiet. God knows we could do
with more like Daniel in this town.'

'I know, but even so—' Maureen began.

'I'll have to help with Gran,' Jenny said hurriedly, squeezing past
her.

Marion had to be taken through to the bedroom and tucked into
the bed shared by Jenny and Lottie because the kitchen was too
crowded for her own bed to be hauled out.

'Anyway, folk would keep steppin' on the old soul,' Mrs Malloy said in a loud whisper as she helped to ease Marion into the room where Helen already slept in her crib. Lottie, who had just arrived home from work, came to see what they were up to and gave a yelp of horror.

'She'll pee the bed! I'm no' sleepin' in a wet bed because of her!'

'Ach, she's been on the bucket, hen,' Mrs Malloy assured her, and the girl sniffed.

'That's no consolation. I've known her tae wet her drawers as soon as they were pulled up again.'

'Listen tae Lady Muck here! What d'ye want us tae dae – wring the poor old soul oot like a floorcloth? Fetch Teeze's coat, someone,' Mrs Malloy ordered, We'll slip it under the sheet tae save the mattress if she has a wee accident.'

Alice brought the coat that Teeze had used in the shipyard, stiff with age and smelling of rubber. Ignoring Lottie's grumbling, Mrs Malloy flipped it under Marion then tucked the old woman in securely. 'There she is – snug as a bug in a rug,' she proclaimed, taking Faith's thin arm in her huge hand and propelling the other woman out of the room. 'Come an' drink tae the happy couple, hen.'

'She's never at a loss for words, is she?' Alice murmured as she and Jenny followed the others into the kitchen, 'I'll never forget her throwin' up the window an' shoutin' "It's a laddie!" before Maureen's cord had even been cut.'

Jenny giggled at the memory. 'And poor Daniel and Walter beating away at their carpet down in the back court. I thought Daniel was going to die on the spot with the shame of it.'

'Ye'll be all right wi' Daniel,' Teeze, glowing with drink, told his daughter for the umpteenth time as his womenfolk tidied the empty kitchen after the well-wishers had gone home. He belched, and scratched his stomach with the base of the glass clutched in his hand. A dribble of beer, unnoticed, ran down his chin.

'An' he doesnae spend all his wages in the pub,' Faith added under her breath, clashing crockery in the sink. 'Ye're blessed there, Jenny.'

The summons to the boardroom was delivered by the Tank super-intendent himself. 'Three o'clock, Mr Archer says.'

'I thought he'd have left things to you.'

Mr Duncan shrugged. 'New brooms like tae dae their own sweepin', I suppose. I told him that as far as I was concerned I'd be happy for ye tae stay on after ye're wed. Ye've done well so far, lassie, and I've nae doubt ye'll dae even better, given the time.'

As the time of her appointment drew nearer Jenny became more and more nervous. She should have confirmed that she could stay on in the tracing office before telling Daniel that she would marry him, she fretted, the line plan on her desk neglected. Again and again she looked up at the clock; sometimes the hands raced towards three, and at others she had to listen for the steady deep ticking to make sure that it hadn't stopped.

Although the boardroom lay directly beneath the tracing office Jenny had never been in it before. Nervously she descended the stairs just before three o'clock, giving herself enough time to pull at her cuffs and run her hands over her neat hair before tapping at the door at the bottom of the staircase.

'Come in.'

The boardroom was small, but luxurious in comparison with the rest of the Tank section. It was carpeted, and the wooden wall panels were hung with portraits of past directors. A highly polished oval table ringed by tall, oval-backed chairs dominated the room. Robert Archer stood by the small window overlooking the yard, his hands clasped behind his back. He turned as Jenny entered, the planes and lines of nose and jaw and mouth and forehead looking as though they had been carved out of granite.

'Sit down.' He repeated the words impatiently as she began to shake her head, drawing a chair out for her. She had no option but to go to it and sit, straight-backed, her hands clasped tightly. To her relief he moved away as soon as she was seated, walking to the other side of the table.

'Mr Duncan tells me you're of a mind to marry. Who's the fortunate man?'

Jenny drew in a deep breath, praying that her voice would be steady. 'Daniel Young.'

'Young?' Robert's voice was astonished; his brows rose, then drew together. 'I've had occasion to deal with him once or twice. He's one of the men that came home from the war with new ideas about the way things should be.'

'He's surely got the right to speak up when he feels that injustice has been done.'

'Some take it too far – and he's one of them. Why, Jenny? Why him?'

'I don't see that that's any business of yours.'

He studied her, his eyes seeming to dig into her heart. Finally he said, 'It's surely not love. There was once a glow about you that I've not seen since I came home. I don't see it now.'

Jenny turned her face away from his scrutiny, biting the insides of her lips, wanting nothing but to get out of the room and away from him.

'Is it for your family's sake? Is that it? For God's sake,' Robert said explosively, 'if it's help you needed for them why couldn't you come to me? You surely know that I'd do anything I could for you.'

'All I'm asking, Mr Archer, is to be kept on after – after my marriage. Mr Duncan says that he's agreeable.'

He tried to catch her eye but she stared over his shoulder, carefully studying every line of the whiskered face in the portrait behind him. Finally Robert said, 'You know I'd not refuse you that. As Mr Duncan says, you're a good supervisor.'

'Thank you.' She got to her feet. 'May I go, Mr Archer?'

His voice was as formal as hers as he said, 'Of course, Miss Gillespie.'

Her hand was on the handle of the boardroom door when he spoke again from just behind her, 'He's not the right man for you, Jen.'

Suddenly angry, she spun round on her heel. 'What right have you to say such a thing?'

'I still care for you, Jen. I'd not want to see you made unhappy.'

'You'll never see that,' she told him, and left the room.

Halfway up the staircase she had to steady herself for a moment with one hand against the wall before she could go any further.

Jenny had started to hate Maurice's photograph. Not a day passed without Faith showing it to little Helen, telling her, 'That's your daddy, hen. Kiss Daddy.' The little girl carefully planted her mouth against the cold glass, which was then re-polished and put back.

When the photograph was taken Helen hadn't been conceived, and Marion and Teeze were both fit and well. On the day Maurice had strutted into the photographer's studio Patrick had been walking on two good legs and Robert and Jenny were still writing to each other, with no thought, on her part at least, that the love between them could so easily wither and die.

It seemed now, to Jenny, that she could detect a smugness in the likeness of her brother's self-conscious young face, as though Maurice had known, even then, that his King and country asked only that he fulfil his duty to them and after that he wouldn't be expected to go on to take the responsibility for his own people.

She held her tongue for as long as she could, then one day, when

Faith and Helen were going through their usual ritual, it became too much to bear. 'You shouldn't do that, Mam,' she protested. 'Helen never knew Maurice and there's no sense in trying to pretend that she did.'

Colour rose in her mother's face. 'I'm makin' sure that she'll know him when he comes walking in that door. I'll not have his own daughter treating him like a stranger when he comes back tae us.'

'But he's not—'

'Hold your tongue!' Faith shouted. 'You just keep your mouth shut or I'll – give him to me, Helen,' she added sharply as the little girl reached up and got a firm grip of the elaborate photograph frame. 'Don't touch! Now look what you've done – you've made a mess of Daddy's nice picture frame!'

She smacked the little girl's fingers until they released their grip then pulled the duster from the pocket of her pinny and started to rub frenziedly at the frame. Helen's eyes filled with tears; her mouth opened into a square and she began to howl her outrage at the unexpected and unwarranted attack. Jenny gathered her up, holding her close and crooning to her as Faith was crooning to the photograph of her son.

Marion, a silver web of spittle between bottom lip and chin, watched the scene before her impassively.

Jenny and Faith walked down the street together, stopping to have a word with some of the women sitting outside their closes. Helen, sure on her feet now, impatient of delays, ran on ahead of them, disappearing into their own close with a whisk of her skirt. When they reached the landing halfway up the stairs she was already sitting on the top step, beaming down at them.

'C'mon, Gran, she shouted, her voice echoing in the stairwell. 'C'mon, Jen!'

'She's lookin' more like her daddy every day.' Faith rested a hand on the damp wall and paused to gather her breath before she started the final climb.

'Give me your bag, Mam.'

Faith held tight to the worn leather shopping bag, its handles mended so often that there was more string than leather now. 'I can manage,' she said, and started toiling up the worn stone steps.

Teeze was well enough now to visit the pub and Marion was alone in the kitchen, slumped as usual against the arm of her chair, her chin sunk on her chest.

'Mind ye don't sit on yer Gran's feet, Helen,' Faith said automatically, putting her shopping bag on the table and reaching

133

for the rag she used to wipe Marion's chin. 'Sit up now, Mother, an' let me get you comfy, then we'll all have a nice cup of—'

She stopped, then broke into a sudden strange keening wail that chilled Jenny's veins and startled Helen into a frightened whimper.

'Mam?'

Faith's knees had given way and she had sunk down on to the floor beside her mother-in-law's chair, her hands clutching at the old woman. For a terrifying moment Jenny thought that her mother, too, had taken a seizure. It was only when she tried to free Marion from the grasping hands and settle her into a more comfortable position in the chair and her hand touched a cold and lifeless face that she realised that her grandmother was dead.

All the life seemed to go out of Faith after Marion's funeral. She spent most of her time huddled in the chair that her mother-in-law had used, Maurice's photograph in her lap, staring into space and scarcely eating or drinking. Now and again she roused herself to answer the women who called to pay their respects and show their sympathy, relapsing back into her inner world when they left.

'She's in shock,' Mrs Malloy diagnosed. 'Sure, she's worked hersel' tae the bone tae look after that old woman an' now she doesnae know what tae dae with hersel''. She looked over her shoulder at Faith, who was staring at the range as though trying to memorise every knob and every hinge. The ball of one thumb moved ceaselessly over the smooth cold glass covering Maurice's face.

'I'll damned soon show her what tae dae wi' hersel',' Teeze snarled. 'She's got a house tae see tae the same as she always had, an' if she doesnae get on with it I'll want tae know the reason why!'

Mrs Malloy was afraid of nobody. It was rumoured in the tenements that Mr Malloy, big man though he was, had only tried to hit her once, in the early days of their marriage, and had got a black eye and a bruised head for his trouble. 'Ye should be ashamed o' yersel', Teeze Gillespie,' she snapped back now. 'Yer own mother no' cold yet an' you foul-mouthin'!'

He glared at her then took refuge, as usual, in the pub. Lottie, as was to be expected, was of little use in this time of crisis, and it was left to Jenny and Alice to keep the house going as best they could.

A week after the funeral Jenny and her mother were alone in the kitchen when a sudden uproar in the close below, the clatter of feet, a man's deep laugh, brought Faith to her feet, her eyes wide, her hands clutching at the air. The photograph that had been lying in her lap fell to the floor.

'Mam?' Jenny had been sitting in her father's chair with a pile of darning, and the work fell from her hands as she scrambled to her feet. Faith was already hurrying to the door and out into the small hall; by the time Jenny reached her she had opened the outside door and was staring out at the landing, one hand fisted at her throat. Two pairs of booted feet were coming up the stairs and someone was whistling 'Tipperary'.

'He's here, Jenny – he's come home and he's brought one of his pals with him.'

'Who?'

'Maurice – who else?' Faith asked impatiently, taking a step on to the landing.

A shiver ran through Jenny, as though something unspeakable had just walked across her grave. 'Mam—'

Two youths swung into sight at the top of the stairs, jostling each other – young Tommy Lang, who lived with his parents in the flat opposite the Gillespies, and one of his friends. When they caught sight of Faith, her hair tousled, her eyes huge and brilliant in the gloom, the whistling faded. They stared, startled, then scurried up the last short flight of stairs, crowding together as they arrived on the landing as though trying to keep as far from Faith's stricken face as possible. Tommy's hand fumbled with the latch, the door opened, and the two of them tumbled inside, almost falling over their feet in their haste to get out of sight. The door slammed and there was a burst of raw, relieved laughter from behind the scarred panels.

Faith's shoulders had slumped at the sight of the youths. She allowed Jenny to draw her back into the house and close the door. In the kitchen, she bent and picked up the photograph. The fall had broken the glass, and a crack ran raggedly across Maurice's solemn young face, distorting his features. Faith's finger traced the crack.

'He's no' comin' back, is he, Jenny?' she said, her voice empty.

'No, Mam, he's not coming back.'

'She was a wicked old bitch, all the years we knew each other. But I thought that if I took care of her, if I was good tae her, my Maurice'd be sent back tae me.' She sank into her chair and looked up at Jenny, struggling to be understood. 'It was as if I was bein' tested, d'ye see? I thought—' The hand holding the photograph began to shake, then a violent trembling took hold of Faith's entire body. Tears pattered down on to Maurice's features and he continued to smile uncaringly through them.

'Oh, Mam!' Jenny dropped to her knees and, for the first time in her life, she put her arms round her mother and held her while she

135

wept, understanding at last why Faith had been so devoted to the woman who had tormented her all her married life.

At last the shuddering and gasping stopped and Faith drew back, her face swollen with grief. 'I'm fine now. Make us a cup of tea, there's a good lass.' She scrubbed the last of the tears away with a piece of faded cloth that Jenny recognised as the rag she had always kept for Marion, then got up and used the poker to lift one of the iron lids on the range. She dropped the rag into the flames, then put Maurice's photograph back on the sideboard and picked up the jar of artificial flowers that had always stood beside the photograph.

'Put that up on the mantelshelf, will you? It doesnae look right there.'

'Mam, mebbe Daniel and me should put the wedding off for a wee while,' Jenny ventured a few minutes later as they sat on either side of the range, cups in hand. Faith's face was still swollen with weeping, yet there was something about the serenity in her eyes and the set of her thin shoulders that indicated that she had at last reached the end of a long hard journey and had come to terms with what had happened to her over the past years.

'Why should ye do that?'

'With Gran dying – I should mebbe stay here for a bit longer. I'm sure Daniel would understand.'

'No,' Faith said swiftly. 'Your Gran would've wanted you to go on with your own plans.' She leaned forward and put a hand over her daughter's fingers. 'Daniel's a good man, and it wouldnae be right tae keep him waitin'.'

Jenny shifted uneasily in her chair, well aware of the meaning behind her mother's words. Now that Faith had finally accepted that Maurice would never come home, Jenny's wage – and the support that Daniel had promised – was all the more important to her.

'All right, Mam,' she said quietly, and Faith relaxed and handed her empty cup over to be washed.

Getting up and taking both cups to the sink, Jenny wondered about the impulse that had made her offer to put the marriage off, and couldn't be certain that it had been done solely for her mother's benefit. She knew that she herself wouldn't have minded the postponement, the chance to put off her future for a little longer.

Carefully, she rinsed both cups under the running tap and put them on to the draining board, trying to ignore the panic that fluttered deep in her heart like a bird trapped in a net.

Daniel was a good man, she reminded herself. Trustworthy,

conscientious, hard-working. There was no doubt of that. And her decision to marry him had already been taken. If she was to voice any doubts now she would only upset her mother, anger her father, and shame Daniel and herself in the eyes of the community.

There was no going back. And there was no other path, now, to take.

14

In May the weather changed for the better. Suddenly summer arrived, marked on the hills around the town with flowering clumps of golden broom, and in the narrow streets beside the river by the familiar smell of poor drains and overcrowded housing.

It was Jenny's turn now to be dressed at work by Kerry and Jinnet and Senga in brightly coloured paper streamers and to jump over the chanty of salt. The faces of the joiners and moulders and clay-workers scratched hers as they took turns to kiss her, and the coins they contributed to the wedding festivities jingled into the old top hat she held. As she was carried through the town on the trolley more coins flashed in the sun as they soared from the hands of the onlookers into her lap. She waved and laughed and did her best to enjoy her moment of fame, acutely aware that none of this harmless nonsense fitted in with the grave solemnity of the man she had promised to marry.

Daniel had insisted on contributing some money to her wedding outfit. 'I know you've got more than enough tae do with your own wage,' he said earnestly when she tried to refuse. 'But it's your wedding day, and I want you tae get somethin' that pleases you.' She gave in, and bought a new costume, a pleated skirt and long, loose-belted jacket striped in bronze and soft rose pink with white collar and cuffs. After a great deal of searching she managed to buy some bronze material to make a blouse and a ribbon to put round the crown of her straw Panama hat.

She and Daniel were married in the vestry of the parish church on a sunny day a month after she had accepted his proposal, with Alice and one of Daniel's workmates as their witnesses.

Afterwards they walked further into the town to a photographic studio where they had their likenesses taken, Jenny sitting erect on an uncomfortable wooden chair, Daniel standing behind her, one hand resting on her shoulder. Then they went back to the Gillespie flat for high tea with Jenny's family and Walter, who was almost inarticulate with shyness in spite of Alice's efforts to winkle him from his shell.

Helen, in a new frock that Jenny had made for her, scampered to the door to meet the wedding party then fell back shyly, intimidated by her aunts' smart clothes and the presence of the two men, and tried to hide herself in her mother's skirt. With an exclamation of disgust, Lottie pushed her away

'It cost me good money, this dress. Don't touch it!'

'Come to me, Helen.' Jenny lifted the little girl up and Helen threw her arms about her and buried her face in her neck. Lottie shrugged and turned her attention to Daniel's best man.

Neighbours came and went, most of them bringing items of food or drink for the wedding party. They drank the health of the bride and groom, and with each toast Teeze grew more inebriated. Daniel, Jenny noticed, only sipped at the glass of beer before him, and quietly but firmly refused to let Teeze refill it every time he filled his own glass. Sitting by his side in the crowded room, aware of the warmth of his shoulder against hers and the clean fresh soapy smell from his skin, she felt a moment's panic as she realised that when he left the house she would go with him as his wife. She swallowed hard and glanced down at the wedding ring on her finger. Her life would never be the same again . . .

Helen fell asleep under the table, and when Jenny would have scooped her up and taken her off to her room, Alice got there before her. 'You stay where you are, Mrs Young,' she said, smiling, and Jenny watched the little girl being carried off, head lolling, relaxed as a contented cat against Alice's shoulder.

Not long after that Daniel got to his feet and courteously thanked his new in-laws for their hospitality. 'It's time we were on our way,' he said, and Walter immediately rose.

To Jenny's horror her father clapped a large hand on Daniel's wrist to detain him. 'Now you look after my wee lassie,' he slurred. 'She's one o' the best an' ye'll no' find a better. See an' look after her, man.'

'I will, Teeze, I will.'

Faith touched Jenny's hand. 'Ye'll be all right, hen?'

'Of course, Mam. I'm only going to be at the other side of the back court – you'll see me every day.'

It was a relief when the three of them finally got out of the place. To mark the solemnity of the day they walked to Daniel's home through the streets instead of crossing the courtyard, stopping every few yards to talk to neighbours who came to closemouths or leaned from open windows to wish them well. Jenny walked with a hand on her husband's arm, while Walter stayed two steps behind them all the time.

Daniel had refused to let Jenny help to prepare his two-roomed flat for its new mistress, insisting that he and Walter could see to it between them. The place was spotless and the shabby suitcase Daniel had collected from her parents' home that morning stood neatly against one wall.

'Walter, away tae yer bed,' Daniel said as soon as they were inside.

'Would you not like a cup of tea first, Walter?'

'He needs sleep more than tea. He's tae be up early in the morning for the milk round.' Daniel led the way into the kitchen and opened the door of a tall narrow closet in one corner, beside a small chest of drawers. 'I'll see tae the tea. I've made room for your clothes in here, and there's two drawers freshly lined for ye.'

He made tea in silence while Jenny hung up her clothes. She opened the wrong drawer by accident and caught a quick glimpse of spotlessly clean, neatly folded long johns and vests before she shut the drawer hurriedly, warmth rising to her cheeks.

The tea was hot and strong; Jenny clutched the cup for comfort, wondering if Lottie would be able to rouse herself if Helen woke in the night, and whether or not Alice would have trouble trying to keep up with her homework without Jenny there to see that she got peace to work on her books.

Daniel washed his empty cup at the sink, dried it and put it away before reaching for his cap. 'I'll just take a turn outside,' he said gruffly.

'What time does Walter have to be up for his milk round?'

'Five o'clock. He gets himself up so there's no need for you tae rouse yourself on his account.'

'He'll need to eat something before he goes out.'

'He breaks his fast when he comes back.'

When he had gone she hurried to wash and dry her own cup and put it away in a cupboard that was clearly cleaned thoroughly once a week. Then she stripped her clothes off and put them neatly over a chair before washing herself and putting on her new nightdress.

Finally she drew back the curtains that masked the wall bed from sight and stood for a moment staring at the patchwork quilt, the sheet folded back neatly over it, the two pillows, side by side. Her fingers ran admiringly over one of the pillowcases. At home she had often had to do without the luxury of a pillowcase and the few that the Gillespies owned were patched and darned and permanently stained, no matter how hard they were scrubbed, from Marion's dribbling and Lottie's habit of tumbling into bed without washing the make-up from her face. But Daniel's pillowcases were snowy white and well ironed, made of the best linen, each case edged with a frill.

Jenny turned back the covers and climbed into the high bed, settling herself carefully so as not to crumple the bedding or tangle her newly brushed hair.

141

A few moments later Daniel tapped lightly on the kitchen door and waited until she called to him to come in. He glanced swiftly at the bed then looked away, saying gruffly, 'I always set the breakfast table last thing.'

'I'm sorry, I didn't know—' She began to sit up, but he said at once, 'Stay where you are, I'll do it.'

Embarrassed by her first mistake, she watched as he prepared the table then took off his jacket and waistcoat and shirt, handling each item carefully and taking time to fold it.

'I left enough hot water for you in the kettle.'

'I always use cold water,' said Daniel, turning one of the gas mantels off. The soft light of the remaining mantel glanced off his muscular arms and neck as he worked at the 'jawbox' – the small sink set beneath the window – and Jenny felt a thrill of anticipation tingling deep within her. Unbidden, the memory of Robert's loving just before he left for Tyneside came back to her. Shocked though she was at herself for thinking of another man's lovemaking on her wedding night, the memory refused to go away once it had arrived. A wave of warmth ran through her body and she moved restlessly, stretching her legs down towards the foot of the bed until her toes were blocked by the sheet tucked tightly round the mattress.

Daniel turned off the second gas mantel and the dark room was filled with the whisper of his movements, his breathing, the rustle of his underclothing being slipped off. Jenny heard a drawer squeak open then shut again, followed by a crisp, hissing sound as Daniel's nightshirt was slipped over his head. She moved in the bed again and ran her hands over her own body, testing the flatness of her stomach, the swell of her hips, the softness and fullness of her breasts beneath the thin material of her gown. She let her fingers slide along the warm valley between her breasts and hoped that she would please Daniel.

There was a flurry of cool air against her calves as the blankets were lifted, then the mattress dipped as her husband slid in beside her. She waited, holding her breath, for his touch. Waited and waited, the air silently, slowly drifting from her lungs. Then, to her astonishment, Daniel said, 'Goodnight, then,' and turned over, his back to her.

For a moment Jenny lay still, unable to believe that he was going to go to sleep, then she raised herself on one elbow. 'Daniel?'

He grunted.

'Daniel, did I do something wrong?'

'No. Go tae sleep.'

'Daniel—' She laid her hand on his cotton-clad shoulder then drew it back with a gasp of fright as he suddenly threw himself over in the bed to face her.

142

'For pity's sake, woman, have ye no decency?' His voice was a harsh whisper. 'D'ye expect me tae take ye when my own son's lyin' eighteen inches away from us?'

'But—' Jenny glanced into the darkness behind her, in the direction of the wall that divided them from Walter's room, '—he'll surely be asleep by now. He'd not hear us.' She pushed away the memories of herself and her brother and sisters as children, awake in the darkness, listening to the sounds from the kitchen wall-bed, the creaking of the bedframe, the grunting, the thudding of her father's large body against the wall until sometimes they feared that he would burst through it, covering them with plaster. She remembered them nudging each other, biting the blanket to stifle their giggles – remembered, too, the undercurrent of nervous fear. In the tenements the walls were thin and the houses so small that every child grew up wise to the facts of life. But Daniel wasn't like her father. He would be gentle and – quiet.

'There'll be no fornicating in this house,' Daniel hissed at her. 'Not in my son's presence. Now go to sleep.' And he turned away from her again, hunching himself to his side of the bed.

She lay awake for a long time, tormented by her own wanting, knowing by his shallow breathing, the tension that she sensed even though their bodies weren't touching, that Daniel, too, was awake.

The Gillespie flat faced on to the back court but Daniel's flat fronted the road and, now and again, the night was disturbed by voices or footsteps, even the squeaking, once, of a perambulator or a handcart. A group of drunks, women as well as men, on their way home from a public house staggered along the street, their voices loud and threatening in the night.

Jenny moved to ease a cramp in her calf and her bare foot brushed lightly against Daniel's. He flinched away and she hurriedly eased her body closer to the wall to avoid any further contact. A tear rolled slowly from beneath one of her lids and eased itself down her cheek. She felt its wetness drip from her to lose itself in the linen pillowcase.

When she woke in grey dawn she didn't know where she was or what had roused her. Then she heard a stealthy sound from the adjoining room and began to push the blanket back so that she could go to help her mother. It was only when her fingers hit against the wall instead of sweeping through thin air that she recalled that she was in Daniel's home, in Daniel's bed. She was Daniel's wife – in name, if not in body.

Memories of his rejection the night before rushed back to her as she lay still, listening to his even breathing. The door of Walter's room gave out a faint squeak of hinges; she heard the boy tiptoe along the hall then the close door opened and closed. At once Daniel startled the life out of her by suddenly bounding from the bed and into the hallway. He was back in the kitchen while she was still struggling to sit up.

'He's gone,' he said, then the bed coverings were thrown aside and he was kneeling over her, his hands reaching for her, pushing beneath the pretty nightgown with its coloured bows, exploring her, claiming her.

'God, ye're bonny,' he said huskily, 'My bonny Jenny!'

Jenny, still struggling to come fully awake, felt as though she had been swept up by a sudden storm and was being tossed and turned in its wake with no time to catch her breath. 'Daniel—' She tried to catch his hands in hers, to make him slow down, but he ignored her. Her nightdress was pushed up as far as it could go and Daniel moved swiftly to straddle her; the ceiling was blotted out by his body as he moved into her swiftly, insistently.

When she cried out in pain and protest at the suddenness of the assault he muttered breathlessly into her ear, 'It's all right, it always hurts the first time.'

A wave of chill realisation swept down Jenny's spine at the words. The first time. Even thinking about Robert the night before, while she was waiting for Daniel to come to bed, it hadn't occurred to her that she was no longer the virgin that Daniel had naturally expected her to be. If he had heard anything of her affair with Robert all those years before he would have assumed, as everyone else had, that it was long over and forgotten. Only she and Robert knew that their love had been consummated.

Daniel rolled away from her, panting, then almost at once he got out of bed, leaving her alone. She swiftly covered herself and the rumpled sheet with the blanket, but he kept his back to her as he pulled on his underdrawers then turned on the tap and began to sluice his hands and face and chest. The storm of his passion had passed as suddenly as it had arrived.

He dried himself and hauled his singlet on, then she heard the clatter as he opened up the range and stirred the embers within into life, followed by the brisk sound of the wooden ladle stirring the oatmeal that had been left to soak in water overnight. He pushed the iron pot over the fire and scooped the rest of his clothes into his arms.

'The laddie'll be back soon. I'll dress in his room,' he said, then the door closed behind him. Jenny jumped out of bed then hurriedly dragged the undersheet free of the mattress, bundling it up to hide the absence of the blood that should have been spilled on it.

By the time Daniel tapped on the door she had washed and dressed and brushed her hair, and was stirring the porridge. The blanket and the patchwork quilt had been smoothed neatly over the bed, and she saw his eyes flicker to the bucket in the corner, where the sheet, and her nightgown for good measure, were soaking in cold water.

'The boy'll no' be long,' he said, whisking the curtains shut to hide the bed from sight. He looked just as he had looked on the morning she had arrived to tell him that she would marry him, though this time even his braces were in place.

'God, but I'm hungry.' He sat down at the table and fingered one of the plain white cups. 'I was thinkin', Jenny, could ye mebbe decorate them a bit when ye've got the time? Just for us,' he added with unexpected, touching shyness, his free hand reaching out to touch hers briefly. 'Tae commemorate us findin' each other?'

Jenny's hopes that she would be able to draw Walter out of his shell once she was his stepmother were soon dashed by Daniel. From the day of his son's birth he had mapped out the boy's life and he was firmly opposed to any attempt she made to ease Walter's regime.

When she tried to encourage her stepson to spend a little time each day on recreation Daniel said that Satan found mischief for idle hands and he'd not have his son lounging on street corners and learning bad habits. When Jenny suggested that the milk round was too much for the boy on top of all the studying he had to do Daniel said, thin-lipped, that Walter had to learn that everyone had to learn to pay their way.

'Don't spoil the boy,' he said impatiently when Jenny made treacle scones, knowing that they were Walter's favourites.

'It's no bother to make a few scones, Daniel. And he's been working hard at his homework all evening. He surely deserves a treat.'

'He knows that the reward for working hard lies in getting good results in his examinations, not in treats.' Daniel spoke the final word scathingly and Walter's long thin hands, busy spreading margarine thinly on a scone still warm from the oven, faltered.

Jenny could have wept for the boy as she watched him force the scone down, bite by bite, all the pleasant anticipation scoured from him by his father's cruelty. She didn't make treacle scones again, knowing from her own experience that Walter would probably hate that particular delicacy for the rest of his life.

The intimate side of her marriage continued to follow the pattern that had been set immediately after their wedding. Daniel appeared to be totally indifferent to her while his son was in the house, but as

145

soon as they were alone he behaved like a starving man falling on a feast. She grew to accept his loving – if what happened between them could be given such a name – but for her there was no joy in it, not even the pleasure of knowing that she had satisfied her husband.

During the day she and Daniel were at work and Walter at school, so their swift couplings only took place in the early mornings. On the rare occasions when she and Daniel were alone at home during the day he eagerly took advantage of his son's absence, whisking her to the bed no matter what task she might be busy with. Confused by the situation, she didn't dare say anything to anyone about it, even to Bella, and was left to wonder if this was what most men and most marriages were like.

At least the tracing office and its familiar, comforting routine were still part of her life. She had heard that some of the yards on the Clyde were beginning to see a drop in orders now, but Dalkieth's Experimental Tank was in use all day and every day, and Jenny and her staff were never short of work. Now and then, hurrying to collect a drum of paper from the truck or to deliver an analysis to Mr Duncan she encountered Robert Archer. Each time, afraid that those searching eyes of his might look deep into her mind, she stared at the floor. She couldn't bear the thought of Robert, of all people, guessing the truth about her bewildering marriage.

But, to her relief, he behaved towards her as he would behave towards any other employee, wishing her a crisp good morning or good afternoon each time they met, then passing her by.

15

Robert Archer was too wrapped up in his own problems to brood over Jenny's marriage. The conflict between himself and George Dalkieth had worsened, and it had become increasingly clear that Isobel Dalkieth was not going to be able to bring herself to vote against her son when he and Robert clashed. Already work had begun on the land they had bought from McWalter. Some of the Dalkieth buildings had been extended, and new machinery, bought with a substantial bank loan, had been brought in.

From his office window Robert stared down at the yard and wondered if the time had come for him to leave Ellerslie once again. Some of the yards on the Clyde were already beginning to feel the first waft of chill air from the economic storms lurking on the horizon, and the same thing was happening to a greater extent on Tyneside. He knew all about it for he kept a close watch on what was happening to shipbuilding all around the globe. But there was still time for a sensible company to evaluate and use its own strengths, to hunt out and eliminate its weak spots. Given a less prejudiced platform where his opinions would be listened to, he could perhaps do some good somewhere else. At the very least he would retain his own self-respect and not let George Dalkieth drag it down together with his own.

Robert Archer didn't believe in brooding over the past and what might have been. He had hoped, on hearing from Tyneside that Anne had plans for marriage to another man, that once his divorce came through and he was free he and Jenny might come together again. But Jenny was married now, and any dreams he had had of winning her back were over. He himself had no strong ties with Ellerslie, no family, and certainly no lingering affection for the place. Shipbuilding was all he cared about, and he could pursue his career in any yard, anywhere.

He ran a finger over his moustache as the idea of killing two birds with one stone came to him. He would suggest to the Board that he should travel to Tyneside soon to get some idea of the problems facing the yards there. What happened in England always affected Scotland later. If he found evidence of trouble on Tyneside that could, with foresight, be avoided here in Ellerslie, surely Isobel Dalkieth wouldn't brush it aside whatever her son might say to the contrary. And he could use his visit to find out which yards might be interested in offering him a post.

Jenny had been used to a household where the men came in filthy from the shipyard. Every working day her mother had dragged out the old hip-bath and put so many pots and kettles of hot water on the range that the kitchen was like a steam-room by the time Teeze and Maurice came home. Teeze, as head of the household, always got first use of the bath and Maurice followed him, while Jenny and her sisters were banished to the other room.

She vividly remembered the day Maurice had rebelled over the filthy state of the water he was expected to step into. Teeze had swung a fist at him, and for the first time Maurice, his muscles developed by a year of hard work at the yard, had retaliated. The resulting uproar had brought Jenny and Bella and Alice running from the bedroom to see, through clouds of steam, two naked bodies, one thick-set and white, the other slim and boyish and still dappled with shipyard grime, grappling with each other while poor Faith knelt at their feet, holding tightly to the bath, which was in danger of being tipped over and flooding the kitchen floor and house below, screaming at her menfolk to behave themselves.

Bella, Jenny recalled with amusement, had clapped her hands over Alice's eyes, but not quickly enough.

Many lessons were learned that day. Teeze discovered that his son was too strong and too old for physical chastisement, and the three sisters, pooling their observations when they were alone in bed later and going into intensive though giggling discussion, had learned quite a lot about the male anatomy. Poor Faith had learned how humiliating shame could be for a previously respectable woman, for the uproar had been so alarming, even in the tenements where fights were commonplace, that the people who lived below had sent for the police.

From then on Maurice had made do with two basins of water in his tiny bedroom, and a head-to-toe scrub each day when he came home from the yard.

The rumours about Daniel Young's visits to the public baths after each day's work turned out to be true. Every morning when he set out for the yard, as clean and neat as an office worker, he carried a shabby

148

carpet bag containing his dinner and his working clothes. Every afternoon he came home in the same spotless fashion, his overalls and working shirt and even his underwear rolled up and stuffed in the bag.

'It's my job to have hot water ready for you, and the tub out,' Jenny argued in the early days of their marriage, but Daniel scowled and shook his head.

'I'll not walk through the streets and in at my own door like a tink,' he said shortly. 'I'll not have my son seeing me like that. The day he was born I swore that he'd never have to do it, either. He'll have work that he can be proud of, clean work.'

'Shipbuilding's a craft to be proud of.'

'Aye – to those that don't have to put up with the noise and the dirt and the humiliations,' Daniel retorted, and refused to change his ways.

He had looked after all his clothes well, including his working clothes, which were darned and patched over and over again and, unlike many of his colleagues, he had managed to get together two sets so that he could change in the middle of the week as well as on Mondays.

Between that, and his insistence that he and Walter changed their shirts more often than most men, Jenny's washload was just as large as it had been in her parents' home, and she took to washing clothes occasionally in the evenings. Although it meant more hard work at the end of a busy day, she enjoyed being in the wash-house at a time when it was quiet. It reminded her then of rainy days spent happily in that same wash-house with the other tenement children, the girls playing at wee houses, or at shops on the broad windowsill, using pebbles for goods; the boys playing with toy soldiers or swinging from ropes suspended from the two hooks set in the ceiling, one at each end of the room. The hooks had been set into the ceiling to take a drying line in wet weather, but they weren't used much, for the wash-house was usually too steamy to allow clothes to dry.

Alice often gave her a hand with the washing and, now and again, if Daniel was out at one of his union meetings and Walter had finished his homework, the boy offered to help. It was during one of those washing sessions, on an August evening a few weeks before she and Walter were due to go back to school, that Alice announced that she had given up her Saturday work in the bakery and found work instead in a local pawnshop.

'And I'm going to start evening classes in book-keeping and typewriting,' she announced. 'Mr Monroe that runs the shop says he'll help to pay for them. He says I've got a good head for figures.'

149

There were four of them in the wash-house that evening – Jenny, Walter, Alice, and Helen, who was toddling around, dragging a piece of wood tied to a string. This was Helen's doggie, and her favourite toy of the moment.

'Oh, Alice! You were doing fine at the bakery. Why give it up?' Jenny plunged Daniel's dungarees into the hot scummy water yet again, rubbing them fiercely against the ribbed washboard.

'The work was awful dull, Jen. I did nothing but sell potato-scones and wee cakes, and the flour made me sneeze.'

'But a pawnshop! Could you not have found something more – more respectable?' Jenny gave a tut of impatience as she reached for the cake of harsh black soap and it skittered off the bench and across the floor. 'Fetch that, will you?'

Alice dropped to her hands and knees to scrabble on the floor for the elusive slippery tablet. Over her shoulder she said breathlessly, 'It's a very respectable pawnshop, and Mr Monroe's a respectable employer, but his chest's bad since he got gassed in the war and he's finding it all too much for him.'

'Poor soul, it's a pity he's got no wife to help him.' Jenny straightened up for a moment, stretching her back and arms. She recalled Alec Monroe, a thin young man who had been invalided out of the army after being gassed in the trenches. At that time his widowed mother had been running the pawnshop, but not long after he came back home she died, leaving the shop and the flat above to Alec.

Alice captured the soap and handed it over. 'At least he's got me now. I'm a great help with the books, he says, and the work's interesting.'

'I'm not certain that I'm happy about you taking on nightschool as well. Your schoolwork'll suffer.'

'Not at all,' said Alice firmly. 'Book-keeping's arithmetic, and the typewriting's interesting.'

Walter was wiping the mangle down with a rag to clear the dust from the rollers before the wet clothes went through. 'I wish I could get another holiday job,' he said over his shoulder. 'It's dull, scrubbing down floors and walls in the dairy.'

'Look for something else, then,' Alice suggested, but he shook his head.

'It was my father that got me that job and he'd not like me looking for something else. Working in a pawnshop's certainly a way of meeting people.' A grin lit up his face as he paused to turn the cloth over in search of a dust-free area. 'I only get to meet cows.'

Seeing the way his whole face changed when he smiled, Jenny

resolved to make sure that it happened more often. Already, in his fourteenth year, she could see that Walter was going to grow up to be a fine-looking young man. He would set many a lassie's heart dancing in another few years or so.

'Oh, it's interesting, right enough.' Alice deftly sidestepped round Helen, who had suddenly veered in front of her, and returned to the tub where she was plunging shirts in fresh rinsing water. 'Mind that Miss Galbraith from the school, Jenny? She came in last Saturday morning and she just about keeled over when she saw me standing behind the counter. I knew the minute I saw the look on her face that she minded me from when I was in her class. She just stuck there in the doorway and didnae know whether to come on in or fight her way out, so I said to her, easy-like, "Good morning, madam, d'you require us to look after your valuables for the week?" When I said it like that, as if it was a sort of favour she was doing us, in she came and not a word was said about us recognising each other.'

'Poor soul, she must have fallen on hard times. What did she pawn?'

'Mind your own business,' Alice rapped back at her. 'And me and Mr Munroe'll mind ours.'

Jenny laughed, knuckling a particularly filthy patch of cloth against another patch so that she could rub harder and deciding that when the washing was finished she was going to give her hands an extra going over. She kept a mixture of glycerine and rosewater in the house at all times, for she had to look after her hands to keep them supple for her work in the tracing office.

'I wish my father would let me do something different,' Walter said.

'Fathers are all the same. My dad's doing everything he can to make me feel foolish about going to nightschool, but he'll not win,' Alice told him. 'And neither should yours. The way I see it, you're the one that's doing all the studying so you're the one that should decide what you want to do with your life, not your father.'

Walter stopped what he was doing and gaped at her as though expecting her to be struck dead on the spot for uttering such sacrilege. Then he said, wonderingly, 'You're right.'

'Of course I'm right.' Alice lifted the lid of the boiler and a cloud of steam enveloped her. Helen, enchanted, giggled and dropped her 'doggie's' string and started windmilling her arms vigorously to disperse the hot damp cloud descending on her.

'Now don't you go putting ideas into Walter's head,' Jenny told her sister nervously, 'Daniel wouldn't like it.'

151

Walter was leaning on the mangle now, the rag dangling from his hand, staring through the steam at Alice's wavering outline. His eyes were glowing with what Jenny could only think of as hero-worship.

'I'm not putting ideas into anyone's head. I'm just saying what I think.'

Jenny looked at her younger sister as the steam began to break up and realised that Alice was growing up. Her sturdy, solid body was beginning to take on a womanly shape, even wrapped as it was at that moment in a sacking apron. Wisps of brown hair with a curl to it fell over a face rosy with heat and exertion, and the lingering steam softened her strong features. Alice might never be pretty, but one day she was going to be attractive in her own way.

The steam from the boiling water, together with the fire beneath the copper, was making the small room unbearably hot and stuffy. Jenny went to open the door and take a few breaths of fresh air before returning to her work.

'What I'd really like to do,' she heard Walter say as she stood in the doorway, 'is work on a ship. In the engine room.'

Dragging an arm across her damp face, Jenny turned in dismay, 'But Walter, your father's set on you working in an office.' It had never occurred to her that Walter himself might have other ideas.

His shoulders slumped. 'I know. It's all I ever hear from him – but what I really want is tae be an engineer.'

'Just mind what I said – it's your life, not your father's. The shirts are done,' Alice said. 'Fetch the pole, Walter.'

He obediently handed her the long wooden pole that had been leaning on the wall and she plunged it into the boiler, twisting it with deft flicks of the wrists so that the clothes would wrap themselves around it. 'Careful Helen pet, the water's burny. Take your wee doggie over to the door so's it doesnae get splashcd. Ready, Walter? One-two-THREE!'

Her voice ended on a shriek and Walter jumped to add his strength to hers as she hoisted the pole out of the copper. It came free with a tangle of sopping, steaming material clinging to the other end and water cascading over the floor as they swung round, working in unison, and deposited their load in the waiting tub of cold clean water.

Walter eased the pole free. 'To my father, engineering's black work, an' he says I'm never going to have to put on dungarees and get my hands oily.' He used the pole to poke the shirts down into the rinsing tub. 'Mebbe when the time comes I'll get him tae change his mind.' He spoke without much hope, and Jenny, returning to the washboard, knew why. Daniel held fast to a dream that had been born on the same day as Walter himself, a dream he would not easily relinquish.

'Nobody should be allowed to decide what someone else should do with the rest of his life. We've only got one each,' Alice said briskly. 'Now then, Walter Young, are you going to stop clinging to that pole like a monkey on a stick and help me to get the rest of the stuff out of this boiler?'

16

The wooden doors between the Palmers' parlour and their dining room had been folded back to accommodate the large number attending their musical soiree. Fiona Dalkieth, who had been there for half an hour and was already bored, drifted from one group to the other, eyeing herself in every mirror she passed, admiring the way the low waistband of her new, deep red gown, embroidered with a pattern of black and silver beading, showed off her figure to advantage. As she paused before one of the mirrors to put a hand up to her hair her sleeve, full from the elbow, fell back from her soft white forearm and tiny diamonds in the gold bracelet clasped about her wrist sparkled in the light from the chandelier.

The expression on her lovely face was one of aloof boredom, but in truth Fiona was becoming more nervous with every day that passed. George was even more determined to father a child and the week before, when she had had to admit to him that her monthly bleeding had started, he had accused her of using some sort of preventative. When she protested that she would never do such a disgusting thing he had snapped back at her, 'Then you must be barren!' Since then he had made one or two veiled references to divorce.

She would not be sent back in disgrace to her family in Glasgow, Fiona vowed as she fidgeted her way round the room, nodding to acquaintances but reluctant to be drawn into idle chatter. Papa had money, but he disliked parting with it unless there was good reason. He had made it very clear to his only daughter that his only reason for spending a fortune on her clothes was so that she would attract a wealthy husband; the thought of his reaction if she returned to the family home, divorced and disgraced, was quite unbearable. To use his own words, she would be shop-soiled goods.

Fiona had quite forgotten where she was and had reached the stage of picturing herself as a poor relation, farmed out to some distant cousin as a companion or, even worse, a housekeeper, when a voice said from behind her, 'You're very solemn tonight, Mrs Dalkieth. I take it that you're missing your husband?'

Fiona turned quickly, her face lighting up. 'Rob – Mr Archer!

I didn't know you were coming here tonight.'

'Nor did I. I had expected to be in Tyneside this week.' There was a decided edge to Robert Archer's voice.

'With George? He left for England this morning. He was looking forward very much to visiting the yards there.' And she herself had been looking forward very much to several days of freedom.

'Instead of George,' he corrected her. 'The visit to Tyneside was my idea but, unfortunately, it was felt that I was needed here to deal with some problem that one of our clients has raised.'

Fiona beamed up at him. 'Well I for one am delighted that—' she began, but just then Mrs Palmer decided that her guests should move to the library across the hall to be entertained by the singer she had engaged for the evening.

Fiona paid scant attention to the musical entertainment, for she was busy making plans. While the cat was away, she thought . . . and felt a delicious squiggle of excitement run through her body. She risked a sidelong glance at her companion, thinking how strange it was that, although he came from the working classes, he wore his clothes with more of an air than George. He seemed to be completely unaware of her appraisal; his gaze, and apparently all his attention, was fixed on the singer.

'You seem to be quite taken with the lady,' she whispered under cover of a polite pattering of applause.

'I was thinking of a cat my aunt once had,' he murmured, his face expressionless. 'Given a hairpiece and a gown that cat would have looked just like her. It would even have sounded like her.'

Shocked, delighted, Fiona clapped a gloved hand over her mouth, but not swiftly enough to smother a peal of laughter. Heads turned in their direction and the singer, about to start her next song, paused.

Robert patted Fiona on the back then took her arm and led her back to the drawing room, where he seated her on an upright chair. 'A sudden fit of coughing,' he explained above her head to Mrs Palmer, who had followed them. 'A glass of water, perhaps?'

By the time it arrived Fiona was recovered and dabbing at her eyes with a lacy handkerchief. She sipped at the water and when their hostess had returned to the library she looked up at Robert reproachfully. 'I doubt if I shall ever be invited here again.'

'Will you mind that?'

'Not in the least.' As he took the glass from her and put it on a nearby table his hand came in contact with hers and the thrill of excitement returned.

The musical interlude ended and the others came in for supper. To Fiona's annoyance she and Robert became separated; occasionally their eyes met and each time they exchanged smiles. When Mrs Palmer began rounding up her guests after supper and sending them back to the music room to hear some violin solos, Fiona, unable to bear the thought of staying a moment longer, made her excuses, pleading a headache.

As the front door closed behind her she paused for a moment, drawing her sable-trimmed coat more closely about her, then walked along the short drive, the sound of violin music becoming more distant until she stepped on to the pavement and it faded away altogether.

The night was pleasantly cool and the roadway quiet. Fiona slowed her steps and had strolled as far as the lamp-post at the corner when she heard someone coming along behind her. She waited until the footsteps were close before turning.

'Mr Archer – we meet again.'

He looked up and down the empty road. 'Hasn't your chauffeur arrived after all?'

'My chauffeur is no doubt sitting snugly in his room reading his newspaper. I told him that someone else would drive me home.'

The light above them revealed amusement in his grey eyes. Usually Robert Archer was serious but, when he smiled, Fiona thought with pleasure, he became almost handsome. 'At times like this I regret that I don't own a car. I could have offered you a lift.'

'I recall you telling me once that you prefer walking. I believe I shall try it for myself,' said Fiona, and placed a gloved hand on the arm he offered.

It was delightful to stroll through the quiet night with someone other than George, who puffed if he had to walk any distance at all and spent most of his time grumbling about something or other.

They reached a corner and he moved towards the kerb, ready to cross the road, then paused when Fiona stopped. 'Isn't this the road where you live?' she asked, the flutter in her throat making her words sound quite breathless.

'Yes, but I intend to walk with you to your own gate.'

'Couldn't we—' She moistened her lips with the tip of her tongue, 'Couldn't we perhaps stop for some refreshment? I feel quite parched.'

'D'you think that's wise, Mrs Dalkieth? I live alone.'

Fiona looked up and down the quiet road. 'There's not a soul here to see us. You surely wouldn't deny me a glass of water to sustain me for the rest of the journey?'

In his hall, she gazed about with interest before following him into a small comfortable parlour.

'A glass of water?'

'I would prefer sherry wine, if you have it,' said Fiona, unfastening the large buttons on her coat. The silk material rustled as he drew the garment from her shoulders and tossed it over his arm. Slowly, her eyes fixed on his, Fiona withdrew the pins from her hat and handed it to him, then peeled off her gloves. He waited, expressionless, until she had handed hat and gloves over, then said, 'Please sit down,' and went back into the hall. Fiona wandered around the room, pausing to examine the bookcase, which held a collection of technical books on shipbuilding. To her disappointment there were no photographs to study.

When Robert came back into the room he was carrying a salver containing two filled glasses. She accepted one and sank on to the comfortable sofa, watching as he removed the guard from before the fireplace and knelt to poke the fire, which had been banked up in readiness for his return, into a blaze. Then he drew the curtains, enclosing the two of them in intimate, flame-splashed darkness for a moment as he crossed the room to switch on the electric light.

'You said that you hadn't intended to visit the Palmers tonight. Did you change your mind because—?' Fiona let the sentence linger unfinished on the air and sipped her wine slowly, watching him over the glass.

Robert Archer hesitated before answering. The directors' decision to send Dalkieth to Tyneside instead of himself had infuriated him. The man knew nothing of the questions that should be asked, the observations that had to be made. He would believe anything he was told and would almost certainly return to Ellerslie with a totally erroneous picture of the economic situation in the Southern yards. Robert had gone to the soiree because he knew that if he stayed at home his anger would gnaw at him until it drove him into a pointless, frustrated rage. At such a time it was never a good idea to be alone. Looking up, looking into Fiona's wide long-lashed eyes, he realised that he had been alone too often lately.

Fiona took his silence as a reluctance to commit himself. 'It was because you guessed that I would be there, and knew that George would not.' She got up and moved with short swift steps to the curtained window, the fringed hem of her elegant gown swirling about her calves. The neckline was cut straight across from shoulder to shoulder and she had recently had her hair bobbed; her skin was very white against the rich red of the dress and, as she bent her head, the nape of her slender neck looked touchingly fragile and vulnerable. 'I'm tired of pretending, Robert,' she said in a rush of words. 'Pretending to be happy with George when I'm wretchedly miserable, pretending that I enjoy going to one silly party after another and seeing the same people all the time. Pretending—' She swung round and the light turned the tears in her blue eyes into sapphires. 'Pretending that I don't care—' She stopped herself with a hand pressed tightly to her lips.

'Fiona—' He put his untouched glass down and went to her and she moved to meet him without hesitation. When he put his arms round her, her hair was soft and smooth against his cheek; she lifted her face to his and her mouth fluttered and opened beneath his, the point of her tongue flickering, warm and moist, along his lips.

The coals of restless anger that had been smouldering in him since he heard that George was to go to Tyneside collapsed and became a consuming heat, and it took all his control to push her gently away from him, his hands on her shoulders.

'Fiona, are you sure?'

She closed her eyes and the tears, caught now among her long fair lashes, became diamonds. 'Yes,' she said. 'Oh – yes!'

Fiona was an avid reader of romantic novels. Before George entered her life she had day-dreamed of being wooed and won by handsome, virile lovers but, even so, her feet had always been kept firmly on the ground and she had assumed that such dreams were no more than the stuff of imagination.

But lying in Robert's bed she discovered that dreams could, after all, come true. After months of celibacy his own needs were urgent, and Fiona found herself swept up in a passion that she had never even dared to dream of, kissed and stroked and coaxed into moaning abandon and surrender that at times became almost too much to bear.

When at last they lay exhausted among the tangled sheets, their limbs still twined round each other, she whispered, 'I'm so glad that you decided to attend the soiree after all.'

'So am I.' Robert, sated and at peace, turned his head lazily to kiss her earlobe. They lay in contented silence for a few moments before his body tensed and he said with sudden urgency, 'I hope to God I've not – we haven't—'

'Sensible women know how to take precautions nowadays,' Fiona murmured reassuringly. 'Any child I bear will be my husband's, I can promise you that.'

As she felt his body relax again in her arms she smiled slowly, lazily, thinking to herself that a man with the ability to pleasure a woman as Robert had pleasured her must surely also have the ability to father on her the fine healthy son she so badly needed . . .

George stayed in Tyneside for longer than he had intended, sending back word that he had important business to see to.

'What sort of business?' Robert demanded anxiously of Fiona when she visited him.

She shrugged. 'He just said that it would be of benefit to the yard.'

'But—'

Fiona pouted. 'Don't let's talk about George, or the yard,' she said, going to him, moving her body against his. A shiver of desire shook him; she sensed it and smiled, a cat-like smile of anticipation. 'Let's just be glad that he's given us more time together,' she murmured, her small soft hands busy with the buttons of his shirt. At the touch of her fingers against his skin Robert shuddered again, then swept her off her feet and into his arms.

She was right – he would know what George was up to soon enough. In the meantime, he had urgent business of his own to see to.

But when George Dalkieth came home the news he brought was far worse than anything Robert had imagined, He had become acquainted with a group of English businessmen who had formed a consortium for the purpose of investing in a number of industries, including shipbuilding. On a wave of euphoria at what he saw as his astute business capabilities George smugly informed the Board that he had agreed to make the Dalkieth yard part of their group.

When Fergus Craig, speaking a mere second before Robert, protested, 'But Dalkieth's has always been an independent yard,' George told him loftily, 'And a number of small independent yards like ourselves are going to the wall in England at this very moment. This way we can prosper on new money, investors' money we can use to buy more modern machinery.'

'And in return you lose control of Dalkieth's.' Robert Archer's voice was like ice.

'Not at all. We benefit by an exchange of shares, including shares in a steelworks. We showed a net profit of two hundred and fifty-four thousand pounds last year,' George told his fellow directors, 'We're on the crest of the wave and by God we're going to ride it! Good shipping's still in demand—'

'For the moment,' Robert put in, but George ignored him.

'—and will be for many years to come,' he continued stiffly. 'We paid out a good dividend to our shareholders last year and all the indications are that we shall be able to do so again this year. Why would the consortium want to invest in us if we were about to fail?'

'Because they know nothing about shipbuilding,' Robert Archer said stubbornly. 'They're only interested in making profits – and if they start to lose money they simply sell out as fast as they can and walk away, regardless of the suffering they might leave behind them. If we become linked to other businesses, companies we have no control over whatsoever, it means that if they fail we fail.'

'The consortium is run by men with good business experience,' George blustered.

'Experience in investing money, not in shipbuilding!' Robert looked round the table, his eyes lingering on Isobel Dalkieth. Her gaze dropped before his and he knew, with dismay, that once again George had gone to her first. She had already pledged her support for this mad scheme.

Fergus Craig hurriedly cleared his throat. 'I can see reason in both arguments. As George says, this may seem like a good time to expand, but on the other hand we don't know what the next few years may bring.'

'By that time we'll have money coming in from businesses outwith shipbuilding to keep us going, thanks to the share-exchange scheme. We ourselves use coal, timber, iron and steel, machinery,' George rushed on, expanding on the shining future that had been spread before his delighted gaze in England. 'Linking this yard with associated companies not only saves cost on materials but shares the incomes of these other industries. Look at the Experimental Tank – it has more work than it can comfortably handle from other yards, let alone from our own. We were the first yard to have such a tank. My grandfather had the foresight to invest hard-earned money in that project and it's paid for itself a hundred times over.'

'The Experimental Tank is specialised, in a category of its own. And your grandfather,' Robert added in a voice that would have cut through iron, 'was a man of vision. He didn't choose to spend his money on consortiums or associated industries because he realised that the more entangled a family business like this becomes with outside interests, the less control it enjoys. Has it ever occurred to you how easily this wonderful consortium could collapse if anything out of the ordinary occurred?'

Isobel Dalkieth's head came up suddenly, her eyes meeting Archer's. He saw the doubt in her gaze and said slowly, deliberately, to her alone, 'Ask yourselves how strong their understanding is of the world-wide problems affecting shipbuilding today. And ask yourselves if this is the right time to hand our future success over to men who have never in their lives built ships.'

Her lips parted, but at that moment George thumped a fist on the table, his face purpling. 'Dammit, man, they have controlling

161

interests in Tyneside yards far larger than Dalkieth's! I can assure you that they know their business better than any jumped-up naval architect!'

Robert was on his way round the table to where George sat before he realised that he had got to his feet. George flinched back in his chair as Fergus Craig reached out to clamp a restraining hand on the office manager's arm.

'Gentlemen!' Isobel Dalkieth's voice cut through the room like a whip. 'I will not allow this meeting to turn into a bear-garden!'

There was a pause during which the air crackled and the men around the table shifted uneasily, their eyes flickering from works' manager to office manager and back again. Then Robert Archer jerked his arm free and returned to his own seat.

'I beg your pardon, Mrs Dalkieth. I would like to record my objection – my strong objection – to the matter of the consortium.'

'Your objection is noted.' Isobel's voice was cold as she called for a vote. It was evenly divided, half the directors agreeing with George Dalkieth, half with Robert Archer.

'Yours is the casting vote, Isobel,' her brother told her, his voice husky with apprehension.

She stared down at her hands. The clock on the wall ticked out sixty seconds before she looked up again to say levelly, 'I vote that we agree to an exchange of shares with the consortium – but I suggest that we restrict the number of Dalkieth shares to a level that leaves control in our hands.'

The crack as the pencil between Robert Archer's fingers snapped rang through the small panelled room. When the meeting ended he walked out without speaking to anyone, almost bumping into Jenny. She stumbled and he caught at her arm to steady her, staring down at her as though she was a stranger.

'Robert? Are you ill?'

Recognition came into his grey eyes but the anger was still there, bright and hard.

'I'm sick to my stomach, Jen.' His voice shook with rage. 'I wish to Christ that I'd never set foot in this damned place!'

He released her and walked away with long, angry strides, moving fast, his shoulders hunched and his head pushed forward, throwing himself through the side door into the yard and out of her sight.

George Dalkieth couldn't be trusted to run a wheelbarrow down the middle of a street, let alone run a shipyard, Robert thought savagely as he sat in his small house that evening, a bottle of whisky by his side and a glass in his hand. George was a fool and, thanks to him, Dalkieth's yard was in danger of slipping into the hands of a group of men whose only interest lay in making money, switching fortunes around at will, pledging the assets from one company under their control to raise funds for another. They played a dangerous game and Robert wanted no part of them.

He emptied the glass then refilled it. 'To your damnation, Mrs Isobel Dalkieth,' he said aloud, and half-emptied it with one swallow.

There had been a moment at the meeting when he had seen doubt in the woman's eyes and thought that perhaps this time she would listen to him; then George had managed to rouse him to unwise fury and the scales had tipped in the wrong direction – just a fraction, but enough. She was well aware that her son had no business sense at all but, even so, her maternal instinct was stronger than her undoubted ability for business. As long as George had his mother's support, albeit reluctantly, Robert Archer might as well save his breath to cool his porridge.

He could still walk out, leave the Dalkieths, mother and son, to their own devices and return to Tyneside. He emptied the glass, put a hand to the bottle, then changed his mind. He would need a clear head in the morning.

A sudden delicate waft of lilies-of-the-valley brushed his nostrils as he got into bed an hour later – Fiona's scent, caught in the threads of the pillowcase, teasing him with the memory of her last visit to his bed, only the day before.

He closed his eyes and her lovely body was imprinted on the darkness behind the lids; he could almost feel its silky nakedness against his own skin. His fingers tightened on the pillow at the memory.

He had assumed that George's imminent return would make this their last time together, but to his surprise Fiona had disagreed. 'There are ways and means – we can go on meeting and George won't find out, I promise you.'

She refused to argue, and Robert soon gave up trying to make her see reason, though he knew in his heart that, for everyone's sakes, the affair couldn't be allowed to continue. But now, finding himself clutching at the pillow that bore her scent like some weak, lovesick youth, he knew that the matter was out of his hands. He wanted her – and if the occasion arose he would not be able to deny himself.

There was, too, a certain satisfaction in knowing that, in one way at least, he was getting the better of George Dalkieth.

17

The old man who lived opposite the Youngs grew too feeble to look after himself and, in September, when he was taken off to a married son's home, Bella and Patrick managed to secure the tenancy of his flat. Although Patrick no longer worked at the yard the fact that he had been injured fighting for his country, coupled with his wife's family's history of employment with Dalkieth's, meant that he and Bella were allowed to continue as tenants.

The new flat was only a single room, the same size as the home they already had, but at least there were no stairs to prevent Patrick from getting outside.

'I'm sure he'll be much better once we make the move and he can start getting out and about again,' Bella said, but without much conviction, rubbing hard at the filthy window-pane. She and Jenny had taken on the task of scrubbing the place out before Daniel and Walter whitewashed the walls.

'You should try to get him to apply for one of those special boots to help him to walk.'

'He wouldnae agree tae it before – but mebbe now that he's had time tae think about it—' Bella stopped as the scrubbing brush slithered from her sister's wet hand and Jenny rose and walked unsteadily towards her. 'Jenny?'

'I'm – I'm fine. It's just the heat of the place—' Jenny brushed Bella aside and struggled with the sash, managing to open it an inch. 'I'll ask Daniel if he can put in a new cord to make this easier for you,' she said automatically, then managed to smile at her sister. 'It was just the heat,' she said again.

'But it's cold in here.' Bella eyed her closely. 'Are you sure you're all right?'

'Of course I'm – oh, Bella,' Jenny clutched at her sister's hand. 'It cannae be a bairn, can it?'

'You'd know that better than me.'

'But we've not been married all that long!'

'Four months. Long enough.'

'I've been worrying about it for the past week. I didnae mean to fall

165

wi' a bairn for a year or more, not till things got a bit easier,' Jenny said in a panic.

Bella's gaze held a mixture of pity and envy. 'What's for us won't go past us. And if it's true, you'll manage. Folk always do. Away home and sit down for a wee while. I'll finish off here.'

'You'll do nothing of the kind. I'm fine now,' Jenny drew a deep breath and went back to her work, plunging her hand into the bucket to retrieve the brush. 'There's no need to treat me like an invalid.'

'Is Daniel pleased?'

'There's plenty of time yet.' She rubbed the cracked yellow soap vigorously over the brush's worn bristles.

'You've not told him? I'd have told Pat the first minute I suspected. We both wanted bairns before – before he was hurt.' Then Bella asked shrewdly, 'You're not scared tae tell Daniel, are you? He'll be pleased, Jen, even if it's happened sooner than you meant it to. Look how proud he is of Walter—'

'If you'd talk less and rub that window harder mebbe you'd get it clean,' Jenny snapped, scrubbing at the floor as if she was trying to force the brush through the planks.

It was precisely because of Walter that she had put off telling Daniel her suspicions about a baby. She was afraid that, wrapped up as he was in his ambitions for his son, he wouldn't want the responsibility of raising a second family. But, if she was indeed pregnant, Daniel would have to know, sooner or later.

She sighed, decided that there was no point in fretting until she had to, and concentrated instead on applying herself to forcing years of ingrained dirt out of the worn floorboards.

The move turned into a festive occasion, with the Malloy clan joining in. Even Teeze was there, making up for his inability to carry anything heavy by directing operations. When his chronic bronchitis had finally forced him to leave the shipyard his wife had feared that he would spend most of his time and what little money he had in the public house where Lottie worked. But Teeze had proved her wrong. At first he lay in bed most mornings until midday and spent the afternoons loitering with his cronies at the corner of the street. Then, to everyone's astonishment, he took to helping a former workmate, now retired, who had an allotment near the river.

As far as his family was concerned he was as surly and uncommunicative as ever, but at least he spent less money on drink, and now and again he stamped into the house to toss a small turnip or greens or a handful of potatoes, the earth still clinging to them, on to the table with a grunted, 'I'll have that wi' my dinner.'

Although he no longer worked at Dalkieth's yard, his experience and knowledge was still sought after, and the fact that his son-in-law was a union representative gave him a certain standing at the meetings, official and unofficial, held on at least one evening every week, usually in a large room in the Burgh Halls.

Jenny and Alice were convinced that their grandmother's death had something to do with the change in Teeze. Marion had dominated him all his life; even when she was a helpless invalid her very presence in his house had unsettled him. It was sad, Jenny thought as she watched him oversee Daniel, Walter and Maureen's husband Jacko struggling to ease the Kerr's bedframe out on to the upper landing, that anyone should be so hated and feared that their death meant liberation for others.

Lottie was the only member of the family who didn't help with the move. Helen was there, scurrying about, wild with excitement and getting in everyone's way.

'Careful, pet, you'll get hurt,' Jenny cautioned as her niece ran across the room and almost collided with the bedframe. She lifted the little girl out of harm's way, cuddling the warm wriggling little body in her arms.

'Here, give her tae me.' Faith ordered, taking Helen from her. 'You go down and make some tea – they'll all be parched by now. Go on,' she added as Jenny began to protest. 'You need a rest, ye shouldnae be doin' too much at a time like this.'

'What's Bella been—'

Faith eyed her daughter, and a faint smile softened her mouth. Since the day she had finally accepted that Maurice would never come home a new understanding had developed between her and Jenny. Not open affection, for the Gillespies weren't an affectionate family, but an almost sisterly rapport, the sort of special relationship that only women can share. 'Bella's not said a word, but I'm no' daft. I've had six of my own and I know the signs.'

When the furniture was in place Mr Malloy sent two of his brood out to the public house for some beer and his wife and Faith produced sandwiches and home-made scones and tea. Bella's habitual air of exhaustion and worry was gone for once and she looked as happy as she had on her wedding day when the future had been spread out before her like a carpet of crimson and gold. Jenny glanced from her to Patrick, clutching a glass of beer, smiling over something Jacko was saying to him. It was only a shadow of the grin that used to split his handsome young face almost in two, but it was a beginning.

Cautiously, Jenny let herself hope that this move would be a new beginning for them all, and that they were finally going to emerge from the shadows of the war that had so cruelly ripped their lives apart in different ways.

'Walter and your sister seem tae know each other well,' Daniel said a few hours later when they were back in their own home and Walter had been packed off to his bed.

'It's just a friendship, Daniel.'

'Aye, well, just you mind that the boy's got a long road tae go if he wants tae get on.' In one gulp he drank down half the scalding tea Jenny had just poured out.

'For goodness' sake! Alice is working hard at school herself, she's got ambitions of her own.'

His dark deep-set eyes studied her suspiciously. 'You think so? Lassies know they can aye get married, but a man has tae make his own way. I'll not have anyone encouraging Walter tae take time away from his books.'

Jenny felt irritation well up and tried to quell it. 'My sister's not interested in marriage.'

'She'll change her mind as soon as she finds some man tae look after her.' He emptied his cup and pushed it over for a refill, wiping his mouth with the back of his free hand. 'Just mind that it's no' goin' tae be my Walter.'

'So you're even going to deny him marriage, are you?'

'He'll find the right wife at the right time. But first he's got the university in front of him.'

Jenny, about to pour more tea into her own cup, set the pot down carefully on the range. 'Daniel, have you ever wondered if Walter wants to go to the university?'

'Eh? What laddie wouldnae want it?'

'He might not be clever enough—'

'He is!' Daniel said fiercely. 'I know he is! I'm warnin' you, Jenny, don't you or yer sister try tae make him think otherwise.' He drained his cup again and got to his feet. 'I'll away an' take a turn round the back yard.'

'Before you go, I've something to tell you.' Jenny smoothed her apron carefully over her flat stomach, suddenly nervous. 'I'm – I'm going to have a bairn.'

He stared, his pale face dismayed, then said, 'Ye're sure?'

'I'm sure.'

'Oh, God.' Daniel sank down into the chair he had just left. 'I thought you said you knew how to take care of that sort of thing.'

'I tried, but—' She had intended to make use of sponges soaked in vinegar and pessaries of water and flour, but she couldn't tell him that his refusal to make love to her with his son in the house, the hurried, urgent couplings whenever Walter happened to be out, gave her little chance to make use of the knowledge she had gleaned from the other tenement women.

'Ye'll have tae stop work, then.'

'Not for a while. I'll not let on to anyone at the Tank until I have to.' She hadn't even thought of having to leave the tracing office, and Daniel's reminder sent a pang through her. She loved her work.

He went without another word and stayed out for longer than usual; Jenny was in bed long before she heard his step in the close. He put out the remaining gas mantel as soon as he came into the room, undressing in the dark, and when at last he came to bed they lay silently apart from each other as usual. She longed to reach out and touch his hand, but didn't dare. Instead she said after the clock on the wall had ticked several minutes by, 'Daniel, are you vexed with me?'

'Go tae sleep,' he said. Then, after another silence, 'No sense in frettin' yerself. We'll manage.'

She released her breath in a long sigh of relief, and was drifting off to sleep when Daniel spoke again, his own voice drowsy, 'This new one'll have Walter as an example. It means I'll have two sons tae be proud of.'

Suddenly sleep fled and Jenny lay awake far into the night, worrying about the child she was carrying, while beside her Daniel slept.

The contract with the English consortium was signed and a generous slice of the Dalkieth shares were relinquished in return for shares in Tyneside yards as well as an iron and steel works. Flushed with success, George paid a second visit to Tyneside in October to cultivate the new friends he had made there.

'As far as I'm concerned he can go to England as often as he wants,' Fiona said happily, making use of her husband's absence to visit Robert.

'The thing is, what harm's he doing while he's there?'

Fiona curled up in the corner of the sofa, tucking her slim, silk-clad legs beneath her and smiling at her lover possessively. 'I don't care, as long as he's doing it elsewhere.' She had never been happier. With George out of the way she was mistress in her own home, freed from his unwelcome attentions, able to visit Robert whenever she could manage to slip away. 'Stop talking about George, and come here.'

Robert, leaning against the mantelshelf, looked down at her. She wore a misty blue tweed suit, the jacket lying open over a cream silk blouse that followed the curves of her breasts. The top button was unfastened, giving a glimpse of smooth skin below the soft hollow at the base of her throat. Her eyes were as blue and clear as a summer sky and her skin glowed. The sulky pout she had always worn when he first knew her had vanished.

'You look more beautiful each time I see you.' He took her hand and let her draw him down to her side.

'That's because I'm happy.' Fiona's hand cupped his face, and he turned and let his mouth nestle into her palm. 'Leave him, Fiona,' he said against her hand. 'Come to me.'

'Leave George? I couldn't do that!'

'Why not?'

'He's my husband.'

'Divorce him.' Robert took her into his arms and kissed her. He hadn't meant to say it so soon, but being with her again, knowing that it couldn't be for long, had given him impetus. Stupidly, he had lost Jenny to another man by leaving Ellerslie and entangling himself in a disastrous marriage, and now that he had found love again he didn't want to lose it in the same way. 'Let him divorce you.'

'But the scandal—'

'We don't have to worry about the scandal. Let Ellerslie topple off its foundations with shock – we'll be far away, you and I. We could start a new life in England, or even abroad. I could find work anywhere.'

Fiona appalled, pushed him away and sat upright. 'Robert, I couldn't possibly. The Dalkieths – my f-father—' Dismay entangled her tongue. This was not part of her plan.

'Your father and the Dalkieths be damned! Fiona, I mean it. I could make you happy, you know I could.'

Fiona liked to be in control of situations, and this one was slipping away from her. She fought to regain it, drawing Robert's head back down to hers, letting her lips flutter against his face as she spoke. 'Please, my love, give me a little time to think about it. Surely that isn't too much to ask?'

Her fingers skilfully loosened his waistcoat, slid between the fastenings of his shirt to stroke his chest. His need for her flared up in him like a forest fire and, with a soft moan, he buried his mouth in the hollow at the base of her throat.

Just over a mile away, on the other side of the river, another fire blazed, this time in the grate of the drawing room in Dalkieth House.

Fergus Craig stretched out his feet and sipped the last of his whisky, drawing comfort from the warmth of the flames and the spirit's excellent bouquet. Isobel paced the room, moving restlessly between

170

fireplace and window, then back again. Her upright figure was clothed, as usual, in black, but even so her silk and wool dress was stylish, cut straight across at the neck from shoulder to shoulder. The bodice was embroidered with jet beading echoed on the three-quarter-length sleeves and the sash at the low waist of the dress was caught by a large square jet buckle. Her diamond and sapphire ring flashed as she fingered her long pearl and jet necklace

'It was a mistake to bring Robert Archer into the company,' she announced. 'A mistake, Fergus! I wish I'd never let myself be persuaded into it.'

Fergus thought longingly of his own comfortable drawing room. He and his wife had intended to have an evening at home together, Elspeth busy with her knitting, he himself studying a new book on ornithology which had been delivered that day from his bookseller. He had been unwrapping it when Isobel's summons had arrived. 'He's proved himself to be very able.' He wrenched his mind from what might have been and forced it back to the present.

'Oh, I grant him that,' Isobel said impatiently, pausing to pick up her own glass and toss down a mouthful of whisky. 'But he and George – they're like chalk and cheese, oil and water. They've each got their own ideas and neither will budge an inch. It's causing confusion to the other directors and considerable worry to me. The Dalkieth Board has always been used to strong leadership, Fergus – always! Now look at us – the minute you put George and young Archer into the same room they're at each other's throats. Dear God, the directors' meetings have become more like dog-fights than anything else.'

'You agreed at the time that we needed a balance of views, Isobel.' He looked down into his empty glass, wondering if he could help himself to more whisky. Isobel was usually very generous with the decanter but today she was in such a pet that she seemed to have forgotten her duties as a hostess. 'George has the family background, and young Archer possesses a very good brain, not to mention his experience. One gives his views, the other counters with his – and the Board weighs up both opinions and makes the final decision. That's what we planned.'

'That might be what we planned, George,' said his sister in ringing tones. 'But in reality if one of them says black's black the other's sure to insist that it's white – while the rest of the directors sit there in utter bewilderment like a flock of hens scared to open their beaks in case either George or young Archer turns on them.' She emptied her own glass and refilled it from the decanter on a side table then stoppered the decanter and banged it down so hard on its silver tray that her

171

brother fully expected the crystal to crack and the whisky he desired more strongly with each passing moment to spill all its goodness into the carpet below.

'The Board members are often waiting for your decision, my dear. They rely heavily on your judgement.'

Isobel passed a hand over her smooth white hair. 'And I find it more and more difficult to make a judgement.'

'I can see that if George wasn't your son, it would be easier for you to form a – more detached opinion of his arguments,' Craig said delicately.

'Fergus, I'm shocked! I have never let favouritism sway me in the slightest and I never will!'

'I didn't say that you favoured the boy, Isobel, I merely said—'

'Besides, you know that I myself can't stand George. He irritates me more and more – and there's Fiona, as flat in the stomach as ever she was with still no sign of a child yet,' Isobel said, off on a tangent. 'Next thing we know the young fool will be talking about divorce again, and how I'll cope with the shame of that I don't know. It's just that—' she stopped, staring down into her glass, her brow furrowed, then said, 'George is family, Fergus, even though he is a fool. And Robert Archer may be very clever – I certainly can't fault his behaviour apart from an occasional abrasive lapse that I'm generously willing to overlook – but when it comes down to it, one can scarcely oppose one's own flesh and blood, not to mention one's own class.'

There was a slight pause before she said more briskly, 'And then there's the unions.'

'The unions?' asked Fergus Craig in bewilderment, then flinched back into the cushions of his chair as his sister suddenly swooped down on him. Memories of nursery fights of sixty years before, when Isobel had been known to use teeth and nails ruthlessly in order to get her own way, suddenly flooded his mind and it was all he could do to suppress an involuntary yelp of fear.

'My dear Fergus, you've clearly had more than enough to drink,' said Isobel, whipping the empty glass from his fingers and returning it to the tray with another crash. 'Your mind's all fuddled, just when I'm relying on you to help me sort things out. Never before have the unions been in Dalkieth's yard – never. Edward and his father must be birling in their graves. It only happened after you talked me into making Robert Archer office manager.'

'Isobel, the war changed the face of Britain. The unions were bound to come in sooner or later.' Privately, Fergus thought that if George had been in sole charge the unions would have run riot over

172

the yard by this time. Thanks to young Archer's level-headedness unions and management worked better together in Dalkieth's yard than in many others, and were set to continue doing so.

'And the workforce expects so much these days,' Isobel was saying. He was glad to note that the whisky's mellowing effect was beginning to show and some of the fire was going out of her. 'They never used to be so demanding, Fergus. They knew their place in the old days, and they were grateful to employers for looking after them. Look at the fine tenements the Dalkieths built for their workers on this side of the river. They cost a great deal of money, but nobody ever stops to think of that when they're talking of labourers being worthy of their hire.'

'Times change, my dear. And, talking of time, I ought to be going.' Craig began to struggle to his feet. His stomach was bothering him again, as often happened when he spent too much time in Isobel's company. And there was a very fine malt waiting for him in a cupboard in his library.

'Can't you stay a little longer?'

Fergus consulted the handsome silver watch slung across his stomach. 'Elspeth will be expecting me back.' His voice was almost pleading.

'The truth of the matter is, Fergus,' his sister sank into a chair, her voice slow and subdued, 'It's all such a burden, and we're none of us getting any younger, are we?' Her fingers caressed her left hand, lingering on the magnificent engagement ring and the worn plain gold band beneath it. 'I wish William was still alive – and Edward. They would know what should be done.'

She looked up, and Fergus saw that her blue eyes sparkled, not with impatience now, but with tears. Isobel had always been undeniably beautiful, and at that moment she was also vulnerable, a mixture of the impetuous child she had once been and the old, rather tired woman she had become. Strangely, his own eyes began to sting a little. He subsided back into the chair he had almost freed himself from.

'Perhaps I can stay – for a little while,' he said gently, round a lump that had begun to form in his throat.

18

'D'you realise the chances you're giving up? You could have been a schoolteacher yourself – anything you put your mind to,' Jenny said in despair. 'Why didn't you tell me that you were planning to leave the Academy?'

'Because I knew you'd talk me out of it. Why else d'you think I waited until I'd got Mr Monroe to agree to take me on full time before I said a word to Mam?' Alice was unrepentant. 'Anyway, I'd never have made a decent teacher – I've not got the patience, for one thing. I'd have become a grumpy old witch by the time I turned twenty-five.'

'You've given up your schooling because of me, haven't you?' Jenny felt guilt settle heavily on her shoulders. 'Just because I'm going to have to stop work. But we've talked about it, me and Daniel, and we can still manage to—'

'It's nothing to do with your baby, so don't start fretting about that. It's what I want to do, Jen. I just wish Mam hadnae told you.'

'But don't you see—'

'Ach, leave her be,' Faith advised from the sink, where she was bathing her little granddaughter. 'Will you keep that towel on, Helen? You'll catch your death of cold!'

Naked, and seemingly oblivious to the cold early December air that blew through the cracks in the ill-fitting window frame beside her, the little girl sat on the draining board with her feet in the sink, bent double so that she could dabble her hands in the water. When Faith tried to tuck the towel more securely round her shoulders, she shrugged it off. 'Don't want it!'

'Well don't expect me tae fret over you when you start coughing,' her grandmother warned. 'Jenny, our Alice was always one tae go her own way and you'll just tire yourself out arguin' with her. Shut your eyes, now, Helen.'

She poured a jugful of warm water over the child's head to rinse the soap out of her hair. Helen squeaked and gurgled then gasped, inhaling water. Alice, laughing, went over to wrap the towel round

175

her plump body then scooped her up, carrying her to Teeze's empty chair where she sat down, the little girl in her lap.

'You're a right water baby, aren't you?' she said as Helen's face emerged from the folds of the towel, blinking.

'I'm not a baby!' three-year-old Helen said indignantly.

Jenny lifted the small patched gown from the wooden clotheshorse before the range, where it had been airing and sat down on Faith's chair. 'Come and sit on my knee, Helen, and I'll help you to put your wee gown on.'

'She's awful heavy now,' Alice said doubtfully.

'Tuts, I'm not made of glass! The bairn's not due until May – I'm scarcely showing yet.'

'Here she comes, then, big heavy lump that she is.' Alice jumped up and with an exaggerated heave swung Helen, squealing with excitement, into the air then down on to Jenny's lap.

'Again!' Helen demanded, holding out her arms and wriggling like an eel in Jenny's arms.

'You behave yourself, young lady, or I'll send you to bed without any supper,' Alice told her, her face twisted into a scowl. 'See, Jen? I'd make a terrible teacher. I'd have all the weans in tears.' Then, dropping back into her chair, she said with a sudden change of voice, 'Anyway, I never wanted to teach.'

'But you never said—'

'It was Maurice's idea, then yours, but never mine,' said Alice. 'I just wanted to please the two of you, but now I've decided that the person I should really try to please is myself.'

Looking at her sister over the damp curls that had already begun to spring back into place on Helen's head, Jenny realised that seemingly overnight her little sister had grown up. Now that Alice was no longer a schoolgirl she had drawn her brown hair into a bun at the back of her head and, under her apron, she wore a black skirt and striped blouse instead of her usual school clothes. There was a new air of purpose about her.

With a sense of shock, Jenny realised that she – and Maurice, when he was alive – had fallen into the same trap as Daniel. Because Alice showed signs of being cleverer than the rest of her family, they had tried to steer her along the path that they themselves might have wanted to take, had they had her abilities. But Alice had had the strength of character to make her own decisions. Would Walter have the courage to do the same?

'If you ask me, it's time this young madam had a good starving anyway,' Alice said just then, prodding Helen in the stomach and making her wriggle so hard that she tumbled off Jenny's knee and on to the floor, howling with laughter just as her mother came into the kitchen on a waft of sharp, cheap scent, her red hair fastened on top of her head, glittering earrings dangling from her ears.

Helen, the nightgown half on and half off, picked herself up and ran over to her, to be pushed away.

'For goodness' sake, don't paw at me like that! Go and get dressed. This place sounds like a bear-garden,' Lottie said, and Alice sniffed loudly then fanned the air, winking at Jenny.

'Funny, that's not what it *smells* like,' she commented blandly. 'I'd say it smells like a bro—'

'That's enough from you, miss!' Faith interrupted loudly while Lottie, slipping her arms into a new coat, glared.

'I'll mebbe be late back tonight,' she told Faith then walked out without a further glance at her daughter. They heard the outside door banging, then Lottie's heels clacking down the stairs.

The laughter had vanished from Helen's face. It crumpled, then was straightened with a visible effort of will as she began to work at pushing her arm into an empty sleeve.

'She'll mebbe not be back at all.' Alice took a small bowl down from a shelf and began to break stale bread into it.

'You mean she stays out all night?' Jenny asked, horrified. 'You never told me about this, Mam.'

'Because it's none of your business,' Faith said brusquely, with a warning glance at the little girl.

'Go and fetch my brush, Helen, and I'll do your hair for you,' Alice suggested. When the three women were alone, she took the weighted muslin cover off the milk jug and stirred milk into the broken bread. 'Lottie does stay out all night sometimes,' she told Jenny, scattering a spoonful of sugar over the mush in the bowl. 'And she never does a thing for that poor wee soul.'

'Is she still walking out with Neil Baker?'

'Aye.' Faith emptied the teapot into the sink then reached up to the high mantelshelf for the caddy. 'He'll be waitin' out in the street for her, tae walk her tae work.'

'It was him that bought her that coat. I just hope they get married.' Alice poured some hot water on to the bread and milk mixture then relinquished the kettle to her mother before adding, 'We'd all be glad to see the back of her.'

'And what'll happen to Helen then?'

'I'd keep her here in a minute,' Faith said at once.

'So would I,' Alice agreed, 'for she's a pleasure to be with. But she's Lottie's bairn, Mam, not ours. And mebbe it would be good for her to have a proper father.'

Helen hurried back into the room just then, the gown now on, though twisted round her plump little body. 'I'll do it myself,' she announced, and started swiping at her own head with the brush.

'And after it's done you'll have to eat up all this break and milk, because we're fattening you up for Christmas, so that we'll have something nice to eat,' Alice told her, and Helen giggled against the outspread fingers of her free hand, then yelled as the hairbrush got caught up in a tangle of red hair.

Although it was only three o'clock in the afternoon the lights were on in George Dalkieth's drawing room, illuminating the silver tinsel that decorated the large Christmas tree in the bay window.

Robert Archer, striding up the driveway, his booted feet splintering thin ice and splashing heedlessly through puddles, ignored the pretty picture that the tree made. He rapped sharply on the front door, then descended the two curved stone steps and paced up and down the drive, impervious to the thin snow that was beginning to fall, spinning round when the door opened to glower at the maidservant.

'Tell Mrs Dalkieth that Robert Archer would like to speak to her,' he snapped, striding up the steps. The girl faltered back and he marched past her into a narrow hallway.

'I'll see if madam—'

'On a matter of some urgency,' said the caller grimly, and the maid, who had begun to hold out her hand for his hat, gave a muffled squeak and let her arm fall back to her side as she turned and scuttled through an adjacent doorway. Archer dropped his hat on to a half-moon table set against one wall and was peeling off his gloves when the girl reappeared.

'This way, sir.'

In the drawing room a fire blazed in the grate. The room was bright with paper chains strung from the light-fitting in the centre of the ceiling to the four corners, and smelled strongly of fresh pine needles. Fiona stood beside a large and handsome sideboard which held a small cardboard box and the model of a stable, together with some figurines. In her hand she held a small plaster statuette of the Madonna, her painted robe the same colour as Fiona's soft woollen dress.

'Mr Archer, this is a surprise.' Her eyes flickered past him to the maid, hovering in the doorway. 'My husband isn't at home—'

'It was you I called to see.' He stood stolidly in the middle of the room, an alien presence in the midst of the cheerful Christmas preparations.

178

'Indeed? You'll take some tea?'

'No thank you.'

'Then you can go, Margaret,' Fiona told the servant calmly. As the door closed, leaving them alone, her tone sharpened.' What are you doing here, Robert? You know you sh—'

'Is it true?'

'Is what true?'

'Don't play games with me, Fiona!' said Archer coldly. Her colour deepened and her eyes slid away from his. She fidgeted with the figurine. 'Are you expecting a child?'

Fiona put the Madonna down very carefully. 'As a matter of fact, I am expecting George's child, but—'

'You're sure that it's his?'

Her gaze was suddenly cold and direct. 'Of course.'

'Are you certain it's not mine, Fiona?'

Her hands flew protectively to her waist. 'I told you – I always took precautions!' Then, as he said nothing, she added defensively, 'I was going to tell you—'

'You haven't come near me for weeks!' He wanted to take hold of her and shake her, but, mindful of the servants nearby, he kept his hands fisted by his sides.

'I – it was difficult for me to get away. And I didn't know how to break the news to you that it must end between us.

'So you decided to let me hear it from my housekeeper!'

Fiona ran the tip of her tongue over her lips and then, aware of the way his eyes followed the movement, turned away and dipped into the open box, bringing out a crib complete with baby. 'So it's all over the town already?'

'Of course it is. This town delights in gossip, and George Dalkieth seems to be a rich source,' he said bitterly. 'Everyone knows he divorced his first wife because she didn't give him an heir. Everyone knew about the child she later bore her second husband.'

Fiona carefully positioned the crib before the stable, then placed Mary and Joseph behind it so that they looked down on the child, Joseph kneeling, Mary standing, serenity painted on both faces.

'Your mother-in-law must be delighted with your – success, Fiona.'

'Robert, I know I should have had the courage to tell y—' Her words ended in a gasp as his impatience got the better of him and he caught her arm, swinging her round to face him. She smelled, as always, of lily-of-the-valley and, beneath the woollen sleeve, he could feel the fragile bones of her elbow, the warmth of her skin.

'I've already asked you to come away with me. I've not changed my mind on that,' he said, his voice low and intense. 'If this child you're carrying is mine, there's no need for you to be afraid to tell me. I promise you that I'll welcome it and love it and care for it—'

'There's no question of it being yours! Is it my fault that my husband's first wife didn't conceive his child, while I did?'

'Swear to me, Fiona, that it's his child you're carrying, and not mine?'

'I will!' She looked up at him, her blue eyes wide and sincere. 'On a Bible, if you wish.'

'That won't be necessary,' he said quietly, and released her.

'Robert – Robert, you were a good friend to me when I badly needed a friend.' She was anxious to keep a pleasant façade between them so that there would be no comment about any sudden hostility towards her on his part on future social occasions.

'I'd hoped I was more than that, Fiona.' He swung out of the door and into the hall, snatching up his hat and gloves, wrenching the front door open.

As he stepped through the open double gates and turned to walk back to his own home a car came towards him, slowing to take the turn into the driveway he had just left. Glancing at it he saw Isobel Dalkieth staring at him through the side window. He nodded to her and walked on, wondering indifferently what explanation Fiona would give for his visit.

No doubt she would think of something, and frankly he didn't care what it was. He was sick with the humiliation of discovering that he hadn't meant as much to Fiona Dalkieth as he had fondly imagined.

The latch of his wrought-iron garden stuck the first time he pushed at it, and he jabbed his hand down again, impatiently, releasing the latch but tearing the skin down the side of his thumb. The wound stung, and when he was inside the house with the lights on he saw that blood dripped from his hand. He sucked it away, and more welled up as he opened the whisky decanter. Impatiently, he held his hand over the hearth and poured whisky on to it, drawing his breath in through set teeth as the alcohol burned through the torn skin. Then he sloshed a generous amount of whisky into a glass, and threw himself down on to a chair.

Three times he had genuinely cared for a woman, and three times he had suffered. His marriage had been a mistake on both sides, and when he and his wife had finally agreed to end it he had known only relief. He had lost Jenny through his own selfish stupidity, and had perhaps lost her again when he returned to Ellerslie because, absorbed in his new career with the Dalkieth shipyard, he hadn't taken the time or the trouble to woo her as he should, to overcome her natural resentment at his earlier desertion.

And then, older and wiser though he should have been by that time, he had fallen for Fiona, believed her when she said that she truly loved him.

She had never intended their affair to be anything but an affair, he told himself bitterly as he refilled his glass. No matter what she thought of George Dalkieth she valued the social position she enjoyed as his wife. Robert, born in the tenements, could never offer her anything as grand as the Dalkieth name.

As for the child – he emptied his glass and got up to fill it again – what did it matter who had fathered it? Clearly Fiona had decided that it would be born a Dalkieth, and there was an end of the matter.

His hand still throbbed, but at least the alcohol was beginning to dull the anger, and the humiliation. A man knew where he stood with a good malt whisky, Robert thought with muzzy satisfaction as he fetched a fresh bottle from the cupboard.

In the first weeks of 1921 one of the building berths in the Dalkieth yard fell vacant unexpectedly, due to the last-minute cancellation of a vessel that had been ordered by one of their major customers. The clients, a firm of shipping merchants in the Far East, were hit by an unexpected world-wide drop in freight charges, and were not the only company to find themselves forced to take a second look at their order books and cut back on planned expansion.

George Dalkieth promptly committed the empty berth to a steam yacht commissioned by an industrialist he had met in Tyneside, a member of the consortium.

'But everyone knows that Dalkieth's yard builds commercial vessels, not pleasure boats!' Daniel fretted to Jenny. 'What are they thinking of, giving up valuable space to pleasure boats?'

It was a Saturday afternoon, with the week's work over, and a pile of ironing to be tackled. Jenny placed two flat-irons on the range where they would heat up quickly. 'It's surely better to use the berth than let it lie idle, Daniel.'

'Aye, but—' A frown puckered his brow, 'They're sayin' that the market's beginnin' tae fail, and surely this is a sign of it. Even George Dalkieth wouldnae give up a good berth tae some rich man's toy if there was the chance of a better order. And I've heard that some of the larger yards down South are askin' their men tae take a cut in wages.'

'That'll not happen up here, surely.' Jenny, spreading a protective blanket over the kitchen table, tried to sound confident, but Daniel's concern worried her, for he wasn't one to fret over unfounded rumour and gossip. She poured water into a bowl to damp the clothes during the ironing.

'I hope not.' He reached for his jacket. 'I'm away tae a meetin'.' It seemed to Jenny that he was always at some meeting or other these days.

When he had gone she made sure that the irons were heating then wrapped a heavy shawl about her head and shoulders and, fetching a basket, went out to the darkening back court, festooned as usual with clothes-lines. It had been a cold day, but dry, and like all the other women in the tenements, she liked to get her washing out in the fresh air whenever possible.

Every item on the line, shirts and blouses, socks and trousers and Daniel's and Walter's vests and long johns, was frozen solid and she had trouble folding them to get them into the basket. The ice through the fabrics crackled and snapped, and her hands were soon numbed with the cold. Bending to push a mutinous pair of trousers into the basket Jenny was suddenly swept by a wave of dizziness and had to clutch at the nearby clothes-pole until the courtyard stopped swinging about her like a carousel and swayed to a standstill.

She heard boots skittering over the cobblestones, then Walter's voice asking sharply, 'Are ye all right? D'ye want me tae fetch Bella?' His hand was firm beneath her elbow, his young face concerned.

'I'm fine.' She blinked and smiled into his steady dark eyes, so like his father's. 'It must have been all that bending and stretching.'

'Sit down for a minute.' He steered her towards an upturned orange box then went back and finished taking in the washing, working swiftly and deftly. When the frozen clothes had all been subdued he scooped the basket under one long arm and came back to ease her to her feet and escort her into the welcome warmth of the kitchen, where he put the basket down near the range to let the clothes thaw out.

'I'll make a cup of tea then see tae the ironin' – you sit down and rest.'

'I'll do nothing of the kind. I'm over it now,' she told him firmly, taking the cups from the dresser.

Walter hesitated, fiddling with the stiff corner of a shirt that poked over the edge of the basket. Watching him from the corner of her eye as she moved about the kitchen, Jenny was aware of a wave of affection for him. In the seven months since her marriage to his father she had come to love Walter, a love born out of pity for the boy who carried such a burden of responsibility and paternal ambition on his thin shoulders. Only ten days away from his fourteenth birthday, Walter was still gawky and awkward, in some ways touchingly young for his age, yet in other ways, such as his concern for her, quite mature.

He had, as was expected, done very well in his scholarship examination, so instead of leaving his schooldays behind he would be moving to the Academy at the end of the month. Then, Jenny knew, Daniel would expect even more effort from him.

'Have you finished your homework?'

'Long since.' The material between his fingers was limp and damp now, and Walter blew on his numbed fingers to warm them.

'Why don't you go out for a wee while, then?'

'My father—'

'Your father's off on union business and he'll not be back for a good hour or more, You can have some time to yourself and be back at your books long before then.' She studied him and saw that although his cheeks and nose were bright red from being out in the yard, his face was pale and he looked tired. 'It's not good for a laddie of your age to be sitting over school-books all the time.'

Hope gleamed in Walter's eyes. 'If you're sure it'd be all right—'

'I'm sure. Go on now – but keep moving, I don't want you to catch cold.' Jenny measured tea-leaves into the pot then added water as Walter ducked into the hall. He re-appeared almost at once to say shyly, 'Jenny?'

'Aye?'

'I'm – I'm pleased you're living here.' His face was flushed now with embarrassment. 'And I'm pleased about the bairn. I hope it's a wee lassie.'

'Your father wants another son.'

'Well, I think a wee sister would be nice,' he said with an almost conspiratorial grin, and went. She caught sight of herself in the mirror on the mantelshelf and saw that there was a broad smile of pleasure on her face.

She had come to realise that giving Walter some freedom when his father was away from the house was the only way in which she could help the boy. The attempts she made to stand up to Daniel on Walter's behalf since her marriage had resulted in him accusing his son unfairly of trying to hide behind a woman's skirts.

Walter was no sooner gone than he was back again. 'There's a visitor for you,' he said, and hurried off to make the most of his unexpected hour of freedom as Lizzie Caldwell walked into the kitchen, smiling self-consciously.

'I'm down from Glasgow for my sister's wedding – you mind Annie? – and I thought I'd just look in and see how you are. I can't stay long.' She took off her stylish woollen coat then settled herself in a chair by the range, glancing around the kitchen. Jenny, hanging the coat behind the kitchen door, was uncomfortably aware of the underwear suspended from the overhead pulley and the ironing blanket spread in readiness over the table. She swooped on the basket of thawing clothes and pushed it under the wall-bed out of sight, then took the cups and saucers down from the shelf.

'This is a pretty cup – did you paint it yourself, Jenny?' Lizzie asked as she accepted her tea. 'It's unusual.'

Daniel had been so pleased with the cups and saucers Jenny had painted at his request that she had gone on to decorate the entire set, teapot and all, using bold bright colours in a mixture of geometrical shapes she had found in one of Walter's mathematics books.

Lizzie surveyed Jenny over the rim of the cup as she took a sip, then returned it to the saucer and said, with a glint of amusement, 'You've – grown.'

Jenny laughed and put a hand to the small bulge below her apron, then looked enviously at her friend's trim figure. 'And you've shrunk!'

Lizzie looked down smugly at her beige skirt and dark green knitted top. Her hat was also beige, like her coat, a small-brimmed cloche trimmed with a green feather. 'To tell you the truth, I'm wearing one of the emporium's best corsets, though I've lost weight since I left Ellerslie. Now that I'm in charge of ladies' underwear I like to look smart for our clients, so I watch what I eat.' She smoothed her skirt. 'I bought this from the emporium, too – I get a discount on clothes there, being a supervisor.'

She wore a discreet touch of lipstick, Jenny noticed, and her thick eyebrows had been plucked out and new brows, delicately arched, pencilled in. They gave her ordinary face a slightly sophisticated, quizzical look that suited it.

'I heard about your gran. Your mother must have taken it hard. I mind how well she looked after the old woman.'

'She's over it now. And our Alice is out of school and all but running Munroe's pawnshop,' Jenny said proudly. 'She's got a great head for business.'

'You didn't do so badly yourself. Supervisor at the tracing office, no less.'

'I'll have to finish there soon.'

Lizzie sipped her tea, then turned the cup round slowly, studying the design. 'I'll need to get you to do a set for me some time.' She accepted more tea, then launched into a vivacious account of her work in Glasgow and the clients who insisted on asking for her personally each time they came in.

'You'd have done well, Jen, if you'd only come with me. Are you sorry you didn't?'

'A wee bit,' Jenny said, then, aware that the words sounded disloyal to Daniel, she added quickly, 'but I'm happy enough in Ellerslie.'

'Are you? Lizzie's eyes beneath the elegant new brows were bird-sharp. 'I heard that Robert Archer's back at the yard,' she added casually, taking cigarettes and matches out of her leather bag.

'He's the office manager there.'

'That's someone else who's done well for himself. Was it not difficult for you, him coming back to Ellerslie, I mean?'

'The past's past,' Jenny told her shortly. 'Anyway, he got married in England – as you no doubt heard.' Lizzie's sister Annie was an incurable gossip and Lizzie must have been kept well informed of everything that had gone on during her absence.

'I'd heard he was divorced and living in a nice house with a housekeeper to look after him.' Lizzie blew out a plume of smoke, the cigarette propped elegantly between plump but well-manicured fingers. 'When you think of him all those years ago, always looking as if that aunt of his didnae give him enough tae eat—' Her genteel tones began to blur at the edges as she slipped smoothly into local gossip.

'Lottie's walking out with Neil Baker these days. D'ye mind him?' Jenny asked.

'That naval architect that couldnae keep his hands tae himself? She's setting her sights high. D'ye think she'll manage tae catch him?' Lizzie asked, diverted. Her voice rose and fell and when Jenny finally looked up at the clock she realised that time had gone by faster than she had thought. Walter hadn't yet returned and Daniel would be home soon.

Lizzie interpreted her glance and got to her feet. 'I'd best go – I told Annie I'd not be long. It was nice seeing you again, Jenny,' she said as she slid her arms into her coat sleeves then drew on her beige kid gloves. 'If you're ever in Glasgow come and visit me.' She reached into her bag and brought out a flat parcel. 'I brought this for you from the emporium – it's a remainder of some of our best material,' she added casually as Jenny unfolded the brown paper and exclaimed with pleasure over the fine cream muslin sprigged with tiny pink and blue flowers. 'I thought you could mebbe make a wee gown for the bairn.'

'More than one – this'll do two or three.' Jenny stroked the material. 'Oh thank you, Lizzie, it's kind of you.'

'It's nothing,' said Lizzie airily. At the close door she said, suddenly wistful, 'I wish you could have come with me, Jen. You'd have loved Glasgow.'

'I'm happy as I am,' Jenny said firmly.

Lizzie's gaze swept over her friend's swelling, aproned figure. 'Well – if it's what you want—' she said, and went off along the close, her heels tapping crisply on the stone flags.

Back in the kitchen Jenny studied herself in the mirror on the mantelshelf. She looked pale and tired; wisps of hair fell across her face, and there was a downward droop that she hadn't been aware of at the corners of her mouth. She was beginning to look like the other housewives in the tenements, the women who had had to struggle all their lives, making ends meet, scraping the rent money together week after week, only just managing to keep themselves and their families going with nothing left over for luxuries.

The latch on the outer door rattled, and Walter hurried in. 'I met some of the lads from school and the time just sort of slipped past,' he said anxiously. 'Is he—' The fingers of one hand fumbled with his jacket buttons as the other whipped off his cap.

'No, but I thought you were going to – quick,' Jenny urged as she heard familiar footsteps in the close. 'Into your room with you!'

Walter didn't need telling twice. He peeled the jacket off and pushed it into her hands as he slid past her. When Daniel came in the jacket was hanging on the back of the door and Jenny was stacking the used cups on the draining board, already scolding herself for getting into a panic just because he had almost caught Walter in his outdoor clothes.

'Where's the boy?' he asked, as he always did.

'In his room, working at his books. Where else would he be?' She hesitated, then said, 'Daniel, d'you not think that Walter should be out in the fresh air more often?'

'He gets fresh air every day, on his milk-round, then going to and from the school.'

'But that's not much, is it? The other laddies get out to play football or play along the riverbank—'

'Has he been whinin' tae you again?' Daniel wanted to know, his voice tense. 'Because if he has I'll soon teach him tae—'

'No!' She caught at his arm as he got up from his chair and began to move towards the door. 'Of course he's said nothing – Walter would never complain! It was just – every boy needs to get fresh air and exercise, Daniel. Maurice used to be out and about all the time, and I'm sure you were too, when you were Walter's age.'

Under her fingers, the muscles in his arm were like steel. 'Aye, I was out in the streets all the time – because my father was a drunkard

186

who cared nothing for his weans. And what happened to me, eh?' He glared down at her and her hand fell away from his arm. 'I'm nothin' but a slave now, dependent on the likes of George Dalkieth for the money tae keep me and mine alive.' His voice rose. 'My son's goin' tae have a better life than I ever did, Jenny. He'll be the one tae give the orders, no' the one tae take them. And until then he'll dae as I say – so don't you try turnin' him against his work with talk of playin' football and runnin' wi' the other laddies that are goin' tae follow their fathers intae the yard. Heed me now, Jenny, for I'll be master in my own house!'

She had never known Daniel to raise a hand to anyone, but she knew now that there was no need for it – his anger was so intense that it radiated into the room from every inch of him and seemed to take on a shape of its own. Its heat scorched Jenny and, trying to contain her shock, she moved away from her husband, back to the stove.

'I've had a visitor.' Despite herself, her voice shook, and so did her hands. 'D'ye mind Lizzie Caldwell who used to work in the yard office? She's in Glasgow now, working in a big store. She brought some bonny cloth to make gowns for the baby.'

'Oh aye?' Daniel said without interest, sitting down and unlacing his boots. The anger had gone out of him almost as suddenly as it had sparked, and he started to talk about the meeting he had just left.

The baby kicked and she put a comforting hand on her swelling belly. She wanted only the best for the child she was carrying, but surely Daniel, too, would want the best for it. After all, it was his child as well. She suddenly recalled Walter saying earlier that he hoped that she would have a daughter.

A cold hand brushed against the skin between Jenny's shoulder-blades at the memory. Had the boy said that because he knew only too well what would be expected of a boy rather than a girl? And if – when – that happened, when Daniel started imposing his own thwarted ambitions on the new baby just as he had done with Walter, would she have the strength to resist him, Jenny wondered. Even for the sake of her own child?

19

Apart from bouts of morning sickness in the first few months Jenny continued to enjoy good health, and she was able to keep on working until March, just over two months before her baby was due.

'I'll be sorry tae lose ye, lass,' Mr Duncan said on her final day at the Experimental Tank. 'Ye've been a grand supervisor.'

'I'll be sorry to go,' Jenny's voice shook. Now that it was coming to an end, she knew that her work in the Tank section had meant more to her than she had realised. She had to swallow hard to keep back the tears when Senga, who was going to take her place as supervisor, presented her with a parcel of baby clothes knitted by the tracing-room staff.

Mr Duncan, with much clearing of the throat, gave her a handsome glass vase, bought by a collection gathered from the other departments in the Tank and, at the end of the day, Robert Archer summoned her to the boardroom. He closed the door, shutting out the clang of the truck, enclosing the two of them in the dusty opulence of the carpeted room.

He had changed, even in the time since he had come back to Ellerslie. He had aged, she realised, looking more closely at him. There was an air of tension about him now, disillusionment in his steady grey eyes, a sharpening of his lean features. Jenny felt a moment's pang for the ambitious young man she had once loved, then reminded herself, briskly, that she too had changed. It was inevitable. Their lives, once apparently destined to be woven together, had taken separate paths after all, and they had grown away from each other in a way that she would never have thought possible in the days of the rhododendrons. There was no sense, now, in thinking about matters that were over and done with.

But when he said, 'How are you, Jenny?' she knew by the tone of his voice that for him, too, the past couldn't be denied. Alone together, with nobody else to overhear, Robert wasn't merely talking to an employee.

'I'm very well.'

His eyes travelled slowly over her face. 'And are you happy?'

'Daniel's a good husband to me.'

'I'm pleased to hear it. You deserve happiness, Jen,' he said gently, then on a more formal note, 'You'll be missed here. Your loyalty and your hard work have been appreciated.'

Carefully, avoiding contact between their fingers, Jenny took the stiff white envelope he proferred, reminded of the envelope that had arrived from Lizzie's aunt, the letter that had fleetingly offered her the chance to leave Ellerslie. If she had been able to take that chance she wouldn't have seen Robert again, wouldn't have married Daniel.

She opened the envelope and gasped as she read the fancy lettering on the treasury note inside. 'Ten pounds? It's too much!'

'As far as Dalkieth's is concerned you've been worth every penny of it. And if ever you need any help—' again, the formality had gone, and it was Robert himself who was speaking, studying her with that gaze that seemed to have the ability to read her very soul, '—remember that *we're* still friends, no matter what's happened between us.'

'Thank you, Mr – thank you, Robert.' She held her hand out and, for a long moment, he took it in his own warm, strong clasp, putting his other hand over their clasped fingers.

'Jen—'

'I must go—' She pulled away from him, and he let her hand slip from between his. As she turned towards the door she heard him say her name again, but she had found the handle, and she opened the door and went through without looking back.

It was too late, now, to think of looking back.

As the weeks passed the routine of Jenny's new life began to take up all her attention and the tracing office was gradually relegated to her past. She was able to take some of the burden from Bella's shoulders now that she was at home all day. She could keep an eye on Patrick and give him his midday meal, saving Bella many a hurried journey across the town to feed him and then rushing back to work.

The move to a ground-floor flat had had little impact on Patrick Kerr after all. He still refused to use the crutches he had been given when he first came home, or to have a special boot made to enable him to walk more comfortably. When Jenny took tea or a meal to him she always found him crouched in a chair, staring at the walls that held him as securely as any prison cell. He scarcely looked at her or answered her when she spoke and, without realising it, she herself started behaving like a gaoler, putting the food down near the edge of the table, within his reach, and withdrawing without a word.

Bella was working as hard as ever to support the two of them. She was up early in the morning and in bed late at night.

'You're killing yourself, d'you know that?' Jenny asked bluntly one day when she had managed to coax her sister to come in for a cup of tea.

'I'm as strong as a horse.' Bella fidgeted, turning away from her sister's scrutiny. Her wedding ring was almost lost in swollen, reddened flesh and Jenny could hear the rasping noise her roughened fingers made as they twisted together.

'Horses are sometimes worked until they fall down in the street, then they're shot,' Jenny pointed out, and Bella laughed.

'You think I'm ready for the catsmeat man, do you?'

'I think that's all you'll *be* fit for, the rate you're going.'

'Ye're havering, Jen.' A strand of hair fell over Bella's wan face; she put her hands up to push it away and one sleeve fell back to reveal an ugly blue and green bruise on the soft inner skin of her thin arm.

'I see you've run into another door,' Jenny said dryly. 'You should try opening them some time.'

Bella flushed crimson, dropping her arm back into her lap, dragging the sleeve down over the tell-tale bruising. 'Mind your own business!'

'It *is* my business. D'you think I want to see you turning yourself into an invalid? What'll happen to Patrick, then?'

Tears flooded at once into Bella's eyes. She put her cup down and made for the door.

'Bella—'

'Patrick'll be wondering where I've got to.' Bella fumbled with the latch of the outer door with shaking hands, taking so long over it that Jenny, large and clumsy as she now was, had time to follow her into the narrow hall.

'Bella, I'm only trying to—'

Bella rounded on her, sobbing freely now. 'Patrick didnae ask tae be turned intae a cripple, Jen! I loved him before, and I love him now. And if I do end up as catsmeat,' she added, her voice rising as the door finally opened for her, 'it's only what he would have done for me if it had been the other way round!'

Then she plunged across the close, disappearing into her own flat and slamming the door in Jenny's face.

On the following day when Jenny took food in to Patrick he was in his usual chair, a discarded newspaper crumpled on the floor by his side. He didn't bother to acknowledge her when she went in. Seeing that the fire was almost out she put the tray down on the table and hurried to replenish it.

'You could surely have managed to keep the fire going, Patrick. Bella left enough coal in the scuttle for you.'

'I'm warm enough.' He glanced at her indifferently. He was thin, pale with lack of fresh air, and unshaven, and his hair needed cutting.

'Mebbe so, but there's a cold wind blowing outside and Bella'll be in need of the fire when she comes home,' Jenny said breathlessly. Stooping over the range was an effort now that the birth of her baby was only a few days away, and when she straightened her back gave a painful twinge.

'Bella's not sitting indoors all day with a blanket over her legs like some people, Patrick. Anyway, she'll be tired enough when she gets back without having to set to and light the range. She works hard to keep the two of you – or haven't you noticed?'

With a sweep of his hand Patrick tossed the blanket to the floor to reveal his twisted foot, covered by a thick sock. 'I'm a cripple,' he said bitterly, 'or haven't you noticed?'

Jenny hadn't had a chance to talk to her sister since Bella had rushed out of her house in tears. She had spent an uncomfortable, sleepless night fretting over the things she had said, wishing they had been left unsaid. Guilt honed the edge of her voice. 'I've seen men in the streets every day since the war with crutches and false limbs. There's a man that sells newspapers in Dreghorn Street who has to go about on a wee sort of cart because he's got no legs at all!' She picked up the tray and put it on a stool beside his chair, so that he could reach it. 'You're fortunate compared to him.'

Patrick's lips pulled back from his teeth in a snarl of rage. 'Fortunate? What d'you know about the way I'm suffering?'

'How did our Bella get those bad bruises on her arm?' Jenny countered and colour stained the skin stretched tightly over his cheekbones.

'Runnin' girnin' tae you, was she? Whinin' for sympathy?'

'Our Bella's got more self-respect than that. She didn't mean me to see, but I did, just as I've seen the black eyes and the bruised mouths. Why should you take your bitterness out on her? It wasn't her that sent you to the war, Patrick. And at least you came back – Maurice didn't, and neither did thousands of other men.'

His hands, still powerful, gripped the wooden arms of his chair, the knuckles white. 'Where's the sense in a man comin' back if he's no' whole any more?' He ground the words between his teeth. 'Who wants a cripple?'

'Our Bella does, for one! She loves you so much she'd have

welcomed you home no matter how bad you were hurt. But that doesn't matter to you, does it? All you want is to make her stop loving you and start hating you instead, so that you can feel even sorrier for yourself. You're more crippled in your head than your leg, Patrick Kerr,' said Jenny with contempt, 'and it's time someone had the sense to tell you the truth of it.'

'Get out of here, you bitch! Mind yer own business!'

'You're just a poor, pathetic, creature, Patrick, without the guts of a flea.'

With a wordless yell he launched himself at her. If he had reached her the two of them would have gone crashing down, but in spite of her added weight Jenny was able to step aside, though, as she turned, she felt a sudden tearing sensation in her back. Patrick's hoarse roar turned to a thin scream of pain as his weight was thrown on to his twisted foot and it buckled beneath him. He caught at the table cover as he went down and an empty bowl and a vegetable knife Bella had left there spun down after him. He measured his length on the rug before the fire, the side of his head narrowly missing the leg of the other fireside chair. He escaped further injury when the falling knife landed on its handle and bounced away from him. The bowl spun into a corner and the tablecloth drifted down to cover his head.

To her own astonishment, Jenny began to laugh. She stood clutching at the corner of the table while her crippled brother-in-law writhed on the floor at her feet, clawing the cloth away from his face, wave after wave of hysterical mirth washing over her.

'Get me up, damn you!' Patrick yelled.

'Get yourself up, if you're still man enough.' Laughing was giving her a stitch in her side and she managed, with an effort, to get it under control as she went to pick up the bowl. It was still intact; Jenny put it back on the table but decided against salvaging the knife and the tablecloth for fear that Patrick might catch at her ankle and pull her off-balance.

At the door she turned. 'The men begging in the streets'd rather let the folk see the poor, maimed things they've become through no fault of their own than let their wives slave for them. Think about *that*, Patrick Kerr.'

Inside her own flat she leaned against the panels of the outer door. She dearly wanted to sit down but she was shaking too much to make her way into the kitchen. She had done a terrible, cruel thing. She should go back to make sure that Patrick was all right, she told herself, then thought of the sharp knife lying within his reach. If he had managed to get to his feet, if he had the knife, there was no telling what he might do if she went back.

But if Patrick killed himself, it would be her fault, she thought. Then she remembered the ugly bruising she had seen on her sister's arm the day before, and all the other bruises Bella had had.

The shaking had eased off a little. She pushed herself away from the door and into the kitchen, trying to think. Someone should go to make sure that Patrick was all right, but Daniel was at work, Walter at school. She wondered if she could ask her mother if she would look in on him, making some excuse for not doing it herself. There was no harm in admitting that she had angered him without saying anything about his fall or the sharp knife that had tumbled from the table. It was the thought of the knife, temptingly close to his hand, that was worrying her more than anything.

She was reaching up to take her coat from the back of the door when a huge, strong hand seemed to take hold of her body, gripping her cruelly round the back and belly.

She gasped and curled one arm protectively round her body, the other hand catching the back of a chair, clutching it tightly. When the pain finally ebbed she lowered herself cautiously into the chair, moving as though she was an old woman, and sat still until she got her breath back.

It was only a touch of cramp, she told herself, getting up to fetch a glass of water and sipping the cold liquid slowly, standing by the sink. Then the tumbler dropped from her fingers to shatter against the tap as the pain struck again and she bowed herself over, trying to hold it in and control it, frightened in case it began to control her.

When it was over she went as quickly as she could to the outer door, ignoring her coat, aware only of the need to get help quickly. The elderly woman who had moved into Bella's old flat was on her way downstairs when she opened the door, a shabby shopping bag in one fist. She nodded, then looked again at Jenny.

'Ye're awful white, hen. Is it the bairn?'

'I think so. But it's not supposed to come for a few days yet.'

'Bairns don't use calendars,' the woman said, dropping her bag and guiding Jenny back indoors. 'You go and lie down and I'll fetch yer mother.'

By the time Faith arrived at a run, accompanied by Mrs Malloy, Jenny had managed to heave her swollen clumsy body on to the bed.

'Sure an' this one's in a hurry tae see the world, is it no'?' the Irishwoman said almost at once. 'It'll be a lassie – the laddies arenae half as nosy.'

Patrick Kerr lay where he had fallen for a long time after Jenny walked out, his cheek pressed painfully into the cracked linoleum, and wept like a child, noisily, angrily, the frustration pouring out of him in a torrent of self-pity that was bitter with salt when it trickled into his mouth.

When, at last, the tears slowed and dried to a snuffling and gasping, he stayed where he was for a while then finally reached out and managed to catch at the leg of Bella's chair. Painfully, laboriously, he pulled himself to his knees, whimpering like a dog when burning needles of pain shot through his wounded foot, which had twisted beneath him when he fell. It took several attempts before he got his good foot under him and stood up, then turned himself about, gripping now at the table, and finally fell back into his chair, his twisted leg throbbing each time it was bumped against the furniture.

He rubbed the sleeve of his jersey across his face again and again until the angry tears and the mucus which had run from his nose were scrubbed away, before realising that one hand was gripped tightly about the wooden handle of the knife that had fallen from the table. He turned it over to let the light from the window kiss the blade into life, running the ball of one thumb over the cutting edge, his breathing still ragged, with the occasional shoulder-heaving gasp. The knife was sharp. Patrick tested the point against the inside of one wrist, where a blue vein was clearly visible just under the white skin.

There had been a man in the trenches, a friend, who had cut his wrists. It was an easy death, someone had said. Patrick pressed a little harder, then pulled the blade away as a glistening bead of blood welled up. He lifted his wrist to his mouth and licked the blood away. He wasn't afraid to die; it would be easy, it would be more fitting than to spend the rest of his life a cripple – but that bitch Jenny had probably left the knife near him on purpose, and he'd not kill himself just to please her! He turned the blade over again, thinking longingly of the pleasure it would give him at that moment to drive it through his interfering sister-in-law's throat.

A piece of driftwood lay on the hearth, a lump of timber that Bella had found on the river shore and brought in to be used as kindling for the range. Patrick bent over and managed to curl the fingers of one hand round it and hoist it to his lap. He stabbed the knife into it savagely, dislodging a flake of wood that fell away, revealing the pale, grained interior. He stabbed again, then again, the breath whistling in his throat. More flakes tumbled down to the floor by his wounded foot and he wielded the knife again, this time with direction and purpose, the neat handle fitting comfortably into his palm. Five minutes later the lump of wood in his hands had taken on the rough shape of a woman, short haired and with a swollen belly. He turned it over, examining it closely, then grinned and twisted the point of the knife deep into the swelling.

'That's done for you, Jenny Young,' he muttered, then paused on the point of tossing the carved figure down and uncurled his fingers to expose it lying in the palm of his hand. He turned it around, studying it from all angles, his mind stirring with memories that had long since been pushed out of sight. Finally he lifted the knife again, this time using the blade carefully to start paring the swollen stomach away, flake by flake, turning the blade deftly this way and that, slipping back into an old and soothing routine.

By the time Walter arrived home from school, Jenny was in the final stages of a short and swift labour, and had forgotten all about Patrick. Her hands gripped her mother's as the pain came and went, advancing a little further each time it came, receding a little less each time it ebbed, until it seemed to be a part of her that would never leave. Dimly she heard Mrs Malloy in the hall, instructing Walter to go round to her house until he was sent for.

'Should I mebbe run to the yard and tell my father?' The boy's voice was high-pitched with tension.

'No! Jenny forced the word through the wall of pain surrounding her, knowing full well, even in the midst of her torment, that Daniel wouldn't want his son to see him at work.

'Best not,' Mrs Malloy told Walter. 'He's played his part – let him come back in his own time. It'll be over by then.'

She was right. By the time Daniel arrived home, scrubbed clean and smelling of carbolic soap as usual, his daughter, also washed and smelling of soap, though in her case a flowery soap that Jenny had saved for the occasion, was gowned, shawled, and asleep in her crib.

'She's healthy lookin',' he said awkwardly, staring down at her.

'Ye're a fortunate man, Daniel. A clever son, an' now a bonny wee daughter,' Faith told him. He nodded, but Jenny, watching from the shadow of the alcove bed, saw the disappointment in his face. He had set his heart on another son.

'Where's Walter?'

'I sent him tae my house. He was best out o' the way,' Mrs Malloy said serenely, and at once he made for the door.

'I'll fetch him,' he said, and hurried out. Mrs Malloy made a face at the closing door.

'An' what's troublin' the man?' she asked with good humour. 'Scared his laddie'll be enjoying himself, for once? Or scared he'll catch somethin' in my house?' Her rich laugh boomed out, filling a room that seldom heard laughter.

'It's just his way,' Jenny found herself defending her husband. 'He doesn't mean anything by it.'

'Now don't you go thinkin' I'm bothered, child. Don't I know Daniel Young well enough by now?' Mrs Malloy said calmly, then, as the baby snuffled, she swooped down on the crib and scooped her up, blankets and all. 'An' no need for you to fret, bonny wee thing that ye are,' she instructed, depositing the sweet-smelling bundle in Jenny's arms. 'Now then, just you enjoy yer wee daughter an' have a good rest. Sure an' ye've earned it.'

The baby had translucent skin like white porcelain, and a lot of soft, black hair. Her wide, serene eyes were dark blue, staring up at Jenny, who held her close, marvelling over the lightness yet compactness of the small body in her arms. She had let Daniel down, she knew that, but, deep in her heart, she was glad that she had given birth to a daughter. This baby would be free to grow up without the responsibility that lay so heavily on poor Walter's young shoulders . . .

Bella came in an hour later, her exhausted face radiant, to croon over the baby.

'Oh Jen, she's beautiful!'

Jenny, more rested now, suddenly remembered the scene in her sister's flat earlier. 'How's Patrick?'

'He's fine. In fact, he's better than fine. You'll never guess what he did today, Jen! He got hold of my wee vegetable knife and a bit of wood I'd brought in for the fire and he started carving a lovely wee figure, just like the sort of things he used tae make before the war. It's like a wee figurehead for a wee toy sailing ship. He was so busy with it he forgot all about eating that dinner you made for him.'

She laughed, and cuddled the baby close. 'Tae think I was worried about leavin' any knives near him in case he hurt himself. It was a daft thought. I should have encouraged him, not tried tae protect him so much, but Jenny, I never thought tae see him workin' away like that again.' She dropped a light kiss on the sleeping baby's forehead. 'Mebbe this bairn's brought luck with her. Mebbe things are goin' tae get better at last!'

20

As Daniel felt that it was unseemly for his son to be in the same house as a woman recovering from childbirth Walter was dispatched to the Gillespies' flat, where he slept in Alice's room. Daniel moved into Walter's room and Alice shared the alcove bed with Jenny so that she was at hand to help with the baby during the night. Faith came in every day, bringing Helen with her.

They had wondered how Helen, the only child in the family for the past three years, would react to her new little cousin, At first sight of the new baby she tossed her faded, battered rag doll out of its 'perambulator' – an old wooden box with rickety wheels and a wooden handle that had been passed to her from the youngest Malloy child – then smoothed out the scrap of blanket in the bottom of the box. Briskly pushing back her sleeves in imitation of the women she had seen about her all her life she confidently held her fat little arms out.

'My babby,' she announced, and her lower lip trembled when Bella, who was holding the shawled bundle, shook her head.

'It's not a dolly, pet, it's a real wee girl, and we've tae be very careful with her. See—' Bella drew a fold of shawl away from the tiny face, and Helen approached on tiptoe to stroke the baby's cheek with a wondering finger, then tugged at Bella's skirt in a sudden fit of jealousy.

'Me now,' she demanded, trying to scramble up on to her aunt's knee, forcing Bella to hand the baby over to her mother and pick Helen up.

'I doubt we've spoiled her over much,' Faith commented, shaking her head.

'Ach, she'll be all right.' Bella cuddled the little girl. 'We'll just need to be sure that she doesnae feel left out of things.'

For the first few days after her daughter's birth Jenny was content to lie back and be cossetted for the first time in her life. She listened to Helen's contented chatter and watched Faith moving competently about the kitchen, marvelling over her mother's renewed energy now that she was free of Marion and had come to terms with Maurice's death.

'He's a nice laddie, that Walter,' Faith said more than once. 'Grateful for everything ye do for him, and awful good with Helen. A nice, quiet laddie.'

'Too quiet, for his age,' Jenny said, sadly.

'Not when him and Alice get together. She'd get a stone tae turn noisy, that one.'

'Is he keeping up with his schoolwork?' Jenny asked anxiously.

'He does more than he should, if you ask me.' Faith removed Helen's clutching hands from the side of the crib. 'That's enough kissin' for now, pet, let the babby get some sleep or she'll grow up crabbit.' She cast an approving glance at her new granddaughter. 'Have you and Daniel thought of a name yet?'

'We both like Shona.' Jenny had had several names in mind, but Daniel had shown little interest, saying to each suggestion, 'Whatever you want.'

'Shona.' Faith tried it on her tongue, then nodded. 'It suits her.'

Bella came in every day to linger over the crib and, if the baby was awake, to hold her and croon over her. There had been no new bruises and she had lost some of her usual tension. Alice and Walter had been combing the riverbanks in search of pieces of timber for Patrick, who had indeed rediscovered his interest in wood carving.

'He's got talent,' Alice told Jenny. Since starting work in the pawnshop she had become quite an expert where ornaments and jewellery were concerned.

Not all Mr Monroe's customers pawned their best clothes – the more affluent survived from month to month on the proceeds of vases and statuettes and even family heirlooms passed down from one generation to the next. Alice had discovered a collection of books on antiques in Alec Monroe's flat and she was working her way through them, one by one, with increasing interest. 'I've told him that I think he might be able to sell some pieces if he works hard enough.'

'What did he say to that?'

Alice shrugged. 'He just gave me one of those looks of his. You know Patrick – he's never got much to say for himself now. But at least he's doing something. I'll keep at him,' she added thoughtfully. 'There are folk that come into the shop sometimes to see what's for sale, not to pawn their own stuff. I'm sure they'd be interested in his carvings. And in your painted china, too,' she added, eyeing her sister.

'D'you not think I've got enough to do now that she's arrived?' Jenny ran a finger gently over the dark fluff that covered her daughter's neat skull and looked down at Shona's tiny face pressed into the curve of her breast, her cheeks rounding then emptying as she sucked strongly.

'Just remember what I'm saying when you do have the time,' Alice said quietly.

Ten days after Shona's birth Jenny was up and about and well enough to gather the reins of the house back into her own hands. Walter came home and was immediately captivated by his tiny half-sister. Shona was a placid and undemanding baby, and the household routine reshaped itself easily to accommodate her.

Robert Archer strode down the cobbled street, skirting groups of toddlers playing in the gutters, tipping his hat to the women who stopped their gossiping at the closemouths to stare as he went by. It had been a good while since he had lived among them but they all knew who he was. He turned in at one particular close and rapped on a ground-floor door with the head of his cane. It opened after a moment and Jenny Young stared at him in astonishment.

'What brings you here?'

'I'd business in the area,' Robert lied blandly. 'And I thought that since I was here I'd pay my respects. Have I called at a bad time?'

'No. I was just putting the bairn down.' She led him into the kitchen, which was neat and bright and welcoming. 'You'll take a cup of tea?'

He nodded and went over to the crib, where the baby lay, wide-eyed. Robert put a finger into a tiny hand which gripped it with surprising strength. 'What are you calling her?'

'Shona.'

'It's a bonny choice.' He stayed where he was, reluctant to break the grip on his finger, while Jenny moved about the room. Her surprise at his arrival was so strong that he could almost taste it. 'She looks like you.'

'I think she's got Daniel's mouth.'

He looked at the tiny rosebud mouth, and disagreed, but silently. To his eyes Jenny's daughter was Jenny in miniature, with her neat little face and her solemn and steady blue-eyed gaze. If things had been different, this could have been his daughter, he thought, and knew why he had suddenly decided to call. He was still smarting over Fiona Dalkieth's sudden rejection and from the suspicion, which had never left him in spite of her denials, that she had made use of him. It came hard to a man with Robert's sturdy independence to think that he had been taken for a fool.

When the tea was ready he carefully eased himself free of the baby's grip and watched Jenny pouring his tea. Her face and body were still softly rounded from childbearing, and there was a new maturity in her blue eyes. 'You look well,' he said, then, catching them both unawares, 'Are you content, Jenny?'

'Yes.' She said it quickly, perhaps too quickly, then, as he stretched out to take a scone from the proffered plate. 'And you?'

The scone had a crisp outer shell, but inside it was light and fluffy, melting on the tongue. Robert laid it carefully on his saucer. 'I suppose you could say that I've got what I deserved.'

'What does that mean?

He looked up at her and was warmed by the concern he saw in her eyes. 'It means that I'm fine.'

'You don't look it.'

'Does that matter to you?

'Of course it matters! We were good friends, you and me.'

'More than friends.'

She flushed slightly. 'Once, mebbe. But I'd always want your happiness, even though we took different roads.'

He looked round the kitchen, then at the baby, still awake. 'I sometimes wonder if I took the wrong turning altogether.'

'You did what you wanted to do.'

'What my head wanted, Jenny.'

Jenny smiled faintly. 'Your head was always stronger than your heart,' she said.

'I suppose so.' He was silent for a moment, then, 'Things are busier than ever at the Tank.'

'So I hear. Senga and Kerry visit me.'

'You're missed, Jenny.'

'What about the yard?' she dared to ask. She knew that Daniel and the others were worried about the yard. There were rumours that orders were hard to find and men might be laid off.

He shifted uneasily in his chair. 'Business could be better than it is. It's the same in every yard just now.'

'But Dalkieth's surely won't fail. Not with the good name it's always had.'

'You heard what happened to the steam yacht George Dalkieth undertook to build?' Robert asked wryly, and she nodded.

'The whole of Ellerslie's heard about it.'

A month after George Dalkieth commandeered the empty dock for his friend's steam yacht an urgent order had come in from a regular client for a passenger steamer to replace one that had been badly damaged in a storm. The yard had no available space and the lucrative order had gone instead to a rival. Not long after that the man who had commissioned the yacht left the country abruptly – one step ahead of his personal creditors, according to the rumours – and, after a fruitless search for another buyer, the half-completed yacht had been abandoned and was now rusting in some corner of the yard. George Dalkieth had shrugged the matter off, refusing to take any blame for it.

'Have you heard of a whipping boy, Jenny? In the old days, when the prince did anything wrong another boy, a commoner, was punished in his place because nobody could be allowed to chastise a member of the royal family.' Robert got up, putting his cup down on the table and walking to the window, where he lifted the neat net curtain aside and stared out at the street without seeing it. 'I sometimes think that that's why I was brought back from England – to take the blame for George Dalkieth's mistakes.'

'But everyone knows who took on the yacht,' Jenny protested. 'They know you'd never have done anything as foolish as that.'

'I work hand in glove with the man. That means that in the eyes of those who matter I'm tarred with the same brush.' His voice was hard, bitter. 'And Mrs Dalkieth has one great weakness – she can't help favouring her own flesh and blood. The other directors follow her blindly because George's a Dalkieth and it sticks in their craws to listen to anyone less well-born than he is.' He swung round and, even though his back was now to the window and his face in shadow, she knew that impotent anger was stamped on it. 'And when George leads them into a pickle, what happens? They can't chastise *him* in front of his mother, so they look for a whipping boy. They're outraged because I let him blunder.'

'Are things going badly for Dalkieth's?'

'What does your husband say?'

'He's concerned,' Jenny said honestly. 'They all are.' She joined him at the window, putting a hand on his arm. 'All the yards are having problems just now, but I'm sure Dalkieth's is strong enough to weather the storms. And so are you. Don't lose heart, Robert.'

The clock ticked on and, from the crib, came a soft snuffling sound. Robert noticed that Jenny's hair, close to his shoulder now, shone in the light coming through the net curtains. She smelled of fresh baking.

He was aware of a great sense of loss. This could have been his – Jenny, the neat, clean kitchen, the baby in the crib. But instead, his damned self-centred ambition had led him to reject her and everything she could have given him. The longing to turn the clock back was suddenly so strong in him that he felt ill.

Her fingers tightened on his arm and concern came into her eyes. 'Robert? Are you all right?'

He wanted to put his arms about her, to bury his face in her hair and to just hold her for the rest of his life. Instead, with an effort, he turned away.

'I'm fine. I'd best get back.' He had already ruined her life once, and he had no right to give in to his own weakness and do so again.

'If you're not happy working for the Dalkieths, mebbe you should go back to England,' she suggested as she handed him his hat and cane.

'Would it matter to you whether I went or stayed?'

'You've not got the right to ask me a thing like that, Robert. Not now.'

'I'm asking you anyway.'

'And I've not got the right to answer you.'

'I suppose not,' he said. 'Thank you for the tea.'

When he had gone Jenny lifted Shona from the crib and sat down, rocking her daughter in her arms, remembering the expressions that had chased each other across his face as they stood together at the window, and her too-swift answer to his question about her contentment. Daniel was a good man, but his continual tension, his treatment of Walter, meant that living with him was like walking on a knife-edge.

Robert, too, was an ambitious man – ambitious for himself and for Dalkieth's. There was a similarity between the two men although their situations – Daniel a worker, Robert one of the 'gaffers' – put them on opposite sides of the fence. It seemed strange, Jenny thought, that the two men in her life were so ambitious in their different ways, when all she herself wanted was to have the right to grasp a handful of happiness, just one handful, and be able to keep it close for always.

'Mebbe folk like us were never meant to be happy,' she said to Shona, her lips moving against the baby's silky little skull. 'Mebbe just making the best of what we've got is our happiness.'

Isobel Dalkieth had been insistent that her first grandchild must be born in Dalkieth House. It took little pressure to get her son's and daughter-in-law's agreement; George because he heartily disliked the thought of childbirth and felt that, with his mother in charge, he himself would be free to continue to live a normal life, and Fiona because it was an extension of the pampering she had been smothered with ever since she had announced the glad news. Since that day, her mother-in-law had been much kinder to her, and her determination to enter Dalkieth House only as its mistress no longer applied.

To her great relief she and George were given separate bedrooms.

He was established in his old room while Fiona was given a large and comfortable bedroom, refurbished to her own taste, at the front of the house. Two rooms on the top floor overlooking the back garden were lavishly fitted out as day and night nurseries, and an experienced nanny and nursery-maid had been appointed. Isobel's own doctor, the most respected medical man in the area, had eased Fiona through the waiting months, and she glowed with health and well-being.

Even so she was apprehensive about the ordeal that lay before her and, as soon as the first pains gripped her, she took to her bed and ordered her maid to fetch Doctor Baillie at once. The maid, acting on instructions from the woman who paid her wages, went first to Isobel Dalkieth.

When the door opened and her mother-in-law appeared, Fiona raised herself on her pillows. 'Where's the doctor?'

'Everything's being attended to, my dear.'

'Have you sent for George?'

Isobel seated herself on a chair near the bed, her hands folded in her lap. 'What use will George be at a time like this? You surely don't want him cluttering up the place.'

'He should be in the house.'

'He'd be of more use at the shipyard, trying to undo some of the harm he's done with his stupid ideas. I've been hearing, though not of course from George, that this combine he insisted on bringing in seems to be having little success and more than a few problems in England. Has he said anything to you about that?'

'George doesn't talk to me about business matters,' Fiona said sulkily from among her pillows, and Isobel raised her eyebrows.

'You mean you don't encourage him to do so? Oh, my dear, you're making a great mistake. A man – any man, but particularly a buffoon like George – needs guidance from his wife. I always thought of you as having the sense to realise that.'

Fiona gaped at the older woman then said in feeble protest, 'Mrs Dalkieth, I cannot listen to you talking of your own son like that! How can you bring yourself to—'

'Don't try to pretend that you're shocked, my dear. George is a buffoon – you know it, and I know it, and we don't have time to waste on pretence. Now – has he said anything to you about this combine he's embroiled us with?'

Fiona shifted uneasily in the bed. 'The shipyard is George's concern, not mine.'

'You should make it your concern. In fact, you *must* make it your concern from now on. I shall insist on it.'

'Mrs Dalkieth—'

Isobel fluttered one hand at her daughter-in-law. 'My dear Fiona – please! You must learn to call me Mother, now that you're about to give birth to my grandchild.'

'—when do you think the doctor will arrive?'

'In plenty of time. I recall that Edward took ten hours in the birthing and, as for George—' Isobel shook her head and tutted. 'A full twenty-four hours. George always was slow to come to a decision.' She fingered her magnificent engagement ring then said bluntly, 'Between ourselves, Fiona, I blame myself for the mess George has made of the yard. I have allowed the fondness I felt for him as a little boy to linger on and, because of that, I've turned a blind eye to his faults instead of dealing with them. I hoped that once he was in charge of the yard he would take his responsibilities more seriously, and that was very foolish of me. I hope that you will never make the same mistake.' She sighed, staring down at the ring. 'And now we're in trouble, Fiona. I've given George his head once too often, and I persuaded the whole Board to support him. I should have listened to Robert Arch—'

She rose quickly and went to the bedside as Fiona's swollen body suddenly went into a spasm, her hands gripping at the quilt. Isobel consulted the small fob watch that hung round her neck by a gold chain then, as the pain receded and Fiona relaxed, she picked up a bottle of Eau de Cologne from the bedside table and dabbed some on to a lacy handkerchief, smoothing it over the girl's forehead.

'Rest, my dear, and gather your strength. You're going to need it before this business is over. So now I must make amends for my foolishness,' she went on, regaining her seat, folding her hands. 'For the sake of Dalkieth's yard, Fiona, I must go to Mr Archer and eat humble pie. It won't be easy, but if we're to have a shipyard for this child to inherit it must be done. What do you think of Robert Archer, Fiona?'

Fiona's blue eyes widened, then, as Isobel looked back steadily at her, she turned her head away. 'I – I scarcely know the man,' she said fretfully. 'Isn't the doctor here yet?'

'There's plenty of time yet. Archer comes from common stock but he talks a great deal of sense and I believe that he genuinely cares about Dalkieth's, just as I do.' Isobel rose and walked to the window to stare down at the driveway.

'Can you see his car coming?' There was a note of panic in Fiona's voice now. Isobel ignored it.

'George doesn't care about the business, not the way he should. He assumes that because it has always been there and always been successful nothing can harm it. He thinks that everything he does and says must be right just because he is a Dalkieth.' She began to move back across the room to the bed. 'But we have to face facts, Fiona, you and I. George is useless.'

Fiona raised herself up clumsily and reached for the bell-rope that hung at the bed-head. Isobel reached it first, tucking it out of her daughter-in-law's reach.

'What are you doing?' Fiona asked, alarmed.

'You mustn't exert yourself, my dear. Everything's under control.' She sat down again. 'There's a difference between being a Dalkieth and having the Dalkieth name, Fiona. George is a Dalkieth by blood but he has no notion whatsoever of what's best for the yard. I, on the other hand, am a Dalkieth only by marriage, yet I've spent all my adult life in the service of the business.'

She studied Fiona, ignoring the tumbled hair, the flushed face, the frightened eyes, seeing only the self-centred ruthlessness that she knew lay beneath the surface.

'Your child, Fiona, will inherit everything. Given proper guidance in his formative years he could do more for the shipyard than George ever will. And he'll have full rights to the Dalkieth name. Whether or not,' she added calmly, 'there's Dalkieth blood in his veins.'

'What do you mean?' Fiona demanded shrilly, forgetting her own problems for the moment, 'Of course he'll have the Dalkieth blood! He'll be your own son's child!'

'Will he? I've been thinking a great deal over the past few months, Fiona, and it seems to me that George's blood may well be altogether too thin to spread to another generation.'

Fiona began to speak then gasped, her hands reaching out, her body stiffening beneath the satin quilt. Isobel hurried to her side again and put her hands in Fiona's, setting her teeth against the pain as the girl's fingers gripped and tightened like bands of steel, her nails digging in. By the time the contraction eased away the backs of Isobel's hands were scored with deep red weals.

'Where's that damned doctor?' Fiona moaned as the dampened handkerchief mopped beads of sweat from her crimson face.

'Don't fret yourself, I'll get word to him in good time,' Isobel said soothingly and her daughter-in-law's blue eyes, which had been screwed tightly shut, flew open in horror.

'You've not sent for him?'

'I thought we should talk first.'

'For God's sake—!' Fiona tried to struggle out of bed and was pushed back on to the pillows.

'Don't upset yourself, my dear. It's bad for the baby.'

'Fetch George! I want George!'

'Only a fool would want George,' said his mother. 'And you're no fool. I've come to realise that over the past few months.'

'You're going to kill me!'

'Nonsense! You're a healthy, well-nourished young woman. If you were a peasant woman in some other country you would think nothing of birthing your baby in a ditch then getting on with your work.'

Fiona lunged up, a hand stretched up towards the bell-pull, but failed to reach it. She dropped back on to the mound of soft pillows like a beached whale, gasping with effort and fear. 'You're trying to destroy my child!'

'On the contrary, your child is extremely important to me. But I need your co-operation, and I need to know the truth.' Isobel moved to sit on the side of the bed, catching her daughter-in-law's wrists in her own strong hands. 'Tell me, Fiona – who is the father of this child?'

'It's George – George – George!' Fiona's voice rose to a scream. 'Who else could it be?'

'There's no sense in shouting, dear,' Isobel told her calmly. 'The servants all know that I am with you and that I can be trusted to decide when the doctor should be sent for.'

'Fetch the nurse!'

'When I'm ready. I pay her wages, Fiona. She'll wait, like the rest of them, until I give her her orders. It can be very useful, holding the purse-strings. You'll learn that in time.'

'George—'

'Forget George,' Isobel advised crisply. 'We don't need him. You were about to tell me who you chose to father your child, weren't you, my dear?'

Tears, born more of anger than fear, glittered in Fiona's eyes. 'Damn you!' She spat the words out, trying without success to free herself from the older woman's grip.

'I already know what it's like to be damned, my dear, and it holds little fear for me now. I've made some very discreet enquiries, Fiona, and I believe that I already know the answer to my question. But I must hear it from you. I must know that the parentage is acceptable. Until I do,' said Isobel Dalkieth clearly, 'there will be no nurse, and no doctor. Do you hear me, Fiona? If necessary, we'll deliver your child together.'

'I'll tell them—' Fiona panted, against the beginning of the next pain.

'And I'll tell them that it all happened more quickly than either of us thought it would. My word will stand against yours. Tell me his

208

name, Fiona,' Isobel added as her daughter-in-law caught desperately at her hands again. The rings on the older woman's fingers hurt them both as Fiona struggled against the contraction. When it finally receded, Isobel said again, mercilessly, 'Tell me!'

'Ro – Robert Archer.' The name came out in a wail, and Isobel nodded her head.

'I was almost certain. A good choice, my dear.'

'Please – the doctor—'

'One more thing before I send for him. No doubt you've had some ideas about holding the truth about your child's parentage over my head or my son's head one day.'

'No!'

'Don't lie to me, Fiona. We're going to need each other from now on. Between us we'll rebuild Dalkieth's for my grandchild – my son's child. But there's to be no thought of using what you know in order to feather your own nest. Do you understand me?'

'Oh God – it's coming—!'

Isobel managed to free one hand and swept the bedclothes aside. 'You're nearer your time than I thought,' she acknowledged. 'Listen to me, my dear – if you are planning to blackmail George or myself in the future then I might well save myself a lot of trouble by letting you and your baby die here and now. Do you understand me?'

'Yes – yes! Help me, you old witch!' Fiona screamed as her mother-in-law moved away from the bed. In a moment Isobel was back, thrusting a leather-bound Bible into the girl's hands. Fiona clutched at the book, sweat breaking out on her forehead.

'Swear to me on this Bible that nobody but the two of us will ever know the truth. Nobody!'

Fiona Dalkieth looked into her mother-in-law's cold green eyes and knew that the woman meant everything she had said. There would be no assistance until Isobel got what she wanted.

'I – I promise!' She forced the words through gritted teeth and felt a cool hand brushing the hair back from her forehead.

Then the door opened and she heard Isobel's voice, far away, calling urgently to the servants.

21

In August Alice, who had, as her mother said, turned into a right wee organiser since she started work, hit on the idea of arranging a trip on the River Clyde for the people living in the tenements.

'One of the women that comes into the pawnshop regularly was telling me the other day that they used to do that sort of thing when she was wee,' she told Jenny. 'We'd a back-court party to celebrate the end of the war, and one when the first peacetime ship was launched – is it not time we were celebrating again?'

Walter's eyes lit up, but Jenny said cautiously, 'I'm not sure there's much to celebrate just now. Daniel says that these folk in England who put money into Dalkieth's are in trouble and two of their yards have had to close down. If it happens here—' She let the words trail away, her eyes drawn to the crib where three-month-old Shona, who had just been fed, lay kicking.

'All the more reason to have something to look forward to just now,' Alice argued, and Walter nodded eager agreement.

'If there's bad times coming we'd at least have something good to remember. I mind once when I was a wee laddie my mother and father took me on a steamer trip down the Clyde. It was grand.'

'I've never been on the river in my life,' Alice put in. 'It's time I tried it, and it's long past time Walter here went on a voyage, since he's set on being a ship's engineer.'

'Alice—' Jenny warned, mindful of the way Daniel would react if he heard such talk. Alice jumped up to croon to the baby, avoiding her sister's eyes.

'It should be a paddle-steamer,' Walter said, his face glowing. 'You can see the engines on a paddle-steamer. You stand at a rail, and they're right there in front of you.'

'You can explain it all to me,' Alice told him as she returned to the table.

'There's nothing much to explain.' He flipped through the exercise book spread open on the table then snatched up a pencil and started drawing diagrams on the inside of the back cover. 'It's all so simple and sensible, that's the beauty of it.'

Alice shuffled her chair round the corner of the table to get a better view of the drawing.

'The steam's forced through here, intae the cylinders there, d'ye see?' Walter talked on, his pencil flying easily across the page. Looking at his absorbed face, the light in his eyes, Jenny was reminded of the way Robert had been before he went off to Tyneside.

'Who'd have the time to organise an outing like that? It'd take a lot of work.'

'No it wouldn't.' Alice assured her sister briskly. 'I'll see to it myself. I'll put a poster up in the pawnshop and mebbe get one in the wee corner shop window too, to make sure everyone gets to hear about it. You'd come, wouldn't you, Jenny?'

'It would depend on what Daniel says. And there's Shona to think of. She's too little to take on a steamer.'

'We'll think of something. And even if Daniel won't go there's no reason why you and Walter shouldn't come along.'

'What about the cost? The folk round here haven't got money to throw away.'

Alice, the bit between her teeth, tossed every objection aside. 'They can bring bread and jam to eat, and bottles of lemonade. Old Mrs Smillie said they all kept back something special to pawn when it was time for the annual outing. Which means,' said Alice airily, winking at Walter, 'that it'll not do our shop any harm either, if I can get everything arranged. We've got almost five weeks before the end of September, I'm sure I can have it all seen to in the next three—'

They were so involved in what they were discussing that for once neither Jenny nor Walter heard Daniel's step in the close and the sound of the outer door opening. When he walked into the kitchen the three of them looked up with a start; Jenny's darning needle missed the heel of the sock she was mending and stabbed into her thumb, and Walter swiftly closed his exercise book, hiding the engine sketch from view as his father's eyes settled on him.

'Walter, have you not got homework to do?'

'He's been working all afternoon,' Jenny rushed to Walter's defence. 'Alice has been helping him with his mathematics.'

'Can you not manage it without help?'

Walter went crimson, opening his mouth to reply then shutting it again when Alice said calmly, 'It was just some problems I was going over with him. Sometimes two heads are better than one.'

'And sometimes peace and quiet are sufficient,' Daniel told her curtly. He jerked his head towards the door, and Walter, the tips of his ears afire with humiliation, scrambled to his feet, gathering his books together. One of them slipped to the floor; Alice and he both stooped to pick it up and for a moment their fingers touched.

'I'll see you again, Walter,' she told him, then turned to Daniel as the boy slipped out of the room. 'I was just telling Jenny and Walter that I'm thinking of arranging a trip down the water. Walter says he went with you and his mother once and fair enjoyed it.'

Daniel grunted noncommittally, taking his jacket off with abrupt movements and hanging it on the nail at the back of the door so sharply that Jenny thought for a moment that the material was going to tear.

Alice raised her eyebrows at her sister behind his back, then, in answer to the silent appeal in Jenny's face, said, 'I'd best get home. Mam'll be wanting me to see to Helen while she gets the dinner ready.'

'What was she doing here?' Daniel wanted to know as soon as she had left. Jenny put her darning aside and dropped to her knees to fetch some potatoes from the box beneath the wall-bed. It still felt good to be able to kneel again after the months of carrying Shona, when she had been too stout to move freely.

'She's my sister and Shona's auntie. She often calls in.'

'And does Walter come into the kitchen every time she calls?'

'No, but I don't see why he shouldn't be allowed to talk to her now and again. He works hard, Daniel, and he doesn't have anything like the freedom the other laddies of his age have.'

'That's because the other lads' parents don't care about their futures. I told you, Jenny, I'll not have him distracted from his studying.'

Daniel unfolded the newspaper he had brought in with him, shaking the creases out of it noisily. Shona, unaware of the tension between her parents, stared up at her own bare toes, flailing through the air, and let out a squeal of amusement at their antics.

Her father tossed a glance at the crib, the first time he had looked in its direction since coming into the room, then turned back to his newspaper.

'Another thing,' his voice said from behind the printed sheet. 'You shouldnae let that bairn lie there with nothing over her legs when Walter's in the room, It's not seemly.'

Jenny said nothing, but her grip on the handle of the potato-peeler tightened until her knuckles stood out sharp and white beneath the skin.

Alice lost no time in going ahead with her plans. With Walter's help, when his father was at work and well out of the way, she called at

213

every single flat in the area, and soon had a healthy list of families eager to take a trip 'doon the water'.

To her delight, Robert Archer looked in at the pawnshop when he heard about the proposed trip, and donated a generous sum from his own pocket. Part of it was used to subsidise the cost of the outing, but Alice kept enough back to pay for a generous boxful of sweeties for the children.

Even Isobel Dalkieth got to hear about the river trip, and offered, in a letter addressed to Alice, to pay for two charabancs to transport the Ellerslie party to Helensburgh, where they were to embark on the paddle-steamer.

Alice brought the letter to Jenny with a gleeful grin. 'I'm going to keep this letter for ever, Jen. Would you listen to the way she's worded it?' She held the paper at arm's length and read aloud in the manner of a herald reading a proclamation, '"—I have pleasure in making this donation to mark the birth of my first grandson, William Dalkieth, in the month of July in the twenty-second year of this century." Have you ever heard such a pompous way of saying that the bairn was born in July 1921?' Alice demanded to know, lowering the letter.

'I suppose the Dalkieths always have to sound different from the rest of us.' Jenny hung one of Shona's small gowns on the clothes-horse to air before the fire.

'At least she gave us money, and I'm grateful for that. I invited Robert to come along with us,' Alice went on, 'but he thought he'd better not. He said most of the folk would want to get away from the yard, not be reminded of it. You know, I like Robert. He might be one of the bosses now, but he's still human.'

Teeze sniffed when he read the letter from Mrs Dalkieth. 'George Dalkieth himsel's too mean tae put his hand in his pocket. He had tae leave it tae his mother.'

'He'd no' want tae waste good money on the likes of us,' Daniel agreed. 'I hope the boy grows up tae be a better man than his father.'

Excitement gripped the tenements as the appointed date approached. Bella offered to look after Shona, who was now bottle-fed and, by waiting until the right time and choosing her words carefully, Jenny managed to persuade Daniel to take herself and Walter on the trip.

'I can pay for it out of the money I got from Dalkieth's when I left,' she offered eagerly. Daniel had refused to take the ten-pound note Robert had handed to her, advising her to put it into the bank in case she ever had need of it.

Again he turned down her offer. 'I've not reached the stage where I

214

have tae be dependent on my wife for money,' he said stiffly. 'And God willing, I never will. I'll pay for the trip myself.'

Once his father had committed himself to going on the outing, Walter relaxed and talked of nothing else, although when Daniel was present he was careful to behave as though the occasion held little importance for him.

It wasn't fair on the boy, Jenny thought, noticing the way Walter hid his thoughts and feelings from his father instead of feeling free to express himself. She was determined to see that he enjoyed every minute of the outing, and that there would be other treats for him in the future, no matter what his father thought.

'Gonny come with us, Walter?' Jamie Preston coaxed for the tenth time. 'It'll no' take long, honest.'

'I'm supposed to go straight home,' Walter argued, though he yearned to go with the other boy.

'Ye will be, in a way. It's on the way home – well, nearly,' Jamie wheedled. 'Look, just down there an' not far intae the yard.'

They had met on the street corner on their way home, Jamie from school, Walter from the Academy. In one direction lay the street that led to the bridge, in the other lay the Dalkieth's shipyard. Walter eased the leather strap holding his school-books on his shoulder and his eyes followed Jamie's grubby finger, pointing towards the forbidden land.

'Can you no' go on your own?'

'Aye, but I'd as soon have comp'ny.'

Walter's eyes flickered towards the road he should be taking, then back to the road he wanted to take. 'You're sure your uncle said it would be all right?'

'I told ye!' An impatient note was creeping into Jamie's voice. He shifted his weight from one booted foot to the other with a rasping sound. 'My uncle's put in a word for me tae be taken on as a 'prentice, an' Mr Osbourne telt him tae tell me tae go tae the yard an' see him mysel' – och, for any favour, man,' he added, the impatience bursting forth, 'the hooter'll be soundin' if we stand here much longer. I'll go on my lone!'

He started down the street, his cracked boots scuffing over the paving stones and, after one last moment of doubt, Walter made up his mind and scampered after him. The opportunity to step inside the yard, even a little way, was too tempting to be resisted.

'I'll come – but we're not tae stay long.'

'I don't suppose Mr Osbourne'll have it in mind tae treat us tae tea an' biscuits,' Jamie said sarcastically, stopping in front of the yard

215

entrance. He scrubbed an arm over his face then spat on his hand before passing it over his tousled hair. 'Here – take these, I don't want tae look like a school-wean.'

He tossed his books, clumsily bundled together with a piece of old string, at Walter, who took them without argument, too busy staring up at the shipyard gates to object.

They were enormous, wide enough to take two lorries side by side, each gate a masterpiece of scrolled black iron, curved at the top in such a way that when they were closed they formed an arch, spiked at the top. The letters D-A-L-K, picked out in gold and a good twelve inches high, marched up the half-arch of the left-hand gate, while I-E-T-H ran from top to the bottom of the right-hand arch. When the gates were closed the name would be laid out like a golden rainbow straddling the sky.

'Come on!' Jamie tugged at his friend's sleeve, almost dislodging the two bundles he carried. Walter dragged his eyes away from the black-and-gold splendour, tightened his grip on the books, and followed the other boy through the gates and over the cobbles, trying to look everywhere at once.   Until then, his only sight of the shipyard had consisted of glimpses of the tops of cranes and derricks from the surrounding streets and the occasional illicit trip along the opposite riverbank. From there the building berths could be seen, with the vessels in them under construction.

Most of the shipyard workers' children had a better knowledge of the yard than Walter; occasionally, if a man forgot to take his midday 'piece' with him one or other of his children had to take it to him. Youngsters whose fathers were given to drinking or gambling their wages as soon as they received them were used to gathering outside the gates with their mothers on Fridays so that desperately needed money could be claimed before the man who had earned it squandered it in the public house nearest to the yard. But Daniel never talked of his work at home, other than to rail at the bosses for their injustices, and Walter had learned early in life that questions about his father's workplace were inevitably answered with, 'That's no place for you. You'll never have tae seek yer living in any shipyard – not while there's breath in my body!'

Once, and only once, he had dared to disagree, pointing out that shipbuilding, particularly on the Clyde, was a hard-learned skill to be proud of. Daniel had rounded on him, tense with anger.

'What d'you know about it? The noise and the filth and the – the degradation of it all!'

In the face of his rage Walter had fallen silent and never dared to broach the subject again, though the word 'degradation' had told him

216

more than his father realised. It told him that in his past, a time that was never mentioned, Daniel Young must have been a scholar, and he guessed that somehow his father's academic thirst had been denied and suppressed. He was trying, Walter realised from then on, to quench that thirst through his son. But knowing that, understanding something of his father's motives, had given Walter no consolation. Daniel had once wanted what Walter had, but ironically Walter craved what his father had – the chance to serve his apprenticeship in a shipyard, then eventually go to sea as a ship's engineer.

At the rickety wooden gatehouse just inside the yard Jamie was talking earnestly over the closed lower half of the door. The watchman leaned out, one arm gesticulating as he gave directions, and Jamie nodded then jerked his head at Walter and set off at a trot.

'I'll be watchin' for yez comin' back,' the watchman shouted as Walter scurried past. 'None o' yer loiterin', mind. An' nae pilferin', or I'll spifflicate yez!'

'It's the machine shed we're lookin' for,' Jamie panted when Walter caught up with him. 'Down on the right he says, across from the berths—'

The rest of his words were drowned out by a thunderous clanging from deep inside the huge building they were passing. Both boys shied away in sudden panic, Jamie clapping his hands to his ears and laughing shame-facedly at his own fright. Walter, hampered by the books he carried, felt his head ringing with the merciless racket of machinery hammering metal into shape.

'Christ—' Jamie shouted as they cleared the building, 'Nae wonder hauf the men that work here are deaf!'

A handcart piled high with copper piping came wavering towards them, the front wheel bouncing from one cobblestone to another and being deflected each time so that the entire cart zig-zagged from side to side as well as inching forward. They skipped out of the way and, as it went past, Walter saw that it was being pushed by a youngster less than half the height of the load which towered above him, threatening all the time to burst the ropes that lashed it to the cart. A large peaked cap of the type all the shipyard workers wore, known as 'doolanders', was jammed down over the boy's ears and almost rested on his nose. Beneath it, what could be seen of his face was purple with effort, his lips drawn back in a grimace and his teeth clenched.

As they went deeper into the yard the clanging from the shed they were leaving behind gave way to a mixture of other sounds – saws ripping their way through timber, hammers bouncing and echoing on metal, men yelling, the hiss and thump of steam-driven machinery. The place was as busy as Ellerslie High Street on a Saturday afternoon, and the broad strip they walked along was edged with great piles of timber, its fresh, sharp, resinous smell enfolding the boys before becoming absorbed in the general smell of heat and metal and oil as they moved on. Great sheets of iron and steel were piled along the roadside, too, and there was even a massive boiler, large enough to hold the Young's two-roomed flat, resting on the cobbles like a whale driven ashore on a beach.

Walter's head swivelled from side to side as he trailed after Jamie, trying to take in everything at once. The sheer size of the place, the activity and even the noise, enthralled him. He detoured, skipping over rails and abandoned scraps of metal as he went, to peer in through a cavernous door larger than the yard entrance. A massive machine rose up into the shadows of the roof, dwarfing the line of men who tended it. The smell of oil caught at his lungs; he sneezed, a sound drowned by the machine's rumbling, and turned away to follow Jamie, realising that they had almost reached the first of the building berths. The first three vessels were in their early stages; within the stocks their shapes were outlined in sturdy timber that from a distance, had a delicate, lacy quality. The metal sheets that would be put in place later were piled on the ground before each berth, sacrificial offerings to heathen gods. Sheer-legs and cranes clustered round the ships and men worked everywhere – on the ground, on the skeleton vessels high above, on the stocks themselves. It seemed to Walter that there were more men in the part of the yard he had seen so far than there were in the whole of Ellerslie.

As they walked further along, jostled out of the way now and again by cursing, hurrying men, more vessels came into view, great ribbed monsters with their graceful sweeping outlines supported on timber struts. One was almost completed, clothed in metal armour, her upper decks already railed in, one propellor in place. Walter stared up at the vast, curved underbelly of the ship, the part that would be below the surface when the vessel was in the water, and knew what an ant must feel like when it looked up at the raised foot of a passing human being.

Jamie, suddenly remembering what he was there for, tugged at his sleeve. 'What was it the man said?' he bellowed in Walter's ear. 'Across from the berths?'

'I don't know,' Walter shouted back, his eyes greedily travelling over the ship. 'I didnae hear him.'

'We'll have tae ask,' Jamie roared, and pulled again at his arm. Reluctantly, knowing that now that he had seen the yard for himself he would never be content to spend his life in an office, Walter lowered his gaze, staggering slightly as dizziness washed over him.

The nape of his neck, which had been bent right back while he gawked up at the ship, reproached him with a twinge of pain and he had to move his head cautiously from side to side to loosen cramped muscles as he followed Jamie away from the building berths and in through another enormous opening. He stepped into the noisy darkness and stopped, appalled.

In the early days of the war Walter's mother had started taking him with her on Sundays to a religious service in a small hall where a powerfully built man with iron grey hair and a thick beard had talked for hours on end about the eternal flames of hell, where the sinful and the damned would toil and burn and suffer for eternity. Daniel Young had a strong mistrust of religion, and so Walter's mother had made him promise not to tell his father when he came home on leave.

The man had painted such a graphic word picture of the torments of hell that Walter, drinking in and believing every word, had started to suffer from nightmares. Unfortunately one of the nightmares occurred while his father was home and Daniel discovered what his wife and child had been up to in his absence. Furious, he had forbidden visits to future services.

The nightmares had gradually stopped after that and Walter had forgotten about them as the years passed, but now, stepping inside the building opposite the berths to be struck by a blast of heat, he was transported back in an instant to the world of eternal hellfire.

Before him lay a huge, dark cavern, splashed by scattered patches of crimson and gold flames from roaring furnaces tended by shadowy figures glimpsed only sporadically against the fires. The merciless crash of hammers beating on metal resounded through the place. It looked and sounded as though a vicious thunderstorm had been trapped inside the building and was crashing round and round, roaring endlessly, fruitlessly, for freedom.

Near the door two men stripped to the waist, their arms and torsos black, worked over an anvil, taking it in turns to hammer at a sheet of metal held in place by a third man. One of them saw the two boys hesitating just inside the doorway and broke the pattern of his work, lowering his hammer to the ground and leaning on the long, sturdy handle. His partner paused, looking round to see what had caused the interruption, his eyes rolling like pale marbles in his filthy face.

The first man's teeth flashed in the gloom as he shouted something at the boys. Jamie, intimidated, stumbled back a step, bumping into Walter, seizing the sleeve of his jacket and urging him forward. 'Tell 'im we only want tae know where the machine shop is,' he said nervously as the second man dropped his hammer and strode towards them.

219

Walter clutched the books to his chest, his mouth dry with fear, the nightmares flooding back into his memory. This was exactly what the preacher had talked about. Surely hell couldn't be any worse than this place and the Devil himself couldn't be any more terrifying than the man who was now standing over him?

His nerve broke. He dropped the books and turned to run, wanting only to get away from this place and out into the blessed cool air. A hand, black and oil-shiny, caught at his shoulder and he was spun back towards the flame-shot, thunderous blackness of the place.

'Walter! What the hell d'ye think ye're up tae?'

He would never have known, if he hadn't heard that familiar voice, that the filthy, half-naked devil looming over him, reeking of oily sweat, was his father . . .

22

'What's that on your jacket?' Jenny peered at the material. 'It looks like oil.'

Walter, who had returned home from school later than usual that day, mumbling something about having had to stay behind to help one of the teachers, pulled the sleeve round and inspected the greasy smudge. His face went red. 'I – I must've leaned on a wall.'

'Take it off and I'll see what I can do with it. Are you all right?' she asked as he obeyed, his head lowered so that his face was hidden from her.

'I'm fine.' He handed the jacket over and went to his room.

'Where's the boy?' Daniel wanted to know as soon as he came into the kitchen an hour later, clean and neat as always, but with a suppressed anger, a deepening of his usual tension, that frightened her.

'Working on his books, the same as he always is at this time. Is there something wrong?' He ignored her, striding to the door and calling his son's name.

Walter came at once. 'I only went because—' he began as soon as he came into the room, but his father interrupted him, his voice thick, the words forced out of his throat.

'You disobeyed me.'

Walter swallowed, then said, 'Jamie Clark had tae see one of the gaffers about work in the yard. He asked me tae—'

'I'd forbidden ye tae go near that yard, and ye deliberately disobeyed me!' The room crackled with menace.

'Daniel,' Jenny said nervously, then flinched back as he rounded on her, his dark eyes blazing.

'You keep yer neb out o' this, it's between me and my son!' he told her harshly.

Walter was white to the lips but he held his ground. 'Is it because I saw you? Is—' his voice suddenly broke and faltered, and he took in a sharp, steadying breath, his eyes still locked with his father's. '—is that why you're angry with me?'

Daniel's hands clenched into fists and for a moment Jenny thought that he was going to hit the boy. Instead he said, his own voice scarcely above a whisper, 'Aye, ye saw me – ye saw how yer own father has tae earn his livin', in filth and sweat. Now ye know why I'll not have ye settin' foot in that place!'

'What's wrong with working with your hands?' Walter's voice was thin but desperate. 'Where's the shame in it? It's surely more honest than letting other men work tae earn for you—'

'Get back tae yer books,' his father told him roughly. 'Ye don't know what ye're talking about!'

'I do! I'm fourteen now, old enough to be out of the school. Old enough tae know what I want.'

'Walter—' Jenny warned, but he paid no heed.

'What you want doesnae come intae it – it's what I want that matters!' Daniel snapped, but Walter obstinately struggled on.

'I want tae leave the Academy and go intae the yard. I want tae learn tae be an engineer, then go tae sea,' he told his father, whose lips thinned with rage.

'Workin' in the filth an' the noise of the engine shop at Dalkieth's, then goin' tae sea buried in the bowels of a ship, at everyone's beck an' call? There'll be none of that for my son!'

'It's my life we're talking about! You can't make me live it your way.'

Daniel's fury had reached white-heat. 'I'll have a bloody good stab at it,' he snarled.

'I want tae be an engineer,' Walter insisted, his hands folded tightly into fists by his side.

'Ye'll dae as ye're told!'

They faced each other, Walter only half a head smaller than his father, both of them whip-thin, though Daniel's body was muscular and strong, Walter's still boyish and unformed. If Daniel chose, Jenny thought fearfully, he could beat the boy into a bloody pulp. Walter must have known it, too, but he had gone too far to back down.

'I'll not always be under your control,' he said, his voice, in the throes of breaking, only just managing to avoid rising to an absurd, childish squeak.

'Ye're under it for now, an' ye'll dae as ye're told! I'll not be crossed! D'ye hear me? I'll not be argued with in my own house!'

Daniel's thin chest was heaving and he was beginning to spit the words out breathlessly between foam-flecked lips. Jenny, suddenly afraid that he was in danger of going into a fit, put a hand on his arm, only to have it violently thrown aside.

'D'ye hear me?' Daniel demanded again. There was a brief pause, then Walter, paper-white but still in control of himself, nodded.

'Aye, I hear ye. But the day'll come, Father, when I'll be old enough tae walk out of this house an' go my own way. And I'll mebbe never come back. You just mind that.'

Daniel gave a strangled yelp and his hands moved swiftly to the buckle of the broad leather belt round his waist. Jenny stepped between father and son again, her own hands reaching to cover his.

'No, Daniel! I'll not have you beating the boy!'

He growled, trying to shake her off again, but she held tight, and he had to give up, glowering at her, so close that she felt his breath warm on her face.

'Have it yer own way,' he said at last, then, looking over her head at Walter, he added, 'But ye can forget about goin' on the steamer trip next week.'

Jenny heard the boy catch his breath with a gasp that was close to a sob. Turning, she saw his eyes flare as though he had just been struck in the face.

'Daniel! You can't do that to the laddie!'

'He went intae the yard when I'd forbidden him tae go near the place. You'll not let me give him the beatin' he deserves for defyin' me, so he'll have another punishment instead. Now get back tae yer books,' he growled at his son.

Walter turned and went without a word. As the door closed on his skinny back Jenny said, 'How could you be so cruel? He's been looking forward to the trip for weeks.'

Daniel picked up his cap. 'Ye've spoiled him long enough, you and that sister o' yours. It'll be her that's put these daft notions intae his head.'

'It wasn't Alice at all. Walter's wanted to be an engineer for a long time.'

His eyes were accusing. 'So ye knew about it all along, did ye?'

'He mentioned it one time.'

'An' ye kept it a secret from me? From now on,' said Daniel viciously, 'Mind yer own business and leave the raising of my son tae me. You've interfered enough!' And he stalked out of the house.

Jenny's hands shook as she made a cup of tea and took it into the narrow, airless little room where Walter spent most of his time. He was staring down at his books, pencil in hand, and didn't look up when she tapped on the door.

She set the saucer down. 'He doesnae really mean it – about you not going on the trip.'

'Aye he does.' Then he added, low-voiced, 'I wish I'd just taken the beatin' instead.'

'I'll talk to him—'

'Leave it!' He looked up and she saw the angry tears glittering in his eyes. 'The harm's done, and you'll make it worse for yourself.' Then he added more gently as she began to argue. 'I don't want you tae get intae bother because of me. And I'll not have the two of us sidin' against him. It'd not be fair.'

'Walter, why did you have to go to the yard when you knew he was so set against it?'

'Jamie asked me tae go. Anyway, I've wanted tae see inside that yard since I was wee. It doesnae do any good,' said Walter with adult wisdom, 'tae deny things tae children. It just makes them hungry tae know more. Mind that when wee Shona starts askin' ye questions.' He stared at the pencil between his fingers. 'It was me seein' him that he couldnae stand. Seein' him covered with the filth of the place, runnin' with sweat.'

Jenny looked at the situation through his eyes and knew why, after what Daniel had done, his son could still find the compassion to understand and pity him. 'Daniel hates dirt. He must hate having to work in it every day.'

'I just wish he was man enough tae understand that I'm proud of what he goes through tae keep me – and you, and the wee one,' said Walter. As she was going out of the room, he added, 'I meant what I said – as soon as I can, I'll be out of here. And I'll no' be back.'

Daniel and his son scarcely spoke to each other after the quarrel. Walter spent all his time in his room when his father was at home, coming into the kitchen only for meals, which were eaten in silence. When Daniel was out Walter played with the baby and helped Jenny as before, but there was a change in him, a withdrawing that worried her.

Alice, too, noticed it, and was furious when Jenny told her what had happened. 'How could Daniel be so hard on him? Walter's always done all he could to please his father.'

'And now he's gone back into his shell. It's as if he's rebuilt the wall that he always had round him.'

'I'll break it down,' Alice said confidently, but even she couldn't reach Walter; this time his defences were impregnable.

Jenny's hopes that Daniel would relent came to nothing. Anger at being defied by his own son continued to burn deep within him and, not content with banning Daniel from the trip on the River Clyde, he introduced a series of other, small punishments. He insisted on being shown the boy's homework every evening, and he was never satisfied

224

with what had been done, demanding that it be re-worked. Walter began to eat most of his meals in his own room, or go without, because Daniel decreed that he couldn't spare the time from his books. Even the boy's milk-round was carefully timed, with Daniel waiting impatiently at the closemouth for his return, and imposing one small punishment after another each time he considered that the boy was later than necessary.

Walter seemed to shrink back into himself, suffering the continual tyranny without complaint, refusing to talk about it to Jenny. When she tried to protest to her husband, she was told shortly that matters between himself and his son were none of her business.

Ashamed to tell anyone, even Alice, what was happening, unable to offer either comfort or hope to her stepson, Jenny felt helplessly that the whole business was slipping out of control.

September had started off as a wet month, the air damp and heavy with reminders that the summer was over and autumn had arrived. But when the Saturday chosen for the trip arrived the clouds were gone and the sun was out. It was clearly going to be one of those perfect autumn days rarely seen in that part of the world.

All morning the streets round the tenements were busy with women darting in and out of closes, borrowing and exchanging pieces of finery, packing food, hurrying to the shops for items that had been forgotten until the last moment, tripping over the excited children who scurried about like frantic mice, unable to stand still for more than ten seconds at a time.

By the time the midday hooter blew in the yard the women and children were dressed and ready and there was scarcely a kitchen where the window wasn't already opaque with steam from the tin bath waiting in front of the range, with soap, towel, clean shirt and freshly pressed suit close to hand.

Walter had taken little Shona to his room, so that Jenny could get on with the housework. When she went in to fetch the baby he looked up, startled, and her heart ached when she saw his red-rimmed eyes and the track of tears on his cheeks.

'She poked her finger in my eye,' he said hurriedly, handing the little bundle over and scrubbing at his face with his sleeve. 'It was watering.'

'Mebbe your father'll change his mind about the trip, now that the day's arrived.'

'Mebbe.' Walter bent over his books, his voice muffled. 'If not, don't go blaming yourself. It's my own fault. I shouldnae have gone tae the yard.'

225

She cuddled the baby, trying to find some words of comfort. 'Time passes, Walter. You'll soon be old enough to do as you want.'

The hooter shrilled from the yard, signalling the end of the Saturday shift.

'I tell myself that,' Walter said as Jenny stepped out into the narrow hall. 'But there's times when I wonder if I'll ever really be free of him, or if he'll be with me wherever I go, no matter how old I am.'

Before the sound of the hooter had died away the first of the men came pounding over the cobbles. Along the streets they poured, peeling off to disappear into this close and that close like rabbits fleeing down their burrows before a fox.

In Jenny's kitchen there was no need for the tin bath. She had to wait longer than the other women for her man to return home but when he did he was clean and neat, already dressed in his best brown suit and clean white shirt. She looked up hopefully as he came in and saw at once that he hadn't changed his mind. For weeks she had looked forward to the outing, but now that Walter was staying home the pleasure had all gone. She would happily have stayed behind to keep the boy company, but when she suggested it, using a sudden concern over leaving Shona as an excuse, Daniel insisted on her going with him. 'You went tae enough trouble tae get me tae agree in the first place,' he said implacably. 'An' we're both goin'. The bairn'll be fine with Bella.'

By the time the menfolk were ready the charabancs had arrived, almost filling George Street from footpath to footpath. As the people poured out of their closes and clambered into the charabancs children were passed from hand to hand and grans and grandpas were cheerfully 'punted' up the high stairs by those queuing behind them. Alice rushed between the two vehicles, exercise book in hand, ticking off names to make sure that nobody was left behind by mistake or, even worse, that no dishonest person had managed to sneak aboard in the hope of getting a free ride.

The loaded buses jerked forward to a great burst of cheering from the loiterers who had gathered to see them off. Faces bobbed at the windows and hands flapped vigorously at those being left behind.

'Ye'd think we were emigratin' tae the other end of the world,' giggled Maureen, sitting by Jenny, her boisterous toddler bouncing on her lap. Helen, only weeks away from her fourth birthday, eyed him disapprovingly from her own seat on Jenny's knee. She wore a new blue dress Alice had made specially for the outing and a straw hat freshly trimmed with a row of little blue silk flowers was perched on her red-gold curls. Lottie was on the outing, but she and Neil had vanished into the other charabanc without a backward glance and

Helen, used to her mother's neglect, had watched them go without complaint then slipped her hand in Jenny's.

Helensburgh, a residential town long popular with rich Glasgow industrialists in search of an attractive riverside area where they could build summer houses well away from the smoke and grime and factories that brought them their wealth, was a graceful town of wide streets and smart shops and an air of serenity. As the charabancs turned from the main street and made for the pier the lusty singing that had started up before they had cleared Ellerslie was replaced by a whoop of excitement at sight of the paddle-steamer, 'Lucy Ashton', waiting for them by the pier.

'Look!' Helen pointed at the trim little steamer, smart in the colours of the North British Fleet. Her hull and paddle-boxes were painted black, picked out in white. Her white deck-saloons shone in the sun like cake icing, and smoke plumed from the single red funnel with its white band and black top. The Union Jack fluttered from the steamer's bows and the house flag, a red pennant with the Scottish thistle inside a white circle, flew from the top of a slim flagpole almost twice the height of the funnel.

'I'm going up there,' Helen shrieked into Jenny's ear, indicating the open upper deck, where wooden seats were laid out in rows for the convenience of passengers. At the upper rail the steamer's ports of call were listed in white letters on a polished wooden notice board. 'Hunter's Quay, Kirn, Dunoon, Rothesay.'

The River Clyde was on its best behaviour as the 'Lucy Ashton' moved serenely across the mouth of the Gareloch. The sun made the water sparkle like a handful of diamonds and the white water in the steamer's wake turned to glittering snow for several yards before breaking up into fine lace and eventually reverting back to water again. Clearing the Gareloch they passed another opening, this time to Loch Long, that narrow, deep stretch of water edged on both sides by heavily wooded hills that plunged down into and below the water like Norwegian fjords.

Daniel, in company with most of the men and boys, went down below at once to watch the engines working. Jenny patiently trailed over every inch of the steamer with Helen, who finally settled for the upper deck where she could wrap her arms around the rail, her red-gold head angled out and down so that she could watch the water sliding past the ship's flank.

'It's spoiled, isn't it, with Walter not being here?' Alice settled on the bench beside her sister.

'I'm trying to remember everything so that I can tell him about it.'

'So am I, but it's not the same,' said Alice, sadly.

227

At the first three destinations they only stopped for long enough to land some passengers and pick others up. The longest stop was at Rothesay, on the Isle of Bute, where the passengers had just over an hour to spend as they pleased. Some explored the shops and a few, including Lottie and Neil, hired bicycles and set off to explore the island. Jenny and Daniel, the Malloys, and Alice and Alec Monroe, her employer, elected to have a picnic on the beach then the men and boys launched themselves into a noisy game of football. Alec, his lungs injured by gas during the war, couldn't join them, but Alice roped him in as her assistant and the two of them took the smaller children to the water's edge to paddle in the sea. Jenny would have been content to watch, her back comfortably settled against a convenient rock, but Mrs Malloy would have none of it.

'Hold my skirts down, lassie,' she ordered, slipping her shoes off and glancing swiftly from side to side to make sure that nobody was watching her. Jenny did as she was told, and after scuffling discreetly beneath her skirt for a moment Mrs Malloy triumphantly flourished a pair of thick, much-darned stockings.

'I'll hold your skirt now. Come on, our Maureen, we could all do with gettin' a bit of salt water round our feet.'

The water was cold and they stood in a huddled group for a moment, shrieking in various sharps and flats each time a small wave broke round their ankles until the chill of the water eased as their skin became used to it.

'Come on, then,' Mrs Malloy boomed, hoicking up her skirt and petticoat to reveal thick, well-muscled calves, so generously roped with bunches of swollen veins that they looked like carved, slightly bent pillars in an old church.

The women followed her, venturing in until the water reached their knees. All too soon the steamer gave a long, mournful bellow on its siren, the signal that it was time for its passengers to return.

'It sounds as sorry to go home as I am,' Alice said as they straggled back along the beach. Wisely, she had decided to hold the sweets, bought with Robert Archer's money, back as a final treat for the homeward journey. She was still close enough to her own childhood to know what was popular, and there were squeals of delight when Alec and Jacko opened the boxes that had been stacked in the purser's office, out of reach of inquisitive fingers, to disclose a rich harvest of boiled sweets, sherberts, 'soor plooms', chews, aniseed balls, midget gems, liquorice straps, toffees, cinammon sticks, and even toffee apples.

As the steamer headed for Helensburgh on the last lap of the journey Jenny glanced at Daniel, leaning now on the railing and looking towards the land that was creeping nearer with every turn of the paddles. He had caught the sun and there was a faint blush of colour over his forehead and cheekbones and nose; he had taken his jacket and tie off and loosened the collar of his shirt. His body, as he leaned over the railing, was relaxed. He turned, caught her eye, and turned away again without speaking or smiling. She wondered if he was regretting his harsh decision to deny this trip to Walter. But regrets weren't enough, she thought, sad for the man as well as the boy, knowing that unless Daniel, by some miracle, learned to unbend, there was little hope for a future relationship with his son. In a few short years, as she had reminded Walter, he would be old enough to live his own life, and if Daniel insisted on continuing down the path he followed now he might never have the chance to know his son as a man.

Jenny shivered as across the water Helensburgh grew from a blurred mass to a collection of roofs and steeples. What did the years ahead hold for her, and for Shona? At some time in his past Daniel Young must have suffered deeply, to have so much bitterness burned into his soul. He was a good provider, an honest man, and she still cared for him, despite his rigid attitude towards Walter. But she knew that now her caring had come to have more pity in it than love.

She was Daniel's wife, she had promised to stay by his side for the rest of their lives, and it was not a promise made lightly. But she had begun to fear for Shona. She couldn't bear to think of her baby being subjected, like Walter, to such a harsh regime as she grew older. Jenny had seen enough of life to know that children brought up without love very often found it impossible to give love themselves, and she didn't want that to happen to either Walter or Shona.

A group of children thundered past, screaming with excitement, and she came out of her thoughts with a start to realise that she could clearly make out the pier and the charabancs waiting to take the Ellerslie party home.

Moments later they were bumping gently against the timbers of the pier and as the great pistons in the engine room below slowed, reversed, then stopped. The paddles came to rest and the water beneath the paddle-boxes calmed.

Once the steamer was safely roped to the pier the gangplank was put into place and the passengers began to surge down it, children's heads bobbing in sleep on their fathers' shoulders, their mouths sticky and stained with raspberry and lime and orange and lemon and liquorice. Daniel, carrying Helen, was loose-limbed with the pleasure of the day as he strode sure-footed down the gangplank, Jenny at his back.

As they stepped on to the pier two uniformed policemen stopped Jacko, several yards ahead, and spoke to him. He turned, his little son sleeping on his shoulder, his cheery face suddenly puzzled and concerned, and indicated Daniel.

The police officers advanced, solemn-faced, drawing Daniel and Jenny out of the throng to tell them, with rough gentleness, that Walter had hanged himself that afternoon from one of the hooks in the back-court wash-house . . .

23

As soon as Robert Archer walked into the general office the supervisor rushed over to him, almost dancing across the floor in his agitation.

'Mrs Dalkieth's been sitting in your office for the past twenty minutes,' he whispered, 'I said you were in the Tank section, and she said she'd wait.' His moustache bristled with anxiety. 'I'd have sent someone to fetch you, or at least taken her to the boardroom where she'd be more comfortable, but she'd have none of it.'

'I'm sure it'll do her no harm to sit on a hard chair for once.' Robert turned away from the man's shocked expression and went towards the door of the small room that led off the general office. George Dalkieth used the comfortable office adjoining the counting house that his father and grandfather had had before him and Robert had had to make do with what was left.

Isobel Dalkieth, straight-backed in an upright chair, extended her hand to him when he went into the room and he took it briefly in his. 'Good afternoon, Mrs Dalkieth. You wish to see me?' He seated himself behind the desk, making no reference to the time she had had to wait. He was in no mood to be pleasant or self-effacing.

'I've come to apologise to you, Mr Archer,' Isobel Dalkieth said flatly, then, as he gaped at her, she allowed herself a slight smile. 'Well may you look surprised. It's not often that I apologise to anyone.'

'Particularly someone so much further down the social scale than yourself.'

'You sound bitter.'

'I believe I have a right to be bitter, Mrs Dalkieth.' He gave her a level look.

'I can understand that.' Isobel smoothed her expensive gloves in her lap then looked the office manager in the eye. 'Mr Archer, my husband was a man of vision and intelligence, and he recognised two things many years ago. One was that, of his two sons, the elder was fit to follow him into the business while the younger was not. The other was that at some time in the future, the yard might have need of a man with experience, intelligence, and a sense of loyalty. Brilliant though he was, I doubt if he could have foreseen the coming of the war and our elder son's tragic death.' She paused for a moment then said more briskly, 'Be that as it may – he looked around for a suitable candidate to fill that need, should it arise—'

'And settled on me,' Robert interrupted, impatience in his voice. 'You mentioned intelligence; I've got enough of that to be aware of my own history, Mrs Dalkieth.'

Her mouth tightened, then she nodded. 'You're quite right, I was being condescending. And I now realise that, without stopping to think of the harm I was doing, I've all but ruined my husband's plans by insisting on keeping control of the shipyard and letting my maternal affection – my natural maternal affection,' she stressed slightly, 'take precedence over my sense of the rightness of William's intentions. In that sense I've done you a grave injustice.'

Robert dismissed the final sentence with a wave of the hand. 'I'll not wither away and die from your lack of understanding, Mrs Dalkieth, but the business might. You may already have delivered it a mortal blow – you and your son and the other Board members.'

'You're being very harsh, Mr Archer.'

'As I'm not a gentleman I see no point in mincing my words.' Robert opened a drawer, rummaged among some papers and withdrew an envelope which he tossed over to her side of the desk. 'I was about to hand this to your son, to be read out at the next Board meeting. You might as well take it.'

'Your resignation?' She made no attempt to pick the envelope up. 'Your decision to desert Dalkieth's?'

His eyes glittered at her from the other side of the desk. 'Don't bother trying to make me feel like the rat deserting the sinking ship, ma'am. I did my best to save this yard and I was thwarted at every turn. My sense of loyalty towards the Dalkieths vanished some time ago.'

'I'm quite aware of that.' Isobel's tone was enigmatic but, as he looked up sharply, she went on, 'However, what's done is done and I'm not here to rake over the past. Do you intend going back to Tyneside?'

'Perhaps – if I can find a place there. It's more likely that I'll have to seek work abroad. I have no ties and I'll go wherever I must.'

She rested her elbows on the wooden arms of her chair and linked her long, slim, fingers together. 'Mr Archer – how, in your opinion, can this yard escape closure?'

His answer was prompt. 'It must break loose of the combine that's strangling it.'

'In order to do that we would have to buy back the shares they hold.'

'Which means applying for a considerable bank loan and running yourselves into a great deal of debt,' he agreed. 'But that is your only hope. You must also look closely at the interests this company holds in other businesses. Some will be worth keeping because they'll pay for themselves with careful management. Others will have to be sold off, if that's possible.' He spoke swiftly and decisively, like a man who had already given a great deal of thought to what he was saying. She watched him, frowning slightly, but not interrupting him.

'You must try to sell off the additional land your son insisted on buying, and try to sell a large part of the new machinery, possibly abroad. It'll never be used here anyway – there won't be enough work coming in to warrant it – and at the rate things are going,' he pressed on ruthlessly, 'you'll be bankrupt in two years. There's no point in letting good machinery rust away to scrap when you might get something back on it. Not as much as you paid, but a few pounds are better than nothing. The Experimental Tank's giving a good account of itself, but you'll have to fine down the main yard, possibly close some of the berths and lay off more workers. Offer to build vessels at more competitive prices.'

'That would leave us very little profit,' she protested.

'Indeed, and it'll lead to bitterness among the workers and the unions. Nobody,' said Robert with feeling, 'likes to see men thrown out of work through no fault of their own. It will also lead to panic among your shareholders; they would need to be carefully handled and assured that if they can stand behind you and give you their continued support they'll get their money back eventually. The market will recover, Mrs Archer. I don't know how long it'll take, but it must recover eventually. All Dalkieth's can do at the moment is try to survive until then.'

'Do you believe that it can be done?'

'Not,' said Robert flatly, 'unless the Board changes its way of thinking.'

'If I guarantee that that will happen—' Isobel picked up the sealed envelope and held it between the tips of her fingers, '—if I give you my word that from now on you will be listened to and your advice will be followed, will you reconsider your resignation?'

'To be honest, Mrs Dalkieth, I doubt if you could bring yourself to vote against your son when it came to it.'

She jutted her chin and said, her voice hard, 'I can do anything I put my mind to.'

233

He leaned forward, propping his elbows on the desk, steepling his fingers. 'Why should I believe that you mean what you say? Why the change of policy now, when it's almost too late?'

'I have my grandson's future to consider now. He may only be a few months old, but I fully intend that he shall inherit the yard one day. If that is to happen the company *must* keep going. I also intend to make certain,' she added, 'that he will be a worthy successor to my husband. But I can't do it alone, Mr Archer. I need your help.'

'Mrs Dalkieth, I've tried to give you assistance in the past and been spurned. Your grandson is no concern of mine, so why should I be willing to put my own interests aside in favour of his?'

She gave him an oblique look from beneath her lashes. 'Give me one year to prove that what I promise, I will do. And, during that year, do all you can to guide the company along the lines you've suggested.'

'You're asking me to act in what the workforce will naturally see as a ruthless manner. Once again I'll be the villain – only this time it'll be more than just the Board opposed to me.'

They eyed each other warily, no longer the elegant lady and the man from the tenements, but equal adversaries, both ruthless, both determined. 'What salary would it take to persuade you to give me that year?' Isobel Dalkieth asked at last, and he gave a bark of impatient laughter.

'You couldn't afford to pay me what I'd deserve, Mrs Dalkieth. Not with the financial problems the yard has at the moment.'

She smiled faintly, and shrugged. 'Your right. Nor can I appeal to your loyalty, for you already offered me that when you came back to Ellerslie – and I threw it back in your face.'

She got up, walked round to the side of the desk, and deliberately dropped the envelope into the waste-basket.

'I can only ask, in the name of my late husband who gave you a chance many years ago – and in the name of my grandson, who deserves the opportunity to prove himself.'

Robert hesitated. 'I like the idea of a challenge.'

'I thought that you might. I *hoped* that you might.' She smiled, a genuine smile, and held out her hand. Her fingers curled about his, strong and bony. 'I promise that you'll not regret your change of heart, Mr Archer.'

As he opened the office door for her she added, 'You will receive an invitation tomorrow morning to my grandson's christening celebration. I promise you that it will be the last unseemly exhibition of wealth in the Dalkieth family until such time as we can celebrate the rebirth of the yard and the end of the downturn in the market. I

234

hope that you will accept. Indeed, I would particularly like you to be present.'

Daniel went through the formalities of arranging his son's funeral impassively, not even uttering a word of protest when he was told that Walter, a suicide, must be buried in a far corner of the parish churchyard instead of being laid to rest beside his mother in the plot that Daniel had bought for himself and his family.

'It was his fault – if he had been kinder to Walter, the poor lad would still be with us,' Alice said fiercely, her own eyes red with weeping as she and Jenny watched Daniel walk alone from the grave without a backward glance. 'He stood there as if he didn't care one whit—' Her voice broke and Jenny put her arms round her sister, holding her as she longed to hold Daniel.

'Ssshh, pet. He's grieving in the only way he knows.'

Alice dug into her pocket for a handkerchief and blew her nose hard. 'We were getting to know each other, Walter and me. I feel – it's as if we'd just managed to touch each other's fingertips. If I'd only had the time to take a good grip on his hand he'd not have fallen the way he did!'

'I know.' Jenny watched her husband's retreating back. 'I know.'

'You must never let him do the same thing to Shona.' Alice pushed the handkerchief back into her pocket. 'Whatever happens, Jen, don't let him!'

On the day after the funeral Daniel got up at the usual time and dressed, not in his good street clothes, but in his dungarees. He went off to work without a word and returned soon after the siren blew to mark the end of the working day, still filthy from the foundry. Jenny, who had half-expected this to happen, said nothing, but fetched the hip-bath from the hall cupboard and filled it with water from the pots she had been heating on the range, just in case. When Daniel stripped and climbed into the bath she helped him to wash, scrubbing his back as her mother had scrubbed her father's and Maurice's at the close of every working day.

When he was clean Daniel dressed and sat down to his meal, leaving her to empty the bath pailful by pailful before drying it and putting it away. Now that Walter was gone there was no reason for him to hide the truth about the work he did.

From then on he only spoke to her when he had to, and paid no attention at all to Shona, even when she crowed and laughed and held out her chubby arms to him. Lying awake by his side in the night, knowing full well that, like her, he was sleepless, Jenny longed to reach out to him. But he made no attempt to touch her, and on the only occasion when she tried to put her arms about him he flung himself violently from the bed and blundered out of the kitchen without a word and into Walter's room. From that night on, he slept in his dead son's room, with Walter's books laid out on the little wooden desk and Walter's coat hanging below his on the nail on the back of the door.

'I can't reach him,' Jenny said miserably to Bella after several weeks had passed and it had become clear to her that Daniel had no intention of letting their lives return to normal. 'If he'd talk about the laddie, or even let himself grieve naturally – but he'll not do it.'

'It's strange the way grief takes different folk. Look at my Pat, now – just when I'd given up all hope of him ever coming back tae himself he began tae change. Mebbe it'll go that way with Daniel.'

'Mebbe you're right, mebbe he just needs time,' Jenny agreed, but without much hope.

It was ironic that just as Daniel was retreating from this world Patrick Kerr had begun to regain something of his old self. He had asked Jacko Livingstone, who worked in the joinery shop at the shipyard, to make him a decent pair of crutches, and had started to go out again. He arranged to be fitted with the special boots he had refused when he first came home from the war, and already Alice had sold about half a dozen of his carvings in the pawnshop and had taken in a few orders for more. He used scraps of discarded wood Jacko brought to him from the shipyard, and driftwood that Bella and Alice found on the shores of Ellerslie Water.

Some of the strain had left Bella's face and she had started to smile again. Nobody seemed to have noticed that Patrick never spoke to Jenny or looked at her. She knew that although her outburst on the day Shona was born was probably responsible for his improvement he would never forgive her for what she had said to him, and the way she had laughed at him as he lay sprawled on the floor at her feet.

Sometimes, when she looked at herself in the mirror and realised that she was still young, only twenty-three years of age, panic rose into her throat, threatening to choke her. The thought of spending year after year in the same small flat with a husband who had become a stranger terrified her. On these days she wanted to gather Shona up and walk out of the house, out of Ellerslie, to a place where the two of them could start a new life. But she couldn't leave Daniel; without her there to cook his meals and keep his house clean and wash his clothes, what would become of him? And how could she cope in a strange town with no friends or family and a small baby to care for?

Fiona Dalkieth studied the people milling round the large drawing room at Dalkieth House and smiled contentedly. This was what she had worked for, planned for. The guests, among them some of the most important and influential people in the district, were all here to attend her son's christening party and, as his mother, she was indispensable and free of any fears that she might be cast aside by George and sent back in disgrace to her father, who was at that moment standing by one of the windows, champagne glass in hand. Beside him, George gulped from his own glass as though trying to slake a burning thirst, although Fiona knew for a fact that he had been drinking steadily since their return from church.

Not that it mattered now if he drank himself to death. She stroked the silky pale fur on the cuffs of her cream and brown brocade jacket and glanced casually to her right, where she could see herself reflected in a long wall mirror. She had lost most of the soft plumpness left by child-bearing, and the long jacket and straight, matching skirt below skilfully slimmed the last lingering traces of excess fat out of existence. Her cream shoes, square-heeled with sequins scattered over the brown rosettes at the insteps, were flattering to her ankles and calves, while the sapphire earrings just seen beneath her brown and cream turban matched her eyes admirably. The earrings, and the bracelet on her right wrist, were a gift from George, to mark his gratitude at the birth of his son.

Fiona's smile widened as she remembered the fuss George had made over the cost of the sapphires. His mother had over-ruled him, telling him sharply that he had waited long enough for this son and heir and that his wife deserved only the best. She herself had paid for Fiona's brocade and fur suit, summoning representatives of a well-known and respected Glasgow fashion house to Ellerslie so that her daughter-in-law could choose the materials and pattern in comfort. Isobel had also decreed that now that a new member had been born into the Dalkieth family the time for dressing in black to mourn the dead was over, and she herself was dressed on this auspicious day in lilac and pale grey.

Fiona moved through the room, assuring a group of gushing women that small William, the guest of honour, would indeed be brought to the drawing room as soon as he had wakened from his afternoon nap, stopping to talk with studied condescension to her father and mother and brother, pausing to rest a hand on George's arm and reach up to kiss his cheek.

'Eat something, my dear,' she breathed into his ear as she did so. 'If you don't you'll probably fall over and you know how displeased your mama would be if that happened in front of her guests.'

She smiled sweetly into his angry eyes and moved on to another group, confirming that yes, the house she and George had lived in until recently was to be sold.

'We've decided to settle in with Mother Dalkieth,' she explained. 'She's been lonely in this large house on her own and, of course, she wants William nearby.'

'I'd not care for the thought of living with my mother-in-law,' one of the women said, and other heads nodded their agreement.

Fiona's blue eyes widened. 'But George's mother and I get on very well indeed. We understand each other perfectly and we both want the same things for George and William.' No need to point out that here, in Dalkieth House, there were enough servants to ensure that Fiona need never be troubled by any of the tiresome duties of motherhood, and enough room to ensure that she and George need never again share the same room, let alone the same bed. She had done her duty by him and now she was about to reap the rewards.

There was a stir as the nurse came in, her arms filled with the imposing christening gown Isobel had bought for her grandson. The baby was carefully laid in his mother's arms, staring solemnly up from beneath the white swansdown trimming of his christening cap at the cooing women who flocked from all sides of the room. Fiona was moving in slow procession down the centre of the room, smiling graciously at the well-wishers, when someone in front of her moved away and she saw Robert Archer standing by the door, watching her.

The breath caught in her throat and her arms tightened protectively round her son as she was transported back to the moment when Robert had stormed into the house she had shared with George to confront her. They hadn't met since that day.

'I'll take William now, my dear,' Isobel said in her ear, and Fiona relinquished the bundle of silk and lace as Robert walked towards her.

'May I offer my congratulations, Mrs Dalkieth?'

'Mr Archer,' she said graciously, offering him her hand. Then, seeing that Isobel had moved away and they weren't being overheard, she added low-voiced, 'What are you doing here?'

'I received an invitation.' His eyes, cold and grey as a misty day, searched hers and he smiled thinly, recognising her panic. 'Afraid that I'll speak out of turn? My dear Fiona, gentlemen aren't always born in mansions and boors aren't always born in tenements. But I don't suppose you'd realise that.'

Looking round to make sure that they were still not overheard Fiona saw that Isobel, sitting on a sofa with the baby in her arms, was watching her closely. She realised that Robert's invitation was the older woman's way of discovering whether he was likely to be a threat to the Dalkieth family.

She took a deep breath and smiled up at him. 'Thank you for your good wishes, Mr Archer,' she said, her voice clear as a bell. 'Excuse me, I must have a word with Mrs Palmer . . .'

24

Isobel Dalkieth kept her word. Despite her son's opposition she had Robert Archer appointed to the Board of Directors and saw to it that he was given the freedom to carry out the changes he had insisted were essential if the Dalkieth yard was to survive.

The results of the ruthless decisions he had to make rocked the town and led to a considerable number of men being laid off from the yard. Daniel Young was one of them. He walked through the yard gates for the last time in the middle of January, 1922.

In the four months since Walter's death Daniel had spent most of his evenings and weekends away from the flat, only coming home to eat and sleep. After being turned away from the shipyard he stayed at home, day and night, staring into space, making no attempt to seek other work and worrying Jenny with his refusal to talk about their future.

It was common knowledge in the town that George Dalkieth had more or less given up all pretence of running the shipyard, and spent most of his time brooding in his office or at home, while Robert Archer had taken over the reins. As a result, Robert was blamed for what was happening in the yard.

'Good men bein' turned off after giving years o' their lives tae the company an' others havin' tae take cuts in wages,' Teeze rumbled, his big scarred hands tightened into knotty bunches on his thighs. 'But whatever happens the Dalkieths'll not go without, ye can be sure of that. An' Archer's done well for himsel', has he no'? The bastard thinks nothin' o' climbin' on the backs o' his own folks tae dae it.'

'It's not Robert's fault,' protested Faith, who still had a soft spot for her dead son's friend. 'All the yards are having a bad time.'

Teeze coughed, then spat with a skill born of years of experience between the bars of the range. The burning coals behind the bars hissed briefly. 'There's no danger o' him bein' turned off, though, is there? He's seen tae that.'

A week after Daniel was laid off Jenny and Robert Archer came face to face in the street. She would have ducked past him with a nod and hurried on but he stopped directly before her, laying a hand on her arm. 'Jenny, I'm vexed about your husband having to be turned off, especially after what happened to the boy. But I've no power to choose that one man should go before another.'

She was uncomfortably aware that the passers-by were staring at Robert, some of them with antagonism. Under the shawl she wore she tightened her arm protectively about Shona, slumbering against her breast. 'I don't blame you for what's happened, I know that all the yards are in a bad way just now.'

He nodded. He looked tired and there was grimness in the set of his mouth. Jenny felt sorry for him. He was basically a good man and she knew that he would take no pleasure in the harsh steps he was having to take to safeguard the yard.

'If Dalkieth's isn't pruned back now it'll be finished once and for all,' he said sombrely. 'I'd as soon see the place staying open and mebbe being able to take the men back eventually than have it closing down and everyone thrown out on to the street. But that's no consolation to men who have no work to do and no pay coming in. But Jenny, there's a place in the main drawing office. It's yours, if you want it.'

'The drawing office?' For a moment excitement leapt up in her, then she came back to earth. 'I don't know how Daniel would feel about that. Then there's the bairn to think of.'

'It'd be a wage coming in. You've got a good, skilful hand, Jenny, and I'm not offering the work out of charity. They could fairly do with you in the drawing office. Can you not speak to Daniel about it?'

'I could try, I suppose . . . I must go, Robert, he'll be wondering where I've got to.'

He touched his hat to her. 'Think about my offer,' he said as she turned away. 'Let me know.'

She thought of nothing else as she hurried home. Since Walter's suicide there had been times when the resentment she had experienced when Maurice's death had forced her to give up her plans to move to Glasgow came flooding back; each time she fought it down, for there was no sense in brooding over what might have been. She tried hard to concentrate instead on keeping the house nice for Daniel, who neither noticed nor cared, and tending Shona, who was growing into a contented affectionate baby. Without her daughter, Jenny knew, life wouldn't be worth living.

But now Robert's offer of work, the sort of work she had always wanted to do, put temptation in her way once again. As she made her way automatically through the streets she tried to think of the best way to put the offer to Daniel. They desperately needed the money she would earn, but she doubted if Daniel would agree to being supported by his wife. He certainly wouldn't consider a reversal of roles, with him looking after the house and caring for Shona. He had done that after his first wife's death, but he had done it all for Walter, and what little interest he had shown in his daughter had died along with the boy. If – Jenny scarcely dared to even think the word – he agreed to her going back to work, she would have to pay Bella or her mother to look after the baby. Lottie had married Neil Baker in the previous November and she and Helen were now living in a smart little tenement flat several streets away, so Faith would be free to take Shona during the day.

But there was another problem. Daniel knew that Robert had been Jenny's sweetheart before going to England, but it was obvious from remarks he had made in the past that he considered the relationship to have been a childish affair, one that was over and forgotten long before Robert's return to Ellerslie. Since then he had grown to dislike Robert simply because he was 'one of the gaffers', and as such he was allied in Daniel's eyes with the Dalkieths. Like Teeze, Daniel put the sole blame for his dismissal at Robert's door.

Walter's short life and tragic death bore witness to the fact that Daniel Young was a man who looked on his family as his possessions rather than human beings with rights of their own. If he was ever to discover that his wife and Robert Archer had been lovers, Jenny thought, there was no telling what he might do. And the very fact that it was Robert who had offered the job to her might be enough to stir suspicion in his mind.

She had no choice – she must turn down Robert's offer of work. But with every step she took she wanted the drawing-office job more and more. She had the ability to do it, they needed the money – by the time she turned in at her own close she had convinced herself that if she was patient, if she waited for the right time to speak, if she used the right words . . .

There was a lightness in her step and a smile on her lips as she lifted the latch and stepped into the tiny hall.

She had left Daniel huddled by the range in the kitchen, but now the room was empty. She put Shona down in her cot and glanced in at Walter's room. It had been left just as it was when Walter walked out of it for the last time, with one of his school-books open on the small table, a pencil lying on top of it. Sometimes Daniel sat in there, but today it, too, was empty.

Jenny returned to the kitchen and was about to see to the baby when she noticed a page torn from one of Walter's exercise books lying on the kitchen table. She read the few words scrawled over it in disbelief.

Daniel wrote, in a scrawl quite unlike his usual neat script, that he had gone to look for work, away from Ellerslie to where nobody knew him. There was no mention of keeping in touch with his wife, or sending for her and his daughter when he could. There was no word of assurance or affection. Just his formal signature, 'Daniel Young,' at the bottom of the page.

At first Jenny was afraid that Daniel planned to kill himself, just as his son had done. Over the next week she attended to Shona mechanically, hurrying to the door every time she heard footsteps in the close, lying awake night after night listening to the wind howling round the building and wondering if he was out in the open, perhaps sleeping rough, or ill and unable to get help. She called on all the men Daniel had worked with, but nobody had seen him or heard from him. She even went to the police station, where she was assured that there had been no word of an accident involving an unknown man, and the river hadn't cast up any bodies.

'There's plenty of poor souls on the roads just now, missus, looking for work,' the police constable told her gruffly. 'Yer man'll probably come back tae ye, and with any luck he'll have found a place for himself. He's mebbe not wantin' tae face ye until he can bring a wage in again.'

Confused and bewildered, Jenny waited for two days, then three, then four. When a week had passed without any word from her husband, she knew that she could wait no longer and she must face up to some hard facts.

She didn't love Daniel, at least not in the way that a woman should love her man. He had been a conscientious husband but as a father he had shown little interest in Shona, and his behaviour towards Walter had been so ambitious and self-centred that he had destroyed the boy. As for Jenny herself, the fact that he had made no attempt to contact her or to find out if she and Shona were managing showed that he had little genuine feeling for her.

She no longer wanted to live with him again, but for Walter's sake more than anyone else's, she needed to know that Daniel was safe and well, that he hadn't, in his misery and guilt over the boy's death, decided to follow the same path and take his own life.

In the past few days, waiting in vain for word of him, she had been haunted by the memory of Walter, wounded beyond bearing by his father's continual bullying, insisting through ashen lips, 'I'll not have the two of us sidin' against him. It'd not be fair.'

If Walter was here, he wouldn't rest until he had made sure that his father was alive, and safe. Since he could no longer do that, Jenny must do it for him, if only to atone for the part she herself had played in his death by standing by instead of finding some way to convince Daniel that he was being unfair to his son. And when she had done her duty by Walter's memory, when she had made certain that Daniel was all right, she would be free to shape a new life for herself and her child.

She wrote at once to Lizzie Caldwell in Glasgow, and when she got Lizzie's reply she took it across the close to show to Bella. Her sister's small face crumpled with dismay as she read the letter.

'Why did ye want tae go askin' her tae find you a job in Glasgow?' she wanted to know. 'This is where you belong.'

'I'm certain now that that's where Daniel's gone, to the big shipyards there. I have to try to find him and I need to support myself while I'm about it.'

'But it's a big place – how could you find one man there? And what about the house, and Shona? Ye'll no' be able tae pay the rent here as well as pay for lodgings for yerself.'

Jenny had thought it all through. 'I'll have to let the house go. Daniel didn't give a thought when he left as to how I was going to manage to keep it on. We can always get somewhere else to live when I find him – we might settle in Glasgow, if he gets work there. As for Shona . . .' She touched the little girl's soft brown hair, knowing that parting with her daughter, even for a short while, was going to be hard. '. . . I'll ask Mam if she'll take her for a wee while. I've still got the money I got when I left the tracing office – that'll help me to pay Mam and keep myself until I get started in the job Lizzie's managed to find for me. It'll not be for long,' she added hopefully. 'Mebbe Daniel's got a job already and he's writing to tell me at this very minute.'

'Jen, let me take Shona,' Bella said on a rush of words, her eyes hungry.

'You? But—' Jenny glanced at Patrick, intent on carving a cat. Before him on the table lay a photograph; obviously someone had put in an order at the pawnshop for a wooden model of a favourite pet. As usual, he hadn't looked up when Jenny came into the room, only grunted a greeting and gone on working.

Bella's hands twisted together in her apron. 'Mam can help out while I'm at Mrs McColl's and anyway, I don't have tae go out working so much now that Pat's bringing a bit in. I'd like tae look

245

after the wee one for you, Jenny.' She went over to the table and put her arms about her husband. 'What d'ye think, Pat? We could manage, couldn't we?'

He laid down his knife – a sharp, small-bladed knife Alice had given him, easier to work with than the vegetable knife he had started with – and looked up at her in silence for a moment. Then he shrugged and went back to his work.

'If that's what you want,' he said indifferently, and Bella looked up at her sister, her face radiant. As far as she was concerned, the matter was settled.

Robert called at the flat and did his best to persuade Jenny to stay in Ellerslie.

'I've already offered you work – take it, and stay here so that when your husband comes back the house'll still be here,' he urged, but she shook her head.

'I'm sure he's in Glasgow and it's not right that he should be alone at a time like this. I need to know he's all right,' she said firmly, and he finally gave in, insisting on accompanying her to the station on the allotted day.

The air was rancid with the lingering remnants of the night's fog and the ground was slippery underfoot. Their breath met and became one white cloud as Robert stood on the platform, still in Ellerslie, while Jenny looked down at him from the carriage, feeling that already she was on foreign ground, almost in limbo.

'D'you think you'll find him?' he asked.

'I must.'

'I think you're frightened in case he's taken his own life, as the boy did.'

'No!' Shaken by his perception, she almost shouted the word out. A man hurrying past paused and stared at her in confusion, then scurried on his way.

'I think you're both sick with guilt over the laddie's death, Jen, you and Daniel,' Robert persisted, and when tears blurred her eyes he reached up and laid a gloved hand over hers where it rested on the window ledge. 'His fault, mebbe, but never yours. Don't go blaming yourself for other folks' wrongs, my dear.'

Further down the snaking train a door slammed, the sound echoing mournfully.

'It seems to me that the man just wants to be on his own,' Robert went on. 'If I'm right, he'll not thank you for the trouble you're taking.'

'Mebbe.' She blinked the weak tears away and his face came

246

into view again, upturned to hers. 'But I have to be sure of his feelings before I can think of trying to make another life for me and Shona.'

'Remember, if there's anything at all that I can do you only have to let me know.'

'I will. Thank you, Robert, you've been a good friend to me.'

A shadow clouded his eyes. 'Not such a good friend in the past,' he said. 'But I intend to make up for that in whatever way I can.'

The whistle blew and as the train jolted forward sudden terror swept over Jenny at the thought of going off to the city on her own. She wanted to open the carriage door, to jump out and bury her face in Robert's shoulder and stay there until, somehow, her world came right again. Instead she waved from the window until he was hidden from her by smoke from the funnel and it was too late to do anything but follow her plans through.

Lizzie was already waiting at the ticket barrier in Queen Street Station, a welcome sight to Jenny, who was quite demoralised by the clamour of the place, including the noisy chirruping of birds in the great iron arches far overhead. With an air of calm confidence Lizzie beckoned to a lad and ordered him to carry Jenny's case.

'I can manage,' she protested, but Lizzie frowned and shook her head.

'You're a Neilson employee now,' she said, her mouth shaping the words primly, like a buttonhole slipping around a button. As they stepped out of the station entrance she pointed proudly to the open square on the opposite side of the street. 'That's George Square, with all the statues. And over there—' her finger stabbed in the direction of a handsome building with pillars and an upper balcony overlooking the square, '—that's the City Chambers.'

The streets round the square were busy with trams and cars and bicycles and horse-drawn carts. Jenny scarcely had time to get used to the noise before Lizzie hurried her away, the boy with the luggage trailing a few steps behind.

'You'll be able to see the emporium on the way to your lodgings in Oswald Street. This is West George Street we're in just now. I've managed to get you into the china and glass department on the first floor. I work on the ground floor myself. The woman you'll be lodging with used to work in the millinery department but she's retired now, and recently widowed. Very respectable. You'll be able to walk to work.'

Lizzie herself, it transpired, lived in a boarding house for young ladies in Tollcross. 'It's very genteel – I was fortunate in getting a room there. I was recommended by Miss Blake, who supervised the drapery department before me. I'd have got you in there, but there are no rooms vacant just now. There's Neilson's down there – see?' They had rounded the corner into Buchanan Street, and she indicated a tall building halfway down the hill. They were on the opposite pavement; as they got nearer Jenny could see the words, 'Neilson and Son' in large gilt letters over the three glassed double-doorways in the centre of the building, between two rows of huge display windows.

As they crossed the street and walked along the frontage of the store, admiring the toy window, the two ladies' fashion windows, the gents' clothing window, and the millinery window, Lizzie bragged about the navy and gold canopies that were pulled out over the windows each morning. Then they walked round the corner of the store and into an alleyway so that Jenny could familiarise herself with the staff entrance, not nearly as grand as the front entrances which were reserved for customers and the more superior staff members, such as the floor-walkers.

At the end of Buchanan Street they turned into Argyle Street where they were separated briefly by a group of people advancing along the pavement towards them. Jenny swerved towards the kerb, the youth with the case following her, while Lizzie moved the other way, towards the shop windows. Reunited, the three of them waited at the junction with Union Street until a policeman held back the traffic for them, then after crossing they plunged beneath the railway bridge known, Lizzie informed Jenny, as the Highland-man's Umbrella because the Gaelic-speaking Highlanders who had flocked to Glasgow for work tended to meet there. At the far side of the bridge they crossed the road again and turned into Oswald Street, where Jenny was to lodge.

Mrs McLean lived in a spotless close where the stairs, even those from the pavement to the close itself, were neatly edged with fresh white pipe clay and the lower sections of the close walls were covered with shining bronze tiles edged with small blue flowers. Her door on the first floor landing was a poem in flawless varnished wood, with brass knocker, nameplate, letter-box, handle and bell-push gleaming as though they had been fashioned from pure gold. While Lizzie rang the bell, Jenny dug in her purse for a coin for the station lad, who handed her case over, skimmed down the stairs, and was whistling his way through the close by the time Mrs McLean opened the door.

The landlady was very small and slight and dressed in black

silk with white lace at collar and cuffs and a black apron. Her grey hair was skewered high on her small head by long pins topped with black jet knobs that matched her bright black eyes almost exactly.

'You buy your own provisions,' she said as she led them along the hall. 'I will cook your breakfast and tea each day, and lunch on Sundays but I don't care for folk in my kitchen. And I do *not* permit gentlemen callers.' She opened a door and stepped back. 'I hope the room's to your liking, Mistress Young.'

The room allocated to Jenny had highly polished linoleum on the floor with a small, handmade rug by the narrow bed, a wardrobe, a chest of drawers, one chair, and a small marble-topped table bearing a flowered bowl and a matching soap dish and water jug.

'It's grand, Mrs McLean, thank you,' Jenny said warmly.

The grey head bobbed briefly in acknowledgement. 'The bathroom's the next door along,' said the woman, and withdrew.

Lizzie sat down on the bed, taking her hat off and looking round. 'It's not bad.'

'It's very nice indeed. Imagine – an indoor bathroom!'

'Glasgow's very modern,' said Lizzie complacently, getting up to tidy her hair before the mirror. 'Jenny, d'you know how difficult it's going to be for you to find Daniel in this city?' she asked as she worked, her voice muffled by a hairpin gripped between her teeth.

'It'll be like looking for a needle in a haystack, but I've got to try. I couldn't just stay in Ellerslie, not knowing what was happening to him.'

Lizzie removed the hairpin from her mouth and stabbed it back in place, then patted her hair. 'There's thousands of places where he could have found lodgings. Are you certain he's in Glasgow at all?'

'I don't even know that. But I have to try,' Jenny repeated, fully aware of how hollow the words sounded.

'Well, I'd better get back, and you'll be tired. You're sure you'll remember how to get to the emporium in the morning?' she asked anxiously as she pinned her hat on.

'Of course I will. If I forget I've got a good Scots tongue in my head,' Jenny said firmly. She was growing a little tired of her friend's patronage.

'If you have to ask anyone for directions, make sure you speak to someone respectable. Mebbe I should come round early tomorrow and walk to the store with you.'

'You'll do nothing of the sort! If I can't manage to find a big place like Neilson's on my own how am I going to find Daniel? I'll need to get used to the streets and I might as well start tomorrow. You've done more than enough for me already.'

At the door Lizzie said anxiously, 'You'll remember to be at the staff entrance at eight o' clock sharp?'

'I'll remember. Goodnight, Lizzie,' Jenny said, and after she had closed the door she took a quick look at the bathroom before going back to her own room. She was gazing in wonder at the white, claw-footed bath, wash-hand basin, and lavatory bowl boxed in with varnished wood when a door further down the hall opened, making her jump guiltily.

'You'll take a cup of tea and a wee bit shortbread with me before you go to your bed?' Mrs McLean suggested.

'Oh, that would be very nice,' Jenny said, gratefully.

'It'll be ready in the kitchen in five minutes,' said the landlady, and Jenny went back to her own room to take a new white blouse and a black skirt out of her case and hang them up in readiness for the morning.

Tired though she was when she went to bed she lay awake for a long time, tossing restlessly in the strange bed, wondering how Shona was settling in, and if she was fretting for her mother as much as Jenny was fretting for her.

By the time the clock in the hall chimed midnight she had made up her mind that she couldn't spend another night away from her baby, and fell asleep on the decision to catch the first train home in the morning. She slept fitfully throughout the night, but by morning her commonsense was restored, and she knew that she had to stay in Glasgow, at least for a while. Shona would be safe with Bella, and Faith was nearby to help out if needed. Lizzie had gone to a great deal of trouble to find a job and a room for Jenny, and she couldn't go back to Ellerslie until she had at least made a good attempt to find Daniel.

She took up her position in a corner by the staff entrance of Neilson and Son's Buchanan Street emporium well before eight o'clock, keeping out of the way of the people who poured down the narrow lane and in at the entrance. They flocked in, some alone, others in groups of two and three, chattering and laughing, some yawning, some of them throwing her inquisitive glances as they swept past her and in at the modest wooden door. She wondered, as they flooded by, if one day soon some of them at least would be known to her.

Lizzie bobbed out at her from the middle of a group. 'There you are,' she said as though she had been searching for Jenny everywhere. 'Come on!'

It was like being five years old all over again, going to school for the first time. Even Jenny's first day in Dalkieth's hadn't been as nerve-wracking as this, because there had been some familiar faces in the wax-model room and Senga, whom she had known well at school, was as new and as nervous as Jenny herself. Here, she knew nobody but Lizzie, who was enviably confident of her surroundings as she showed Jenny where to put her coat and where she could tidy her hair.

'I forgot to say last night that I'd be grateful if you'd call me Eliza from now on,' she murmured as they stepped from the ladies' cloakroom into a narrow corridor. 'Lizzie's too common, now that I'm supervising my own department.'

'D'you think I should call myself Janet, then?' Jenny asked in amusement, but Lizzie – Eliza, Jenny reminded herself – was quite serious.

'Oh no, Jenny'll do. After all, you'll just be a salesgirl.'

As they made their way along the corridor they were jostled by women in crisp white blouses and neat dark skirts and men in smart suits. Some of the older men wore grey striped trousers, stiff high collars, and frock-coats.

'Are they customers?' Jenny asked in a whisper, and her friend gave her a withering look.

'Not at all – they're the floor-walkers. They oversee everyone and make sure the customers are kept happy.' Colour flooded her plain face as one of the frock-coated men paused on his way past to greet her by name. 'That's Mr Scott of Gents' Suits,' she murmured as he passed on. 'He's very genteel.'

'Is he married?'

'His wife died two years a – what d'you want to know that for?'

'You went as red as a poppy when you saw him.'

'Don't be daft!' Lizzie snapped, her colour deepening, reminding Jenny of carefree days in the school playground when romance was still something to be dreamed about and whispered over. 'Come on – I've got special permission to take you into the foyer before we go to our departments, but we'll have to be quick because the customers'll be coming in soon.'

They turned down a short corridor, leaving the bustle of incoming employees behind, then Lizzie opened a door and Jenny followed her into a dazzle of light and space. She had never in her life seen such a handsome place as the entrance foyer of Neilson and Son. Marble flooring stretched from where she stood to the huge plate-glass doors some distance away, and five galleries rose overhead, each supported on huge pillars garlanded with wreaths of gilded flowers. The galleries culminated in a great glass cupola high above, and the overall effect was one of light and space and opulence.

In the summer, Jenny realised, natural light would pour in through the glass frontage and the cupola, but on that late February morning it was still dark outside, and the place was lit by chandeliers on every floor and suspended from the roof.

'This is my department,' Lizzie said proudly, leading Jenny forward. 'Neilson's started in drapery and it's always been one of their main departments.'

The space in the middle of the huge foyer was empty, but to the sides, beneath the first gallery, ran a series of long, polished counters with shelving on the walls behind them. Between the shelves stands draped with materials blazed with jewelled colour, from shell-pink to crimson, pale lilac to royal purple, soft cream to burning orange. As well as self-colours there were floral patterns and stripes and polka-dots, and every type of material from thick warm velvet to delicate summery muslin. Women, neatly dressed in blouses and skirts, were beginning to come through the small baize door behind Jenny to take their places behind the counters, each murmuring, 'Good morning, Miss Caldwell,' as she slipped past. Lizzie greeted each one by name, giving stiff little nods of the head almost as though she was royalty.

'My staff,' she explained.

'Did you arrange all those stands, Li – Eliza?'

'Of course not, they've got folk specially paid to do that, and the windows too.'

Craning her neck Jenny saw that a wide marble staircase rose from the foyer, directly opposite the entrance, dividing at the back wall to lead off left and right towards the first gallery. The pillars edging the stairs were draped in generous swathes of material in shades of green varying from a deep woodland green at the bottom of the stairs to a delicate pale shade at the landing, each swathe draped as though it was a wide sleeve being held up and out to indicate the way to the floor above.

Lizzie's voice brought her back to the foyer itself. 'These are the lifts – for customers and management only.' She indicated two tiny apartments, one at each side of the foyer, well lit by electric lighting, the walls padded with pleated gold cloth. Wrought-iron sliding doors had been folded back, and a uniformed white-gloved page-boy in Neilson's navy blue and gold colours stood beside one of the lifts. Three doormen in uniforms heavy with gold braid stood conferring by the main doors from the street.

'It's all – beautiful!' Jenny said in awe. A scamper of feet came from behind them and a second page-boy, still fixing his pill-box hat in position, swept past to take his place beside the unattended lift.

'Come on, it's almost time to open and I've to see you settled in first.' Lizzie – *Eliza*, Jenny reminded herself – led the way back through the discreet baize door and into the plain narrow corridors that the store's customers never saw, to a flight of narrow wooden stairs that the customers would never be expected to use.

25

In the china and glass department the brilliance from a battery of skilfully placed electric lighting was echoed again and again in glass drops and prisms, crystal and cut-glass vases on the stands and tables. At the other side of the gallery tables covered with snowy napery were placed strategically in such a way that they allowed ample room for customers to move between them, each table set with a different china display. More china stood on stands between the counters which, as on the ground floor, were placed against the walls. The whole gallery was radiant with colour and pattern and reflections.

'My God,' said Jenny without thinking, 'I'd hate to see what a clumsy person could do in a place like this!'

'Ssshh!' Eliza was shocked. 'Our customers are never clumsy – and neither are the staff, if they know what's good for them.'

She led Jenny over to a grey-haired man, immaculately moustached and dressed in a grey frock-coat, grey-striped trousers, a snowy shirt with a grey bow-tie, and immaculate white gloves, and introduced her to the floor-walker, Mr Davidson. He inclined his head then said, 'You may go to your own department now, Miss Caldwell.'

'Yes, Mr Davidson,' Eliza said demurely, and slipped back through the baize door, leaving Jenny with the floor-walker. A very superior-looking lady standing behind one of the counters was introduced as Miss Lang, the china supervisor.

Her voice was frosty. 'What experience have you had in retailing?'

'None – but I worked for years as a tracer and analyst in a shipyard. A very delicate touch was needed for that – and a sense of responsibility. I learn quickly.' Jenny was determined not to be intimidated.

'Hmmph. Well, you'll assist Miss Ballantyne.'

Miss Ballantyne was an angular young woman of Jenny's own age, with curly red hair, more carrotty than the red-gold of Helen's and Lottie's hair. 'You'll be fine with me,' she said reassuringly when the supervisor had left them alone. 'Just don't knock anything over, and don't let Miss Lang get you down. Her bark's worse than her—'

She stopped abruptly as Mr Davidson, who had been standing by the low wall and looking down on the foyer, turned with one hand raised, palm out, the other reaching for the handsome watch chained to his waistcoat. The assistants behind the counters, mainly women, straightened their shoulders, their eyes fixed on the floorwalker.

Jenny sensed anticipation sweeping through the department, brushing against her, then moving on and upwards. She was suddenly keenly aware of the staff on the gallery above, and the galleries higher up, all standing to attention, all waiting for some signal. After a moment Mr Davidson nodded slightly, returned his watch to its pocket, and began to parade slowly round the gallery, hands clasped behind him.

'That's us open for the public now,' Miss Ballantyne said on an outgoing breath. 'They'll not start arriving for a while yet – this isn't the sort of store where the folk rush in as soon as the doors are opened. At least, not unless we're having our Christmas Bazaar. Now just watch me and remember that the customer's always in the right, even if she's a nasty old cat out to make trouble. And keep a smile on your face if you don't want Miss Lang or Mr Davidson giving you one of their looks.'

Within the hour the public had begun to invade the department, some using the marble staircase, others preferring to be whisked from floor to floor by lift. At first Jenny stood well back, watching and listening as her companion dealt with the ladies who approached their counter; later, when the department had become quite busy, she stepped forward nervously and managed to achieve her first sale without offending the customer or dropping any of the merchandise. As the woman walked away Miss Ballantyne gave Jenny an encouraging smile. 'You did fine. Now—' She nodded up towards the overhead wires, 'Let's see if you know how to work the cash system.'

Jenny had intended to spend every spare moment searching for Daniel, but at the end of her first day at work her feet and legs were so sore that it was all she could do to make her way downstairs, collect her coat and hat, and walk the short distance to her lodgings, where Mrs McLean awaited her in the kitchen with a cup of strong tea and a basin of hot water and mustard for her feet.

'I mind what it was like on my first day,' she said briskly, stirring the tea and handing it over. 'You'll get used to it – everyone does. Take your stockings off, my dear, there's alum and zinc in there to ease your feet, and I'll give you a recipe for some soothing powder to sprinkle inside your stockings in the mornings. You'll be fine inside a week.'

Jenny, gratefully flexing her stiff aching toes in the basin, doubted it. She was used to standing for hours at a time on the stone floor of the wash-house at home, but had had no idea that standing on carpeted flooring while wearing the smart shoes demanded by Neilson and Son could be so exhausting.

But her kindly landlady was right – after her first week the fatigue eased off and she began to settle into the store's routine. Under Kate Ballantyne's placid supervision she learned how to cope confidently with the customers, even the more difficult and arrogant of the women who came to their counter. She was fascinated by the girl's ability to speak 'pan loaf' to the clients then lapse easily into her own plain Glaswegian accent when there was nobody near enough to hear her but Jenny.

The plainer crockery on show at their counter meant that most of their clients were ordinary working-class women like themselves, but now and again wealthier clients, used to being treated with servility, would step from the lift – in some cases like a crab emerging from a pretty shell, Jenny thought privately – and advance on their counter.

'They're no' daft, the Scots wifies,' Kate said candidly when Jenny remarked on it. 'Those that don't have much tae spend want the best value for their money. And most of them that have plenty only have it because they wouldnae spend a penny more than they had tae. That's why you'll often get someone with a big house at Kelvinside and furs on her back walking past all the good china and coming to our counter. They want the best they can get – but they want it for as little as they have tae spend. And even our plain stuff's good quality, the Neilsons insist on that.'

Jenny learned to cope with the sophisticated pneumatic cash-carrying system, tucking money into hollow cups with screw-tops, sending them flying off along the overhead tracks to the change desk, and receiving the receipts and change by the same route within minutes. She learned how to recognise the 'tabbies' – the women who were only in the store to look, and had no intention of buying – and to give them enough attention to keep them happy without wasting too much time and energy on them. She absorbed the art of watching everything that was going on without seeming to watch, and how to keep a discreet look-out for kleptomaniacs.

'Not that we have many of them in this department, but some folk just can't keep their fingers to themselves,' Kate told her. 'Not just the poor-looking souls either – we've had real ladies trying tae slip a wee figurine into a pocket before this.'

For the first week it was all Jenny could do to keep up, let alone start looking for Daniel. By the second week she had begun to feel more confident about her own ability and had stopped crying herself to sleep every night, though not a minute went by, sleeping or waking, without her thinking longingly of Shona. She wrote to Bella almost every day and to her mother and Robert once a week, posting the letters on her way to work in the mornings.

'Now that I've settled in and stopped falling asleep every time I sit down I am about to start my search for Daniel,' she wrote to Robert at the end of the first week, her stomach turning over with nervousness as she re-read the words. Now that she was actually in the city, and had seen for herself now huge and how busy it was, she knew that she had little chance of finding her husband. But she had to try. She licked the envelope then sealed it, thumping the flap down with a determined fist to make certain that it was properly sealed.

She began her search in the area where she was lodging, for Oswald Street was close to the river and Daniel just might be nearby. She knocked at lodging-house doors, went into little corner shops, and summoned the courage to make enquiries of the men hanging about at street corners. There were plenty out of work in the city, gaunt men with little hope in their eyes, standing about in groups of anything from three to a dozen, clustered together for comfort. Many of them had fought all through the war, only to find on coming home that Lloyd George's promise of a land fit for heroes to live in was an empty boast as far as they were concerned. By day, every street had its share of maimed ex-servicemen begging for coins, and at night they slept in doorways.

Jenny, passing their huddled shadows on her way back to Oswald Street after yet another fruitless search, had to fight back the desire to shake each shoulder, peer into each wan face, to make sure that Daniel wasn't among their number. She couldn't bear to think of him reduced to such poverty and homelessness. When the rain hissed outside, or the wind beat against the sturdy tenement walls, she lay awake, dividing her time between worrying about Shona and worrying about Daniel.

She began to get up early, tiptoeing out of the house and down the stairs, joining the flow of men on their way to the shipyards, asking here and there if anyone knew Daniel Young. Nobody ever did, so she extended her search to the yards themselves on Sundays and Tuesday afternoons, her only time off, travelling on the trams that rocked self-importantly through the city streets, swaying from side to side like land-ships – or drunk men, Jenny often thought as she stood at the stop, hand outstretched, watching a tram speeding towards her, sparks shooting from the harness connected to the overhead rail.

She confided her real reason for coming to Glasgow to Kate, who at once circulated Daniel's name round her family and friends in the hope that someone might have heard of him. 'You must really love him, to leave your own folk and your bairn behind,' she said wistfully.

'He's my husband,' Jenny said and left it at that.

Letters arrived regularly from Alice, assuring her that everything was fine at home and that Shona was happy and being well looked after. 'Bella dotes on her and Patrick's taken to her as well,' she wrote. 'When I visited them last night Shona was on his knee while Bella got her supper ready.'

Robert, too, kept in touch with her. Seeing his confident handwriting on the first envelope that arrived from him Jenny was swept back over the years to the day when she had received that final short note from Tyneside, telling her that he was to be married. She remembered the disbelief, the heartbreak, the terrible sense of loss. She hadn't experienced any of these emotions when Daniel left her, she now realised, and tried to tell herself that that was because she was older and wiser.

She sat holding the envelope for a while, tracing her name, written in Robert's hand, with the tip of a finger, before finally opening it.

Robert wrote that he thought that he had managed to turn the tide of misfortune, and the yard may well be saved. 'I wish you were here in Ellerslie, among your own folk,' he ended the latest letter. 'But knowing you I realise that you have to make your own decisions.'

Occasionally Eliza or Kate, insisting that Jenny needed to take some time to herself, persuaded her to go window-shopping or to take a tramcar ride to one of Glasgow's handsome large parks. She enjoyed herself on these outings, but while she was admiring the fine clothes in the windows of Fraser and Sons or Pettigrew and Stephens or Treron & Cie, or hurtling along the streets in a swaying tramcar, or walking by the boating pond in Queen's Park, she was also searching the faces around her, hoping against hope that one of them would be Daniel's.

When she went to the music-hall with Eliza she even scanned the people in the gods when the interval came, though she knew full well that unless he had changed a great deal her husband wouldn't frequent such a place, with its comedians and jugglers and bosomy singers. Then she remembered, wryly, that she herself had enjoyed the first half just as much as anyone else, though not all that long ago she would have claimed that she had no interest in such frivolity.

'What are you grinning at?' Eliza wanted to know, and laughed when Jenny told her. 'I mind being shocked the first time someone asked if I'd like to come here. But there's something about the atmosphere of the place, and everyone else enjoying themselves.' She rummaged in the paper bag of boiled sweets she had brought with her, selecting one and passing the bag to Jenny. 'Would you look at that hat over there? I'd not even take it home for the cat, let alone be seen in public underneath it!'

Kate had taken Jenny home in the first week to meet her family, and since then Jenny had become a regular visitor. The Ballantynes, almost as large a mob as the Malloys in Ellerslie, lived in a two-room-and-kitchen; Mrs Ballantyne was as bony and as placid as her daughter, and always managed to find room for someone else at her table. The vicious 'flu epidemic that had ravaged the country just after the war had carried off her husband and two of their younger children. Kate was the second eldest, and she and three others who were also working supported the rest. A brother worked in an abattoir and Evie, just out of school, was behind the counter of a local greengrocer's shop. Evie was the artistic member of the family and would have liked to stay on at school to gain some extra qualifications, but her father's death had ended her hopes. Jenny, remembering her own frustration when she had to stay in Ellerslie after Maurice went missing in action, sympathised with the girl. Doris, Kate's elder sister, was a clippie on the trams.

'She got the job near the end of the war when they were glad enough to get women to do the work,' Kate explained proudly to Jenny. 'And she was so good at it that she managed to keep it on. And why shouldn't women be as good as men? Just because we sit down to pee it doesnae mean we're stupid.'

Four members of the family were still at school, though the two older boys were shop messengers in their spare time and the girl helped behind the counter of a nearby baker's shop. The youngest child, Timmy, was only six years old, and it was some time before Jenny realised that Timmy was Kate's own child and not a brother.

'His dad and me was going to get wed but he got killed. He was a builder and he lost his footing one day,' Kate said without a shred of self-pity. 'I was working in Fraser's then, but I lost my job when they found out that Timmy was on the way. Nobody at Neilson's knows about him, so keep it to yourself.'

Kate herself turned out to be ambitious; she was determined, one day, to become a floor-walker.

'Why not? We'd two lady floor-walkers in Neilson's during the war when I first started, replacing men who'd gone off to fight. One of them, Miss Cameron her name was, was good to me, she taught me how important it was to speak right, and how to look after my clothes properly. But both the men came home and they'd been promised their jobs back, so the ladies had to go. Miss Cameron went to Stirling to look after her brother's family because his wife was poorly, so I didn't see her again.'

For a moment she looked sad, then she squared her shoulders and picked Timmy up for a cuddle. Jenny watched enviously, thinking of Shona. 'But she was good at her work, Miss Cameron,' Kate went on, 'and there's no reason why Neilson's shouldn't start taking on women again, one day.'

The Ballantyne household re-awakened Jenny's homesickness, and she broke her own rule and managed a swift trip back to Ellerslie, travelling home after work on the Saturday evening and returning on the last train on Sunday. The sight of Robert waiting on the platform when she stepped down from the train at Ellerslie brought a strange mixture of happiness and guilt – happiness at the sight of him, guilt because she hadn't told him that she was coming home.

'Alice told me,' he said before she had a chance to speak, taking her bag from her. 'Otherwise you might have come and gone without me knowing a thing about it. Fortunately I've got into the habit of looking in at the pawnshop now and again to exchange news about you.' He put a firm hand beneath her elbow and led her from the station to where a hansom cab waited. 'Get in.'

'I could easily have walked,' she protested as he joined her in the leather-smelling interior, and he let his face relax into a faint smile.

'You've only got a short time, remember? No point in wasting some of it by walking home. Besides, you spend enough time on your feet, what with your work and the search for your husband.' He sat back in the opposite corner and studied her. 'You look tired.'

'I'm managing. How's the shipyard?'

'Holding on, now that George's grip's broken at last. I think there'll be something for Mrs Dalkieth's precious grandson to inherit after all.'

When they reached the tenements he ordered the driver to stop. 'I don't suppose you'll want to be seen driving up to your father's close in my company.'

Jenny reached for the door, but Robert stretched a long arm past her and she pulled her fingers hurriedly from beneath his. As he opened the door she was aware of the masculine smell that came from him of soap and tobacco and hair-oil . . .

Her mother and two sisters were waiting for her in the flat, Faith washing dishes at the sink, Alice working at the table, once spread with homework, now with what looked like account books, and Bella nursing Shona by the fire.

'Jen! Look, pet,' she lifted the baby, turning her round towards the door. 'Here's your mammy come tae see you.'

To Jenny's dismay Shona's brows puckered uncertainly, then she let out a whimper and burrowed into Bella's neck.

'They forget fast at that age,' Faith's voice was brisk. She dried her hands and reached for the teapot on the range. 'Give her a minute tae get used tae ye. Ye'll be ready for a cup of tea.'

Jenny sipped obediently at her tea, answering Alice's questions about Glasgow without really hearing them, waiting in an agony of impatience to hold her daughter again. After a few minutes Shona got over her shyness but, even so, she twisted her head round to make sure that Bella and Faith were within reach when Jenny at last gathered her into her arms.

'Oh, lovey, you've grown since I saw you last! Look what I've brought for you.' She held out the little cloth kitten she had bought from Neilson's toy department and Shona's eyes widened. She reached for the toy, then, a few minutes later, discovering that the cat was inedible, tried to claim the biscuit her mother was eating. Faith cut a thick crust from the end of the loaf and dipped it in tea, then in sugar.

'I'll take her now,' Bella offered. 'She'll get your nice skirt in a mess.'

Jenny clung to her baby. 'That doesn't matter.'

Faith fetched a cloth and tucked it round Shona's neck. The baby submitted impatiently, then grabbed at the proferred crust.

'She likes tae fill her belly, that one,' Bella said fondly.

'You're sure she's not too much for you, or a nuisance to Patrick?'

'Not a bit of it. She's given him a new interest in life. And you'll never guess—' Bella's face lit up; she looked very like the happy young girl Patrick Kerr had courted and married. 'The gatekeeper at the yard's retiring, and Robert Archer's offered the job tae Patrick. He's tae start at the end of the month.'

'Bella, that's grand! Will he manage all right?'

Her sister nodded. 'He'll not have a lot of walking to do once he gets tae the yard, and there's a seat, Robert says, for when he's not havin' tae talk tae folk going in and out. That special boot's made it much easier for him tae get out and about.'

'He'll still have to go on with his carving,' Alice put in. 'You've no idea how much folk like them. I can sell as many as he can make.'

Shona gradually settled down in her mother's embrace while Jenny talked about her work in the emporium and her fruitless search for Daniel. It was amazing that there was so much Ellerslie news for her to hear in return after an absence of only four weeks. Maureen was pregnant again, and Alice was of the opinion that she and Jacko were determined to have just as many children as Maureen's parents had had. Jacko had managed to keep his job at the yard and so had Neil Baker. Lottie was becoming more and more stuck up and hadn't visited for several weeks.

'I don't bother about her, but I miss wee Helen,' Faith said wistfully.

Alec Monroe's gas-damaged lungs had been giving him trouble, forcing him to spend a week in his bed in the flat above the pawnshop. 'But he's back on his feet again,' said Alice, who had not only coped with the shop on her own but had managed to find time to look after Alec as well.

There was a rumour going around that George Dalkieth was drinking more than was good for him. He wasn't seen around the yard much, which was a blessing as far as the workers were concerned, and Robert was taking on more to do with the running of the place than ever before. Bella had met a former schoolfriend now in service at Dalkieth House, who told her that the two Mrs Dalkieths, matriarch and daughter-in-law, were real cronies these days, though they'd scarcely looked at each other before.

'It's the bairn,' Faith said wisely. 'A bairn can either heal trouble or cause it.'

'There's no doubt that the wee one's the centre of that family,' Bella agreed. 'Annie tells me that his mother and his gran dote on him, though his father doesnae bother his backside.'

'Mebbe his nose is out of joint,' Alice put in. 'He was aye his mother's favourite, from what I've heard.'

Shona's eyelids had begun to droop and her head was heavy

against Jenny's arm. Now she yawned, and Bella reached over and gently took the half-chewed crust out of her fingers. 'I'd best get her home and intae her bed.'

'Can she not sleep here tonight, with me?'

'Her wee crib's not here,' Bella said. 'It's no' fair at her age tae expect her tae chop and change. I'll bring her back tomorrow morning.'

Reluctantly, Jenny handed the sleepy baby over, winding Bella's shawl about the two of them. Her arms felt strangely light and empty without Shona.

'I wish I could find Daniel then come back home,' she said later when she and Alice were lying together in the double bed she had once shared with Lottie. Alice had elected to desert her own small room for the night so that she and Jenny could talk. Through the wall Teeze, who had reacted indifferently to Jenny's presence when he came home from the pub, was snoring loudly.

'If it's Shona you're fretting about, she's contented enough. Bella and Pat are both good to her.'

'I know that,' Jenny said. 'It's me that's missing her . . .'

26

It was even harder to leave Shona a second time. By Sunday afternoon the baby had spent so much time with her mother that she wailed and held her arms out to Jenny when she was handed over to Bella.

Jenny's own eyes filled as she blundered out of Bella's house and through the close where she had once lived. She walked past Robert, waiting for her at the end of the street, without noticing him, and he hurried after her and put a hand on her arm. 'What's wrong?'

Jenny rubbed at her face with the heel of her hand and sniffed as he relieved her of her bag. 'It – it was just having to leave the wee one.'

He shook his head, frowning. 'Stay with her, Jen, and I'll find someone to look for your husband.'

'I can manage,' she said curtly, marching ahead of him, angry that he had seen her weakness.

'That's your trouble, Jenny Gillespie,' he said from behind her. 'You're altogether too independent.'

'I've had to be. And my name's Young, not Gillespie. Give me my bag, I can—'

'I know,' he said dryly. 'You can manage.'

The next day started badly in the store. Among the people at Jenny's counter was a plump, well-dressed woman with a discontented mouth who insisted on seeing every decorative wall-plate poor Kate could find, and turning up her nose at each and every one of them.

'It's ridiculous,' the customer complained, 'All I want is something simple and you can't supply it.' Her gloved finger stabbed at one offering after another and her voice became shrill with impatience. 'This shape is right but the pattern is wrong, while this pattern's more what I'm looking for, but the colours aren't right.'

'There are other wall-plates over at that counter, madam,' Kate told her hopefully.

'I'm aware of that, but the prices on that counter are ridiculous.'

'What about this one?'

'Aren't you listening to me? I already told you, the colour is wrong.'

'You said yellow, madam.'

'Precisely. I said yellow, not orange. These flowers are orange.'

'They're daffodils, madam, and daffodils are yellow,' Kate pointed out and the woman stared at her then turned towards her companion, who was half her width but just as sour looking.

'Come along, Muriel, we'll try Dallas's. Perhaps the staff there will be more helpful. As for you, miss, I shall be complaining about your impudence, make no mistake about that,' she added sharply to Kate. 'Mrs Neilson happens to be a friend of mine and she'll hear about this.'

'But—'

Jenny broke in hastily, realising that her friend had been driven to the end of her tether and was about to make matters worse for herself. 'I believe that madam was thinking of pure yellow flowers, Miss Ballantyne. Pansies, for instance.'

'Pansies – exactly.' The woman swung round to look at her.

'Yellow pansies, with velvety-brown centres?'

'That would match my dining room. You have a plate like that in stock?'

'I could make one up.'

'You? Make one?'

'If madam would choose the right shape,' Jenny indicated a shelf of plain plates, 'I could paint it for her.'

'How long would it take?'

'We could have it delivered to you on Saturday morning, madam.'

The woman hesitated, then said grudgingly, 'Very well – but I'll come in myself on Saturday. If I'm not satisfied I'll not buy it.'

'Of course not, madam.'

'Are you daft?' Kate wanted to know as the two women walked away.

'I can do it, I used to paint china at home for people and I've got my paints with me.'

'But Mrs Provan's terribly hard to satisfy,' Kate protested. 'You'll get yourself into trouble.'

'At least it's kept her from complaining.'

'She'll probably have us both out of work on Saturday,' Kate predicted gloomily. 'What about Miss Lang and Mr Davidson? What are you going to tell them?'

'We'll wait to see what happens. I'll pay for the plate out of my own pocket for the moment. Can I paint it in your house? I need an oven and my landlady'll not let me use hers.'

For the next three evenings all thought of looking for Daniel had to be put aside while Jenny worked at the Ballantyne's kitchen table. The family watched, enthralled, as a cluster of yellow pansies, fringed with leaves and with deep brown hearts began to fill the centre of the plate, with the yellows and browns of the blossoms echoed round the rim, mingled with leaf-green in a series of feathery outlines.

'Imagine having a talent like that!' Mrs Ballantyne said in awe, and Evie, the thwarted artist languishing behind the counter of a greengrocer's shop, watched every stroke of the brush with rapt attention.

Seeing her interest, Jenny showed the girl how to paint one of her mother's saucers, which could be used to test the oven before the pansy plate was entrusted to the heat. The girl picked up the idea quickly and chose an imaginative design of green leaves.

On Thursday afternoon Mrs Ballantyne did a baking and, by the evening, Jenny judged the oven section of the range to be at just the right temperature for the saucer. She tested the design with the tip of a finger to satisfy herself that the paint was dry then slid the saucer into the oven and closed the door.

'If it's too hot the colours'll lose their freshness and if it's too cool they'll not bake in properly, then they'll be spoiled when the saucer's washed,' she explained, a worried frown tucking itself between her brows. It stayed there until the saucer was brought out half an hour later, the pattern baked firmly on to it, the leaves Evie had painted looking fresh and green.

'They're so real they look as if you could just pick them off,' Kate marvelled, and Evie flushed with pride and pleasure as she gazed at her own handiwork.

Mrs Ballantyne willingly did another baking on Friday afternoon, and that evening it was the pansy plate's turn to go in to the oven. While she waited to see the results Jenny's tea cooled in its cup and she was too nervous to do more than nibble at the scones Kate's mother had made that afternoon.

'Oh, Jenny—' Kate whispered when the moment came and the oven door was opened. 'Then, 'Oh, Jenny!' she squealed as the plate emerged. 'It's beautiful!'

Jenny gazed down at the pansies, bright and pure, half-hidden by the cloth she was using to protect her fingers from the heat. 'The thing is – what will Mrs Provan think of it?'

As soon as Jenny produced the plate on Saturday Mrs Provan's friend, the woman who had been with her on Monday, gave a squeak of delight. 'Marion, it's awfully bonny!'

Mrs Provan withered her with a look, then studied the plate carefully, peering at it then holding it at arm's length, turning it this way and that to catch the light before finally saying in a grudging voice, 'Mmhhmm, it's quite nice. Certainly more like what I had in mind in the first place. How much is it?'

Jenny, who had been hiding her nervousness behind an impassive face, felt such a wave of relief wash over her that she almost had to clutch at the edge of the counter to keep herself upright. She named the sum that she and Kate had earlier agreed would be fair and acceptable.

'Though it's my belief that you could charge a lot more,' Kate had said. 'It's worth it.'

Mrs Provan handed the money over without protest, left instructions for the plate to be delivered to her house that afternoon, and sailed away, her friend bobbing in her wake.

'You'd have thought she could have carried it herself, ' Jenny said as she deftly packed the plate in tissue paper.

'That sort wouldn't carry a bite of food to their own mouths if they could get someone else to do it for them,' Kate told her, adding, 'I still think you should take the difference between the price of the plate the way it was before and the price Mrs Provan paid.'

'It wouldn't be right to take some of her money.'

'But it means that Neilson's is getting more than the original plate cost and you're getting nothing for your work,' Kate argued, but Jenny was adamant.

'If they found out, I'd not want to be accused of taking money from them. But your mother should get something for the use of her oven.'

It was Kate's turn to shake her head. 'You're not going to pay her out of your own pocket. We all did well out of the extra baking.'

They were still arguing about the matter when Mrs Provan's friend came back on her own, scurrying across the carpet with an occasional guilty glance over her shoulder, for all the world like an escaped fugitive, to ask Jenny if she would decorate a plate for her as well, 'Any flowers you like, as long as they're in different shades of red,' she murmured, and scuttled off.

Over the next few weeks word began to spread among the customers. A third order came in, then another, and Jenny was soon in a quandary. Evenings that should have been devoted to looking for Daniel were spent instead working in the Ballantynes' little kitchen. Evie was pressed into service to do some of the plainer work and

Jenny had to buy more paints and brushes and was therefore forced to take some money to cover her own expenses and pay Mrs Ballantyne for the extra fuel needed to keep her oven at the necessary temperature.

'It'll have to stop,' she told Kate when the work began to spill over into the weekends. 'I've got a bairn waiting for me at home and I'll have to get back to her soon. And there's still Daniel.'

'You'll have to tell Miss Lang what's going on.'

'And lose my job?'

'Jenny, you're beginning to bring custom to Neilson's. We're getting folk in that I've never seen before, looking for hand-painted china because they've seen your work in someone else's house. You'd not lose your job, not now.'

'She'll not be pleased at me keeping it quiet all those weeks, nor will Mr Davidson. It's ridiculous,' said Jenny, shaking her head. 'I ran my own department at Dalkieth's, I'm a married woman with a child, yet I'm scared of Miss Lang. She's like all the schoolteachers I ever had rolled into one. But you're right, Kate, I'll have to tell her.'

But Kate wasn't listening. Instead she was gaping at a tall, fair-haired young man who was making his way across the carpet towards their counter. 'That's Mr Matthew!'

'Who?'

Miss Lang and Mr Davidson had seen the newcomer and were converging on him from different points of the gallery. But he moved faster than they did, and Kate just had time to hiss, 'Matthew Neilson, Mr Neilson's son,' before he was standing in front of them, looking from one to the other and asking with interest, 'Which of you paints plates?'

'I – I do,' Jenny confessed, horrified that he knew.

Clear blue eyes settled on Jenny's face. 'And you are Miss—?'

Miss Lang, only just beating Mr Davidson to the counter, supplied the information in a voice fluting with nervousness. 'This is Mrs Young, Mr Matthew. She's been working with us for about six weeks now. Is there—'

'—anything wrong, sir?' Mr Davidson took up the sentence as he arrived.

'Nothing wrong,' Matthew Neilson said crisply. 'I want a word with Mrs Young, that's all. In my office, if you can spare her for a while.'

'I gather,' he said dryly a moment later, as he and Jenny left the counter, 'that your superiors know nothing about your – activities?'

She kept her eyes on the door leading to the back stairs, not daring to look up at him. 'I was just about to tell Miss Lang.'

269

A firm grip on her elbow turned her towards one of the lifts. 'This way,' Matthew Neilson said, and within moments the three of them – Jenny, the lift attendant, and the store owner's son – were caged in a padded silken box and the china department was dropping away from them. Jenny tensed and the fingers still holding her elbow tightened slightly. 'Your first time in a lift?'

'Y-yes.'

'Don't worry, it's quite safe.'

Ladies' Fashions and Gents' Suitings flashed by, moving disconcertingly from top to bottom of the latticed iron doors enclosing the lift, then the tearoom appeared and, after a slight bounce, the floor settled and the gates rattled open.

'This way.' Matthew Neilson led her past the tearoom, through a door marked 'Private' and into a short corridor with more doors to the left and right. He opened one and ushered her into a fairly small, plain room dominated by a large desk.

'Sit down, Mrs Young. You'll have a cup of tea - or would you prefer coffee?'

'Neither, thank you.'

He grinned. 'Even a condemned murderer gets something,' he told her, opening an inner door. 'Muriel, could you bring tea for two, please?' he asked someone out of Jenny's line of vision, then returned to lean against the edge of the desk.

'My parents and I dined with friends of theirs last night,' he said conversationally. 'I believe you've met Mrs Provan?'

'She's a good customer of Neilson's,' Jenny said nervously.

'She showed us a handsome new wall-plate that had been specially designed and painted for her and congratulated my father and I on our new service to customers. We had to confess that we knew nothing about it. Nor, I gather, does anyone else.'

Jenny took a deep breath and launched into an explanation about Mrs Provan and her insistence on a plate with a yellow pattern, pausing when an efficient-looking woman brought a tea-tray from the inner room.

When the secretary had returned to her own office Matthew Neilson picked up the teapot. 'I understand from Mrs Provan that you've painted plates for other customers,' he said, pouring tea as though accustomed to it.

'One or two ladies who saw Mrs Provan's asked me to decorate plates for them. I didn't like to refuse.' Jenny accepted the cup he held out to her. The tea had a refreshing, slightly lemony scent; she sipped at it appreciatively, then said, 'I've charged the customers the same price they would have paid for a decorated plate, and only kept back enough to cover the cost of the paints and the fuel Mrs Ballantyne used. I've not taken a penny away from the store, Mr Neilson.'

His eyes were on her wedding ring. 'Are you a widow, Mrs Young?'

'No.'

'A deserted wife?'

Jenny's face grew hot. She got to her feet, carefully setting the cup and saucer on the tray. 'That's none of your business, Mr Neilson.'

'As an employee—'

'I am no longer an employee,' she told him.

'And what about the people who are still waiting for orders to be completed? What about Mrs McNeill? She's a very good customer of ours and she was at Mrs Provan's last night too,' he added as Jenny, confused, stared at him. 'She asked me if Neilson's could supply a specially decorated tea-service for her. I said I'd see to it.'

'Then you must employ a china-painter.' Jenny opened the door, determined to retain her dignity. She would not allow this inquisitive young man to dismiss her, order her from his father's store. She would leave of her own free will.

'That,' said Matthew Neilson, 'is an excellent idea. Will you accept the post, Mrs Young?'

She turned to face him, astonished. 'Me?'

'You're a china-painter, aren't you?'

Yes, but—'

He came round the desk, closed the door, and led her back to her chair. 'I see no reason to look for someone else when you've not only got the talent to do the job, but the sense to recognise the gap in our services to our customers. Naturally there will be a considerable increase. After all, you'll be starting a new department for us.' He took an ornate box from the desk and offered it to her. 'Cigarette?'

She shook her head, still bewildered by the turn the interview had taken.

'My father,' he explained, lighting a cigarette for himself, 'is always looking for new ways to please our clients and there seems little sense in advertising for a china-painter when you're right here. You'll have your own workroom, of course, and if you give me a list of the necessary paints and so on I'll see that they're supplied.'

Jenny felt as though the world was spinning too fast. 'I haven't said that I'll do it,' she said faintly.

'Why let someone else make money out of your idea, Mrs Young?'

Jenny thought of Ellerslie, and Shona. She wanted to go home to her baby, but she still hadn't found Daniel; leaving Glasgow now

271

would be like turning her back on him. If the job that Matthew Neilson was offering paid well enough then maybe she could find some way of bringing Shona to Glasgow for the time being. And her evenings and weekends would be free again now.

'Well?' His voice nudged at her. The smell of cigarette smoke was sharp in her nostrils.

'I accept,' said Jenny.

27

A former store-room off the china department, well-lit by a row of windows looking down on Buchanan Street, became Jenny's workshop, and within two weeks Matthew Neilson saw to it that the room was freshly painted and well equipped with everything she needed, including a compact gas-fired oven.

At Jenny's request Kate's sister Evie was brought in as her assistant and, to Matthew's delight, the handsome posters he set up in the foyer and in the china department advertising the store's new facility for its customers resulted in a lot of interest in the new department from the start.

'I knew we'd do well,' he exulted, strolling round the workroom, examining a row of plates waiting to be fired.

Jenny took time to complete an ivy leaf, the tip of her tongue between her teeth as she concentrated on the work, then she laid down her brush. 'I didn't. Anyone can paint china; I can't think why folk should want to spend good money getting someone to do it for them when they could easily do it for themselves.'

'You've not got the right commercial attitude.' He picked up a book of flower plates that she had bought and flipped through the pages. 'People with money prefer to have things done for them. Which is fortunate for Neilson's, and for you, too, Mrs Young.'

The last words were delivered in amused tones. He had taken to calling her by her first name almost at once, but when he thought that she was being too serious and stuffy he reverted to her title. The two of them had worked together on renovating the workroom, Jenny planning it and Matthew Neilson making sure that everything was done just as she wanted it. During that time he had tried to find out more about her, but Jenny had calmly but firmly declined to answer his probing questions or volunteer any information.

She liked him, but his conviction that money could buy anything troubled her. If he knew why she was in Glasgow he would be quite likely to offer to pay someone to find Daniel for her, and she had no wish to expose her husband to that sort of prying.

She picked up a fresh paint-brush, wishing that Matthew would go back to his office and leave her to get on with her own work. Instead he said suddenly, 'Let's go out for a drive this evening.'

'What?' She was confused.

'It's a lovely day outside. You need a break, and I'm looking for an excuse to give the car a spin.'

'I'm sure you don't need to find an excuse.' Jenny loaded her brush with paint and turned back to her work. To her annoyance, her fingers shook slightly and her heart had speeded up; his interest in her was certainly flattering.

Two large, well-cared-for hands were planted on the table in front of her and he said from above her head, 'Be a sport, Jenny. There's no fun in driving about on my own.'

'Mr Neilson, I'm an employee of your father's.'

'And a married woman. I'm only suggesting a drive, not an elopement.'

'Surely you can invite someone more suitable?'

'I can't think of anyone else that I particularly want to spend the evening with. Besides, you need to get some fresh air after slaving away all day.'

Jenny put the brush down again and rested her elbows on the table, glancing out of the window. The sky was hidden from sight by the building opposite, but it had been a clear blue when she went out for a breath of fresh air during the midday break and the sun sparkled back at her from the windows across the road.

She had intended to take a tram out to Govan that evening and walk along some streets near the shipyards in the hope of catching sight of Daniel.

'The snowdrops and crocuses and daffodils are coming out in the parks. Jenny, you're forever painting flowers – you should really have a good look at the real thing now and again,' the voice above her head coaxed.

'It would be nice, but—'

'Good! I'll pick you up at eight,' Matthew said, and whisked out of the room.

Jenny had fully intended, once she was earning more money, to find a place of her own so that she could bring Shona to Glasgow. But when she suggested it in a letter home Alice wrote back that the family were opposed to the prospect.

'Shona would have to spend her days with a stranger while you were at work, and how could you look for Daniel when you'd have her to see to in the evenings and at weekends?' Alice wrote. 'I think

Mam and Bella are right when they say that she's best left where she is, with people she knows. The sooner you find Daniel, or decide that you've done all you could to find him, the sooner you'll be back here, with Shona.'

Jenny read the letter over several times, and knew that her family was right. Shona was best left in Ellerslie.

The days and weeks had rushed past while she was busy setting up the new workshop. Unable to bear too many partings from Shona she had decided that it was best if she didn't return to Ellerslie frequently, electing, instead, to spend her weekends searching for word or sight of her husband.

By April her outings with Matthew had somehow become weekly events, usually visiting one of the many beautiful parks within easy reach of the city centre. As their friendship developed she steadfastly continued to refuse to say much about herself and where she came from, knowing full well that he would insist on meeting her family or, even worse, would turn up in Ellerslie uninvited when she had gone back there. Good company though he was, there was a possessive side to Matthew's nature that bothered Jenny. They had all but quarrelled one Sunday evening when, returning footsore and tired from another fruitless search round the streets by the river, she found him comfortably settled in her landlady's parlour, with Mrs McLean bright-eyed with excitement, plying him with fruit loaf and tea out of her best china cups, taken from the display cabinet for the occasion.

'I thought we might discuss a new pattern I've had in mind,' he said blandly, smiling up at Jenny as she stopped in the doorway.

'I told Mr Matthew you'd not be long,' Mrs McLean chirped, pouring out fresh tea for Jenny before refilling Matthew's cup.

'Did you not tell him that gentlemen callers aren't encouraged?' Jenny asked with a slight edge to her voice, and her landlady coloured and tutted.

'I didnae mean Mr *Matthew*,' she said reprovingly, and Matthew himself added, 'Besides, I'm not a gentleman caller. I'm here on business.'

'Sit down here, my dear. I'm just off to evening service, so you can have some time on your own,' Mrs McLean gathered up her own cup and plate and whisked out of the room with a final girlish simper in Matthew's direction.

'Mr Neilson—'

'It's usually Matthew out of shop hours, Jenny.'

'You said you were here on business,' she reminded him. 'Though I'd prefer it if you didn't call at my lodgings.'

'I wouldn't have to, if you'd only agree to see me more often.'

'We see quite enough of each other as it is. Anyway, I'm too tired to talk business tonight.' She had come back feeling dispirited after yet another fruitless search, and had been looking forward to going to bed early.

'You shouldn't walk so far, then. Mrs McLean said you go out walking a lot when you're not at work. Maybe we could take walks together.'

'I don't think so.'

'Why not?' Matthew wanted to know, maddeningly.

'Because—' Jenny stopped abruptly as her landlady popped her head, now topped by a black straw hat with a bunch of daisies pinned to the brim, round the door.

'Don't trouble to put the dishes in the kitchen, dear,' she said brightly. 'I'll see to them when I get back.'

'—because I like to walk on my own sometimes,' Jenny finished when the landing door closed and they were alone.

'Come for a drive.'

'I'm not in the mood for a drive, Matthew! Why don't you take your mother out for a nice run in the car?'

He scowled, sliding down in his chair and stretching long legs across Mrs McLean's brown and red carpet. 'My mother has other fish to fry. My sister's honoured us with one of her rare visits. She's brought the infant with her and there are nursemaids and cribs and toys all over the place. I barked my shins on a perambulator this morning. Walked out of the drawing room and almost fell over the damned thing in the hall, waiting for his majesty.'

'You don't care for children?' Jenny thought of Shona, never far from her mind.

'Oh, they're well enough in their proper place, which is the nursery, with the door closed. That's where we lived until we reached an interesting age. But this brat's the first grandchild and my parents are besotted. Everywhere I turn there he is being passed from hand to hand and fussed over.'

Jenny was glad that she hadn't said anything about Shona. Not that Matthew's opinions would have been of any importance.

'At least her husband's not with her,' Matthew said. 'He's a terrible bore. I can't think what she ever saw in the fellow.' Then he brightened. 'They're going to have a party on Tuesday evening for some friends. Why don't you come along as my guest?'

'Don't be ridiculous, Matthew. I'm an employee.'

'But a special kind of employee. You started up a new department for us.'

'That doesn't mean that it would be fitting for me to visit your parents' home as a guest.'

'You got on well enough with my father when he had a look at your workshop. You impressed him.'

'We met in the emporium on business terms, not social.' James Neilson, a smaller, stockier man than his son but with the same thick hair and moustache, except that his was grey instead of fair, had asked a number of practical questions and listened carefully to the answers, studying Jenny with eyes that were shrewd, though kindly enough.

To her relief, Matthew finally took no for an answer, and left before Mrs McLean came back and invited him to stay for supper. Washing the good china carefully in the kitchen after he had gone Jenny shook her head over his naive assumption that his mother would willingly play hostess to one of her husband's employees. Besides, Mrs Neilson was sure to ask questions about her, questions which couldn't be fobbed off the way Matthew's were.

As April gave way to May Jenny felt that she had travelled on every tram in Glasgow and walked through every street, but still there was no sign of Daniel. He had made no attempt to contact her or anyone else in Ellerslie, and even the Ballantyne clan had found nothing out.

She managed to get a few days off from the store, making the excuse that there was illness in her family and went home for Shona's first birthday, taking with her a handsome baby doll complete with cradle, bought from Neilson's toy department. After such a long time apart it took Shona, who had taken her first shaky steps only a week before, longer to get to know her mother again; at first she held tightly to her grandmother and aunts, particularly to Bella, and when she finally came to Jenny and allowed her to cuddle her she soon wanted to get down on the floor, where she was eager to toddle around, holding on to the furniture.

'They don't stay babies for long,' Faith said, watching the little girl stagger from table to chair. Her voice was wistful with the memories of her own babies, some dead, the others grown now.

'I know that,' Jenny agreed, and wished that she had stopped to think before sacrificing months of Shona's precious babyhood to the search for Daniel.

She was kneeling on the floor, helping Shona to put her new dolly to bed, when Patrick came in, pausing briefly in the doorway to clutch at the frame for balance after the journey upstairs.

'Hello, Pat', she said. 'You're doing well.'

'Well enough,' he said shortly. He had discarded the crutch and was using a stick now; he swayed from side to side as he walked into the room, reminding Jenny of the Glasgow trams, but for all that he moved confidently and without pain.

Shona, who had been intent on her doll until then, glanced up and saw him. Her pretty little face broke into a broad grin and she held her arms up to him.

'Pat!'

'Here, here, let me sit down, hen. Don't rush at me like a bull at a barn door,' he said, his face softening as he looked down at the baby. She caught hold of the table leg and scrambled to her feet as he lowered himself into a chair, then toddled over to him, swaying from side to side much as he had done, the doll dragged along by the skirt after her. Patrick leaned down to her, hoisting her into his lap and she held her new present up to be admired. Solemnly, he studied the doll's golden curls and the tucked and embroidered muslin dress, then his eyes, following Shona's pointing finger, travelled to the lace-covered crib in the middle of the kitchen floor.

'Aye, it's bonny,' he said and Shona, satisfied, scrambled down from his knee and went back to the crib.

'It must have cost a fair bit, too,' Patrick added almost accusingly, his gaze moving to Jenny's face then down over the striped green crepe de chine blouse and matching skirt she wore.

She flushed, keenly aware as usual of his dislike and his resentment.

'It's grand to see Pat and Bella getting on together,' Alice said as she and Jenny set out for Lottie's flat the next day. 'He's got his self-respect back now that he's earning again, and he's good to Shona, so you've got no reason to worry about her.' Then she added with a sidelong glance at her sister, 'He seems to have some bee in his bonnet about you, though.'

'What makes you say that?'

'His mouth tightens whenever your name's mentioned, and he goes quiet when you're in the same room as him. Did the two of you quarrel?'

'Why should we?' Jenny asked evasively. As far as she knew nobody, not even Bella, knew about the confrontation between herself and Patrick on the day Shona was born. And nobody would ever hear as much as a hint of it from her.

As they turned the corner into Mayfield Street she changed the subject, eyeing the three-storey greystone tenements. 'Lottie's fairly come up in the world. But I can't see her down on her knees taking her turn of scrubbing the stairs.'

'Neil pays a woman to do the heavy work, I believe.' Alice's voice was heavy with disapproval. She turned in at a close tiled like Mrs McLean's and added, as Jenny followed her up the stairs, 'I come here when I can, for Helen's sake, but Lottie doesn't make any of us welcome. She doesn't like to be reminded of us, or our house, now that she's done so well for herself.' She knocked on the door then said as they waited, 'You'll – you'll see a difference in Helen.'

'She'll be quite grown up now – she'll be five in October,' Jenny replied as Lottie opened the door, a cigarette smouldering between the red-tipped fingers of one hand, her red hair frizzed on either side of her carefully made-up face. She led the way into the 'drawing room', where a low table had been laid for afternoon tea.

When her guests had been supplied with tea and shop-bought gingerbread Lottie dropped into a comfortable arm-chair and tapped the ash from her cigarette into a convenient ashtray, studying Jenny openly. 'You look smarter now that you're living in the city,' she said at last.

'You look very smart yourself, Lottie.'

The other girl glanced complacently down at her low-necked, knitted blue jumper and slender black calf-length skirt, with fine pleats at each side. She stretched out one slender leg, twisting her foot this way and that to admire her buckled, wedge-heeled shoes and silk stockings.

'Neil makes a good wage.'

'Is Helen in?' Alice wanted to know, and Lottie's red mouth turned down in a scowl.

'She's been a right pest all morning, so I sent her out to play. Thank goodness she'll be old enough to go to school in September. Mebbe I'll get some peace from her then. She likes attention, does that little madam,' she said impatiently, then began to question Jenny about Glasgow, the people she met there, the clothes the women wore.

'I've been to Glasgow with Neil several times and he's promised to take me to Edinburgh soon for a holiday,' she remarked, stubbing her cigarette out and selecting a fresh one from an ornate box. She lit it and blew a smoke ring across the room. 'I thought mebbe your mother would take Helen while we're gone. There'd be no pleasure in trailing her round the shops, listening to her whining all the time.'

Alice and Jenny exchanged glances as a gentle, tentative tapping was heard at the door of the flat. Lottie, ignoring it, went on talking.

279

When Jenny finally interrupted her to say, 'I think there's someone at the door,' she frowned.

'It'll be Helen, I suppose. That lassie never gives me a minute's peace.' She got up, sighing ostentatiously, and flounced out into the hall. The sisters exchanged glances, and Alice raised her eyes to the ceiling.

'Well – come in if you're coming,' they heard Lottie say crossly. 'Don't hang about on the landing letting me catch my death of cold.' The door shut then Lottie reappeared, looking back over her shoulder. 'Come and say hello to Mama's visitors. Come on,' she added sharply, 'D'ye want them to think you're a naughty little girl?'

Helen edged into the room, sliding her small body round the doorframe as though trying to keep as far as possible from her mother. Jenny stared, shocked, at the little girl's pale face. The soft brown eyes that had once sparkled with life were now wary and guarded.

'Helen! My, what a big lassie you are now.' Jenny got up, holding her hands out to the little girl, who took a swift step back, her own hands tucked behind her pink silk frock.

'D'you not remember me, Helen?' Jenny asked, dismayed.

'Of course she does,' Lottie said sharply. 'She's just being silly as usual. Shake hands with your Aunt Jenny the way you've been taught,' she ordered her daughter and Helen did as she was told.

'How d'ye do?' she murmured. For a moment her small hand rested submissively in Jenny's, then it slid away. When Alice held out her hand she went over to her at once to lean against her knee.

'She's never seen you looking so grand, Jenny, that's what it is.' There was malice in Lottie's voice.

Jenny ignored her. 'Your hand's cold, pet.'

'So it is.' Alice rubbed the small fingers. 'You should have put a coat on her, Lottie.'

'It's her own fault, she refuses to run about like the other children.' Lottie poured more tea for herself. 'Just stands in a corner like a daftie. She's needing to go to the school – they'll mebbe learn her some sense there. They take the strap to naughty little girls there,' she added, raising her voice.

'Mebbe Helen should have some tea to warm her up,' Jenny said, suppressing her anger, and Lottie shrugged.

'Fetch your mug, then,' she told her daughter. Helen obediently scurried from the room and it was all Jenny could do to blink back tears when she returned clutching a familiar tin mug, the elves and flowers painted on it still visible, though the colours had faded over the years.

'She's still got the mug I painted for her!'

Lottie shrugged. 'She'll not be parted from it. Anyway, it keeps her from breaking my good stuff,' she said carelessly as Alice poured a little tea into the mug then topped it up with milk and stirred in some sugar. 'Don't you go messing up that frock, mind,' she added sharply as Alice proffered the plate of gingerbread. Helen's reaching fingers fell back to her lap, empty, and she sat down on a pouffe near her mother, the mug in her two hands.

Jenny waited until the little girl had finished her tea before handing over the brightly wrapped parcel she had brought. 'This is for you, Helen. It comes from the big shop where I work in Glasgow.'

Shyly, prodded forward by her mother, Helen accepted the parcel with a whispered 'Thank you,' and turned it over, her wide eyes greedily devouring the gay pattern on the wrapping paper.

'Hurry up and open it, then,' Lottie told her daughter impatiently, then snatched the parcel out of Helen's hands. 'Oh, I'll do it – we'll be here all day if we wait for you.'

She ripped off the paper that Jenny had chosen so carefully and withdrew a clockwork bear. 'Very nice, I'm sure,' she said.

Jenny took the bear from her and knelt on the carpet to wind it up. 'He's got his own little key in his back, Helen – see? You turn it like this, then he plays on the drum.'

She set the bear down and they all watched as the arms moved jerkily. Helen gave a giggle of delight, and when the tapping on the drum slowed to a standstill Jenny handed her the bear and showed her how to turn the key. Carefully, she wound the bear up and when it started beating its drum she smiled up at Jenny with genuine pleasure, a smile that died away when Lottie, crossing her legs and swinging one foot idly, remarked, 'We'll need to see if we can get a key to put in your back, won't we, Helen? Mebbe then we could get you to move a bit faster.'

'I'm having a wee party for Shona's first birthday tomorrow,' Jenny said as she and Alice prepared to go. 'I'd like Helen to come.'

The little girl's face lit up. 'Oh yes!' she said, then added, with a swift glance at her mother, 'Yes – please.'

'I'll come round and fetch her at two o'clock,' Alice offered.

'Or you could bring her yourself, Lottie. You'd be welcome,' Jenny lied with a small, polite smile.

'If she's going to be out of the way for the afternoon, I'll make the most of it and go to the shops in Helensburgh,' Lottie said.

'That poor wee soul!' Jenny exploded when the sisters were out in the street again. 'She used to be such a happy bairn!'

Alice's normally cheerful face was troubled. 'I'm quite sure they're

281

not cruel to her, Jen. She's always got pretty clothes on and she seems to be fed well enough. It's just that Lottie has no patience with her.'

'She never did have. Mam's house might not be as smart as Lottie's, or in such a good neighbourhood, but at least Helen had plenty of love in it.'

'Mebbe it'd have been better for the wee soul if Maurice had come home. Though I doubt if he'd've been able to stomach Lottie for long,' Alice said. Then, as they walked over the bridge spanning Ellerslie Water, she cautioned, 'Don't say anything to Mam, Jenny. She frets over Helen enough as it is.'

When Helen arrived at the Gillespie flat the next day she had exchanged the pink silk frock for a pretty hand-embroidered dress in pale cream muslin with a broad sash and frills round the hem. Lottie had sent a stuffed toy rabbit for Shona.

'She says to tell you,' Alice whispered, wrinkling her nose, 'that it's not much but we can't all buy our toys from a big Glasgow store.' Then, raising her voice again, she said cheerfully, 'Now then, Miss Helen, I'm going to put one of my aprons round you so that you can eat the birthday cake your gran made and the nice jelly Auntie Bella's brought without having to worry about your pretty dress.'

It took a full hour before they could persuade Helen to relax. Comparing her tense little face with Shona's beaming grin, Jenny felt helpless anger against Lottie and Neil. Helen had brought the clockwork bear with her and, throughout the afternoon, she kept a tight hold of it, shaking her head and backing away when Shona, well aware that on that day she was the centre of attention although she was too young to know why, reached out an imperious hand and tried to take it away from her.

Lottie had told Alice that Neil would call after work to take Helen home. When five o'clock came and the town's hooters began to shrill, Helen jumped and her eyes grew moist. Bella, talking cheerfully all the time, washed her face and hands and combed her hair, and when Neil came tramping heavily up the stairs, she was buttoned into her coat and all ready to go home.

It was the first time Jenny had seen Neil since his marriage. Always inclined to plumpness, he had become downright fat, with the slight thickening of advancing years already beginning to overlie his good-looking features. Like Lottie, he was complacent and self-confident and his pale blue eyes roamed over Jenny from her short hair, which had been styled, to her ankles.

'Glasgow suits ye,' he said, then added with a sly grin, 'Or is it bein' fancy free again that's doin' it?'

282

'I've still got Daniel's ring on my finger,' she retorted tartly, the memory of Neil's clumsy attempt to force himself on her on the night she had ridden the Tank truck flooding back.

He grinned, then looked down at Helen, who stood meekly before him.

'Come on then, home tae yer ma. Here—' he stooped and put a hand on the clockwork bear. 'Give that back.'

Her eyes darkened with alarm as she locked both arms tightly about the bear, pressing her lips together with such determination that they almost disappeared.

'That's Helen's bear,' Jenny interceded swiftly. 'I gave it to her yesterday.'

'Did ye?' Neil's voice was indifferent. 'Come on, then,' he ordered his stepdaughter, who followed him without a backward glance. Her tears had been blinked back fiercely while she was being helped into her coat.

Faith's face was shadowed as she watched them go and Jenny could almost feel her mother's longing, just like her own, to catch Helen up and refuse to let her go back to Lottie. As the door closed she picked Shona up without thinking, her mind on her forlorn little niece. It was only when the baby squeaked a protest that she realised she was clutching her almost as tightly as Helen had clutched the toy bear.

'I think Neil's kind enough to Helen,' Alice said later, when the sisters were in bed. 'It's just that he doesnae know anything about bairns. He'd probably be just the same with his own.'

'For the bairns' sakes,' Jenny said into the darkness, 'I hope he and Lottie never have any.'

28

'Daniel might not even be in Glasgow,' Robert said as the door closed behind his housekeeper. 'Have you thought of that?'

'I know.' Jenny poured tea for him, then herself. Shona, sitting on the rug at her mother's feet, stared round Robert's parlour with open curiosity.

'He might have gone to Tyneside. You're surely not going to start looking down there, are you?' Robert accepted his tea and went back to stand by the mantelshelf. 'Jenny, you've done all you can. That place in the drawing office is still yours, and I'm quite sure this young lady would be better off with you at home instead of coming and going like a visitor.'

Shona began to haul herself to her feet, using her mother's skirt for support, and Jenny put out a hand to stop her. 'Mind the teapot, pet.'

'Here's something for you to play with.' Robert discarded his cup and knelt down beside the little girl, unfastening the silver watch from his waistcoat then holding it against Shona's ear. 'Hear that?' The baby listened, wide-eyed, then reached for the watch and chain.

'Don't let her touch it, Robert, she might break it,' Jenny protested.

He laughed, relinquishing the watch. 'If she manages to do that it won't have been very good to start with. Anyway, it's only a possession. No, like this,' he explained gravely to Shona, who was frowningly pressing the watch-face against her cheek and wondering why there was no sound from it. 'Against your ear. This is your ear, round the corner.' He tickled the tiny lobe and Shona giggled, tucking her head against her shoulder.

'I never realised you were so good with children,' Jenny said, surprised.

'I might be a hard taskmaster at the yard, but I'm not an ogre. I like bairns well enough.'

'You'd make a fine father.'

'I'd like that,' he said, looking up at her. His face was on a level with Jenny's and, as his eyes caught and held hers she felt herself flush.

'Get up before you ruin your nice clothes,' she scolded him, busying herself with Shona, who was trying to eat the watch.

He did as he was told, brushing the knees of his grey trousers. 'As I was saying, the place in the drawing office is still yours.'

'It's kind of you, but I must go back to Glasgow. I've got work to do there and, now that the lighter nights are in, I can spend more time looking for Daniel.'

Robert frowned. 'Does he still matter so much to you, Jen?'

She was saved from having to answer when Shona, deprived of the watch, began to protest noisily.

'She's getting tired, we'll have to go home,' Jenny said hastily.

'When are you going to let me drive you to wherever it is, and meet your family?' Matthew Neilson wanted to know when Jenny returned to work.

'I'm not.' Eliza and Kate and Evie were the only people in the store who knew Jenny's story, and she had made them both promise that they wouldn't say a word to anyone, particularly Matthew, about Ellerslie or Daniel or her reason for being in Glasgow.

'Does that mean that I'm not good enough for them?'

'It's got nothing to do with that. I just like to keep my private life and my working life separate.'

'But I want to know you better.'

'I don't see why.'

'Don't you?' They were alone in the workshop, and he put a hand over hers as she reached out to pick up a fresh brush. 'I like you, Jenny Young. I like you very much. I want to meet your family and your friends, and see the place where you grew up. I want to show you off to my friends and take you to see my home.'

'Matthew—' Gently, she removed her hand from beneath his and picked up the brush. 'I've got work to do, and so have you.'

He sighed, then straightened up. 'You're a hard woman, d'you know that?'

'I'm a working woman.'

'Come out with me tonight.'

'I can't, Matthew.'

'We'll go to a music-hall and join in the songs,' he murmured, leaning over her as she worked at the table. 'We'll laugh at the comedy acts and ooh at the dancing ladies kicking their legs, then we'll go somewhere pleasant for supper and I'll get you home at a respectable time. What do you say?'

Jenny put her brush aside. On the previous evening she had grown more and more depressed with each turn of the wheels as the train carried her away from Ellerslie, and she had scarcely slept all night. She knew that she would more than likely sit in her room that evening thinking about Shona and Helen and home instead of forcing herself out to look for Daniel.

'Yes?' Matthew coaxed, sensing surrender, and she looked up at him and smiled faintly. At times she found his self-assurance and his conviction that life held nothing but comfort and enjoyment quite insufferable but, on the other hand, he was kind, and good company.

'Do we visit the music-hall tonight, or do I go and toss myself off Kelvin Bridge with a brick in my pocket and a note saying that Mrs Young drove me to it?'

'It would take more than me to send you off Kelvin Bridge!' Jenny laughed.

'It would be quicker than dying of boredom, which is what I'll catch if I don't have anywhere to go. Yes or no – and if it's yes, I promise you I'll leave you in peace for the rest of the day.'

'In that case,' she said, smiling at him, 'It's yes.'

When he had gone back to his office and she was alone again she wondered if she had done the right thing in giving in to him. Clearly, he was reading more than he should into their friendship, and perhaps she should be warding him off rather than agreeing to go out with him. But at that moment, missing Ellerslie and Shona, worrying about Daniel and now Helen, she had enough to do without fretting over Matthew as well.

After three months Jenny felt that she had covered most of the area round the river without even a hint of success.

'I keep thinking that mebbe Daniel's turning the corner into a street just as I'm turning the far corner out of it, or that he left a shop five minutes before I went into it,' she told Kate and her mother. 'I'm losing hope.'

Mrs Ballantyne reached across the kitchen table and put a warm work-roughened hand over hers. 'Mebbe it's time tae think o' yer bairn now, hen,' she said gently. 'Ye've done yer best by yer man, an' nob'dy can say otherwise. Ye've got yer future tae consider.'

'Mebbe you're right,' Jenny agreed. Without letting Matthew know what she was doing she began to organise the china-painting department so that it could go on without her. The work was flowing in and she suggested to him that it was time they brought in another worker – someone with experience.

'Evie's talented and she's going to be very good for the department, but she still has to take time over her work. It should be easy enough to find someone like me.'

287

'I don't agree at all about that,' Matthew told her, his voice and his expression serious for once. 'As far as I'm concerned you're a very special lady, Jenny Young.'

She felt colour flooding into her face, and turned away from him, fidgeting with her brushes. 'I'm talking about someone who's done china-painting at home for some time and knows what she's about.'

Miss Beckett, a former schoolteacher who had had to give up work to nurse ageing parents through their final illnesses and was now alone in the world, proved to be just the right person. She was a talented painter with a flair for colour and an eye for design and, within two weeks of her arrival, Jenny was able to leave her to get on with her work unsupervised, confident that the finished produce would be of a high standard.

'I've had an idea,' Matthew said one evening when they were out together in his new car, a racy American sports car known affectionately as 'The Wasp' because its bodywork was bright yellow picked out in black and it was useful for buzzing about in. 'My sister's brat's heading for his first birthday and, of course, Uncle Matt's expected to come up with a decent present. D'you think you could paint a set of nursery dishes for him?'

'Of course.' They were driving near the river and Jenny, as usual, was watching the passers-by, just in case. She dragged her attention away from the pavements to glance at him. 'What sort of design would you like?'

He swung the car round a corner and blared the horn at a group of youngsters playing football in the centre of the street. They scattered, grinning and cheering, some whistling shrilly, fingers in their mouths, as the car swept past them.

Matthew gave the lads a lordly wave and parped the horn again. 'Oh, whatever you think the kiddy would like. Something with lots of colour – I'll leave it to you.' He had to raise his voice above the noise of the wind rushing past them as he put his foot down on the accelerator. They had reached a wider road and the tenements were being left behind.

'When do you want it for?'

'The beginning of July – can't remember the exact date,' said the fond uncle. 'My mama's going to visit them for the actual birthday and she can take my gift with her. My sister's coming back to Glasgow with her for a couple of weeks later in the month.' He groaned loudly, then said, 'If I know my mama, she'll want another celebration here for the kid. The house'll be full of brats and I'll probably be expected to be there playing the jolly uncle. And I expect it'll mean a second present – I shall raid the toy department for that.'

The wind had strengthened now that there were fewer high buildings to hold it back. It caught at Jenny's hair and she was glad that she had kept to the short style she had decided on so suddenly several years ago. It was becoming fashionable now and more and more young women were having their hair bobbed.

'You could have the party in the toy department itself instead of the house.' The suggestion was put idly, but Matthew's reaction was instant, and enthusiastic.

'By Jove, Jenny, that's a terrific idea! We could hold it on a Tuesday afternoon when the store's shut. Pack everything away except some toys for the kiddies to keep. Some of the staff might be willing to come in and help get the place ready, and we could get people in to see to the food.'

'You'd have to offer the staff extra payment for giving up their free time.'

Matthew grinned. 'The old man won't like it, but Mother'll make him toe the line.'

A man was tramping along the pavement ahead of them, thin-backed, shabbily dressed, his shoulders rounded against the wind. Jenny felt her throat tighten; she twisted round as they drew level then passed him, straining to see the face beneath the peaked cap.

'Someone you know?' Matthew yelled cheerfully.

'No.' She turned to look through the windscreen again, the familiar dull ache of disappointment and anti-climax nagging behind her breastbone. 'Nobody I know . . .'

Jenny's casual suggestion about the party was taken up enthusiastically by Mrs Neilson when Matthew passed it on. On the day of the birthday party staff members who had agreed to stay behind flocked to the toy department as soon as the glass double doors below closed behind the last customer.

Everything was packed away except a selection of less expensive toys so that each small guest could be given something to take home at the end of the party and, upstairs in the tearoom, the hired caterers started laying out sandwiches and cakes, jellies and trifles.

'It's like watching Santa Claus's little gnomes at work.' Matthew surveyed the army of workers, some packing toys and dismantling display stands and spiriting them out of sight, others setting out small gilt chairs for the children and larger chairs round the sides of the department for nannies and nursemaids.

A gramophone was brought in, together with a pile of records. Ladders appeared and, in no time, the large room became bright with paper streamers suspended from corner to corner across the ceiling and paper bells and balls hanging from the chandeliers. Kate and Evie Ballantyne, pink with excitement, were among those who had offered to help, though Miss Beckett, announcing that she was altogether too elderly for such goings on, had departed homewards. Jenny would have preferred to spend the afternoon doing the rounds of the shipyards, asking the gatemen if they knew anything of Daniel, but Matthew had insisted on her being in the store. 'It was your idea,' he told her, 'and you're going to be there. Besides, I'll finally get the chance to introduce you to my mother.'

'Who's that?' she asked now as one of the lift doors rattled back and a tired, elderly man shuffled out as though his feet hurt him. He was carrying a large carpet bag and the woman who followed him from the lift had a shabby, bulging suitcase. Matthew's secretary, who had undertaken to organise the party, scurried over to the new arrivals and led them into a sideroom.

'It must be the magician.' Matthew shook his head. 'The brat's only a year old. He can't walk or talk yet – how's he going to appreciate a magician?'

'The other children will.' Jenny had been told that there would be about thirty small guests up to four or five years old. Looking at the bustle before her she wondered at people who thought nothing of spending at least a year's wages for the average shipyard worker on celebrating the birthday of one little boy . . .

As the lifts brought the first guests up with their nursemaids Jenny slipped through the discreet baize door and down the plain narrow staircase to her workroom, where she settled down at the table. The party preparations for Matthew's nephew had brought back memories of Shona's birthday tea; the wonder on her baby's small face at first sight of the birthday cake Bella had made for her: the way Helen had clutched the clockwork bear throughout the afternoon, and cried when it was time to go home. Remembering that day, Jenny had no wish to be part of the party for the pampered, wealthy children upstairs.

She had almost completed an elaborately decorated teapot for a customer; she put it on a high stool and studied it from all angles for some time, then slipped a smock over her blue-and-white striped blouse and blue skirt, and started work, her sudden bout of homesickness eased and comforted by the work.

A full hour passed before the door opened and Matthew said, 'There you are! I thought you'd taken fright and run away. Come on, my dear mama and my sister want to meet you.'

'Can't you tell them I've gone home?'

'No, I can't. Come on,' he said insistently.

Reluctantly, Jenny put the teapot aside and unfastened her smock, hanging it on the row of pegs by the door then pausing to take a quick look in the mirror.

'You look fine.' Matthew's hands fell gently on to her shoulders and he turned her round to face him. 'I tell a lie – you look lovely,' he said, then drew her into his arms and kissed her. Taken by surprise she yielded for a moment, lifting her arms to hold him, letting her mouth soften and part beneath the gentle pressure of his lips. It had been a long time since a man had kissed her. Too long. But as his own arms tightened about her and the kiss began to intensify she came to her senses and pushed him away.

'Matthew! What d'you think you're doing?

'Kissing you.' He tried to draw her back into his embrace, but this time she resisted, pulling back and almost stumbling against the corner of one of the work tables.

'You've no right—' she said feebly.

He raised his brows, amusement mingling with the tenderness in his eyes. 'You seemed to be enjoying it as much as I was.'

'I – I thought you wanted me to meet your family.'

'Oh – we've got five minutes before we go up,' he said, advancing on her. 'Maybe even ten.'

'For goodness' sake, Matthew—' She pushed him away again, confused and alarmed by her own response earlier. 'We're in your own father's store!'

'If that's all that's fretting you we can easily arrange to go somewhere less – businesslike,' he teased, but she was already at the door, turning the handle, stepping out into the china gallery, which looked more like a large cluttered room than a store department now that the chandeliers had been switched off and the place was only lit by the afternoon light from the large windows. She made for the door leading to the back stairs but Matthew got to it first, brushing past her and holding the door open for her.

'Come out for a drive tonight,' he said as she passed him.

Jenny started up the stairs. 'I've got things to do tonight.'

He arrived on the toy department landing a fraction of a second behind her, catching at her hand as she reached for the handle of the door. 'Please, Jenny. I want to talk to you.' His voice had lost its teasing note now and his eyes were serious when she looked up at him. She felt shaky, and unsure of herself.

'I'm a married woman, Matthew, it's not seemly for us to—'

'A married woman lives at home with her husband,' he said sharply. 'Where is *your* husband? Why isn't he looking after you? It's time I knew more, Jenny.'

'There's no reason for you to know anything,' she protested defensively.

'Oh yes there is, my dear,' he said, with the slightest catch in his voice. For a moment she thought that he was going to kiss her again and a tingle ran, unbidden, through her body. She put her hands behind her back as though to prevent them from betraying her and reaching for him. But Matthew stepped back and turned towards the door.

'Oh yes there is,' he said again, under his breath, and opened the door. She walked past him into a clamour of noise, music blaring from the gramophone mingling with squeals of excitement from the children who sat in two circles on the floor. A large parcel was being passed quickly round each circle.

'Wait here,' Matthew said, his lips brushing the lobe of her ear as he spoke, then he made off, his tall figure, elegant in a well-cut blue suit, skirting one of the circles and blending into a group of women, some in nannies' uniforms, gathered round a long table set with refreshments.

The small guests were all beautifully dressed, well-fed, confident, so unlike the children Jenny had been used to all her life, many of whom were undernourished and grimy, some with legs bowed by rickets and heads shaved because of ringworm or lice. She wouldn't have wished any of that on the children here, but the contrast was painful . . .

The music suddenly stopped and a plump toddler seated near her gaped in dismay at the parcel in his hands then tried to push it at the girl beside him. She resisted fiercely and, as Jenny took an involuntary step towards them, a grey-clad woman swooped.

'Now then, Master Kenneth, out you come like a good little sportsman.'

'Nooooo!' screamed Master Kenneth, kicking fat little legs. The music started up again and the game went on as the nurse gathered her charge up and carried him off, kicking and screaming, to the other end of the room.

Smiling, Jenny turned away and was suddenly and unexpectedly transported back in time to Dalkieth's Experimental Tank section and the first peacetime launch and the line of tracers waiting at the foot of the wooden stairs to be presented to the official guests. On that day Fiona Dalkieth had worn mourning black. Today, walking with Matthew towards Jenny, she wore a leaf-green silky dress with long loose sleeves and a skirt that drifted in layers about her slim calves. A broad, dark green girdle was fastened about her hips by a glittering clasp and a boa of pale brown feathers was draped casually over her shoulders.

Young Mrs Dalkieth's soft fair hair was now cut fashionably short, and the discontented look had left her lovely face, replaced by self-satisfaction and determination. For the first time, seeing her close to Matthew, Jenny recognised the strong family likeness between brother and sister.

One thing hadn't changed – Fiona Dalkieth was as indifferent to Jenny now as she had been at their first meeting. Then, as now, Jenny was merely an employee and of no importance. Matthew was angered by his sister's attitude; Jenny could tell it by the tightening of his jawline, the sharpening of his voice as he said, 'It was Jenny who painted the nursery china I gave to young William.'

'Indeed?' Fiona murmured. It was left to Mrs Neilson, plump and fair and far more friendly than her daughter, to say how sweet the china was and how pleased William would be with it when he was old enough to appreciate it.

Matthew, who had moved away from his sister and mother to stand by Jenny, slid a hand beneath her elbow. 'Come and have a cup of tea with us,' he said firmly. She would have preferred to return to her workroom but, when she started to say so, he ignored the words, steering her towards the long table with Mrs Neilson trotting after them. Fiona drifted off to where a nursemaid stood holding her son.

Jenny, teacup in hand, answering Mrs Neilson's questions about where she had learned to paint china, noticed the way Fiona's face softened as she took the child from his nurse and kissed his brown hair. She settled the baby on one hip and picked up a wafer biscuit with her free hand, offering it to her son, who grabbed at it.

'He'll ruin his suit,' her mother pointed out, and Fiona shrugged. 'He's got plenty of clothes.'

The game of pass-the-parcel had ended and the other children were being shepherded to the opposite end of the room, where the little gilt chairs waited in rows before a small stage.

'Do you and your husband belong to Glasgow, Mrs Young?' Mrs Neilson asked.

'I've not been able to find that out,' Matthew's voice was lightly mocking. 'Jenny guards her privacy jealously – don't you, Jenny?'

His mother's eyes sharpened with curiosity. 'Don't be silly, dear, I'm sure Mrs Young has nothing to hide – have you, my dear?'

There was a burst of ragged applause as the magician stepped on to the stage, resplendent in an evening suit, crimson-lined cloak, and shiny top hat. He looked quite unlike the tired, shabby man Jenny had seen earlier.

293

'You were saying, Mrs Young—?' Matthew's mother said, raising her voice slightly above the noise.

'We – I came to Glasgow this year.'

'Oh? Where did you live before then?'

One of the lift gates rattled open and Fiona squealed as little William Dalkieth, startled, dropped his sticky, half-eaten biscuit on to the bodice of her smart dress. His head, capped with soft brown curly hair, swung sharply towards the noise in a movement that seemed to Jenny to be oddly familiar.

'Look what he's done!' Fiona wailed, holding the baby at arms' length and staring down at the wet smear on her dress. 'Take him, someone!'

Automatically, Jenny put her cup down and lifted the baby into her own arms. Fiona snatched the folded handkerchief from her brother's breast pocket and began to dab at her dress then stopped, staring at the two men advancing across the carpet from the lift, one in the Neilson uniform, the other in a dark lounge suit. Following her gaze, Jenny saw Robert Archer striding across the carpeting so quickly that the doorman accompanying him had to run to keep up with him.

'This gentleman insisted on being brought up to see you, Mrs Young,' the man said breathlessly when they arrived within earshot. 'I told him that—'

'Robert?' Fiona stepped in front of him, putting a hand on his arm. 'What on earth are you doing here?'

His dark head snapped round in a swift, surprised movement. It was the second time within a minute that Jenny had seen that distinctive turn of the head.

'Fiona?' Robert said, puzzled, briefly diverted, then looked back at Jenny, continuing unchecked towards her, his momentum brushing Fiona's hand from his arm. 'I've come to take you home, Jenny,' he said.

There was a burst of clapping and cheering from the other end of the room and the baby in Jenny's arms joggled up and down, his round head – the head, she now realised, that had just the same way of turning in surprise as Robert's – bumping against her chin. The magician, who had produced a large bunch of paper flowers from thin air, bowed to his audience, his crimson-lined cloak swirling wide.

'I've come to take you home, Jenny,' Robert repeated. 'It's Daniel – he's come back to Ellerslie.'

29

The tenement Daniel was staying in was near the quarry. It was old and damp and smelled of neglect and cats and too many years of human habitation. In some places the stone stairs were almost worn down to the level of the tread below and Jenny had to ascend cautiously through the semi-gloom, putting a hand from time to time on the slimy, flaking walls for balance. She had refused to allow Robert or Alice to accompany her. This was a meeting she knew she had to face on her own.

She reached the landing, hesitated, then knocked on the centre door. Daniel himself opened it. For a long moment husband and wife looked at each other, then he said, without surprise, 'You'd best come in.'

The door opened into a single room, much the same as the room Bella and Patrick lived in. There was scarcely any furniture – a table, a shabby sideboard, and a single upright wooden chair. Daniel drew it forward for Jenny.

'It's no' much,' he said, indicating his surroundings. 'But – it'll do for the short while I'm here.'

He was clean and neat, as always, but his face was positively gaunt and, as he moved restlessly to the small window, she saw that his dark hair was streaked with grey.

'Patrick told me you were in Glasgow, looking for me. There was no need.'

'I had to make sure you were all right.' Then, when he said nothing, she added, 'Shona's well. Bella's been caring for her. Patrick mebbe told you that?'

'Aye.' He had gone to the tenement where they had lived and, finding strangers in his former home, had knocked at the door on the opposite side of the close and had spoken briefly to Patrick. Jenny knew from what Bella had told her that he *had* been in Glasgow, working in one of the smaller yards, until suddenly deciding to return to Ellerslie.

'I'd have brought the wee one with me today, but I thought it might be best to wait until the next time.'

He shook his head. 'I'm not staying in Ellerslie. I'm moving on.'

'Where?' She was confused.

He ignored her. 'I had tae come back tae see—' He swallowed hard, '—tae see the lad's grave. But I cannae stay.'

'But what about me and Shona?' she asked, and he looked at her as though she was a stranger.

'We should never have got wed, you and me,' he said coldly. 'Me and Walter should have stayed as we were. I thought it was my duty tae give him a mother, but I was wrong.'

She stared at him, shocked, then asked quietly, 'Is that the only reason you wanted me to marry you, Daniel? To be a mother to your son?'

He glanced away, refusing to meet her eyes. 'We should never have got wed,' he said again. 'We were all right until you came intae the house an' started tae encourage him tae rebel against me.'

Jenny's nails dug into her palms. The man's injustice and self-centredness suddenly infuriated her. 'Don't try to blame me for what happened to Walter,' she began, then stopped. There was no sense now in quarrelling over the past, and it was clear that Daniel had turned his own feelings of guilt around in an attempt to clear himself of blame over his son's death.

'But we did get wed,' she said instead, 'and Shona's the result. What's to happen to her?'

He shrugged, an impatient twitch of the shoulders. 'She's your bairn. I only wanted Walter.' His voice broke on the name, and when Jenny, suddenly full of pity, tried to put a hand on his arm, he turned away from her, dragging the door open with one of the abrupt, jerky movements she remembered so well. 'Ye'd best go.'

She made one last attempt. 'I'll come back tomorrow and we can talk about—'

He looked at her as though they were strangers. 'We've got nothin' tae talk about,' he said, and she knew that he meant it, and that her marriage was over, once and for all.

At the end of the street she turned the corner, walking fast, head down to hide her tears from passers-by, and walked into a man standing there. As she rebounded he caught at her arms to steady her and she stared up at him through a mist, then said on a half-laugh, half-sob, 'You keep turning up at the most unexpected times, Robert Archer!'

'I followed you,' he admitted, 'and waited just in case.'

'In case of what?'

He shrugged impatiently. 'Are you all right?'

'Why wouldn't I be?'

'Oh, no reason,' said Robert. He brought a neatly folded white handkerchief from his pocket and lifted her chin with his free hand so that he could dab at her eyes. 'What did he say?' he asked, his tone softer.

She took the handkerchief from him. 'I can manage,' she said sharply and began to walk away. He caught up and fell into step beside her.

'What did he say, Jenny?'

'He's going off again, on his own. He doesn't want me, or Shona. She's his child, and he doesn't even care about what happens to her. I should never have married him, Robert!' she said on a sudden wave of anguish, and he put a comforting arm about her shoulders.

'We all do things we shouldn't. It's just the way folk are, though knowing that doesn't make it any easier,' he said. They walked on together in silence for a moment before he asked, 'So what are you going to do?'

'I don't know,' said Jenny. 'I just don't know.'

'Why didn't you tell me?' Matthew asked two days later, hurt in his voice. 'I'd have helped you to find this husband of yours if you'd only had enough trust in me to tell me the truth.'

Jenny had dreaded this meeting, but she had had to return to Glasgow to talk to him face to face. 'It was my business, I had to see to it alone.' They were in his office, untouched cups of tea cooling on the desk between them.

'What sort of man would go off and leave his wife to fend for herself the way he did?' he asked angrily. 'And how can you think that you owe him any duty after that?'

'I told you – he didn't know what he was doing after his son died. He was out of his mind with grief.'

'And now you're going back to Ellerslie, back to him.'

It would have been easier to let him think that, but he deserved the truth. 'No, I'm not going back to him. Daniel's left the town. He wants to be on his own from now on.'

Hope flared in Matthew's eyes. 'That means that you can stay here, in Glasgow, in the store—'

She shook her head. 'I only came to Glasgow to look for Daniel.

My family are in Ellerslie, and my daughter. It's where I belong, Matthew.'

'And how are you going to support yourself?' he demanded. 'You've got a job right here; you can bring the child to Glasgow.'

'She's best where there are folk she knows. And so am I,' Jenny said, getting to her feet. 'I've had a word with Miss Beckett – she can run the workroom just as well as I did, and Evie's a good worker. They can manage fine without me.'

'And what about me?' He got to his feet and came round the desk to her. 'What about me?' he asked again. 'Jenny, I love you, and you love me, I know you do.'

'I'm not sure if I know what love is, Matthew.'

'I'll teach you,' he offered eagerly. 'I promise you that I'll wait until you're sure, then we can be married, once you're free.'

'I don't know if I'll ever want to marry anyone again.' Jenny felt very tired, and unsure of her own feelings. 'All I know at the moment is that I need to go back to Ellerslie, back to Shona.'

'And what about me? I don't want to lose you.'

'You'll manage fine, Matthew,' she said gently. 'We all have to manage as best we can.'

A week later she left Glasgow for the last time and returned to Ellerslie. Sitting in the train, her gloved fingers twisted together in her lap, she stared into the future, with little idea of what it would hold for her. She had been asked to continue doing some work from home for the store, and she had agreed, for she was going to need all the money she could earn. She was going to live for the time being with her parents and take up Robert's offer of work in the yard's drawing office, but she must find a flat for herself and Shona as soon as possible. She had no intention of settling back into her parents' home, becoming a daughter again instead of a mother and an independent woman.

'Are you all right, my dear?' the elderly woman on the other side of the carriage asked, and Jenny suddenly realised that she had raised a hand to her forehead in an attempt to ease the beginnings of a headache.

She summoned up a smile, assured the woman that she was quite well, and stared out of the window to avoid further conversation.

Robert met her at the station and this time he told the cab driver to take them both right to her parents' closemouth. Ignoring the stares of the children playing in the gutters and the women loitering in gossiping groups he assisted her from the cab and carried her case into the close.

'My father might be home—' she warned.

'To hell with your father!' Robert tossed the words over his shoulder as he mounted the stairs ahead of her. 'He'll have to get used to seeing me around – and so will everyone else,' he added, raising his voice as the door opposite the Gillespies' opened a crack. It closed at once, on an offended sniff.

A mixture of expressions flitted across Faith's face when she opened the door to them. 'Teeze is in,' she faltered, then fell back as Robert stepped into the hall.

'Good,' he said calmly. 'I'll have a word with him before I go.'

Teeze, reading his newspaper in his favourite chair, glanced up, his face stiffening when Robert appeared in the doorway.

'I told you no' tae come here again!' He tossed the paper aside and began to struggle to his feet.

'Teeze—'

'Don't fret yourself, Mrs Gillespie.' Robert put Jenny's case down and faced the older man. 'It's time you faced facts, Teeze Gillespie. Whether you like it or not I'm here, and I'm here to stay. Jenny's forgiven me for the wrong I did her all those years ago, and it's time you forgave me too. As to Maurice, I'm sorry he's dead, but I'm not going to go on apologising to you just because I'm still alive.'

He held a hand out but Teeze struck it aside.

'I'll not take the hand o' a traitor tae his own sort,' he roared. His other fist, bunched and knobbly with age, but still strong, came up fast and sailed past Robert's ear as he stepped aside. Before Teeze could recover his balance his outflung arm was twisted behind him, and he was spun round.

'Call me a traitor again, Teeze, and I'll ram your teeth down your throat,' said Robert as he forced the older man towards the sink. 'I've worked bloody hard for what I've got. I've taken that shipyard out of the gutter where George Dalkieth put it and made it whole again and by God, I'll get the respect I'm due from now on!'

'Robert!' Jenny dragged at his arm. 'He's an old man!'

'Who are you callin' old?' Teeze yelled as he was forced down over the sink.

'Mind your own business, Jen,' Robert grunted, pressing down hard on the back of Teeze's grizzled head with his free hand. 'This is between your father and me.' Teeze, bellowing like a bull, tried to kick back and only succeeded in losing his balance. Robert's fingers curled into Teeze's hair and prevented his face from smashing into the sink, while with his elbow he managed to jerk the brass tap on. Cold water jetted out, hit the back of Teeze's head, and sprayed into the room, soaking Robert and Jenny and Faith, on either side of him now, trying to break his grip.

The older man's roar turned into a gurgle. 'Ye'll drown him!' Faith screamed, beating at Robert's shoulder with frenzied fists.

'It'll take more than a wee bit water to drown this old devil,' he told her grimly, and held his victim down for a further moment before hauling him upright and releasing him. Teeze clutched at the edge of the sink, water and mucus spraying from his mouth and nose as he wheezed and choked and blew.

'Now then,' said Robert, shaking his own head so that drops flew from his hair, 'If it's further humiliation you want we'll go downstairs and I'll deal it out to you in front of the whole street. But speaking for myself I'd as soon shake you by the hand then buy you a pint.'

Teeze, still unsteady on his feet, glowered at the younger man, clearly considering another lunge at him.

'For pity's sake, don't be such a stubborn old fool!' Faith snapped at him with a vigour unusual for her. 'D'ye want him tae drown you altogether? The matter's settled, so away and have a pint and stop your nonsense!'

Teeze, accepting the wisdom of her advice, gave a mighty sneeze and dragged his arm across his face, then pushed wet grey hair out of his eyes. 'Ye'll buy me a whisky,' he growled.

'A whisky, then,' said Robert, and walked out of the kitchen. Teeze, pawing Faith aside when she tried to mop with a towel at his wet shirt, took his jacket from behind the door and followed the office manager. Alone, Jenny and her mother looked at each other.

'What would ye dae with them?' Faith finally asked helplessly, and for the first time in a week Jenny felt a smile pull the corners of her mouth up.

'Nothing,' she said. 'Nothing at all. Let them sort it out over a drink, Mam.'

As she fetched a cloth and got down on her knees to mop at the puddles on the linoleum her thoughts moved from Robert to the moment at the birthday party in the store when little William Dalkieth had reminded her so sharply of him.

As office manager Robert would often meet Fiona socially. He

300

was an attractive man and she was a beautiful young woman. And like everyone else in Ellerslie Jenny knew of the rumours that George Dalkieth had been unable to father children on his first wife.

If her suspicions were correct and Robert had been Fiona Dalkieth's lover, how did matters stand between them now? Rinsing the cloth at the sink, she told herself that whatever had happened between Robert and Fiona Dalkieth, and whatever might happen in the future, was none of her business.

Shona was almost ready for bed when Jenny went into her sister's flat. She was newly washed and in a clean gown, and her blue eyes, almost as dark as her father's, were heavy-lidded with sleepiness. From her seat on Patrick's knee she looked up at her mother with wonder at first, a slight frown between her brows. When Jenny spoke to her the frown cleared and she smiled, showing two tiny white teeth. Jenny stooped to take her and Patrick let the small warm body go with some reluctance then picked up a half-carved piece of wood. Bella took his knife from a drawer and carefully laid some sheets of newspaper about his chair to catch the shavings. She had put on weight and her shoulders had straightened; her movements, as she knelt at Patrick's feet, smoothing the newspaper out, were deft and controlled instead of jerky and nervous. The little room was spotlessly clean and cosy, with an air of serenity about it, and Jenny suddenly felt uncomfortable.

'Will you not be sorry to leave Glasgow, now that you've made a place for yourself there?' Patrick wanted to know, his eyes intent on his work. Tiny pale shavings dropped from beneath the knife-blade, reminding Jenny of the pale gold wax shavings that had lain thickly on the floor of the Experimental Tank section beneath the tables that held the models.

'Glasgow's not my home.' Once she had wanted so badly to get away from Ellerslie, but now she knew that it was where she belonged – for the moment at least.

Shona yawned and her eyelids drooped. Bella immediately held out her arms. 'I'll put her down.'

'I'll do it. No sense in disturbing her more than we have to.'

Bella lifted back the crib blankets. 'She gives us a goodnight kiss,' she explained as Shona wriggled and girned when Jenny began to lower her into the crib. 'First Pat, then me.'

Jenny carried her daughter over to Patrick and watched as he was kissed soundly on the cheek.

''Night, 'night, pet,' he said gruffly. The ritual was repeated with

301

Bella, who then said encouragingly, 'A wee kiss for yer mammy now, hen.'

Shona's mouth, butterfly soft, brushed Jenny's cheek, then she allowed herself to be tucked into the crib.

'Where'll you live, Jen?' Bella wanted to know when the clothes-horse, draped with an old bit of sheeting to shut out as much light as possible, had been angled beside the crib. She drew the curtain across the single window and lit a taper at the range then reached up to light the two gas mantels. They came to life with a soft popping sound, the flames moving quickly from blue to steady gold. 'How'll you support yourself?'

'I'm going to work in Dalkieth's drawing office, and the store where I worked in Glasgow's offered to sell any china I can paint for them in my spare time. I'll stay with Mam and Dad for now, till I find somewhere to rent for me and Shona.'

'Did Mam tell you that Lottie and Neil are going to Edinburgh for a week soon? Mam's going to look after Helen while they're away. You'd best leave Shona with us until after that.' Bella's fingers pleated the folds of her skirt. 'It'll be too much of a crowd in the one house and you don't want to move Shona round too much.'

'You've had her for long enough, Bella – it's time I took over.'

'Bella's right,' Patrick said unexpectedly, his eyes on his work, his hands sure and quick. Beneath his fingers a dog was emerging from the block of wood, one paw delicately lifted, head turned, ears sharp, as though its nocturnal prowl had been alerted by an unexpected sound. It looked for all the world as though the animal had been imprisoned in the block and Patrick was freeing it. 'No sense in unsettling the bairn when she's contented with us.'

Walking back to her parents' flat along the darkening street later, hands pushed deep into her pockets, Jenny thought of how well Shona got on with her aunt and uncle. When the time came for her to take Shona back it would hurt Bella. The prospect nagged at Jenny. Her sister had suffered enough, and Jenny didn't want to inflict more pain on her. But on the other hand, Shona was all that she had left of her marriage, and she ached to be reunited with her own child.

As she walked through the close and began to ascend the stairs she wondered if she was being selfish in wanting Shona back. Should she put Bella's happiness before her own, and accept the fact that the little girl was contented where she was?

Then her thoughts flew to the years ahead, to Shona growing up, discovering that her father had deserted her without a backward glance, and her own mother had handed her over to someone else to care for. And as she stepped into her parents' home she knew that she could never let that happen. Shona's place was with her, in a home of their own, a haven where they could shut out the rest of the world and make their own happiness.

30

George Dalkieth's initial triumph at fathering a healthy son and heir had been quickly soured by what he saw as his mother's betrayal – her sudden and inexplicable tendency to rely more and more on Robert Archer's advice and to vote in his favour at the Board meetings.

'The man's a damned upstart and yet you listen to his every word and vote for him over me,' he complained bitterly again and again.

'Mr Archer knows a great deal about shipbuilding and I've come to realise that what he says makes sense,' Isobel retorted crisply, then added, her voice noticeably chilling, 'As for those precious friends of yours, the English yards they invested in are in trouble. They're selling the machinery off and putting men out of work. That's not what I want for Dalkieth's.'

'But we'd not be out of pocket if it happened here,' her son protested mulishly. 'The machinery and the ground are worth a fair amount. If the yard did have to be sold off we could live comfortably on the proceeds.'

'That,' said Isobel, disgusted, 'is not what your father and grandfather – and your great-grandfather, too – intended. Don't be so selfish, George. You've got a son to think of now. You want him to inherit the yard, don't you?'

George wasn't so sure. Some of his newfound friends had introduced him to the delights of shooting parties and fishing parties in the North of England and the Scottish Highlands. He had had a taste of the life that the landed gentry led, and he liked it. If he had money he could buy himself a small estate, with a house grander than Dalkieth House as well as fishing and shooting rights. He could invite his friends to stay and Fiona would make an ideal hostess. Such a life would be much more convivial than the existence he led now, living under his mother's roof, being expected to make the shipyard the centre of his world, and continually having to put up with Robert Archer's cool manner and insufferable self-importance.

He put this proposition to Fiona but, to his astonishment, she didn't agree with him at all. Wrapped up in caring for her beloved son, basking in her new-found and very welcome rapport with her

305

mother-in-law, pampered by servants and soothed by her comfortable life in Dalkieth House, Fiona was happy at last. She had no desire to give everything up in order to become a hostess to George's boring hunting, shooting and fishing friends.

Another problem had arisen for Fiona, a problem that she couldn't discuss with her mother-in-law. Rampaging across the moors and splashing into rivers, killing defenceless creatures, or at least trying to kill them with gun and fishing-rod, seemed to go straight to George's loins. He came back from his hunting forays with renewed desire for his wife's company, and Fiona's hopes that he might lose interest in her once she had presented him with an heir had come to nothing.

It would have helped, she thought wistfully, if he had found some female companionship on his longer trips and at least learned some of the niceties of lovemaking but, as she already knew from bitter experience, the women who took part in these country house parties tended to be large and hearty, with few feminine subtleties.

Often, lying in George's arms, Fiona recalled Robert Archer and the passion she had known with him. Once or twice she even considered approaching Robert again, but she knew that that was impossible. Believing that she had no further need of him she had ended their affair in a tactless and humiliating manner – and Robert wasn't the sort of man who would easily forgive and forget. She couldn't even tell him the truth about William, for she had made a solemn promise to Isobel.

It was a relief to Fiona when George came home from one of his trips wheezing and sneezing and had to take to his own bedroom with a chill, leaving his wife in peace. She showed her gratitude by pampering him, feeding him calves' foot jelly and insisting on his staying in bed until the chill was completely cured. As he slumped against a mound of pillows and announced his intention of being up and about in time for the following week's launch Fiona eyed him critically. He had put on weight since their marriage, mainly by dint of self-indulgence and comfortable living, and not even his half-hearted scrambling over heather moors had done much to trim him down.

'We'll see what the doctor says, dear,' she told him firmly.

'Nonsense! My own wife has been invited to launch this vessel and I shall be there to support her.' George took her hand, which almost disappeared into his beefy palm and Fiona patted his cheek with her free hand in a maternal way.

'We'll see,' she said lightly, and began to free herself from his hot, moist grip. He tugged unexpectedly, and Fiona, taken unawares, lost her balance and fell on to the bed, against him.

'George!'

'Dammit, Fiona,' said George Dalkieth, his mouth soft and rubbery against her cheek, his free arm tightening about her waist, 'it's damned lonely in this bed all by myself.'

The drawing office was a large, airy room with windows along three of the four walls and counter-balance lamps hung from the ceiling above large, flat tables. At first there was some awkwardness among the draughtsmen as Jenny was the only woman in the place but, as far as she was concerned, she was there purely to work and, to her relief, the men soon accepted that.

She loved the precision and fine detail of the work she was required to do, relishing the sight of a great, empty sweep of paper laid out before her, waiting for her pen to enrich it with detail and colour and purpose. She loved the way an entire ship could come into being in theory beneath her hands from sketches and drawings passed from the naval architects.

There was always plenty to do during her free time. She went round to Bella's at least once every day to help with Shona and, now that Neil had taken Lottie off to Edinburgh on the trip he had promised her, there was Helen to see to at home. Neil's parents didn't want to take her in. They disapproved of Lottie, Alice told Jenny, and would have nothing to do with Helen, born out of wedlock.

The child, who had once scampered cheerfully about the tiny flat dressed in cut-downs made out of old blouses and skirts that nobody wanted, now wore pretty clothes, and sat silently in a corner, watching and listening, flinching if anyone tried to talk to her. She had just had her fifth birthday, and had started attending school the month before. She slept on the truckle-bed Marion had once used, set up in the larger bedroom which she shared with Jenny; she often woke screaming from nightmares and they had had to put a waterproof sheet over the mattress because Helen quite often wet the bed. Slowly, patiently, Jenny and Alice worked on her, coaxing her to go out with them, reading to her, teaching her games. Shona, now sixteen months old and becoming more steady on her feet every day, often came to the flat with Bella, but even her company had little effect on Helen.

'It's as if she's tied into knots and she's scared to unloosen them in case she falls apart,' Alice said one evening as she and Jenny left the house together. 'Mam asked me to fetch her home from school the other day, and when I got there she was just waiting in a corner of the playground on her own, with all the other children playing round her.'

307

'I never thought I'd see Helen so quiet and timid,' Jenny agreed, her voice concerned. 'She used to be so lively.'

'It's that Lottie, always nagging at her and criticising her. Sometimes she puts me in mind of Gran before she fell ill.' Alice bounced the bundle of the account books into a more secure position beneath her arm as she walked. She had brought them home from the pawnshop and worked on them at the table while Jenny decorated a plate she was working on for the store. It had been like old times again. When she had finished, Alice, gathering the books together, had suggested that Jenny should walk round with her to deliver them.

'I'd as soon get them back where they belong, and we could both do with a breath of fresh air. And you've not had a look at the shop since I started in it, have you?'

They left Helen sleeping and Faith darning by the range. It was early October, and dark outside. 'D'you mind the times we used to pretend to run three-legged races down the street?' Alice asked, tucking her free arm into Jenny's.

'I do – but if you've got it in mind to try it now you can forget it. These cobblestones are in a terrible state.'

'Ach, they're no worse than they always were,' Alice countered blithely. 'It's us that's getting older, and more scared of breaking our legs. Getting older's sad, isn't it?' she said from the lofty heights of seventeen.

When they reached the shop she produced a bunch of keys on a ring. 'If I knock, Alec'll come hurrying down to open the door and that'll start him coughing, poor man. He can come down the stairs in his own good time when he hears us.'

While her sister unlocked the door, Jenny studied the two small shop windows where once there had been a clutter of dusty items on view. Now there were far fewer, all neatly laid out, including a group of familiar wood carvings varnished to a high gloss.

'These windows've changed a lot. It looks like a proper shop now.'

'There was no sense in holding on to goods that hadn't been redeemed.' Alice said over her shoulder. 'When they're laid out properly folk are more interested in coming in to buy.'

A bell tinged as she opened the door and led the way inside. 'Wait until I've lit the mantel,' her voice floated through the darkness. Jenny heard the rattle of matches in their box, then there was the scrape of a match-head and a tiny flame blossomed. She looked around when Alice had lit the mantles. 'My – there's been a lot of changes here!'

'It was high time. The place was so crowded that it had almost come to a standstill. We still get plenty of stuff brought in every Monday to be redeemed on Fridays but now it's all stored in the back, out of sight.'

Jenny looked round, remembering the days when she had often scurried into this same shop to pawn her father's Sunday suit on a Monday or redeem it on a Friday night. During the war, when Maurice was in France, his best suit had lived here, being redeemed every three months to ensure that it wasn't lost for ever, then instantly re-pawned, brought home only when Maurice was due home on leave.

'D'you mind the time Maurice came home without letting us know and giving us time to redeem his good suit?'

Alice giggled. 'How could I forget? He was furious because he'd to go out in his uniform until we got it back.'

'Do folk still pawn the same thing, week in and week out?'

'Of course. It's usually the only item they can spare,' Alice told her. 'When folk you know keep bringing in the same thing it fairly colours your thinking towards them. There's one poor soul I can't pass in the street now without seeing her as a big chanty covered with bright blue flowers.'

Even Alec Monroe, who came slowly down the stairs from the upper flat while the two of them were laughing, had changed. Although he was only a few years older than Jenny he, like the shop, had always seemed to her to be dusty and grey and rather sad. But now his movements were more brisk than she remembered, and he looked quite smart and cheerful. When he asked her, 'What d'ye think of the old place now?' his voice was confident and he looked round with a complacent air.

'It's changed a great deal, Alec.'

'For the better, thanks to yer wee sister here. When she first marched in here and told me I should give her a job I nearly sent her packing, d'ye know that? Deciding tae give her a chance was one of the best things I ever did.'

'Ach, away with you,' Alice said calmly. 'He's an awful flatterer, this man.' She fixed her employer with a stern eye. 'Have you finished up that soup I made yesterday?'

'He fancies you,' Jenny teased when they were on their way home, and stopped dead in her tracks when Alice said calmly, 'I should hope so, for I think I'm going to marry him.'

'What? I never heard anything about this!'

'Neither has anyone else, including Alec, so I'd be grateful if you'd say nothing for the meantime.'

'Alice, you're only just seventeen years of age! And the man's ailing, he always will be.'

Alice's expression, as they stepped out of a pool of shadow into the light from a streetlamp, was serene. 'All the more need for a wife to look after him.'

'He's a lot older than you are.'

'He's only thirty. I'm not going to rush into anything,' Alice said practically. 'I'm only thinking about it – I'll give it another year before I make up my mind.'

'You could do better for yourself.'

Alice snorted and gave her sister an old-fashioned look. 'I've no wish to marry someone of my own age and raise a brood of children and worry about feeding and clothing them like Mam's always had to, hoping my man doesn't lose his job or spend all his pay in the pub. Alec's gentle and caring – and I'm no oil painting, Jenny. It seems to me that we could be contented together.'

They walked in silence for a moment, then she added, 'If we do get wed I'll do my best to keep him alive for as long as I can, but if it turns out that we don't have all that long together – well, at least we'll have been happy. And I'll inherit the shop, for he's not got any other family to worry about,' she added with self-mocking amusement, then was serious again. 'I think a good partnership and a proper understanding of each other's more important than romance for folk like us.'

As the day of her mother's return from Edinburgh approached, Helen, who had begun to emerge slightly from her shell, grew quieter again. She followed Jenny about the small flat like a shadow, accompanying her tearfully to the door when she went to work, waiting on the top step for her when she returned, as though she hadn't moved from the same spot all day.

Clutching the clockwork bear, her favourite toy, she watched as Jenny, talking cheerfully all the time, packed her few belongings.

'I'll visit you often, pet, now that I'm back in Ellerslie. And we'll go to the park sometimes, you and me and Shona and Aunt Alice.'

Helen sucked in her lower lip and wriggled her back against the wall, as though trying to burrow through the flaking plaster.

'It's breaking my heart to see her,' Jenny confided low-voiced to Alice as the two of them waited outside the landing privy for the little girl. She was old enough now to go to the lavatory on her own, but insisted on someone – Jenny, if she was available – going with her and waiting outside for her.

'I don't think they're bad parents. I mean, I don't think they beat her,' Alice's brow was furrowed with concern. 'If you ask me, Lottie and Neil see her as a nuisance, and that's a terrible burden for a wee girl to carry.'

The cistern flushed and, after a moment, Helen came out, the bear jammed tightly beneath one arm. She took Jenny's hand and together the two of them, with Alice following, climbed the stairs back to the Gillespie flat.

Darkness came, and there was no sign of Lottie or Neil. The hands of the clock on the mantelshelf ticked past Helen's bedtime and her small body relaxed a little as Jenny washed her, dressed her in the new nightgown she had bought to replace the well-worn, too-tight garment Helen had brought with her, and put her to bed. A few hours later Helen, screaming in a nightmare, woke the entire household, and most of the other folk in the building. Jenny took her into her own bed, risking wet sheets and, long after Helen had fallen asleep, clutching her aunt tightly, her entire body convulsed every now and then with a massive shudder, Jenny stayed awake, thinking about Shona, asleep now in Bella's house. Would she, like Helen, change from a contented baby to a frightened little girl because of the changes in her young life? Bella was right – it was best to leave Shona where she was until Jenny could find a home for them both.

She longed to turn over and re-settle the pillow, which had bunched itself uncomfortably beneath her neck, but Helen's grip was so strong that she couldn't break it without wakening the child. So she suffered the discomfort and lay still, fretting over Shona, wondering how long it would be before she could claim her own baby back.

In the morning Robert came into the drawing office, frowning, to ask Jenny if she knew why Neil Baker hadn't turned up for work on his first day back.

'Mebbe his father's heard from him.'

Robert shook his head. 'His father knows no more than you do,' he said irritably.

'D'you think there's been an accident?'

'I think,' said Robert, 'that the two of them are too busy enjoying themselves to give a thought for anyone else.'

Two more days went by without a word from Lottie, then Jenny came home from work to find Faith sitting in the kitchen, empty-handed for once, staring at the gleaming black-leaded range as though she had never seen it in her life before.

'Mam?' Memories of the day the telegram about Maurice had arrived from the War Office swept in on Jenny. Her heart seemed to falter then patter on its way twice as fast as usual.

'Neil's been here.'

'For Helen? And I wasn't here to tell her I'd be sure to visit—'

311

'Lottie's left him, Jenny. He says she's staying in Edinburgh and she's not coming back. He was in such a taking – I'd not give much for her chances if she ever does come back,' said Faith. 'Not with the look he had on his face.'

'What about Helen?'

'He doesnae want her, and neither does Lottie. He told her that to her face, poor wee fatherless bairn that she is—'

'Where is she?'

'Through there,' said Faith with a jerk of the head. Jenny hurried at once to the bedroom. Helen, spurning her own small bed, had climbed into Jenny's and was sound asleep there, sprawled on her back instead of in her usual tight knot. Her mouth was soft and full and her hands, relaxed and half-curled like little shells, lay on either side of her face. The clockwork bear, carefully tucked up, lay close to her, but out of her arms for once, with its bright-eyed, furry head on Jenny's pillow . . .

31

For once, Jenny gave her reflection in the mirror more than a brief glance as she pulled off her close-fitting hat and ran her fingers through her short hair to fluff it up. The glass, a pleasant oval within an elaborate gilt rim, reflected a woman thinner in the face than before, with serious eyes and a mouth that had been firmed by the events of the past few years.

Deliberately, she smiled at her reflection and was relieved to see that the mirrored mouth still curved easily and a light came into the blue eyes. Then the smile faded, and the serious look returned.

As she turned away from the mirror and moved to the sofa, drawn up before a welcoming fire, Robert came into the little parlour, balancing the tea-tray on one upraised hand like a butler.

'Tea, m'lady?' He set the tray on the small table before her, and sat in the armchair opposite. 'My housekeeper's rheumatism's bothering her today so I said I'd bring the tray through. I'm afraid I'm going to lose her – she's talking of giving up work. I'd be grateful if you'd see to the rest. I'd probably spill it into the saucers.'

As she poured the tea and handed a cup to Robert she took time to study him. He looked tired and there was an almost grim set to his mouth. She had heard from Teeze that, while she was in Glasgow, there had been serious fears in the town over the future of the Dalkieth shipyard, but now the orders were coming in again and the yard was beginning to recover, unlike others on the Clyde hit by the sudden backlash after the war. It was generally agreed, though grudgingly in some cases, that Robert Archer had been instrumental in the yard's survival.

'How's Mr Dalkieth?' she asked. Robert shrugged. 'Back in his bed as far as I know, and being cossetted by his womenfolk.' His mouth turned down in derision. 'His mother claims now that he always had a weak chest. As far as I'm concerned he can stay where he is. Running the yard's easier when he's not around the place issuing counter orders and getting everyone's backs up. When he came in for that launch last week he caused nothing but trouble.'

'You know, Robert,' Jenny said, shaking her head, 'we never dreamed when you used to run around with Maurice that one day you'd be in charge of the shipyard.'

'We've both found ourselves on unexpected roads, haven't we?' Robert asked, then, as she glanced down at the gold band on her left hand he said, with a slight bleakness in his voice, 'Are you still fretting over Daniel Young?'

'I wonder at times what's happened to him.'

'He wanted to be on his own, Jenny, and you could do nothing about that – just as you could do no more than you did to prevent the boy's death,' he added with the uncanny knack he sometimes had of reading her mind. 'There's no sense in wishing that you could turn the clock back and change what's happened. We all wish that now and again, but it's not possible. You've got a child of your own, now. All you can do is try to give her a good life.' Then, leaning forward to look more closely at her, 'Is there something wrong with the wee lass?'

Jenny put her cup down carefully. 'She's fine. It's just—' she hesitated, then said in a rush of words, 'I'm beginning to wonder if she's still mine, Robert, or if she's Bella's child now.'

'Your sister's only looking after her until such time as you've got a place of your own.'

'That's what we all say, but it's been over seven months since she and Patrick took Shona in. That's a long time in a wee girl's life.' Jenny's fingers pleated the material of her grey woollen skirt. 'There's me and Mam and Dad and Alice in the house I was born in – and now Helen's back with us and it's as if I've never been away, never married Daniel or had Shona or gone to Glasgow.' She stopped, then said, 'The other day we were all in my mother's kitchen when the bairns came in from playing in the other room. Helen came straight to me, the way she always does, and Shona went to Bella. And nobody seemed to think anything of it. A bairn for me, a bairn for my sister.' She swallowed hard, then said, low-voiced, blinking tears back, 'I love Helen – but she's not Shona.'

'Jen—' He came to sit beside her, putting a hand over hers. 'I didn't realise it was so hard for you.'

'Nobody does, and that's what's worrying me. They're all beginning to accept things as they are.' Then she squared her shoulders, forcing a smile. 'But I should be doing something about it instead of sitting here girning and grizzling at you like a bairn that's been left out of a game.'

She leaned forward to pick up her cup, but Robert moved his grasp from her hand to her arm, stopping her. 'There's more than enough

314

room in this house for you and Shona. Hear me out, Jenny,' he went on swiftly as she started to speak. 'I've already said that we can't turn the clock back, but we can change the course of our lives if we put our minds to it. I still want to marry you, Jenny, more than ever before.'

'I've already told you that—'

'And what about what's best for Shona?' he interrupted impatiently. 'You want to be with her, don't you? You could bring her here tomorrow – today, if you want. Jen—' He reached out to her. It would have been so easy to lean towards him, to go into his arms and stay there, but instead Jenny got to her feet with an abrupt movement. Letting Robert look after her and Shona for the rest of their lives would be too easy. She had made the decision to manage on her own, and she would stay with it.

'You're wrong, Robert. What's over is over and there's no sense in thinking otherwise.'

His face darkened as he stood up. 'Am I to be condemned for ever because of a mistake I made eight years ago?'

'I'm not condemning you, Robert. We're good friends and I hope we always will be. But we're nothing more than friends.'

'You know that's not so,' he said quietly. 'But you'll just not admit the truth to yourself. You've been badly hurt, Jen, but don't let that spoil the rest of your life – and mine.'

'It's time I was off home.' Jenny went into the hall. The breath was catching in her throat and she felt a desperate need to get out of the house, away from the man whose hand reached past her and took her coat from the stand.

'You said yourself, we've travelled roads we never thought to travel, you and me. Our paths crossed once before and it seems to me that they should cross again, Jenny.' His hands lingered on her shoulders as he helped her on with her coat.

She stepped away from him and opened the front door. 'It wouldn't work, Robert, not now.'

'You're too independent for your own good.'

'I've had to learn to stand on my own feet and I'll go on doing it,' Jenny told him from the bottom step. 'It's safer that way.'

'And lonelier,' she heard Robert say as she fled down the path. Walking along the pavement on her way home, listening to the brisk tapping of her heels on the hard stone, she told herself that she was right in what she had said to him – she had to be right. She had trusted in Robert once before and she had trusted in Daniel, too, and both times her trust had been destroyed. For her own sake, for Shona's sake, she must retain her independence, even if it meant, as Robert had said, leading a lonely life.

315

Fergus Craig got to his feet as quickly as his girth and age would allow as the door opened and his sister came into the room.

'How is he?'

Isobel crossed to the window. November was halfway through and winter was on the other side of the glass; remnants of the fog that had smothered the town since early morning still hovered in wisps over the river and the lawn was patched with frost. In the flower beds beyond the terrace the pruned rose bushes were skeletal and soggy.

'He's dying, Fergus,' she said without looking round.

'Surely not! He's still a young man – he's strong enough to fight off a bout of pneumonia.'

'George,' said his mother, 'was never strong. I always said so, but people thought that I was being over-protective. D'you remember that rheumatic fever he had as a child? Doctor Harkness has confirmed that his heart was damaged at the time.' She turned to face her brother. 'I always felt that George wasn't meant to make old bones. Edward now – he was different. Much stronger in every way. It's strange that the war took him first when I thought he'd have been the survivor.'

Fergus, his normally ruddy face pallid with shock, put a hand on her shoulder. 'Come over to the fire, my dear, it's too chilly by the window.'

'George's room's so warm,' Isobel said, allowing herself to be drawn to the fire. 'I needed to look out at the cold for a minute.' Her rings flashed as she spread her hands to the blaze.

'Brandy—' Fergus bustled over to the table that held the decanters, but his sister shook her head.

'Not for me.'

'I need one,' he said bluntly, picking up the decanter. 'George should never have insisted on attending that last launch while the chill was still on him.'

Isobel shrugged. 'I tried to tell him that, and so did Fiona, but George is never one to listen to advice when his mind's made up, as you well know.'

Her brother downed his brandy in two gulps then set the glass down as the door opened again, this time to admit the younger Mrs Dalkieth, slender and graceful in a drifting grey dress with rose-pink panels.

'My dear—' he hurried to take her hands in his. 'Isobel has just told me – dreadful news, dreadful! If there's anything I can do, you only need to ask.'

She smiled faintly. 'Thank you, Uncle Fergus.'

'How is George?'

'Asleep now, with the nurse in attendance. The doctor's just leaving, Mother Dalkieth. He'll be back this evening.'

'Thank you, my dear.' Isobel held her hand out and the younger woman went to her.

Fergus hesitated, then said, 'Perhaps I should have a word with the doctor—'

'By all means,' his sister said, and he escaped thankfully. Fiona sat down beside her mother-in-law, who retained her hand.

'We must be very brave, my dear,' she said at last.

'Yes, Mother Dalkieth.'

'And be grateful that at least George has been blessed by a healthy son to follow him in the family business.' Isobel's voice was serene. In Fiona she had found a daughter she could both admire and cherish; who had given her a grandson she loved as much as she'd ever loved his supposed father.

Fiona raised her blue eyes to her mother-in-law's face. They had grown to respect each other a great deal in the past fifteen months or so. 'Yes, Mother Dalkieth,' she said.

32

Although few people had had much time for George Dalkieth as a person, his family background decreed that his funeral would be a splendid affair. The shipyard was closed down for the day and most of the workers, under the watchful eye of the foremen, lined the streets to watch the funeral procession pass by on its way to the cemetery, where George was to be buried in the family lair. The hearse, drawn by two black horses, their plumes dancing in the wintry sunshine, was piled high with flowers.

Isobel and Fiona Dalkieth, both in unrelieved mourning black and both veiled, led the cavalcade of mourners, with Robert Archer in the second car.

Robert had always hated funerals, despising what he saw as the hypocrisy often shown by mourners who didn't, in truth, care a whit about the dear departed. But he had been summoned to Dalkieth House on the day before to be instructed by Isobel Dalkieth herself on the part he would be expected to play in the ceremony.

'You will be one of the cord-bearers, Mr Archer,' she told him, standing erect before the drawing-room fireplace, dressed in black from throat to ankle, a piece of fine veiling over her white hair. 'My brother will stand by my side during the service at the cemetery, and I would like you to stand beside my daughter-in-law.'

'Surely, Mrs Dalkieth, her own father or brother should support her.'

'They will also be cord-bearers, of course, but as our office manager I feel that you should be the one to stand by George's widow,' she told him, her voice clear and firm.

As the minister's rounded syllables rolled over the assembled mourners Robert stared up at the massive white marble statue towering above them all, solid against the browns and golds of the autumnal trees beyond, and set about with columns and angels. The name DALKIETH arched across the large facing panel in ornate black and gold letters, very similar to the letters curving over the main gates of the yard. Below the surname were listed the names and dates of the past three generations of Dalkieths, ending in William and Edward, George's father and brother.

This, Robert realised, was the third family funeral Isobel Dalkieth had had to attend in recent years. First her husband, then her elder son, and now her younger son. He stole a sidelong glance at her; even the black veiling over her face couldn't hide the sharpness and strength of her profile.

A heavy, sickly scent rose from the wreaths piled to one side, waiting to be laid over the black scar of the filled-in grave, and above it wafted the delicate perfume of lily-of-the-valley, bringing Robert's mind sharply back to the slim young woman who stood unmoving by his side. She had been dressed in black the first time they had met, he recalled, but this time her hat was small and neat and heavily veiled.

Two years had passed since their brief, passionate affair. Since then they hadn't seen each other very often, and never alone. Their most recent meeting had been during the last launch from the yard, a month earlier. On that day, Robert remembered, Fiona had looked into his face for the first time since she had ended their affair and, to his consternation, he thought he had glimpsed a faint stirring of the warmth and intimacy she had once shown towards him. But now, although he couldn't see her face, he could tell by the way she had tensed beneath his touch as he helped her out of the car at the graveside and by the way she stood erect, alone, not deigning to rely on him for support, that he was no longer part of any plans Fiona Dalkieth might have for the future. Now that she was widowed, she would be aiming her sights higher than an employee, a man who had come from humble beginnings. If there was to be another man in her life it would be someone with money and position.

A grim smile brushed his mouth at the thought and he stepped forward at a nod from the minister to grasp one of the cords supporting the casket that held George Dalkieth. The other cords were held by Fergus Craig, Matthew Neilson and his father, a Dalkieth cousin who had travelled from the Borders for the funeral, and one of the foremen, a burly man who had worked for the Dalkieths for over forty years.

As the cords were laid down on the sides of the grave, their work done, Isobel Dalkieth stepped forward and picked up a handful of soil. As it pattered on to the lid of the casket below, Fiona stooped gracefully and picked up a handful of soil in her turn. She opened her gloved fingers to release the earth, then dusted her hands together to dismiss the final stray fragments of soil.

Isobel Dalkieth, who had stood straight-backed throughout the ceremony, put a hand on her brother's arm as she turned to where the cars waited on the wide gravelled drive. From where he stood Robert could see that for once the woman was leaning heavily on her escort. But Fiona, following her mother-in-law, walked alone.

The people who thronged the Dalkieth drawing room were, to a large extent, the same guests who had gathered not much more than a year before to celebrate the christening of William George Dalkieth, heir to the shipyard. Then they had worn bright colours, now they were all in black, milling across the rich Persian carpet like a flock of crows about to take wing.

At first, gathering in the dining room for refreshments on their return from the cemetery, they had been subdued and solemn-faced, keeping their voices down to a discreet sorrowful murmur. Time had passed since then; stomachs were comfortably filled, the funeral lay behind them and, as the servants, magpie-like among the crows in their black and white uniforms, circulated with trays bearing glasses filled with clear or amber-coloured liquids, the noise had risen to an animated chatter of voices, with here and there a cry of recognition and greeting, and even the occasional laugh.

That, Robert thought, standing alone in a window-bay, sipping at his whisky, was what he disliked most about funerals. No matter how dearly the deceased may have been loved the predominant emotion once the interment was over tended to be one of relief that it was someone else who had had to be left behind in the cemetery and that, for the rest of them, life was still there to be lived. He watched Fiona, making her way through the room group by group, accepting condolences with her usual composure. She had folded her veil back on returning to the house; within its sombre folds her face was like a flower, her mouth pale.

She had come to him not long after the funeral party returned to the house to thank him formally for his presence. Her voice and eyes had been cool and her gloved hand had barely brushed his. As she turned away from him Robert had noticed Isobel Dalkieth watching the two of them, her face expressionless.

'Mr Archer—' Isobel's voice broke into his thoughts now, harsh and steady. 'I wonder if I might have a word with you?'

In the small, book-lined library across the hall, the door closed against the noise of her guests, she motioned Robert to a chair then moved behind the large desk. Waiting for her to sit down before he took his own seat he remembered the last time he had been in this room, the night that Fiona had driven him to his home. George had been present at that meeting, lowering and sulking, picking at his lower lip, his pale blue eyes sliding between Robert and his mother.

Isobel folded her hands, still gloved, on the desk before her, and plunged into business without wasting any time. 'Mr Archer, at the next Board meeting you will be invited to take on the duties of general manager, with a new office manager and a works manager to be appointed by the Board with your approval, to work under your supervision. I'm telling you now because I want you to have time to make your plans.'

Robert gaped at her for a moment. He had expected to stay on in the yard, but not to be offered full control. 'You're inviting me to take over the entire shipyard?'

'I am.'

'But surely the Board should be consulted over such a step.'

She waved his protest aside. 'The matter can't wait until then. Decisions have to be made as soon as possible. Now that I've lost both my sons I have to think of my duty towards my grandchild. In any case,' she added calmly, 'I'm confident that the Board will do as I say. They always have. And as I said, I want you to be able to present your plans as soon as the position is offered to you.'

'Mrs Dalkieth, if I am to be offered and accept the appointment you suggest,' he said levelly, putting a faint emphasis on the word 'if', 'I must point out that from that I will not necessarily do as you wish. I will make my own decisions.'

'So I would hope. You've got a sensible head on your shoulders, Mr Archer. I know I haven't always acted on your suggestions,' she went on, her mouth curving in a dry smile that didn't reach her eyes, 'but I believe that we can still work together. Will you accept?'

'If you don't mind, Mrs Dalkieth, I'd rather be approached by the Board officially before I give my answer.'

Irritation swept across her features. 'You're being very cautious.'

'I don't believe in getting my fingers burned twice,' he told her bluntly.

'Let's suppose the Board does make the proposals I've just put to you. Will you accept them?'

'I may well accept them – and that's as much as I'm prepared to say for the moment.'

'Very well, I'll accept that – for the moment.' She put her hands on the edge of the desk and got to her feet slowly and a little stiffly.

Robert went before her to open the door. 'Thank you for your faith in me.'

Isobel Dalkieth paused and looked him up and down, the dry smile lingering again on her pale mouth.

'Not at all, Mr Archer,' she said at last. 'After all, we do owe you a debt of gratitude. And I have always paid my debts.'

Then she went out of the room and across the hall, back to her guests, with Robert Archer following behind, puzzling over the debt of gratitude, and her use of the word 'we'. Was the old woman, he wondered, quickening his pace to pass her in order to open the drawing-room door, beginning to get delusions of grandeur? Had she taken to using the word 'we' in its Royal sense?

As the yard was closed on the day of George Dalkieth's funeral Jenny had decided to work at the kitchen table on a set of decorative plates for Neilson's store. Her mother and father were out and she had covered the linoleum floor with newspaper and set Shona and Helen, smocks covering their clothes, to some painting of their own. Helen was working on a doll's teaset Alice had given her while Shona was busy lathering paint from her brush on to some unwanted wallpaper Jenny had found in a cupboard.

When the doorknocker rattled, Jenny tutted with annoyance and put her brush down carefully then hurried to the door, the children squeezing into the hall after her. She threw open the door then stared up at the dark-suited young man on the doorstep.

'I've been attending my brother-in-law's funeral, Jen, and you don't think I'd come to Ellerslie without calling in on you, do you?' Matthew Neilson said.

Flustered, pulling at the ties on her overall, Jenny was suddenly aware of two heads, one dark, one auburn, poking inquisitively round her legs. 'Into the kitchen, the pair of you,' she ordered, backing along the narrow hall so that Matthew could step inside. In the kitchen he smiled down at Shona and Helen.

'I thought you had one child, not two.'

'This is Shona, my daughter, and this is Helen, my niece. Say good afternoon to Mr Neilson,' Jenny instructed the little girls, who backed away, hand in hand. 'Watch where you're putting your feet or you'll get paint on your shoes,' she added to Matthew, who picked his way across the sheets of newspaper towards the table where the half-finished plates lay.

'They're good.'

Jenny filled the kettle, feeling, as Helen and Shona both clamped a fist on her skirt, like a liner escorted by two reluctant tugs.

'They should be finished in another three days. They're a special order for Miss Beckett. Sit in that armchair, it's the most comfortable.'

He sat on Teeze's chair and Jenny snatched sidelong glances at him as she bustled about, gathering up the newspaper from the floor, picking up discarded toys. She saw by the expression on his face as he

323

studied the room that he was taken aback by the shabbiness of the place, and longed to tell him sharply that it might not be much, but it was clean and respectable, but held her tongue.

'How's the workroom getting on?' she asked instead. She was dismayed by his unexpected appearance, and irked with herself for not realising that he would be attending the funeral. If she had thought of it, she would have made a point of keeping out of the way.

'Well enough, but we could do with you back in charge.'

Jenny measured tea into the pot and wished that her mother was there. She could have done with someone to take the children off her hands. Or, to be more exact, off her skirt. 'I'm sure Miss Beckett and Evie are managing fine.'

'Maybe they are, but I'm not,' said Matthew. She ignored him, concentrating her attention on making tea and persuading the little girls to go back to their painting. Free of them at last, she set out cups and saucers, moving her work carefully aside.

'Are your parents not in?' Matthew asked.

'Not just now.'

'I was hoping to meet them.'

Jenny, thinking of Teeze's probable reaction to her visitor, was glad that he, at least, wasn't at home. 'How is your sister, and Mr George's mother?'

'Remarkably calm. They seem to have built up quite a strong bond since the boy's birth.'

'Will your sister go back to Glasgow now?'

'Good lord, no. She intends to stay in Dalkieth House and bring the child up within sight of this precious shipyard of theirs.' Matthew sipped at his tea, then put the cup down. 'Are you happy, being back home?'

'It's where I belong.'

'People shouldn't belong anywhere,' Matthew said firmly. 'They should be free to go wherever they want.'

'That takes money.'

'So you'd not stay here if you had the money to move?'

'I didn't say that. Careful, Shona—' Jenny, uncomfortable under the intensity of his gaze, bent down and guided her daughter's paintbrush away from the linoleum and back towards the paper, now slashed with bright colours.

When she straightened up again Matthew said, 'I miss you, Jenny. Come to Glasgow – for a holiday.'

'I've got my work to do.'

'You could surely arrange to get some time off. You work at Dalkieth's, don't you? I'll arrange it for you, if you like.'

The sheer arrogance of the man almost took her breath away. She began to speak, but he swept on enthusiastically. 'Bring the child with you.'

'You don't like children, Matthew.'

'I didn't say that.' Matthew's voice was hurt. 'I said I didn't care for Fiona's. Yours would be different. I know you think I'm too easy-going, Jenny, but I've had time to think things over since you ran away.'

'I didn't run away, I came back to Ellerslie because my husband was here.'

'And where is he now? You're young yet, Jenny. You deserve the chance of happiness with someone else, someone more worthy of you. And what about your daughter – doesn't she deserve a good future?'

Irritation flashed through Jenny. She had heard enough. 'Yes, Matthew, she does, and I intend to see that she gets it.' She got to her feet. 'But I'll manage it on my own, without having to be grateful to anyone else. And now, if you've finished your tea, I'd like to get on with my work,' she went on, removing the cup and saucer from his hands.

'But—' Matthew spluttered, scrambling with difficulty out of Teeze's shabby chair.

'You're a nice enough person, Matthew, but you and me come from different worlds,' Jenny told him ruthlessly. She had tried to tell him politely that she wanted to get on with her own life, but men like Matthew could only understand the blunt truth. 'You think that just having plenty of money gives you the right to do anything you want and get whatever – or whoever – you want. But you're wrong.'

'But Jenny, I only – oh, blast!' Matthew said as the latch was lifted on the outer door.

Helen, followed by Shona, ran to open the kitchen door as Robert, dressed, like Matthew, in funeral black, stepped into the kitchen. He halted abruptly at the sight of Jenny's visitor.

'Archer—' Matthew's voice was cool.

Robert nodded curtly to him, then as Shona clutched at his trouser-leg he bent and swung her into his arms. 'Is this a bad time to call?' he asked Jenny over Shona's bobbing head.

'Not at all. Mr Neilson was just about to go back to Dalkieth House. I'll see you out, Matthew.'

At the landing door, Matthew said, 'Are you rejecting me because of him?'

'It's got nothing to do with Robert. I told you – we're not suited, you and me.'

He left without another word, his mouth turned down at the corners in the sulky pout Jenny had come to know well. It was an expression he and his sister shared.

Robert, who was admiring Shona's painting, looked up as she went back into the room. 'Sorry if I chased your admirer away,' he said, his voice heavy with sarcasm.

She ignored the jibe, asking automatically, 'Will you have some tea?

'I've had enough tea today to launch a ship.' He got to his feet and inspected his trousers for paint smears.

'How's Mrs Dalkieth?' Jenny asked.

'They're both fine. I get the feeling that there's not much sorrow there. I never liked the man myself but he was entitled to more grief than his wife and his mother showed today. I believe his son's of more importance to them than George ever was, poor soul. Fathering that child was the only thing he did right, in his mother's eyes.'

The final sentence brought back her earlier thoughts about the child's true parentage. Still unsettled by Matthew's unexpected and unwelcome appearance she asked, before she could stop herself, 'How well d'you know Fiona Dalkieth, Robert?'

Taken aback by the question, he looked up at her with the familiar twist of the head that the baby had used on the day of his birthday party in the Neilson store. And she knew then that her earlier suspicions had been correct.

'What made you ask a thing like that?'

'That day when you walked into the store I saw—' she hesitated, then said carefully, 'I saw the way she looked at you. She thought you'd come to see her.'

'Is that why you refused me when I asked you to come and live with me?' Robert asked levelly, 'Because you think there's something going on between me and Fiona Dalkieth?'

'I gave you my reasons and they have nothing to do with her.' Then she said again, 'Robert, how well d'you know her?'

He looked for a moment as though he was going to protest, then shrugged. 'I don't like keeping secrets from you of all people, Jen. It happened after you got married. I was lonely, and so was she. It only lasted for a month or two.' His mouth twisted wryly. 'If it gives you any satisfaction to know it, she jilted me, just as I jilted you. She threw me over when she discovered that poor George had managed to give her a child after all.'

'Are you so sure that the wee boy is George Dalkieth's son, and not yours?'

There was a pause, then Robert said, his eyes holding hers, 'She swore to me that the child was her husband's. Whether he is or whether he isn't, he's a Dalkieth and I have no claim on him whatsoever. As you've said yourself, Jenny, the past is past.'

'But Fiona Dalkieth's free now, and so are you,' Jenny pointed out, and his brows rose.

'Are you trying to match-make?'

'I'm just – wondering.'

Robert gave a bark of laughter. 'You've been reading too many romantic novels, Jen. I told you – it was loneliness on both sides, and mebbe it amused her to deceive her husband with someone he couldn't stand. It meant very little as far as she was concerned, though at the time I foolishly chose to believe that I was – important to her.' His voice was self-mocking. 'There you have it – the truth about what a fool I've been. But believe me, we'd not look at each other now if we were the last man and woman alive.'

Shona toddled over to Robert and he put a hand on her head, smiling down at her absently as Jenny picked up Matthew's empty cup and took it to the sink. She was so intent on her thoughts that she turned the tap on too hard.

A jet of water deflected off the cup and shot up to soak her hair and face and the front of her painting smock. The little girls squealed with startled laughter as she reeled back from the sink and Robert snatched at a towel hanging over the back of a chair then reached through the spray to turn the tap off.

'Mercy,' said Faith from the doorway above the children's squeals, surveying her dripping daughter and the puddles on the linoleum round the sink. 'Are ye no' content wi' almost drownin' my man, Robert Archer, without trying tae drown my lassie as well?'

33

'The two pennies first, then the wee bar of chocolate, then this,' Alice instructed, handing over a tiny flaxen-haired doll. 'Then the tangerine on top so that it's the first thing she sees.'

It was Christmas Eve and she and Jenny were busy making up a stocking for Helen, sound asleep in the next room.

Christmas, well celebrated by the English, was a festival that passed by almost unnoticed in Scotland, other than with small gifts for the children.

Pushing the golden tangerine down into the stocking, Jenny remembered her own childhood Christmasses and the breathless excitement of pulling a knobbly stocking down from the range and plunging greedy fingers into its depths. In a good year she and her brother and sisters could count on the sort of stocking she was making up now for Maurice's daughter, but there had been a few bad years as well.

'D'you mind one Christmas when Dad was out of work and our stockings were padded with cold ashes from the range with a penny poke of sweeties sitting on the top?'

'I'll never forget it,' her sister said with feeling. 'I cried and cried, for I'd set my heart on a wee teddy-bear I'd seen in a shop window.' She reached over to touch Jenny's hand lightly. 'Next Christmas you and Shona'll be in a place of your own, you'll see.'

Jenny sighed and shook her head. 'I'm beginning to wonder about that. She's getting more and more settled with Bella and I don't seem to be any nearer finding somewhere for us both. I need to go on working, and it means getting someone to look after her while I'm at the shipyard.'

'You will,' Alice said with conviction. 'It'll all work out. It has to.'

New Year was the special celebration in Scotland, with the yards and quarries and factories closing down for the day. Every house had to be cleaned from top to bottom so that the new year could get off to a good start, and every range or stove in the town was put to good use as the women made the traditional rich fruity 'black bun' or dumpling. Both Robert Archer and Alec Monroe first-footed the

Gillespies, arriving together on the landing as the church bells began to ring 1922 out and 1923 in, each man with a piece of coal for good luck in one hand and a bottle of whisky in the other, much to Teeze's delight. There was more whisky flowing on New Year's Day itself, when Kerry Malloy became engaged to a riveter in Dalkieth's yard.

It was as well that Jenny was staying with her parents, for both Teeze and Faith suffered poor health during the early wintry months of the new year. Jenny was kept busy looking after her parents as well as seeing to Helen and working in the drawing office. Bella helped as much as she could, for Alice had her hands full keeping the pawn-shop going and nursing Alec Monroe, who, like Teeze, was unable to cope with cold wet weather.

At the end of March, when the three invalids were on their way back to health, Alice announced that she and Alec were to be married on the same April day as Kerry and her sweetheart, with a joint back-court party after the ceremonies.

'Mebbe you could bring Shona to live with you once I'm wed,' she said to Jenny. 'The bedroom's big enough for you and the two bairns, or you could mebbe sleep in the wee room if you wanted to be on your own.'

'Never mind me – are you sure you're doing the right thing? You're not eighteen yet, Alice. You told me you'd wait till then to decide.'

Alice surveyed her sister defiantly. 'I know that, but Alec's chest was awful bad this time and—' she stopped, then went on slowly, 'I'm sure enough to know that if he's only going to be with me for a short while I don't want to waste the time we have. Me and Alec are going to reach out and take what happiness we can, while we can. That's what we decided together.'

'Your sister might still be very young but she's got her head screwed on the right way,' Robert said a week later as he and Jenny walked out along the riverbank with Helen trotting between them, one small hand firmly gripping Jenny's fingers.

'It's strange to think that in a few weeks' time she'll be out of the house and I'll be the only one left with my parents.'

He walked on in silence for a moment, then with a sidelong glance he said, 'D'you mind me telling you my housekeeper had decided it was time she gave up working for other folk? She's leaving at the end of this week, though she's been good enough to arrange for someone to take her place. It seems that she's got an extra room in her house and she's been thinking of taking in a lodger. I wondered if you'd be interested. She lives in Chapel Street.'

'I'd need a place where I could have Shona with me.'

'As to that, Mrs Kennedy's fond of children. In fact,' said Robert casually, 'we've talked about it, and if you became her lodger she'd not be averse to looking after Shona while you're working.'

Jenny stopped so quickly that Helen almost fell over. 'Does she mean it?'

'I've never known Mrs Kennedy to say anything she didn't mean. I told her you'd go along and see her tomorrow evening.' He glanced over at Jenny and grinned at the look on her face. 'I thought you'd be pleased,' he said smugly, catching Helen's free hand in his. 'Come on then – one, two, three – and up we go!'

Helen squealed as the two adults swung her forward between them and up into the air. 'Again!' she demanded as soon as her feet thumped back down on the earthen path. An elderly couple approaching them sedately, arm in arm, beamed at the little girl's pleasure, and the woman said to Jenny as they passed, 'I mind when we used to do that with our wee lass. Make the most of her while she's still a bairn. They grow up too soon.'

'We will,' Robert assured her, his grin widening. 'Won't we, dear?'

'You're impossible!' she hissed at him as the older couple moved on.

'That's only because I don't know any better. One, two three—'

As they walked on, swinging Helen between them, it was Shona that Jenny was thinking of, and the wondrous possibility that all the days and weeks and months they had been apart might at last be coming to an end . . .

Mrs Kennedy lived in a neat little terraced house with a wrought-iron gate leading from the pavement into a minute front garden.

'My man was a supervisor in Craig's Quarry,' she told Jenny proudly as she led her into the hall. 'He saved for most of his life tae buy this house, and managed tae leave enough tae let me keep it on after he died, together with the money I earned looking after Mr Archer. I'd not like tae have to sell it after all those years, and when Mr Archer came up with the idea of renting out the spare room it was a godsend.'

'I didn't realise that it was Mr Archer's idea.'

'Oh yes, indeed.' said Mrs Kennedy innocently, putting a plump hand on the gleaming banister and beginning to mount the stairs. 'He's a good man, Mr Archer,' she said over her shoulder as she went.

The room she was offering to rent was a good size, furnished with a large polished walnut wardrobe, matching chest of drawers, and a double bed as well as a small fireplace. The flowered wallpaper was fresh, with no sign of the damp patches Jenny had been used to all her life, and cream lace curtains hung in the bay window. Heavier cretonne curtains, also flowered, could be drawn over at night. There was even electric lighting.

'My son saw tae that,' Mrs Kennedy boasted, clicking the switch on and off. 'He's an electrician tae trade. He's married now, and living in Dumfries. My daughter's in Paisley, and I don't see them or their families all that often, so it would be nice tae have a bairn about the place.' She looked round the spotless room. 'This was ours when my man was living and the bairns were at home. I sleep downstairs now that the rheumatism's settled intae my knees. The wee one'll be no bother tae me while you're at work, Mrs Young, and I've got a folding bed that can be set up for her.'

She led the way back on to the small square landing and opened another door. Jenny, craning past her, saw a lavatory seat, a tiny wash-hand basin, and a small bath. Her eyes widened and Mrs Kennedy, watching her closely, beamed.

'I can see why you don't want to sell the house,' Jenny said, admiringly.

'Oh, my man was away ahead in his thinkin',' the older woman said. 'There's still the privy out the back door, an' I just use that myself. But it's grand tae have a bath in comfort when I want one, without havin' tae heave buckets of water up and down the stairs.'

'As to the rent—' Jenny ventured as Mrs Kennedy started back down the stairs.

'Och, don't fret yourself about that, my dear, I'm sure we can come tae some arrangement. Come down tae the kitchen and we'll talk about it over a cup of tea.'

As she followed Mrs Kennedy into the cosy kitchen, where steam plumed gently from the kettle waiting on the range, Jenny knew that whatever the rent might be she would find it. At last she had discovered a home where she and her baby could be together.

Alice prudently took Shona and Helen out for a walk so that Jenny could tell Bella her news without the distraction of the children underfoot. Bella and Patrick heard what Jenny had to say in silence, then Bella said slowly, 'You mean you're going tae take Shona away from us?'

'That's why I've been looking for somewhere to live, so that we can be together.'

'But—' Bella looked at Patrick then back at Jenny, her fingers twisting together, her small face stricken. 'You've got your work tae do. You'll not be able tae be with her during the day. Who'll see tae her then?'

'Mrs Kennedy's raised a family of her own and she likes bairns. Shona'll be fine with her.'

'But she doesnae know this woman, Jen!'

'She's met her at Robert's house and they've always got on well together.' Jenny's heart chilled within her as she saw the look on her sister's face.

'It's one thing being friendly on a visit, an' another bein' left alone with someone she doesnae know!' Bella said, desperation in her voice. 'Shona's used tae being here, with us. It's wrong tae move her again, just when she's settled.'

'Bella, I have to have my baby with me,' Jenny said, her voice pleading for understanding.

Bella moved away from her sister, going to stand by Patrick, who reached out a hand and clasped hers. He struggled to his feet and shoulder to shoulder they confronted Jenny, faces set.

'That's not what ye thought when ye went off tae Glasgow after Daniel and left the bairn behind,' Patrick said belligerently, his brows drawn together.

'Oh Patrick, I had to make sure Daniel was all right. You knew it was only for a wee while, didn't you, Bella?'

'But it wasnae for a wee while, was it? It was more than a year ago.' The hostility Patrick had only covertly shown towards Jenny since Shona's birth was out in the open now, twisting his mouth, hardening his eyes. 'A whole year Bella's looked after that wean like a mother while you've been busy with your own life!'

Jenny tried to speak but his voice rose, drowning her out. 'An' now you come walkin' in here, bold as brass, an' expect us just tae hand her back tae you as if she's of no more importance than – than a piece of clothing ye'd loaned us!' Patrick spat the words out.

'Let her stay, Jenny,' Bella begged. 'She's been happy with us. Let her stay – until ye're settled in, just.'

'And then you'll find another reason and another reason why I shouldn't take her back.' Looking at her sister's stricken face, Jenny felt as though she was being cut in two, but at the same time she was keenly aware that she was on the verge of losing her baby, the only person who truly belonged to her.

'What about Helen?' she heard herself saying. 'She needs parents to love her and look after her. Why don't you—' She stopped as she heard the latch on the outer door being lifted.

'It's not Helen I want!' Bella's voice was shrill with pain. 'It's Shona, not *Helen*!'

'For God's sake!' Alice swept into the middle of the room, her face tight with anger as she glared round the small circle. 'Keep your voices down, will you, you could be heard out there in the close!'

She left the room quickly and Jenny and Bella stared at each other, appalled.

'Ye don't think the bairns heard us?' Bella whispered through stiff lips.

'Ach, they're too wee tae understand what we're sayin'. And if they did, it's her fault!' Patrick stabbed an accusing finger in Jenny's direction then snatched his jacket from the nail hammered into the door and caught up his stick. He pushed his way past the sisters, ignoring Bella's pleading, 'Pat—' and disappeared out of the open door.

After a moment Alice re-entered, Shona and Helen trailing after her. The little girls' faces were dark-smeared round the mouth and in their hands they each clutched a half-chewed liquorice strap.

Bella immediately stepped forward and scooped Shona up into her arms. 'Look at the state of you,' she scolded lovingly, rubbing with the ball of one thumb at the corner of Shona's mouth as she sat down by the range, the child in her lap.

Jenny held out a hand to Helen, who hovered by the door, looking from one to the other of the adults. 'Come to the fire and get your coat off, love.'

Alice's voice was determinedly bright and cheerful, though above her smiling mouth her eyes were still stormy as they surveyed her older sisters. 'They were desperate for a sweetie, so I thought it wouldn't hurt, just this once. We'd a grand walk, didn't we Helen?'

The little girl nodded, clambering on to Jenny's knee.

'Horsie.' Shona wriggled on Bella's lap, reluctantly allowing the shiny black liquorice sweet to be prised from her fingers so that first one arm and then the other could be freed from her coat sleeves.

'That's right, we saw a big horsie pulling a cart, and a blue motor car. Didn't we, Helen?' Alice dampened the corner of a towel at the kitchen tap and brought it to Jenny, who used it to wipe the stickiness from Helen's face.

Bella spat efficiently on a corner of her handkerchief and wiped Shona's face and hands. Shona turned her face away impatiently, squirming down from Bella's lap and reclaiming the liquorice strap. She toddled over to Jenny and offered her the sweet.

'Thank you.' Jenny bent her head and was about to pretend to nibble at the liquorice when Helen, with a sharp cry of 'No!' leaned forward on her knee and struck it out of Shona's hand, at the same time aiming a kick at the smaller child.

A week later Jenny moved herself and her daughter into the Chapel Street house. At first Shona pined for Bella and Patrick and the single end that had been the only home she remembered. Walking the floor with her when she refused to settle in her new bed, reading stories and reciting nursery rhymes and listening to her over-tired daughter crying for Auntie Bella and Uncle Pat, wondering if she had done the right thing after all, Jenny came close to despair. She had been looking forward to being on her own with her baby, but now all the pleasure had gone out of it.

'I feel like a murderer,' she said shakily to Robert when he called on her a few days after she moved in. They were in Mrs Kennedy's f ront parlour; his former housekeeper had just brought some tea in and borne Shona off with her to the kitchen. 'You should have seen Bella's face when I picked Shona up and carried her out of the house. She looked as though I'd just slapped her.'

'You've got every right to have your own child with you.'

'That's no consolation to Bella – or Patrick. Mebbe they're right, mebbe I'm being selfish and putting myself first instead of thinking about what's best for Shona.'

Robert took her by the shoulders and gave her a little shake. 'The best place for Shona is with her own mother. There are times when we have to stop thinking about other folk and pay heed to what we want ourselves,' he lectured. 'She's all that's left to you of your marriage. If you hand her back to your sister you'll not just break your own heart, you'll be turning your back on your own flesh and blood and giving away months and years out of your own life.'

He released her with one final, admonishing shake. 'And what would she think in the years to come when she heard that her own mother had walked away from her and left someone else to raise her?'

She stared at him, astonished. 'I never thought I'd hear you say things like that.'

'Just because you know me better than most it doesn't mean that you know me well,' said Robert. 'Don't forget that I was raised by an aunt and I've got no happy memories of it.'

'That's because your auntie was a hard kind of woman, not like Bella at all.'

'Perhaps,' said Robert, his mouth grim. 'And perhaps a lot of my unhappiness in those days was knowing that my own parents hadn't cared enough to keep me.'

'But your mother and father died—' Jenny began, and he held up a hand to stop her.

'Enough! Will you stop talking, woman, and pour out my tea before it grows stone cold?'

335

34

'This,' said Alice, 'is going to be the society wedding of the year – at least as far as the Dalkieth tenements are concerned. Have you not finished with my hair yet?'

'Nearly – and I'd be done if you'd stop jumping about,' Bella said through the hair-grip between her teeth. She took it from her mouth and pushed it into the soft knot of hair at the nape of Alice's neck, then stood back. 'There.'

Now it was Jenny's turn. She took Bella's place, and carefully placed the blue cloche hat, the same colour as Alice's eyes, on her sister's head. The brim dipped at one side; Jenny tugged it slightly to a rakish angle before skewering it in place with two pearl-topped hatpins then adjusting the cream-coloured bow at the side. Alice peered into the cloudy mirror and nodded, then swung round on the chair and stuck out her feet.

'Come on, slaves – put my shoes on.'

Shona, in a pink embroidered dress, bustled importantly forward and squatted to push a smart fawn shoe on to one of her aunt's feet, but Helen hung back, the other shoe dangling from a limp hand.

'Come on, slowcoach.' Bella tried to pull her forward, then, as Helen resisted she shook her head. 'I don't know – you're a big schoolgirl now, not a baby.' Impatiently, she took the shoe from the little girl and knelt to fit it on to Alice's foot herself. Helen watched, the hand that had held the shoe fidgeting with the skirt of the new yellow dress Jenny had made for her.

'There! How do I look?' Alice jumped up and pirouetted as well as she could in the small space between bed and orange box.

'You're lovely,' Jenny said sincerely. The fawn silk and wool dress Alice had chosen to wear at her wedding fell from the neck to the loosely-belted dropped waistline, then to mid-calf, in straight folds that had the effect of slimming down the girl's solid body. There was blue bead embroidery on the bodice and along the edges of the loose sleeves, and the high-heeled shoes, each with a shining silver buckle, made the most of Alice's surprisingly slender ankles, her best feature.

Blue pendant earrings gave added length to her neck, and a long necklace of blue and cream beads cascaded down to the loose-fitting sash round her hips.

'You look so – lady-like,' Bella chimed in, her eyes dampening.

'So I should hope, on my wedding day. Now don't you go crying, Bella, or I'll have to slap you, and I don't want to have to go hitting people on a day like this, do I, girls?' Alice demanded of her nieces.

Bella sniffed hard, and blinked. 'I still think you should have had your own special day instead of sharing it with Kerry.'

'Not at all. This way I get to have a big party in the back court. The Malloys know how to do these things in style. Come on, young ladies, and we'll see what Gran thinks.' Alice whisked out of the room, and Shona followed, catching at Helen's hand and dragging her along.

Bella took a handkerchief from the pocket of her knitted jacket and dabbed at her eyes. 'I know I'll not be able to stop myself from crying. She's still so young.'

'She'll be fine.' Jenny put a tentative hand on her sister's arm, half expecting to have it shaken off.

Instead, Bella put her own fingers, still roughened by hard work, on top of hers.

'I hope so.' Bella gave her eyes a final dab then said shyly, 'Jen, I think I'm expectin'.'

'What? Oh, Bella!'

Bella's eyes, still damp, were blazing with happiness. 'It's early days yet, and I've said nothing tae anybody else, but Pat. But I feel – different. I'm sure in my own mind that we're to have a bairn of our own. Just when I thought it would never happen, too!'

Jenny hugged her, and Bella returned the embrace warmly. 'Now I know how you must have felt about wee Shona,' she murmured into Jenny's ear. 'For there's nobody ever going to be allowed to take this bairn away from me!'

They beamed at each other, both on the verge of tears, then Bella gave a loud sniff and put the handkerchief away. She picked up her hat, a brown felt cloche. 'Come on,' she commanded briskly, 'it's nearly time tae go tae the church.'

Alice and Alec had asked Bella and Patrick to be their witnesses. 'You don't mind, do you?' Alice had asked Jenny anxiously. 'I'd sooner have had you to stand by me, but Alec and me both felt that it would be a kindness to Bella and Patrick.'

'Of course I don't mind,' Jenny had assured her, and meant it. Alice was being married by the same minister who had performed the ceremony for Jenny and Daniel, and she had no wish to be reminded of the past. Instead, while the small marriage ceremony was taking

338

place, she was kept busy hurrying up and down the stairs, helping to set out the tables in the back court, spreading tablecloths and linen sheets over them, anchoring the material with jam jars crammed with wild flowers. The weather had decided to bless the double wedding day and the sky overhead was the same blue as Alice's eyes.

By the time the happy couples had arrived, Kerry and her new husband from the Catholic church, Alice and Alec from the Protestant manse, where they had been married in the minister's parlour, Peter McLellan's fiddle was piping away and the men, led by Teeze and Mr Malloy, had already broached the bottles of whisky and barrel of beer bought for the occasion, in spite of their womenfolk's scowls of disapproval.

Robert Archer arrived halfway through the festivities, long after the last crumb had been eaten. He brought some bottles with him, and was noisily welcomed by Teeze and his cronies. When at last he was free to search Jenny out and draw her into the group of dancers there was whisky on his breath.

'They look very happy.' He indicated the newly married couples, standing together in a group of young people. Kerry had tossed her hat aside and her red head flamed in the sun; Alice, with Alec's arm looped possessively about her shoulders, was radiant. 'Does it not put you in the notion for a wedding of your own?'

'I've already had my wedding, Robert Archer, and so have you.'

'We both made a mistake. Mebbe,' said Robert, holding her back slightly so that he could look down at her, 'we're the sort of people that need to learn the hard way. The next time'll be better.'

'There won't be a next time for me,' Jenny told him firmly, but he had drawn her back against him, his arm hard about her, and she was talking into his jacket. She doubted if he heard her.

When the dance was over she noticed Helen standing against the wall, alone, watching the revellers, just as Walter had stood years ago, alone and aloof. Jenny left Robert and went to the little girl, taking her hand, leading her to where the other children, Shona among them, were playing a noisy game of Blind Man's Buff. Helen stood back, watching them, and when Jenny moved away, she followed like a small shadow, staying close to her for the rest of the afternoon.

The party continued after Kerry and her new husband and Alice and Alec left, then gradually the adults began to withdraw from the court, small children drooped over their shoulders, sound asleep. Jenny gathered Shona up and bent down to smooth the tumbled red curls back from Helen's face. 'I'll need to take Shona home to bed now, pet. You go and find Gran. Go on,' she urged as Helen shook her head. The little girl went, step by step, looking back over her shoulder.

'D'ye think she's all right?' Bella murmured from behind Jenny. 'I mean, in her head?'

'Of course she's all right! She does well enough at the school,' Jenny told her sharply.

'She's got no life in her any more. Well, mebbe she's sickening for something.'

'She's just – unsettled, with Lottie deserting her. She'll be fine,' Jenny said, but she was worried as she watched Helen disappear into the crowd.

At home in Chapel Street she settled Shona in her crib and went back down to the kitchen to make a cup of tea for herself. Mrs Kennedy was in Paisley, looking after her daughter and her new baby, and she had the house to herself. The room was warm and peaceful, the clock's ticking soothing, and she was almost asleep in her fireside chair when the doorknocker rattled, making her jump.

Bella stood on the doorstep, still in her wedding finery, her brows knotted with worry.

'Jenny, is Helen with you? She's gone,' she went on as Jenny shook her head. 'Mam thought she'd mebbe followed you.'

'I've not seen her since she went off to look for Mam. Are you sure she's not just put herself to bed?' Helen had taken, lately, to going to bed without a word to anyone.

'It was the first place we looked.'

'The river—' Jenny felt her heart constrict.

'There's folk looking by the river and all over. The Malloys are out helping, and Robert. He was still there when Mam discovered that she was missing. I'd best go to Mam – she's in a right state about it,' Bella said hurriedly and turned towards the gate.

'I can't leave Shona. Let me know if you – when you find her,' Jenny called after her.

'Aye—' Bella was already out on the pavement, hurrying off into the night. Jenny shivered, realising that although it had been a lovely day, there was frost in the air. She closed the door and went upstairs to look at Shona, who was sleeping peacefully, then prowled restlessly about the ground floor, hurrying to open the back and front doors now and again, fancying that she heard a child crying, or a light scratching on the panels. But there was never anyone there.

The clock's ticking had a menacing note now, each second extending the time since Helen had last been seen. Jenny was tormented by mind-pictures of the small figure trudging slowly, reluctantly, away from her, into the crowd.

340

She paced from parlour to kitchen and back to the parlour again, thinking of the fields edging the town, where a little girl could easily be lost, and of the river, deep and cold and fast-running. Sometimes there were tramps and beggars around the area, unknown people who just might take it into their heads to harm a little girl, or steal her away, if they found her wandering alone.

Several times she put on her coat then took it off again, knowing that she couldn't leave Shona on her own. She was pacing the parlour for the hundredth time, wishing that tonight of all nights Mrs Kennedy could have been home, when the doorknocker crashed against its metal plate.

Although she had been praying for contact from the outside world Jenny screamed at the sound, then almost fell over a large horse-hair chair in the darkness in her haste to reach the front door. As soon as she opened it Robert swept in on a wave of frosty air, shirt-sleeved, his jacket wrapped about the bundle his arms.

'She's fine, she's fine,' he said at once. 'I found her huddled under a bush down by the shore and she wouldn't let me take her anywhere but here.'

'Helen?' With trembling hands Jenny unfolded the jacket to reveal a familiar tumble of red curls and a dirty, tear-streaked face pressed against Robert's arm.

'She needs to go to bed,' he said, low-voiced. 'You lead the way.'

'No, let me take her.' As Jenny gathered Helen into her arms the little girl woke with a yelp of fright, then recognised her aunt and started to cry, wrapping her arms tightly around Jenny's neck.

'It's all right, love, you're all right,' Jenny told her over and over again. Forgetting Robert, forgetting everything but the joy of holding Helen again and knowing that she was safe, Jenny began to climb the stairs.

When she came back down half an hour later the house was silent and she thought that Robert had left. But he was in the kitchen, sprawled back in one of the cushioned chairs by the range, sound asleep, his legs stretched out across the rag rug. Carefully stepping around them, Jenny made fresh tea then put a hand on his shoulder. His grey eyes opened at once, blinking up at her as he struggled upright in the chair. 'The warmth must have got to me,' he said, yawning. 'How is she?'

'Sound asleep in my bed. Does Mam know she's safe, and Bella?'

'I sent word to them that she was fine and that I was bringing her here.'

She put a mug of tea into his hands and sat down opposite him.

341

'What did she think she was doing, Robert? Mam's always loved her, there was no reason for her to run away.'

He swallowed some tea and knuckled the last of the sleep out of his eyes, then ran a hand through his hair, lifting it into tufts all over his head. 'She doesn't belong,' he said simply. 'Bella's got Patrick, Shona's got you, and now Alice has her own husband. Helen doesn't have anyone.'

Jenny remembered the day Bella had shouted at her, 'I want Shona, not Helen.' The little girl must have heard, after all. 'Did she tell you that?'

'She didn't need to tell me. I know what it feels like not to belong.' He emptied his mug and held it out to be refilled, grinning ruefully at her. 'I ran away more than once when I was about her age, but I wasn't very good at it, I kept being brought back.' The grin faded. 'That's why I was so eager to be Maurice's friend, to be part of his family for a while. Then I made the greatest mistake of all. I ran off again to Tyneside when old Mr Dalkieth gave me the chance.'

He drained his cup and went to the sink to rinse it out, speaking over his shoulder. 'I don't know who my father was. My mother apparently went off with someone else when I was about a year old and left me with my aunt.' He turned to face her, wiping his hands on a towel. He looked tired. 'The shame of it haunted her for the rest of her life – though, as she kept telling me, she did her duty by me. But children need love, Jen, not duty.'

'You've never told me anything of this before,' she said, stunned. 'Not even when we were courting. I thought I knew everything about you in those days.' The thought of the misery he must have suffered, the secret he had locked away from everyone, horrified her, even though it had happened so long ago.

'Why should I? I didn't want your pity – I didn't want anyone's pity. I'm telling you now because I know how Helen feels. It's you she wants, Jen. Not your mother.'

'I know that. And I'm going to keep her.'

'Good,' said Robert, then was overcome by a huge, jaw-cracking yawn.

'It's time you were in bed. In your own bed,' she added swiftly as he raised an eyebrow at her.

'You're a hard woman, Jenny Young. You've only just decided to take one orphan in, and now you're throwing another out into the street.'

'You're old enough now to look after yourself,' she told him, taking his jacket from where she had laid it over the back of a chair, and holding it out to him. He sighed, but took it, shrugging it on.

342

'One day,' he said, 'I'll get the answer I want. I'll let myself out.'

The kitchen door closed quietly behind him and she heard him go along the hallway, then the front door opened and closed. She was alone, apart from the two little girls sleeping above.

Jenny picked up her own empty mug and took it to the sink, telling herself that she had done the right thing in sending Robert away. She had responsibilities now, and it wouldn't be fair to burden anyone else with them.

Then, as her hand tightened on the tap, Alice's voice seemed to ring out in the silence of the room. 'Me and Alec are going to reach out and take what happiness we can, while we can,' she had said, when she announced her forthcoming marriage.

Jenny hesitated, her fingers falling away from the tap. Young as she was, Alice had had the sense to recognise where her own happiness lay. And she had had the courage to grasp at it firmly, to hold for as long as she could and to remember for always. Alice, Jenny realised suddenly, had the right way of it.

She hurried out of the kitchen, along the hall, towards the front door, fumbling with the latch, the sense of urgency, of time slipping away from her, suddenly strong.

The cold night air hit her as she went through the door and out on to the little path. The wrought-iron gate was so cold beneath her clutching fingers that they felt as though they had been burned.

She had dithered for too long; the street was silent and empty. Still holding on to the gate she looked one way then the other, a sense of loss welling up in her, then spun round as Robert said from the doorway, 'You'll catch your death of cold standing out there.'

'Where were you?'

'Sitting on the stairs, waiting for you. I decided it was too cold to venture outside. I was certain,' he said reproachfully, 'that you'd have caught up with me before I reached the front door, but I was wrong. As I said before, you're a hard woman, Jenny Young.'

'Robert—'

'Don't say another word. Just come here, to me.' He held out his hand and Jenny's own arm lifted as she went towards him along the paved path, glittering with frost in the light from the hall. She put a foot on the first step, then on the second step, and then she was within reach and Robert's fingers closed about hers, warm and strong, driving away the chill left by her contact with the gate.

The heat from his hand spread like a fire up her arm and deep into her body. Her own fingers tightened about his as he drew her into the light and comfort of the hall, his free hand swinging the door shut behind her, closing out the darkness and the cold . . .